THE KILLING GAME

THE KILLING GAME

TONI ANDERSON

PRAISE FOR TONI ANDERSON

"The Killing Game is exceptionally written and insightful." ⭐⭐⭐⭐⭐ Reader Review.

"Great action, political intrigue, spies and endangered species. Added spice in a hot, alpha special forces soldier and a stubborn, smart and sexy doctor. From Afghanistan, to England and America. Do not miss this novel!!!" ⭐⭐⭐⭐⭐ Reader Review.

"Wow, I loved this book. Loved staying on edge. Wildlife biologist Axelle Dean really takes her job seriously. British SAS soldier Ty Dempsey is great at keeping her safe, he's so protective." ⭐⭐⭐⭐⭐ Reader Review.

"I highly recommend this book to anyone who loves this genre and is looking for your next 5 star read!" ⭐⭐⭐⭐⭐ Reader Review.

ALSO BY TONI ANDERSON

THE BARKLEY SOUND SERIES

Dangerous Waters (Book #1)

Dark Waters (Book #2)

SINGLE TITLES

The Killing Game

Edge of Survival

Storm Warning

Sea of Suspicion

We are the Pilgrims, master; we shall go
Always a little further: it may be
Beyond that last blue mountain barred with snow
Across that angry or that glimmering sea...

The Golden Journey to Samarkand
James Elroy Flecker

For my dad who served in the Parachute Regiment and raised me on a diet of military history and healthy skepticism.

ABOUT THE BOOK

A snow leopard biologist becomes the prey when Cold War secrets threaten to expose a modern-day spy ring, and an elite British soldier is forced to choose between his country and his heart.

Wildlife biologist Axelle Dehn isn't about to let anyone harm her endangered snow leopards—not the poacher intent on killing them, nor the soldier who wants to use them as bait. But Axelle is unknowingly entangled in a conflict that stretches back three decades, a conflict that could spark a war between two of the world's great nations.

British SAS soldier, Ty Dempsey, is on a mission to hunt down an infamous Russian terrorist in a remote region of Afghanistan. Dempsey hasn't failed a mission yet, but when Axelle is kidnapped by the Russian, he is forced to choose between duty and his heart. He risks everything to save the determined, prickly woman he's fallen for, but in doing so sparks a deadly series of events that threaten to expose the most successful spy in history. A spy who will destroy anyone who gets in his way.

PROLOGUE

PRESENT DAY

DMITRI CHEWED a piece of dried meat, then swallowed a lump of gristle. Camp was a cave in the mountainside, three hundred meters above the valley floor. Rain dripped past the entranceway, and cold snaked through layers of cloth and bit into his flesh like the metal teeth of a gin trap. He heaved on his heavy sheepskin jerkin, the muscles across his shoulders burning from wear and tear. Skin itched where coarse wool met his neck. The sun had risen but the world outside remained as empty and barren as his carved-out heart.

Charcoal boulders merged with steep scree slopes, forming an impenetrable wall of bleak granite. He drained his coffee and cleaned out his cup with a small splash of river water he'd carried up the narrow path yesterday. He checked the homemade receiver and GPS unit and picked up his hunting rifle. Cautiously he peered from his cave and raised his whiskered chin to the sky, testing the clouds for any hint of pity for an old man's bones.

And found none.

Dmitri grabbed his water canteen and filled his pocket with ammunition. He pulled his pakol hat low over his brow and stepped into the murk of the day. He wore the clothes of local herders, though up-close his fair hair, towering height and distant

1

blue eyes betrayed a different heritage. He walked cautiously along a path made by goatherds and yaks. The snow was gone from the lower gullies, the grass beginning to ripen and green. Perhaps the weather would aid his cause. Perhaps not.

He checked the receiver again and froze. The target was close. Very close. He used a large boulder for support, sank to his knees, and scanned the countryside. He flipped the safety off the rifle and waited. Less than a minute later one of the most beautiful creatures in the world padded into view.

The snow leopard's tread was silent. Blue-gray eyes and smoky coloring blended perfectly into the landscape. Even though Dmitri knew the animal was right there in front of him, it was still hard to pick out. He held his breath in awe. Then the image of his grandson's sallow face filled his mind, and his finger stroked over the trigger. For one split second the leopard met his gaze and his tail snapped taut. Dmitri exhaled and pulled the trigger.

Percussion pounded the rocks, and a smattering of shale clattered down the hillside behind him. Dmitri checked his shoulder but it was just a small rockslide, nothing to worry about.

He picked his way carefully to the valley floor. His aim was true. The animal was dead. His stomach churned. Thirty years ago, he'd stopped his own men from shooting these beautiful beasts, prevented uneducated pigs from raping the land. But he'd been one man in the giant Soviet machine. Now he was performing his own desecration—not for sport or out of anger, but for cold hard cash and desperation born of need.

He sank to his knees beside the carcass. Dug his fingers into the luxurious fur on the leopard's neck and popped the animal's radio collar. Then he began his trek. Laying down bait. A mile or more, up, and over the ridge, onto the top of a high sheer cliff that overlooked the plains below. He stood, breathing heavily, on the edge of the rocky escarpment, and flung the collar with all his might through the fragile mountain air.

Permanent winter cloaked the Pamirs in the north. His home-land. The home of his heart.

Time was slipping through his gnarled fingers. So many years wasted, so little time left. His grandson was dying. Sergei's son, dying. And the only person willing to save him was Dmitri Volkov. Defector. Betrayer. Child killer.

CHAPTER
ONE

IT LOOKED and felt like the dominion of Gods.

Special Air Service trooper Ty Dempsey had been catapulted from a rural English market town into the heart of a colossal mountain range full of pristine snow-capped peaks which glowed against a glassy blue sky. Many of the summits in the Hindu Kush were over five miles high. The utter peace and tranquility of this region was an illusion that hid death, danger and uncertainty beneath every elegant precipice. No place on earth was more treacherous or more beautiful than the high mountains.

He was an anomaly here.

Life was an anomaly here.

Thin sharp needles pierced his lungs every time he took a breath. But his prey was as hampered by the landscape as they were, and Ty Dempsey wasn't going to let a former Russian Special Forces operative-turned-terrorist get the better of an elite modern-day military force. Especially a man who'd shockingly betrayed not only his country, but humanity itself.

They needed to find him. They needed to stop the bastard from killing again.

The only noise in this arena was boots punching through the crust of frozen snow, and the harshness of puny human lungs struggling to draw oxygen out of the fragile atmosphere. The shriek of a golden eagle pierced the vastness overhead, warning the world that there were strangers here and to beware. Dempsey raised his sunglasses to peer back over his shoulder at the snaking trail he and his squad had laid down. Any fool could follow that trail, but only a real fool would track them across the Roof of the World to a place so remote not even war lingered.

But the world was full of fools.

As part of the British SAS's Sabre Squadron A's Mountain Troop, Dempsey was familiar with the terrain. He knew the perils of mountains and altitude, understood the raw omnipotent power of nature. This was what he trained for. This was his job. This was his life. He'd climbed Everest and K2, though the latter had nearly killed him. He understood that there were places on earth that were blisteringly hostile, that could obliterate you in a split second, but they held no malice, no evil. Unlike people...

He relaxed his grip on his carbine and adjusted the weight of his bergen. None of the men said a word as they climbed ever higher, one by one disappearing over the crest of the ridge and dropping down into the snowy wilderness beyond. With an icy breath Dempsey followed his men on the next impossible mission. Hunting a ghost.

———

The small plane taxied down the runway at Kurut in the Wakhan Corridor, a tiny panhandle of land in the far northeast of Afghanistan. Thankfully the runway was clear of snow—a miracle in itself.

Dr. Axelle Dehn stared out of the plane window and tried to relax her grip on the seat in front of her. She'd been traveling for thirty hours straight, leveraging every contact she'd ever made to get flights and temporary visas for her and her graduate student.

Something was going on with her leopards and she was determined to find out what.

Last fall, they'd attached satellite radio collars to ten highly-endangered snow leopards here in the Wakhan. This past week, in the space of a few days, they'd lost one signal completely, and another signal was now coming from a talus-riddled slope where no shelter existed. This latter signal was from a collar that had been attached to a leopard called Sheba, one of only two female snow leopards they'd caught. Just ten days ago, for the first time ever, they'd captured photos from one of their remote camera traps of the same leopard moving two newborn cubs. If Sheba had been killed, the cubs were out there, hungry and defenseless. Emotion tried to crowd her mind but she thrust it aside.

The cats might be fine.

The collar might have malfunctioned and dropped off before it was programmed to. Or maybe she hadn't fastened it tight enough when they'd trapped Sheba, and the leopard had somehow slipped it off.

But two collars in two days…?

The plane came to a stop and the pilot turned off the propellers. The glacier-fed river gushed silkily down the wide, flat valley. Goats grazed beside a couple of rough adobe houses where smoke drifted through the holes in the roof. Bactrian camels and small, sturdy horses were corralled nearby. A line of yaks packed with supplies waited patiently in a row. Yaks were the backbone of survival in this remote valley, especially once you headed east beyond the so-called *road*. People used them for everything from milk, food, transportation and even fuel in this frigid treeless moonscape.

It was early spring—the fields were being tilled in preparation to plant barley in the short but vital growing season. A group of children ran toward the plane, the girls dressed in red dresses with pink headscarves, the boys wearing jewel-bright green and blue sweaters over dusty pants. Hospitality was legendary in this savagely poor region, but with the possibility of only a few hundred snow leopards left in Afghanistan's wilderness, Axelle didn't have time to squander.

Her assistant, a Dane called Josef Vidler, gathered his things beside her. She adjusted her hat and scarf to cover her hair. The type of Islam practiced here was moderate and respectful.

"Hello, Dr. Dehn," the children chimed as the pilot opened the door. A mix of different colored irises and features reflected the diverse genetic makeup of this ancient spit of land.

"*As-Salaam Alaikum.*" She gave them a tired smile. The children's faces were gaunt but wreathed in happiness. Malnourishment was common in the Wakhan, and after a brutal winter most families were only a goat short of starvation.

Despite the worry for her cats, it humbled her. These people, who struggled with survival every single day, were doing their best to live in harmony with the snow leopard. And a large part of this change in attitude toward one of the region's top predators was due to the work of the Conservation Trust. It was a privilege to work for them, a privilege she didn't intend to screw up. She dug into her day pack and pulled out two canisters of children's multi-vitamins she'd found in Frankfurt Airport. She rattled one of the canisters and they all jumped back in surprise. She pointed to Keeta, a teenage girl whose eyes were as blue as Josef's and whose English was excellent thanks to some recent schooling. "These are *not* candy so only eat one a day." She held up a single finger. Then handed them over and the children chorused a thank you before running back to their homes.

Anji Waheed, their local guide and wildlife ranger-in-training, rattled toward them in their sturdy Russian van.

"*As-Salaam Alaikum*, Mr. Josef, Doctor Axelle," Anji called out as he pulled up beside them. The relief in the Wakhi man's deep brown eyes reinforced the seriousness of the situation.

"*Wa-Alaikum Salaam.*" They could all do with a little peace. The men patted each other on the back, and they began hauling their belongings out of the plane and into the van.

Axelle took a deep breath. "Did you find any sign of the cubs?"

Anji shook his head. "No, but as soon as I heard you were on your way, I took some men up to base camp to set up the yurts, then came back to get you." Although only a few miles up the side valley, it was two bone-rattling hours of travel on a barely-there gravel road to their encampment. During winter, they did their tracking online from back home at Montana State University. In summer, they took a more hands-on approach.

"Thanks." Axelle stowed her frustration and smiled her gratitude. From their tracking data she had a good idea where Sheba might have denned up. Barring accidents or breakdowns they might get there before nightfall.

She was praying for a collar malfunction even though that would put their million-dollar project way behind schedule. The alternative meant the cubs and their mother were probably dead. Her instinct told her losing two cats in a couple of days wasn't coincidence, nor was it a local herder protecting livestock. A professional poacher was going after her animals for their fur and bones to feed China's ravenous appetite for traditional medicine. It was imperative to find out exactly what was going on, and with the continuing conflict in Afghanistan it wasn't going to be easy.

"Do the elders know anything about what might be happening?" she asked. Only twelve miles wide in places, the Wakhan Valley was a tiny finger of flat fertile ground separating some of the tallest mountains in the world—the magnificent and treacherous Hindu Kush to the south and the impenetrable Pamir Range to the north. Harsh winters trapped locals inside for seven months of the year. Wildlife was scarce and the region mercilessly inaccessible, but these people knew the land better than a visitor ever could.

"No." His eyes shot between her and Josef. "They are scared that if the snow leopards are dead, you will blame them and they will lose their clinic."

The Trust not only had an anti-poaching scheme, they also

vaccinated local livestock once a year against common diseases, *gratis*. The program promoted healthier livestock and reduced the losses herders suffered to sickness, which in turn compensated for the occasional snow leopard kill. So far the scheme was working, except now they had two missing, possibly dead leopards and two tiny cubs unaccounted for.

The weight of responsibility sat like an elephant on her chest.

"Josef, run over and reassure them while Anji and I finish loading." She held his gaze when he looked like he'd argue. The village elders sometimes struggled to deal with a woman. She didn't mind because she loathed politics. "Be quick. We don't have time for tea—you'll have to make your excuses."

It wasn't how things were done here and she didn't want to offend these people, but the survival of a species trumped social niceties today. Ten more minutes and they were finished packing. Anji tied the spare gasoline canisters onto the roof and made sure both big gas tanks were full. They honked and Josef jogged over and jumped into the van.

"Everything be okay." Lines creased Anji's leathery skin. "*Inshallah.*"

God willing, indeed.

She and Josef exchanged a look as Anji gunned the engine over the rough road marked only by a line of pale stones. Dust flew, stirred up by the tires, the land still soft from the thaw. They bounced over rivers, ruts and alluvial fans. Axelle craned her neck to stare at the imposing mountains.

"If the collars *are* working"—Josef spoke from the backseat—"there could be some crackpot in these hills picking off critically endangered animals for money. Anyone that desperate isn't going to care if a couple of foreigners end up as collateral damage."

They'd left some weapons with their other belongings last fall. Her father had insisted she have some sort of protection when he'd heard she was conducting her research in Afghanistan. Now she was grateful.

She glanced at Josef sharply. "Do you want to go home?"

"I'm just saying this could be dangerous." His hands gripped the back of the seat as they bounced over a rickety bridge.

"If you want to go back you should say so now. The pilot can fly you out in the morning." She kept her voice soft. They were almost the same age but he was her responsibility and she had no right to place him in danger. "I don't want you thinking you don't have a choice. I can handle this." He had a life. He had a future. She only had her passion for saving things that needed saving.

"Ya, I run away and leave you alone in the wilderness." Josef sat back and crossed his arms, muttering angrily.

She held back an instinctive retort. She didn't care about being alone in the wilderness, but with this amount of ground to cover, she needed all the help she could get. "I have Anji," she said instead. "We can get more men from the village."

The Wakhi man grinned a gap-toothed smile, his eyes dancing. After generations of war and decades of being ignored by the government in Kabul, a few missing teeth were the least of anyone's problems. A few dead leopards might not rank high in the concerns of government either, not with the resurgence of the Taliban, not with the constant threat of assassination, insurgents and death.

"If we find sign of a poacher we will gather men from the village and hunt him down," the smaller man said.

Axelle nodded, but she was worried. This would be Anji's responsibility when he finished training and was appointed the wildlife officer for this region. He needed to be confident enough to take charge of dangerous situations like this. She bit her lip. He was such a sweet little guy she didn't know how he'd confront armed poachers. The idea of him hurt didn't sit well. He had a family. People who cared.

Isolation pressed down on her shoulders. All she had was an estranged father and a grandfather she hadn't visited in two long years.

Energetic clouds boiled over the top of the mountains. A spring storm was building, but it was nothing to the growing sense of unease that filled her when she thought of someone lining up her cats in the crosshairs of a hunting scope.

———

Two hours later the sun was sinking into the west. Desperation and the need to hurry pulsed through her blood and made her head pound with frustration. The van got stuck twice but they'd managed to push free of the freshly thawing ground. The shock absorbers were toast. Ahead she could make out the faint outline of pale yurts set deep in the shadow of the mountains.

A sonorous snore resonated from the back seat where Anji slept. Josef's cheeks were ruddy from the exertion of driving in such demanding conditions. They'd all taken a turn behind the wheel.

"Keep going," she urged as they passed the yurts. To save time they needed to drive as far as they dared toward where she figured Sheba had denned up. Half a mile later they bumped over a rock the size of a football, and her head glanced off the side window. *Dammit.*

"I can't go much further without breaking an axle," Josef warned.

"Stop here." She scrabbled in her bag for a head-torch and flashlight. "We'll hike the rest of the way."

"We go now?" Anji asked groggily, throwing a blanket off his lap.

"You take the van back to camp and man the radio, Anji." They needed someone back at base camp in case they ran into trouble. "There's a cave over this ridge that Sheba used as a den. If the cubs aren't there—" Her voice wavered. She didn't want to think what would happen if the cubs weren't there. The Hindu Kush was no place for babies to wander alone in the dark.

Even though they'd traveled as fast as they could, it was probably already too late. Swallowing her concern, she jumped out of the van. Josef joined her with a flashlight and radio.

"Let's go." She started along the path, running because it was still twilight and the precious light wouldn't last long.

She tripped over a rock and Josef grabbed her arm. "Careful."

But she didn't want to slow down. Despite the icy mountain air, heat poured off her body and her heart thumped like her veins were empty and desperate for blood. So many predators roamed these lands—bears, wolves, lynx, leopards, humans— how could two young cubs survive without their mother's protection?

They clambered over large rocks at the top of the ridge and moved cautiously down the steep slope on the other side. The sky shifted to velvet blackness with nothing but ice-encased peaks to cast a faint silvery haze over the lower slopes. Axelle worked her way along a tiny goat path carved in ancient stone. Slippery and dangerous. The narrow beams of their flashlights provided the only clue as to where to put her feet while strung high above a cliff face. She slipped, slamming her knee into a rock. Stones trickled down the mountainside, lending a soundtrack of granite rain to their frantic search.

Her heart revved. She held tight to Josef's hand as he hauled her to her feet. "Thanks."

"We should go back." Every crease on his face told her he didn't want to be here.

"We're almost there." She pulled away. "Two more minutes and we'll know for sure if the cubs are in that den."

Axelle inched along the path, the sound of Josef's footsteps crunching in her wake. *There*. A few yards away she saw the narrow opening of the den. There was a tingle between her shoulder blades that made her hesitate, alert for danger.

They'd rushed here worried the leopard was dead, but if they were wrong, they were approaching the den of a large feline with young cubs. Snow leopards were nowhere near the size of lions or tigers, but she and Josef were balanced on the edge of a cliff face.

The leopards could dance down these rocks; she and Josef would smash and burn.

Josef went to move ahead but she raised her hand to stop him. "Wait."

"Why?"

"Because I'm the boss and I said so."

He grunted, less than impressed. She knew how he felt.

There was no clever way to do this. She inched forward on all fours, the sharp rocks digging into her knees. She held her breath, listening, then shone her beam straight into the mouth of the den. Bare rock reflected back at her.

Nothing.

She ran the beam of light across the floor of the entranceway and saw animal bones—standard snow leopard fare. This was definitely a den. She inched forward, Josef close enough she couldn't turn without knocking into him. A part of her welcomed his body heat in the ever-deepening cold. The other part didn't like to be reminded about how it felt to touch a man. Memories could be colder than an Afghan winter.

They peered silently inside the shallow cave. More bones lay scattered on the bare rock and what looked like a bed of fur was nestled against one side of the cave. There were no green reflective retinas or bad-tempered snarls. An outcrop of rock blocked her view of the back of the cave where the cubs might have wandered in search of food or warmth.

She needed to get in there and take a better look.

Tension built in her muscles and sweat suddenly slid down the groove of her spine. Her mouth went dry and she forced several swallows to moisten it. Her hands shook. God, the last thing she wanted to do was crawl inside that dark hole and take a look behind that rock. Josef grabbed the belt of her pants before she started inside.

She dangled like a rag doll. "Put me down, dammit." She managed to shake off his grip. "I've got to see if the cubs are behind that rock."

"I'll go," he offered.

"You won't fit." Without wasting another moment, she wriggled through the tight opening. Stupid childhood fears would not stop her from doing her job.

Pressure pounded her immediately and made every pore on her body swell. Memories betrayed her, recollections from a time so long ago the images were more like visions of another lifetime. The silence. The immense weight above her that could shift and crush at any moment.

Concentrate. She swung the light around but saw nothing except bare rock. Her pulse sped up. Walls pressed in on her. Gnawed bones poked at her palms as she dragged herself across the ground. Dust and dirt flew through the air and she wheezed. The thought of the cave collapsing, of all that mighty rock crushing her, made her mouth parch and her heart drum.

She breathed in, in, in. Short little breaths that expanded her lungs to bursting. Finally she released the breath and was able to move again. She stuck her hand in the nest of fur. Cold. No remnant of warmth from soft delicate bodies. Josef grabbed tight to her ankle and, despite the bruising pressure, she welcomed the connection.

She shuffled forward, concentrated on the beam from her headlight as she squeezed through the narrow gap and finally got a look behind the outcrop of rock.

Dirt, rock, and white bleached bones.

Disappointment slammed hard into her chest and she swallowed the awful sensation of failure as she shuffled backwards. "Nothing."

Josef's eyes were wide in the glare of her lamp. She brushed the dust and fur that stuck to her clothing, dropping her head to hide the tumult of emotions.

"What do we do now?"

"Go back to camp." There was nothing else to do in the dark. Anger and anguish knotted in her throat.

Wearily Josef turned and began picking his way along the

trail. Axelle wanted to look for the collar but the risk was too high and she hadn't brought a radio receiver. A harsh wind blew down from the mountain and sliced through the layers of clothing, freezing her to the bone. She hugged herself and trudged onward. The radio squawked and they both startled.

"I find the cubs. I find the cubs!"

Anji.

Axelle grabbed the handset. "What do you mean you found the cubs? Where are you?"

"They in box in yurt." It sounded like he was jumping up and down in excitement.

This didn't make any sense. The wind gusted in her face as she frowned at the stars.

"What the hell is going on?" Josef murmured.

She didn't know. "Let's go find out."

———

Dempsey and his soldiers remained fixed in position as the strangers disappeared over the ridge. To the east, wolves howled, the cries echoing off giant pinnacles that edged the corridor like row upon row of shark's teeth. Awareness rippled over Dempsey's skin like hives.

"What was that was all about?" Baxter whispered into his personal role radio, which connected the four of them over short distances. Dempsey didn't answer. He sprinted up the craggy face to see what they'd been looking at. It took him less than a minute to climb there and back again.

"Empty animal den. Some kind of predator," he told his unit.

"Two Westerners? In these mountains? In the middle of the bloody night?" Baxter raised a skeptical brow. "They're either up to no good or they're bloody loonies."

"And yet, here we are, in these mountains, in the middle of the bloody night," Taz commented dryly.

"Aye, but we *are* up to no good," said Baxter.

"And you're a loony," Cullen added. The Scots' amusement faded as an oppressive silence swept around them.

"You really think we're going to find this guy out here?" Baxter asked dubiously.

They had eyes in the sky, but in a wilderness this vast?

"That's the mission," Dempsey said, moving out.

The terrorist they were tracking had connections that gave politicians hard-ons the size of Cleopatra's Needle. The brass said they were working on intelligence reports that this guy was heading to the Wakhan Corridor through the Boroghill Pass. In Dempsey's experience "intelligence" was as trustworthy as a three-year-old with a Kalashnikov.

So far they'd found sweet FA.

"Tell us again what we're doing here?" Baxter grumbled.

"Following orders." Dempsey hadn't failed a mission yet—a soldier with his background couldn't afford failure of any kind, not if he hoped to stay in the Regiment. And although this part of Afghanistan was not a hot zone for terrorist activity, it might be the best hideout for bad guys avoiding the limelight. Men like their quarry who'd supposedly been dead for the past decade.

"What now?" Taz asked. Tariq Moheek was an Iraqi-born Christian who'd been forced into exile under Saddam Hussein's regime. His grandmother had stayed in Iraq, enduring Saddam's iron fist only to be killed in an American bombing raid during the liberation. The guy spoke eight languages and looked like a local —Taz was the best asset the Regiment had when it came to the Middle Eastern crises. Pity they couldn't clone him.

Dempsey pulled his pack onto his back and looked at his squad. They wore gear suitable for high-altitude work, no identifying insignia. They were heavily armed, with webbed vests to keep vital supplies close at hand, and they could survive for weeks without resupply, even in this bleak sterile land.

He didn't want to be in this high hostile arena for that long. "Let's follow these clowns and set up OPs." Observation posts were best constructed during the hours of darkness. "I want to know who they are and what they're doing." Good guys or bad? Either way he could use them.

"What are the chances of finding one old bugger out here when we don't even know which direction he took off in or if he's really still alive?" Baxter griped.

Four-man teams had been dropped at each of the three mountain passes that joined Pakistan to the Wakhan Corridor. Twelve soldiers surveying an area the length of Wales. On the plus side, most of the peaks were too sheer to climb without equipment and most of the valleys were permanently blocked by snow.

Chances were they were following a man who only bore an unfortunate resemblance to a dead Russian terrorist who, a decade earlier, had left only a finger at the site of the British Embassy bombing in Yemen. And the poor bugger was in for a helluva shock when they found him.

"If he's alive, we'll find him." Because those were his orders. At his signal they disappeared silently into the night like wraiths.

CHAPTER TWO

AXELLE SLIPPED inside the yurt to find Anji cradling a tiny squalling snow leopard against his chest. Every muscle ached with fatigue, exhaustion scratched at her eyeballs, but she couldn't help smile at the impossibly beautiful, totally improbable scrap of fur. Then it struck her. If the cubs were in a box in their yurt, then Sheba was unquestionably dead.

Everything she feared had come true. Except the cubs *were* alive...for now. "Do you have any yak's milk we can feed them?" she asked.

He nodded. The cubs were thin and cold and wouldn't survive long without nourishment.

"They were right here, in this box." The Wakhi man tapped the cardboard box on the floor with his boot, his brown eyes shining as he jiggled the cub like a baby.

A mewling sound from inside the box had her reaching down and pulling out a soft tawny bundle covered in inky black spots. The bundle cuddled into her chest for warmth. Axelle's eyes rose to Josef's as he came in behind her. "I don't get it. Who brought them here?"

He held out his hand and she passed him the cub. "I'll get the fire going while you feed them."

The cubs looked at her with bright blue eyes, and Axelle's heart squeezed as she reached out a hand to stroke a tiny fluffy ear. They reminded her why the work was so important. There were so few of these creatures left on earth, and they were being forced into the narrowest, most unforgiving of margins.

"What kind of person kills the mother but saves the cubs?" Josef asked.

It wasn't rational to destroy with one hand and save with another and yet humans did it all the time. She squatted and opened the door of the little cast-iron stove they'd dragged from Kabul two summers ago when they'd launched this project. She lit a match to the yak dung that was already set. It spluttered and caught, the orange flames flickering and dancing as they licked the pungent fuel.

She looked up to find both men staring at her expectantly, awaiting instruction. She was one of the world's foremost experts on conserving endangered cats. Poachers weren't new to her. Death wasn't new. But this was different. The location made finding the culprit extremely problematic. The remoteness of the area, the geographical and political factors all weighed heavily against their chances of stopping this sonofabitch.

Her eyes took in the bare walls of the tent. Normally the walls were plastered with territorial zones for each collared leopard. "At least we didn't have the maps on display when he left the cubs here."

"He doesn't need them," Josef tucked the cub inside his jacket and eyed her from beneath thick brows. "I think someone is using our collars to track the cats."

Axelle opened her mouth to argue, but Josef didn't let her.

"Think about it—to find Aslan and Sheba so quickly? Finding two of our collared cats in a couple of days when it took us nearly two months of constant trapping to even *see* any?" He sucked in a deep breath. "Someone is using our radio frequencies or the satellite feed and picking off our leopards like fairground ducks."

"Impossible." She considered Josef's words. *Unthinkable, but not impossible.* "Aslan might not even be dead," she pointed out.

Anji spoke hesitantly. "I found his collar today. There was blood on it."

Her stomach flipped.

Josef settled next to the metal stove as the flames finally started to expel heat. "You know how hard it is to catch one snow leopard, let alone two, within forty-eight hours."

She was intimately acquainted with the difficulties.

Most people who spent years living in the wilderness never saw one. It had taken a large team of big-cat experts weeks of careful observation and planning before they'd begun to have any success with their state-of-the-art snaring techniques. However, this poacher could have been here for months, or he could be a local, or he could be very, very lucky.

She wrapped her arms around herself as cold swept through her. Even though she wanted to reject Josef's idea, he might be right. An ominous disquiet slid through her chest. "That means we've signed a death warrant for every cat we collared."

Dread wove itself into a thick mass inside her lungs and she found it hard to draw in a full breath. The International Conservation Trust's project had achieved unprecedented success when they'd collared ten individuals last fall. If a poacher targeted all their leopards, they could wipe out a significant proportion of the Afghan snow leopard population in a matter of weeks. It would be her fault. The Trust would never get a permit to work in Afghanistan again—and they might never be able to radio collar another animal in the wild. It would knock conservation efforts back thirty years. More important, *her* leopards were the ones in the firing line.

The lanterns flickered erratically as the wind started to howl.

"Why would this bastard shoot the mother but take the time to bring the cubs to safety?" Axelle shook her head. It didn't make sense. Her head hurt trying to figure it out.

Josef held the cub high, its soft belly curved into his palm. It started to mewl as Anji handed him a small bowl of yak milk and a tiny medicine dispensing cup he'd dug from somewhere.

"These fellows would fetch good money on the black market," Josef remarked.

"But he'd have had to feed them and transport them straight away," Axelle added as comprehension dawned.

"And he didn't have time…" Josef met her gaze.

"Because he isn't finished yet. Oh, God."

"Maybe someone else find the cubs?" Anji suggested hopefully. "Someone who knows about the project and saw the camp? Maybe they find them and bring them here?" He eyed her and Josef uncertainly. There weren't exactly a lot of passersby, and the people who did travel this region could easily be drug dealers moving their opium hauls or arms dealers supplying the insurgents to the south.

"Perhaps," she said doubtfully. She tried to reassure him with a smile but her face felt nerveless and numb. Maybe she smiled. Maybe she didn't. She couldn't tell anymore.

He looked away. The cub tried to crawl up his chest and Anji disengaged the needle-sharp claws that tore small holes in the fabric.

The poacher had stood right here and looked around this tent. It gave her the creeps to think that a killer—the antithesis of her life's work—had been in her space. Saving these animals was what she did, it was an anathema to try to understand someone who'd take their lives—for something as inert and valueless as money.

She climbed slowly to her feet, her head pounding with a mixture of altitude, exhaustion, and anger.

"What are you going to do?" Josef asked.

She booted up her laptop and Sat Link device. "I need to inform the Trust's HQ." The unsettled feeling in her stomach refused to quit. All the months of hard work had to be sacrificed. Scientific knowledge did not trump survival of a species. The stakes were too high for her to falter.

Anji threw another piece of dried dung onto the fire. She felt as if she'd never be warm again.

"I'm going to email the Trust and see if they can send an expert to deal with the cubs with a view to future release." It took eighteen months for a snow leopard mother to rear her cubs. The thought of these wild creatures stuffed into a zoo because of her research project was sickening.

"What else?" Josef gently placed the fat, content cub back in the box next to its sibling. His voice vibrated with emotion.

She narrowed her eyes. "I'll email HQ about what we suspect is going on—"

"If we wait for their permission we'll lose more animals."

She met his anger with resolute calm. "We won't be waiting for anything. We need to re-trap each leopard and remove the collars." It might cost her the one thing in the world she cared about—her job—but there was no alternative.

The collars were programmed to drop off after two years. She rubbed her tired eyes. Why hadn't she chosen an option where they could have blasted the collars off remotely? Those models were less reliable, but...*damn.* She'd never imagined a scenario where a sophisticated poacher would turn their technology against them.

"In the future we'll get the collar company to figure out a way to encrypt the data so this can't happen again." In the meantime it was a race against time. Frustration wanted to force its way out of her throat in a scream. Instead she started typing. "Get some sleep, Josef. We begin at dawn."

Clumsy with exhaustion, Josef and Anji got into their sleeping bags and curled up on bedrolls beside the box of kittens. The fire radiated a steady heat that tempered the fierce wind that shrieked down the mountains and rustled the heavy felt of the yurt.

She hoped the bastard hunting her leopards was caught out in this weather. She hoped the sonofabitch was freezing his ass off on the side of the mountain. She went and grabbed her sleeping bag and pulled it over her shoulders as she typed the message that might destroy her reputation as a conservation biologist.

Once that was gone, what the hell did she have left?

————

Wakhan Corridor, Afghanistan, July 1979

Through the scope of his Dragunov sniper rifle Dmitri tracked two Westerners on horseback followed by three local men leading Bactrian camels heavily loaded with supplies.

"*Kapitán?*" His lieutenant whispered into his ear. "If these are the men we are after do we kill them?"

"*Nyet.* I need to interrogate them." Dmitri stared at their fresh round faces. It wouldn't take long. His masters in Moscow would be pleased his unit had found definitive proof of agents spreading Western propaganda in this region. "Take them."

His troops burst out of the ground and encircled the ragged caravan. The Westerners fumbled for their weapons as they were dragged from their horses and kicked to the ground. They quickly found themselves at the wrong end of a rifle. One of the guides ran for it. Dmitri almost shouted to let the man go but it was too late. He crumpled to the dirt as a bullet pierced his heart. Dmitri would have been content to let the man spread rumors of soldiers who appeared like ghosts out of the earth, but it was not to be. He strode down the hillside, his long stride rapidly covering the ground. The locals and Westerners were separated, stripped of weaponry, pockets emptied, contents laid out in front of them.

The men's wrists were tied behind their backs.

"Comrade." He tilted his head and smiled into a pair of furious blue eyes. From a distance Dmitri had thought the man younger, weaker, but the blond curls gave him a falsely angelic aspect. Up close there was something hard about that face. Something unexpectedly dangerous.

Lack of fear? Or that flicker of contempt in his deceptively youthful face?

He did not trust those blue eyes. Only lies would come out of this man's mouth.

"What do you want? Why have you captured us? The Soviet Union has no jurisdiction here." The man spoke first in English, then repeated his words in perfect Russian. Even the accent was excellent.

"I commend you on your language skills, comrade." He examined one of the leaflets that had been stuffed in the man's pocket. "You speak Arabic too, I see?" He shook his head at the foolishness of the anti-Soviet propaganda. "Pity most of the people in this region cannot read."

The other foreigner was younger, his face softer—too soft to be involved in such worldly machinations. He was the weaker of the two. He was the one to break.

"Where are you from? What are you doing here?" Dmitri addressed the dark-haired man with the scared brown eyes.

"We're explorers. We were going to climb Mount Noshaq but you just shot our guide." There was enough righteous condemnation in his voice to be convincing, but Dmitri wasn't fooled. Amateurs. The world was full of amateurs.

"His own fault." Dmitri spread his fingers and shrugged. "He should not have run." The warning was clear.

The dark-haired man choked out an affronted breath and started to bluster.

"Say nothing, Sebastian." The blond cherub ordered.

Dmitri smashed the butt of his rifle into his face. The man screamed and rolled in the dirt, blood dripping from his nose into the dust.

Dmitri ignored him and concentrated on the dark-haired man, Sebastian. "Do you work for the Americans?" No reaction, "The British?" He found his answer in a flash of the man's pupils. He paced. "So once again the Wakhan Corridor hosts the Great Game." He sighed and tossed the crumpled leaflet at the man, whose eyes were now huge with fear and uncertainty. The other man lay on the ground, blood smeared across his upper lip.

Dmitri narrowed his gaze. He was a dangerous man, no doubt. But Dmitri was also a dangerous man with the might of the USSR backing him. "Take photographs of everything, then burn the leaflets," he ordered his soldiers, who immediately started unloading the sacks from the camels.

One of his soldiers took their photographs, and the blond man boiled with emotion palpable even in the bitter silence.

"What should we do with the guides?" The *starshiná* asked.

Dmitri saw bloodlust in his men's eyes but he was clear on the rules of engagement. "Let them go, and let them take their animals."

"No!" the blond man shouted as if he was in charge of this operation. *Mudak.*

Dmitri went to kick the worm again but the man's pathetic cowering made him spit on him in disgust. The sound of a rifle being cocked split the air.

"Shall I finish him, *Kapitán*?"

Spies were subject to different rules than civilians and soldiers.

"We only need one alive," the lieutenant reminded him.

One to break and find out what else the British imperialists were plotting. He watched the unease build on the blond man's face and felt a moment of pleasure that he'd unsettled him.

The dark-haired man stuttered, "You can't just shoot us. You'll start a full-scale war."

"You and your US allies are the ones inciting war." And the USSR was being drawn in despite itself. A mistake in his opinion, but no one had wanted to listen to him. Dmitri crouched beside the weaker man. "Your masters will never admit they know who you are, let alone claim you. No one will care when you die."

"We are mountaineers—"

"Your family will never know where your body lies." Dmitri

pulled his Stechkin APB out of the holster and checked the chamber. He pointed it at the blond man. Smiled. "Tell me you're a British spy."

"You'll shoot me anyway." The blond man sneered, but his eyes flared as Dmitri began squeezing the trigger. "Stop! I need to talk to you in private."

Dmitri laughed. "The time for privacy expired."

"*Ya russki agent!*"

Dmitri froze and the brown-haired man spluttered, "What the hell are you telling them that for. Now they'll just shoot me."

"Shut your stupid fucking mouth, Sebastian."

Dmitri stood and narrowed his eyes. "Tell me your code name and handler." Patriotism demanded he check the man's story, but Dmitri was looking forward to personally taking care of the arrogant little shit when the GRU denied ever hearing of him.

———

Axelle dragged herself from her sleeping bag in the main yurt and lit the burner for tea. She was wearing the same clothes she'd worn yesterday and was pretty sure she stank worse than the resident yak. Personal hygiene would have to wait. Normally she slept in one of the smaller structures, but because of their late arrival last night and their need to bottle-feed the cubs she hadn't bothered to seek her own bed. She'd simply laid her sleeping bag on the floor and closed her eyes. Josef lay, open-mouthed, snoring. Anji hugged a pallet in the corner, curled protectively close to the cubs who, thankfully, were still sleeping. They'd fed them once in the night, all three of them being woken by the insistent cries of the helpless creatures. If that was any indication about having a baby, no wonder her mother had stopped at one.

Thoughts of her mother came out of nowhere and she blocked them fast.

She made tea for everyone and thought about checking her email but didn't want to receive orders she couldn't follow—like leaving the collars in place until they had a better understanding of the situation. Because if they lost one more leopard she didn't think she could live with herself.

She downloaded the latest positional data from the satellites and made notes about GPS coordinates. They had eight animals to try to capture. Eight of the most elusive cats in the world, who'd all been caught before, and were all pretty savvy about not being caught again. She went over to the gun rack and, soundlessly as possible, started mixing the drugs and packing the tranquilizer darts and antidote, assembling the kit they'd need, along with daypacks full of water bottles and food.

She made two feeds of milk for the cubs and left them on the food counter. Then she shook Josef awake and bade him to silence with a finger across her lips and a glance at the still sleeping trio. He nodded, slipped on his boots, grabbed his pack and the tranquilizer gun and followed her into the silence of the morning. It was cold and they both pulled fleeces tighter around their torsos to keep out the breeze as they sipped warm tea from thermoses. She went to the equipment tent and took out the heavy cable traps and spring mechanisms. She heaved four over her shoulder, nearly sinking beneath the weight. She also grabbed a hammer. Josef picked up the other six snares and the shovel, and they carried them over to where the animals were corralled. They had a dirt bike but no way could they carry everything they needed on that machine. Josef hated horseback riding but they had too much ground to cover and too much at stake for him to balk.

She saddled two horses while Josef packed the equipment onto the back of the yak.

"Ready?" she asked.

Josef nodded, and they both mounted up.

An hour later, Axelle dragged the reluctant bovine to one of their most successful trapping sites—an area that intersected the home range of two collared males. The foothills were drenched in sepia tones, while the Hindu Kush stabbed into a veil of dreary cloud that matched the sullen rock.

Usually it took hours to set each snare but they didn't have hours. Her heart beat like a countdown to disaster and every inhalation hurt. At more than nine thousand feet, the dilute air didn't help.

"We'll use previous trap sites." That would save time digging fresh holes in half-frozen earth and also from having to choose new locations. The disadvantage was the cats might not be dumb enough to fall for the same trick twice.

They approached the first site as the sun conquered the jagged rim of the mountains. Gold and pink bathed the snowcapped peaks and began to burn off the cloud, but neither she nor Josef had time to give the spectacular view more than a cursory glance. She checked the ground and found fresh scrape markings along the canyon floor.

"Looks like they're still using this area." Which confirmed what the collar data told them. They tethered the horses and mule, then she dropped to her knees and started clearing loose gravel out of the pit where they'd previously set the snare. She worked frantically, smashing the stones with a small spade, Josef arranging the spring to attach to the snare that would hold the leopard in place. Satisfied her hole was big enough, she set the loop over a piece of plastic sheeting, disguising the metal with a thin layer of dirt. They checked the snare mechanism—it worked. Finally she set up the radio transmitter, which would send out a signal when the snare was sprung.

Her heart pounded from exertion, and her lungs heaved. It had taken less than an hour to complete but they needed to work faster.

"Let's set another snare in Sven's zone." The neighboring male's territory abutted this one.

They followed the edge of the escarpment a mile north, eating lunch on horseback, without talking, without rest. Axelle's throat was raw from the effort of subduing the emotion rioting inside her. The unseen threat of a bullet in the back made her feel paranoid and small. She straightened her spine and forged onward. There was no alternative and only the leopards mattered.

By midafternoon the sun blazed down and the wind burned her cheeks.

There was a sense of loss and abandonment to the foothills. The only living things they'd encountered thus far were sage bushes and birds. By 6:00 p.m., they'd ridden twenty miles in a rough circle around base camp and set eight traps. It was a record-breaking achievement but hard to celebrate. They had two snares left and both she and Josef were exhausted. They headed into a short bottleneck canyon along a narrow stream that was in full spate from the glacier melt under the afternoon sun. The sense of being watched intensified, and the hair on her arms rose. She glanced up and froze.

A snow leopard with fierce gray eyes sat sphinx-like on an overhang above them. Axelle recognized him from the yellow tags in both ears. It was the cat they'd named Samson—a large male with blood staining his jaw as he guarded the dead markhor at his side. He was the dominant male in the area, 120 pounds of sublime feline, and though snow leopards didn't attack humans, he was aggressive when cornered.

Axelle's horse snorted and danced sideways beneath her.

"Keep going," she urged Josef while kicking her horse past the watchful eyes of the cat.

"He'll never step in a trap if he sees us setting it," Josef protested.

They rounded a corner and she pulled the yak alongside her horse and grabbed the tranquilizer gun from the pack. She loaded a dart and swung her leg over the front of the mare's neck and jumped down.

"You can't dart him without him being snared." Josef grabbed her arm. "Axelle, the Trust will dismiss you on the spot if they find out."

She pulled away from him. "He's here. Now. By the time we

see him again—*if* we see him again—that poacher could have already skinned the hide from his back." Her voice shook and she tried to calm herself. Getting overemotional solved nothing. She'd learned that as a skinny little brat buried under a pile of rubble. "I'll make sure your Ph.D. position isn't jeopardized. You won't be held responsible for anything I do." She swallowed dirt and grit and something that felt suspiciously like tears. "And if they fire me? So what? I'll find you a new supervisor. A better one." Even though this job was the only thing that mattered in her life.

"There isn't a better supervisor." Josef's jaw clenched. "I'm not worried about my Ph.D."

"Well you should be." Her eyes scanned the western horizon. "The sun's going down. We need to hurry." She started climbing to get above the cat. "Tie the animals and be ready to give chase with blankets and the antidote." The leopards tended to head for high ground when scared, but she needed Samson to go down, away from the steep precipices and bone-breaking falls.

She climbed swiftly into position. The cat hadn't moved. He eyed Josef, who he perceived as the bigger threat, and protected his kill. She took aim and hesitated, knowing she was breaking the exact protocol she'd helped instigate, but couldn't think of a single viable alternative.

What if she released the collars and it turned out this was a short-term glitch with the data? She'd be screwed.

Anji had gone searching for Sheba's collar today but she hadn't heard from him and she didn't have time to call him now. What if they were wrong about the poacher?

What if they were right? Was taking a chance worth the life of this leopard?

Dammit.

She shook off the paralyzing indecision, took aim and breathed out. Then she squeezed the trigger. The dart hit Samson square in the flank and he swung around to face her with a snarling hiss. She stood and waved the rifle over her head, making herself big and tall and scary. Hell, scary didn't begin to describe how she was feeling right now. The cat's upper lip drew back over gleaming teeth and he advanced a step. She growled right back at him, and he whirled and leapt straight over the edge of the cliff.

Axelle scrambled down the rocks, slipping and skidding, trying to hold the rifle high so it didn't get damaged. She hopped to the floor of the canyon, raced around the corner to find the cat and Josef in a face-off, and now she was blocking the cat's escape route. The cat froze. The horses jerked on their reins, eyes rolling, hooves stamping, stirring the dust as they smelled the predator. Quickly, she loaded another dart.

"Hurry. Up," Josef ground out as the cat advanced a pace toward him.

She aimed just as the leopard tensed to spring. The shot echoed around the canyon and immediately Samson started to stagger.

It only took a moment for him to go completely under the influence of the tranquilizer. She grabbed a sleeping bag to cover him because the drugs lowered heart rate and could lead to hypothermia, especially as the sun slipped ever lower in the sky. She wrapped him gently as Josef popped the collar. It took a few seconds. She stroked the animal's luxurious thick fur and absorbed his warmth as she felt his pulse. They should be collecting samples and doing weights and measurements, but she didn't have the heart until she knew all her cats were safe.

"Let's move the horses out of the canyon and give him the antidote." It was almost dark and they needed to get back to camp.

Josef sat back on his heels. Worry crinkled his craggy brow. "I hate this."

He wasn't talking about losing data.

Emotions scrambled around her chest and wouldn't settle no matter how deeply she sucked in air. "I hate it, too." The lump grew in her throat until she couldn't speak.

She hadn't cried since her husband died, over a decade ago,

and she wasn't about to start now. Ignoring the unexpected wash of black emotions, she helped Josef move the horses. Then she stood back as one of the most beautiful creatures on earth woke to a better chance of survival.

———

Jonathon Boyle ignored the sweat that dampened his armpits as he sat outside the prime minister's office. The atmosphere in Number 10 was stuffy in the extreme. The weather outside was a record high for May but nary a window was cracked in the hopes of snagging a breeze. The new leader of the British people seemed to have an unhealthy aversion to fresh air.

The door opened and his eyes widened a fraction as his gaze met that of Franklin Dehn, the U.S. Ambassador to the Court of St. James's. Despite their connection by marriage, the man walked past him without a word and Jonathon allowed himself a moment of quiet loathing. Even in the grips of intense heat the other man was a cold fish. Nothing fazed the American. God knew, Jonathon had tried.

The PM's secretary stood in the doorway, ushering him inside with a clawed hand and impatient twist of her lips. Scrawny old bat. He picked up his jacket and briefcase from the plush burgundy chair and went to greet the new British PM.

"Thanks for seeing me at such short notice, Prime Minister." He held out his hand.

"I think we can dispense with the formalities, considering how long we've known each other, Jonathon." David Allworth shook his hand as if he were pumping iron and waved him to a hard-back chair. "I don't have much time"—he checked his watch—"but I suppose you're here because of the rumor that Dmitri Volkov surfaced again after all these years?"

Jonathon folded his hands one over the other. An effeminate gesture he'd cultivated years ago that served him well. Despite having had a wife and child, people believed he was homosexual, and he used the misconception to his advantage. Women certainly seemed to like it. Maybe it made them feel safe.

"I know it is none of my business. Although the man did try to bomb the British embassy in Sana'a, with me in it. That does tend to make it rather personal."

The clock ticked on the mantel. How many prime ministers had that clock marked time for? At least three that he knew of.

"I doubt *you* were the intended target in Yemen." A smile accompanied the soft laugh.

Which proved exactly how little the man knew about the world of espionage and counter-espionage. And that, Jonathon figured with an imaginary shrug, was the whole point of being good at keeping secrets.

"Of course not." He waved the notion away. "I'm hardly important enough to warrant my own bomb." That bomb had pissed him off. He hadn't expected it and it was the second time the Russian had got the best of him. "But I don't understand why they think the man has surfaced now, after all these years. He's supposed to be dead…" It was a risk coming here for information, showing an interest, but espionage was all about playing the odds.

"He probably is dead," Allworth told him with a patronizing little smile. "It was just a rumor that he was seen in Pakistan. I sent someone to check it out anyway."

"Someone?" Jonathon's gaze sharpened.

"Soldiers," the prime minister admitted.

Good news or bad? Jonathon chewed his bottom lip, allowing a little doubt to leak out. After all, he was an old man who'd almost been blown up during the service of his country. "You think they'll find a trace of this ghost? We believed him dead for nearly a decade. Plus he knows those mountains the same way you know politics…"

He really was an obsequious little bastard but it couldn't be helped.

"I sent the SAS." David's stoic expression couldn't hide his nationalistic pride. Jonathon mentally rolled his eyes—as if Britain was the only country in the world to have Special Forces. "If he's alive, they'll find him."

"Of course." Jonathon once again inclined his head and gathered his things to leave. "Your father would have been proud to see how much you've accomplished, David. Very proud indeed."

"You think so?" A contemplative light entered the younger man's eyes.

"Oh, I know so." Orphans hungered for mention of their parents. This he knew from personal experience. "Your father and I often talked about you and your mother when we were sitting in some hut in the middle of nowhere. You've fulfilled every dream he ever envisioned for his son."

"I don't remember him at all." The tone was wistful.

"Trust me," Jonathon smiled, "he'd be proud." He thrust out his hand. "You must be busy. You don't want a useless old fart like me hanging around."

David Allworth leaned forward. "I heard you were finally retiring from the Foreign Office."

"Whether I like it or not, I'm afraid." Jonathon's smile slipped. He was over seventy years old but his brain and body were both sharper than Toledo steel. He wasn't ready to bloody retire. He didn't think he'd ever be ready.

"You don't plan to take up golf and sudoku?"

He shuddered. "I'd rather drink myself to death on cheap French wine."

The PM stared at him with the sort of sympathy in his eyes that Jonathon detested—as if *he* had the right to feel sorry for him. But Jonathon's time was nearly over and he might as well get used to the idea. He was being kicked out on his bony old arse by impatient youngsters he could snap with his pinkie.

He sighed and forced a smile. Nothing to be done except keep his ears to the ground and maintain his contacts. Maybe he'd pay a visit to David's mother. He'd occasionally comforted the widow in the years after her husband's death. But she'd been too needy and he'd tired of her quickly. Perhaps now was the time to renew that acquaintance.

"Actually…"

Jonathon froze mid-step.

David Allworth rose to his feet and paced to the window overlooking the garden. "I do have something you might like to consider. A place on an advisory committee."

Jonathon raised his brows but kept his mouth shut. He wasn't spending his dotage overseeing NHS reforms or pension plans—not even for Mother Russia. "Doing?"

The PM frowned. "Overseeing weapon development at Aldermaston. It requires top-level security clearance." Dark brown eyes started to twinkle. "Would you be interested?"

Jonathon's mouth dropped in genuine shock. *Finally.*

"Me, Prime Minister?" Inside he pumped his fists wildly. He was back in the game. They shook hands and, despite his exultation and the intense heat, his skin was cold. "Anything to help my country."

CHAPTER
THREE

DEMPSEY AND BAXTER had crawled into a hole in the side of a mountain that overlooked this treeless, rock-strewn valley approximately thirty-six hours ago. A million hours later, they were still here, Dempsey lying prone on top of his sleeping bag while he kept watch. The entrance of the OP was well hidden behind straggly bushes, and he and Baxter had cleared the area of spiders and scorpions and checked for snakes before they'd settled in. They needed to be vigilant for unwanted wildlife because neither wanted a medivac out of here. Plus, they could use the protein.

Taz and Cullen were on the same mountain but on the south side, getting the benefit of the rising sun while Dempsey and Baxter froze their asses off in the shadows. The two men they'd spotted that first night had been gone all day yesterday and hadn't returned until after dark last night. Dempsey didn't know what they were up to.

The man they'd left behind in camp looked local. He wore an AK-47 slung across his back with familiar ease, as did most men in this godforsaken country. Yesterday he'd taken a dirt bike into some of the adjacent hills. Dempsey had followed a short distance behind but the guy returned within the hour.

Dempsey glanced down at the three yurts settled into the base of the mountain like circus tents. A couple of horses and a yak were corralled nearby and they had that bike and an old Russian van parked besides it.

Who are you? What are you doing? Can I use you?

He'd contacted HQ to track down more information but so far zilch on confirmed identities. Intel in this region was iffy at best. No one operated here during the winter because it was completely cut off by snow in the mountains and the sort of temperatures that snapped off appendages. This part of Afghanistan was surprisingly peaceful considering it was surrounded by unfriendly borders: Tajikistan, China and Pakistan. The bulk of the Northern Province of Badakhshan lay west, home of the mujahedeen's Northern Alliance, which had battled the Soviets and Taliban for decades. Westerners were rare in this part of the world but not unknown: NGOs and charities carried out work here. In summer they even got tourists. But the valley was also used by gunrunners and drug smugglers.

So who the feck are you? Friend or foe?

The stone of the mountain was unrelenting beneath his body. His legs ached, he felt like he had Sumo wrestlers pounding the muscles in his back. Those who joined Special Forces for the adrenaline rush should try holding this sort of position long-term. It was boring as hell and tested his endurance more than any ice climb. Maybe he was getting too old for this kind of shit. At thirty-nine he was among the older soldiers in the Regiment and, with twenty-two years' service, one of the longest serving. But he'd never struggled physically. He had no clue what he going to do when he quit the SAS and didn't want to think about it.

Getting old was brutal but then so was growing up in Ulster during the Troubles.

The Troubles.

Ha. As if the conflict had been a few boys throwing stones at one another. It had been war. A bloody, vicious battle, fought by ruthless killers brimming with nationalistic zeal and a total lack of human empathy, played out on streets full of innocent civilians. The terrorists hadn't cared who died in the crossfire any more than the British government. He wasn't blind to the hypocrisy. He'd joined up to hurt his family. To destroy them if he could. He'd joined the most hated regiment in the British Army—the paras—then set his sights on becoming one of the most feared soldiers in the world, certainly in Northern Ireland. There could be no doubt of the total rejection of his family's values when he'd passed the grueling selection process and been allowed into the ranks of the SAS.

He'd made his choice. He'd built a life of integrity and honor, and that was more than he could have hoped for as the youngest son of the most notorious bomb maker in Northern Ireland.

He blanked the memories from his mind. Too many years. Too much ancient grief. What was done was done. The Regiment was his family now and protecting innocents by eliminating the bad guys was what he did.

He glanced at Baxter who was out cold after taking the earlier stag duty. He turned back to the camp using his high-powered day/night scope, looking for clues about these people. He saw no weapons except the basic rifle they'd taken off with yesterday and the old AK-47 which was as ubiquitous as a dick in this part of the world. There was a solar panel mounted beside the biggest yurt, and he suspected they had a satellite phone—stupid not to. He'd seen walkie-talkies and some sort of handheld receiver he couldn't identify.

A tent flap was flung back and the tall skinny guy who'd ridden off yesterday morning emerged, carrying two buckets of steaming hot water. He strode over to a curtained-off area that must be a jerry-rigged washing area. Dempsey felt a moment of extreme envy because he itched with grime from scalp to toes. It would be cold but it would be worth it to feel clean even for a short time.

From this elevation he had a clear view of the cubicle. He looked back at the yurts but out of the corner of his eye caught a glimpse of the guy pulling off his hat and shirt. Dempsey's gaze swung back. Suddenly his skin felt too tight, and heat rapid-fired through his veins.

There was enough skin on display to convince him *that* was no man. Long brown hair, the color of rich mahogany, tumbled in a straight line down her back. She grabbed the soap and turned to face him, small breasts with high pink nipples, pebbled from cold, waving hello.

It was a hell of a scope.

And he shouldn't be looking.

She dipped a washcloth into a bucket and started cleaning herself. Water slid over her skin and her body sparkled in the newborn rays of the sun. His mouth went dry as she sluiced water through her hair. There were no weapons hidden anywhere on her person—he could verify that. She was lean and muscled—hard for a trained observer not to notice.

Heat flooded his body. Finally he dragged his gaze away and sweated out the next couple of minutes of torture as she finished her impromptu shower.

Which he now needed more than ever.

She didn't look like a local. Her body was pale as cream and she had a healthy well-nourished glow that people here did not have. Out of his peripheral vision he saw her reach out to grab a towel. His earpiece crackled.

Holy Mary, Mother of God. He felt like his CO had caught him masturbating.

"Nothing to report except a couple of mountain goats, over." Cullen checked in through the PRR.

Dempsey touched the button on his wrist, relieved Baxter hadn't woken and shared in the morning's entertainment. "One subject moving around camp, female. Over and out."

She dressed quickly in jeans, baggy T-shirt, green fleece and vest, her body disappearing beneath shapeless cloth—which was a crying shame. Her features were even and narrow, especially her jaw. Beautiful—when you realized you were looking at a girl and not a guy. She dried her hair with the towel then jerked her head and looked straight at him. *No frickin' way*. He held perfectly still as she pinned him through the straggly sage bushes that covered their hideout. She pulled on her boots after shaking them out—smart girl—picked up the handheld unit he hadn't identified and hopped on the dirt bike.

Kicking the pedal to start it up, the accompanying noise of the engine shattered the tranquility of the morning.

She headed straight for the trail behind the camp, making a beeline for their position.

"Bloody fecking hell."

He held perfectly still, glancing around without moving his head, looking for anything that might have given them away. But there was nothing. He nudged Baxter gently with his boot because the last thing he needed was the Scot starting to snore if she got too close.

Had she seen them?

His brain said no way, no fecking way. He remained still even as she got nearer and nearer to where they lay prone in the dirt concealed by rocks and bushes. He held his breath and felt Baxter tense beside him. Then she veered right and went to the top of the ridge.

What was she doing? Where was she going? He pressed the button on his wrist. "Subject on ridge between us. See if you can see what she's up to, over," he murmured.

"No visual. Out."

The redheaded man stepped out of the central yurts and turned toward them, shading his eyes with his palm. Dempsey dropped his eye to the scope. The guy was tall and bulky, Scandinavian looking with a meaty jaw and cold blue eyes. Too young to be their target though.

Lovers? The woman's husband? Serf? Minion? Slave?

He took some photos—something he should have done of the woman, but had forgotten because his small brain had taken command of the mission.

"She's checking some sort of radio receiver. Can't get a decent look at it but it doesn't look military. Looks like she's heading back your way," Cullen said. Nerves buzzed. "She's pretty once you realize she's a lass and not a bloke."

He rolled his eyes. Craig Cullen was a lady's man and never missed an opportunity to score. Even in the Wakhan Corridor, Dempsey could sense him calculating his odds of seducing this woman. The sound of the bike engine amplified against the rock, grew louder as she crested the ridge and spat dust in her wake as she careened down the trail toward camp. He had an idea what these people might be, but until he knew for sure he had to assume they were hostile. Which was a damn shame, because not only was he hoping to borrow that makeshift shower, his body was telling him in no uncertain terms exactly who he'd like to share it with.

She parked the bike, and Dempsey watched her expression through the scope. Her mouth was pressed into a determined line, her eyes narrowed into a glare. Not a happy camper. The local guy came outside wringing his hands in an agitated gesture of distress. She stormed past both men into the tent, the redheaded giant's shoulders sagging as he followed. The body language was undeniable. She was the leader of this little ragtag band of warriors, and whatever she was telling her cronies was going down as smoothly as a suicide pill at a birthday party.

———

"One of the snares has been triggered." Axelle strode into the tent to check the satellite download. She needed to know where each of the collared cats was. "What's the data telling us?"

When in range of the satellite, the units transmitted positional data every hour. The rest of the GPS coordinates were stored ready to be downloaded when they retrieved the device after the collar fell off—theoretically two years after they were deployed. Anji had found Sheba's collar yesterday—sans snow leopard— which left no doubt in her mind that they had a poacher on their hands. A big, fat, murdering poacher who was targeting the animals using telemetry devices she'd attached.

They had to be careful how this played out. It was a political and ecological nightmare.

She stabbed her keyboard. Wanted to rip out the sonofabitch's heart with her bare hands and stomp on his fingers so he could never hold a rifle ever again.

Josef grabbed the backpack of supplies, slung the tranquilizer rifle across his chest. "Which snare?" he asked, eyeing her as she rapidly typed instructions into the computer.

"Sector three. The first one we set yesterday." She'd fallen in love with the sublime beauty of cats and had discovered something worth living for. Now someone was trying to rip that away from her, the way an IED had ripped away her husband all those years ago. If she weren't so insignificant she'd think this was divine payback for her mistakes, but it was man who craved vengeance, not God.

She wiped the dust from her cheeks. Despite her morning wash she already felt grimy and hot. Tension drew tight across her chest. They needed to move fast because theoretically the snares could be used the same way the collars were. If the hunter took a leopard out of one of her traps she would track him to the end of the earth and crucify him. Forget justice and the law. You couldn't bring back a snow leopard with a heavy fine or prison sentence. You couldn't revive a species from an expensive fur coat.

She pushed away from the computer and grabbed her water canteen. "Sven's signal is closest to the snare. Let's get over there before this bastard beats us to it."

"Can we both make it on the bike?"

"Damn straight." Axelle went outside and swung onto the dirt bike and started it. The suspension sank considerably under the additional strain of Josef's weight. She took a moment to readjust her balance. "Hold on," she yelled and opened up the throttle.

She couldn't go as fast as she wanted, the terrain was too rocky. She reminded herself that whoever was hunting these animals was either on horseback or on foot, and the bike was faster. "Come on, baby," she urged the Yamaha.

They sped past scrubby bushes and over shallow streambeds that were bursting with spring melt. They slid sideways in the shale but Josef put his boots down and steadied the machine. Her heart sped as they climbed the last ridge into the canyon where they'd set the snare. The collars had an accuracy of about five meters so even though the signal showed Sven was nearby, it didn't mean he was actually caught in the snare. A markhor or wolf could have been captured, and Sven could be nearby hoping to score an easy meal. If so, she didn't want to scare the leopard away. Josef muttered under his breath in Danish.

She cut the engine at the entrance to the gully and waited for Josef to get off the bike before she lowered the kickstand and hopped off. They jogged cautiously forward, glancing uneasily around them as they made their way along the worn animal trail. A pissed-off hiss warned them to back off as soon as they came into view.

Relief hit her solar plexus like an explosive fist.

"Sven," she whispered. Named after Josef's late father, this was the first leopard they'd caught and collared. He wasn't as aggressive or as liable to attack as Samson, but he was a fine, healthy specimen complete with requisite claws and teeth.

Josef loaded a dart, walked forward to take aim at the cat. Aside from an angry swipe of his extra-long tail, Sven seemed resigned to what happened next. Josef darted him in the rump and within a few minutes the cat was completely out of it.

Axelle strode forward and covered Sven in a sleeping bag to keep him warm while Josef worked on the collar. She released the cat's front paw from the snare, checked for damage but there was none. She examined his other massive front paw and noted he'd lost a toe—probably to a wolf trap. Unfortunately one of the most endangered species in the world had more to worry about than losing a toe. Josef popped the collar and Axelle prepared the antidote to bring the cat around. Just as she was about to stick it into his flank, the sound of two rifle shots split the air in quick succession.

Shock ripped the air from her lungs. Distress flashed along every nerve ending and over her skin like a blast wave. It took a moment to catch her breath and swallow her anger before she stabbed the needle into Sven's lax flank. They backed away to let the animal recover.

"Maybe he missed." Josef's voice was gruff.

She stared at the blue sky and cursed.

Sven clambered slowly to his feet and staggered in a circle.

"Go!" she yelled. "Go, go!" *Run from this terrible place.* The cat turned to growl at her before bounding away. She stalked over and reset the trap because Goran also patrolled this canyon, and Sven better have enough sense to avoid the area for the next few days.

Dammit. She rested her forehead in her palm. Josef moved closer and put his hand between her shoulder blades. She might have taken that simple comfort if she didn't think she'd buckle under the knowledge that one of her beloved animals was probably dead or dying.

She jerked away and looked over the valley with the jagged ramparts of the Hindu Kush bearing down on them from the south. Afghanistan was locked down by violence. Even if they got a message through to the right person in Kabul, the officials there might rate the plight of the snow leopard a poor runner-up to the troubles of their people.

The enormity of the task began to seep in and overwhelm her. Why were humans so callous? What made them think they had the right to destroy something as rare and precious as a snow leopard for something as unquenchable as greed? She didn't understand and knew she never would.

She needed to act now or the leopards could be annihilated by the end of the week. It was a race against time and she didn't know who she was racing with or how to stop them. A fine tremor of rage vibrated through her bones.

She set the receiver on the ground and checked the other snare frequencies. The base camp was too low to catch the signals but they were more elevated here. No point heading home if another trap had been sprung. All the signals beeped slow and constant, indicating the snares were empty.

"Let's head back to camp."

Josef nodded.

"Then I'm going to see if I can locate the cats south of the camp." In the direction of the gunshot.

His skin paled beneath his tan. "We'll go together—"

"No." She took in the commanding panorama of mountains and wanted to raise her fists in challenge. "One of us needs to be at base camp in case one of the snares gets tripped. Anji has to take care of the cubs."

Josef's blue eyes protested. "It's too dangerous."

"I'll be careful." Damned if she was going to sit around while some asshole took potshots at her animals.

Josef grabbed her arm, his fingers digging into her flesh as he shook her. She blinked at him in shock.

"It is too dangerous," he repeated firmly.

She broke his grip and glared at him. "There's no choice."

"We can monitor the snares and wait for the Trust to send back-up."

"This country is shut down, Josef. It'll take weeks to get people in here." She fisted her hands, wanting to punch something. "I'm not waiting. You're capable of managing a release on your own and that's what I'm telling you to do." Fury against the poacher burned the back of her throat. Anger seared her body.

Josef stood straighter, ready to argue.

"What if he got another one?" Her voice cracked in the

morning quiet. She snatched up a rock and hurled it against the canyon wall.

"What if he's still there, skinning his prize?" Revulsion swirled in his blue eyes, making them darken with rage. "What do you think a man like that would do to a woman like you?"

Pent-up energy raged inside her with nowhere to go. "I don't care!" The thought of these innocent creatures being hurt tore her apart. "I won't approach if I see anyone." *Liar, liar pants on fire.* "I'll track the collars. We'll send Anji down to the village to hire men to help us search."

He muttered something blasphemous.

She climbed back on the bike.

His fingers touched her arm. "Axelle, you can't put yourself at risk." The gentleness startled her.

"I'll be back before nightfall."

"And if you're not?" His hand dropped away.

"Then I'll be keeping my promise." She twisted to hold his stare. "Helping save an endangered species."

———

Dmitri Volkov knelt on the bare earth, slid his knife into the mechanism that secured the tracking-collar and popped the device. He tossed it aside and rolled the snow leopard onto its back and pulled the plush fur away from clinging sinew. He made a hole in the pelt with the tip of his curved blade and carefully drew the whetted edge down the animal's still-warm belly. He avoided nicking the gut, and took a moment to remove the intestines and stomach, and throw them in an opalescent heap where they couldn't mar the prized pelt.

Using fingers and the blade, he worked the skin off the muscle in small, circular motions, revealing an intricate weave of deep pink fibers beneath. The tail took time, as did the legs and the head. The enormous paws were heavy and soft like velvet against his fingers, reminding him of the curtains in his grandmother's house when he was a young child. He squeezed them regretfully, but refused to think about the animal it had once been.

Fifteen minutes after he'd shot the beast, he had his hide. He climbed to his feet, ignoring the pain in his knee as he batted away clumps of lingering snow. He wiped away a single smear of blood that somehow streaked the inside of his wrist. Then, with agonizing care, he rolled the pelt inside a blanket and tied the roll to the back of his yak.

There were men in Xinjiang who'd pay tens of thousands of dollars for each animal. The rarer they became, the more the pelts were worth. The money would help pay for the transplant his grandson needed, just as soon as he got his family out of Russia. Suddenly wary, he scanned the hillside—heard no one, saw no one. Sweat beaded his upper lip as he stood staring down at the glistening corpse. A sense of danger and urgency drove him even though he was tired and needed rest. He spotted the discarded collar and swore, snatching the thing and striding to the edge of the nearest cliff and flinging it over the edge. Fool. He would be caught out by his own cunning if he wasn't careful.

The hair on his nape prickled.

He touched the rifle strung across his back like an old friend, the weight feeling right again after all these years. His breath steamed the air as he looked across the narrow corridor that fingered its way between these formidable mountain ranges. The ancient Silk Road was a barren wasteland since Mao Zedong had blocked the eastern passage to China.

He should have died in these mountains thirty years ago but fate had intervened. He recognized the remorseless weaving of timely threads leading him back to this valley at this moment in time. He just prayed he was smart enough and lucky enough to rescue the one thing that truly mattered. He hurried back to the leopard. There was no time to waste. Skinning was the easy task. Getting the bones was a bitch.

———

Dempsey did not like what he was seeing. They'd moved their OP that morning after the man and the woman had raced off on the bike looking like *Mad Max* and *Xena*. Now he and Baxter were embedded southwest, in a small cave that gave them better cover, farther away from the well-worn trail up the side of the mountain where the camp inhabitants seemed to travel on an hourly basis.

Down below, the woman was saddling the gray gelding and packing her saddlebags, obviously arguing with the redheaded giant and the short local man. From the set of her jaw she wasn't budging, and something told him he'd have sided with the guys if he could hear the conversation.

She wore her androgynous clothing and hid her long brown hair beneath a woolly hat. Because of her height, from a distance she could pass for a male—unless you'd seen her naked. Then even the heavy sheepskin jerkin and canvas trousers didn't disguise the subtle curves or delicate bone structure she was trying hard to obliterate. She mounted the horse, which whirled in a tight circle, and then she urged the animal south, toward the direction of this morning's gunshot.

It had sounded like a high-powered hunting rifle, the sort of weapon their target had been reported purchasing in Pakistan. All they needed was a starting place and they could hunt this bastard down and neutralize his ass.

But now the woman was going toward the shooter. *Shit.*

Taz and Cullen were off searching for the source of the gunshot but, given the steep terrain, not to mention the fifteen square miles it could have originated from, he doubted they'd find any trace. Even if they did, it didn't mean the shooter was the guy they were looking for, though instinct told him it was. Unfortunately, the British Army needed more than his instincts.

They wanted a flesh-and-blood terrorist to hang on their placard.

He checked his belt kit and pockets for gear, then grabbed his bergen.

"Where we off to?" Baxter asked, grabbing his pack.

"*I'm* following the woman. You're watching the camp."

"Bollocks." Baxter blew out a frustrated laugh. "The excitement might kill me." He settled back in his trench. "She packed a gun."

Dempsey tapped his carbine. "Mine's bigger." He was beginning to think he knew who these people might be, or at least, what they were doing here. He slipped out the OP and up behind the knoll of the mountain. He could see the trail of dust her horse left and started moving parallel to her wake.

"Don't wait up. I should be back in a few hours," he said into his mike. The headsets had limited range so he was surprised when Taz responded.

"*Inshallah.*"

Got that right. "See anything?" he asked the trooper.

"Not even a mouse."

"Eyes open, boys and girls. Something tells me our prey is near. Let's wrap up this mission and get back to the lads."

"Amen, to that," Cullen intoned.

Dempsey moved quiet but fast over the rocky land. The first blades of grass had started to sprout, and buds were swelling on the bushes, preparing to take advantage of the brisk alpine summer. The sky was a cloudless blue, the tips of the mountains so high they seemed to rend the fabric of the atmosphere. Nothing moved. There was an eerie silence to the world that felt like watching eyes, or ears pressed tight against stone.

Mile after mile, he followed the woman's trail, shadowing her on the opposite side of the ridge. She raised enough dust he didn't have to see her to know where she was headed.

Was she meeting their quarry? Was the Russian someone she knew? Someone she worked with? Or was this some unconnected scouting trip? The idea that she might lead him directly to his target made him increase his speed while doubling his caution. She scaled a bare hillside and Dempsey waited until she was out of sight, then hauled ass up and over the slope. At the summit he found an area he could crawl over without making a noticeable silhouette against the skyline. He slid behind a rock and caught his breath. It was cold at this altitude, but in the bright sunshine and heavy clothing, he was starting to sweat—not a good thing. He kept hydrated.

She wasn't doing anything to conceal her presence, which made him wary. She didn't seem to be bothered by the idea of the shooter seeing her. She was looking at something in her hands. He raised the scope to his eye and spotted a GPS unit and a radio receiver.

There was snow on the ground here. Large patches of ice trapped in the constant freeze-thaw cycle of night and day. She got off the horse and tied it to an anemic-looking sage bush. Dempsey edged closer, keeping out of her line of vision. She took out the handheld receiver and he heard a faint beep, then she attached an antenna and held it like someone trying to get the picture on an old telly.

She was tracking a signal.

Her head shot up and left, and she disappeared into undergrowth along a dry streambed. Dempsey moved closer to the horse, who raised its nose and then shook his mane. He did a quick search of the saddlebags. Food, water, notebooks, sleeping bag, tranquilizer darts. He pulled the latter out and inspected it carefully. Animal tranqs. It fit with his theory about who and what the woman was.

The clatter of a stone behind him made him freeze. *Shit*.

CHAPTER
FOUR

HE HELD up his hands and turned, relieved to see the woman and not some Taliban nutter or aging Russian terrorist squaring off with him.

Unfortunately the woman was holding a Glock-17 as though she knew how to use it.

"Afternoon," he observed calmly.

"Give me one good reason I shouldn't put a bullet in you right now." Her accent told him she was American.

A joke about the second commandment probably wouldn't work considering his Diemaco and SIG Sauer were locked and loaded with one in the chamber.

"Is there anyone who'd actually give a damn about a man like you?" Her throat convulsed, and hatred sculpted the lines of her mouth.

The question jolted him. He had mates in the Regiment, but no one else really cared if he lived or died. But *she* didn't know that.

He looked at her white knuckles and the pulse beating frantically at the base of her throat. There was something going on here that he didn't understand.

She stood close. Not close enough.

"You need to put the gun down," he told her calmly.

"You sonofabitch, you don't even care, do you?" Her eyes narrowed into glinting slits of rage. *Not good.* "You think it's all right for you to murder and kill, but as soon as someone turns the tables—"

"Not true." He edged closer. "I care very much."

Her accent was definitely Yankee but held a hint of European. French, maybe. He moved another inch, saw her chest rapidly pump oxygen. He worked on calming her down, talking quietly so she had to lean forward to hear. "I don't know who you are or what you're talking about, but I'd hate for somebody to get hurt because of a case of mistaken identity." Did she have some anti-western affiliation? Anti-war agenda?

"There's no mistake." Her lips quivered. "How much money were you offered? I'd have paid you double to leave them alone."

He frowned. He didn't have a clue what she was talking about, but she was within reach now. She blinked against the sun so he lunged, grabbing the gun, aiming it away from their bodies and snatching it out of her hands before tossing it out of reach. She struggled and kicked and punched at him, landing one solid blow to his nose, driving white-hot agony through his brain.

Suck it up, Buttercup.

She fought like a rabid wolf, and he could barely keep hold of the seething, whirling mass of fury without hurting her. He finally captured both her hands in one of his, forcing her onto her knees and down onto the ground, face first in the dirt. He used his weight to pin her while he searched for the flexicuffs he kept in his pockets. They took a moment to locate as he was distracted by all that wriggling.

She froze, perhaps realizing that hard thing in his pocket wasn't another gun. She twisted around to stare at him with hate-filled eyes. He pressed his lips together and tugged the cuffs around a pair of wrists so slim he could circle both with one hand. Then he ran his hands over her body, searching for hidden weapons, making it quick, impersonal but thorough. She flinched when he reached between her legs.

"I'm not going to hurt you."

"Sure you're not." The sarcasm dripped from her words and set his teeth on edge. He wasn't the bad guy. He wasn't the one who'd pulled a gun on someone. He finished the search and sat back on his heels. *Jesus*. This slip of a female had done something no one had in years. Gotten the drop on him. He was thankful none of the lads were here to witness his humiliation.

Underestimating the enemy. Stupid.

He frowned at her as she lay muttering and fighting her bonds. She tried to roll away but he grabbed her and hauled her back. He had questions. Lots of questions, but the high color burning across her cheeks warned him he needed to cool things down a bit. Change direction.

Right now he was an adversary. The chance of winning hearts and minds had never been more unlikely.

He slipped off his pack, went and retrieved her pistol, stuffed it in his pocket, grabbed both their water canteens. The horse stood with one foot cocked. Dozing in the afternoon sun, despite all the excitement.

Dempsey towered over her. She glared up at him and he had to suppress a grin because she wasn't in the least cowed by the difference in size or weaponry. She had courage but—despite the Glock—little training in the art of close-quarter combat. Crouching, he offered her a drink. To his surprise she rolled onto her side and parted her lips. He cupped her head as he poured a little water inside her mouth. Her hair felt soft against his calloused palms.

She swallowed before jerking free of his touch.

He sat on the cold hard earth and drank his own water, wiping his mouth with the back of his hand.

"What?" She glared.

He said nothing. Just looked off toward where the sun was starting its slow descent in the sky.

"Are you just going to leave me tied up?" She started fighting her bonds again.

He grunted. *I wish.* "You're going to hurt yourself if you don't stop that." He didn't shift his gaze from the horizon. Why should he care?

A slight flicker of movement in the distance caught his eye. A subtle shift of shadows high above him on the slope. He brought his scope to his eye to check it out. It took forever to make out the cunning camouflage of a snow leopard against the tawny browns and moss green of the hillside. A smile tugged his lips. They were rare, and he'd never seen one in the wild before. It wore a collar, which was what he figured was going on with these people in their little camp on the edge of nowhere. Although he hadn't figured on being held at gunpoint by someone he assumed was a wildlife biologist.

The leopard stepped delicately across the rocks, beautifully balanced with strong back legs and that humungous tail, but something looked off with its gait.

The woman crashed into his thigh and knocked him sideways. Her face was distorted and there was a ferocity in her eyes that made her look feral.

He rubbed a hand over his dust-covered face. "You've got to be the craziest woman I've ever met."

"Says the man who has shot three of the world's most endangered species—"

He opened his mouth to correct her but she bulldozered right over him.

"Please don't kill any more, I have money. I'll pay whatever you want *not* to kill him." She sobbed and it sounded awful in the peacefulness of the mountains. "I'll do *anything* you want." She froze, and then steeled herself as she realized what she'd offered.

Whoa. What the hell? There was a beat of tense silence.

"Really? You'll do anything I want?" He let his eyes scrape down her body. "As long as I don't shoot that leopard?"

She nodded although she looked like she'd rather puke. He was torn between humiliation, irritation, and amusement. What the hell was she *thinking*? He pushed her onto her front and straddled her thighs from behind. Because he was angry he paused for a moment and let his weight sink against her. She felt as rigid and sexy as a tank but he *had* seen her naked.

"Tempting." He pulled out his knife and cut the cuffs. "Thankfully I don't have to tie up women for sex. Well," he amended, "only if they want me to." He climbed off her and brushed the dust off his trousers. Gazed at the leopard who turned briefly to look at them before disappearing over the hill's crest. His anger had burned down to a low simmer and he savored the peace and quiet for a moment before he spoke. "For your information, lady, I was never going to shoot that leopard, so your generous...sacrifice...was unnecessary. Although if you get the urge again just let me know." He let his eyes drift over her. "I'll think about it."

She sat up, looking dazed. There was a smudge of dirt across her cheek and a graze on the end of her stubborn chin. He refused to feel bad about it. She'd pulled a gun on him. She was lucky she wasn't dead.

She rubbed her wrists, ringed red from her struggles against the cuffs, shaking her hands to get the blood back into her fingers. "I don't understand."

"I'm not desperate for female companionship."

Her lips twisted. "That bit I understood."

He held out his hand. This was a peace offering and if she wasn't smart enough to take it that was her problem. "Sergeant Dempsey, British Army."

"British Army?" She swept her gaze over him suspiciously. "You don't look like Army and you don't sound British. You sound Irish."

"Some parts of Ireland are British and wars've been fought to prove it." Anyone who thought the Northern Ireland he'd grown up in wasn't a war zone hadn't set foot in Ulster in the seventies or eighties.

Hesitantly, she placed cool fingers in his and allowed him to pull her to her feet. Her skin was soft and smooth. "Dr. Axelle Dehn."

She retrieved her fingers immediately, which was fine by him, although he was a little chagrined when she wiped her hands up and down her thighs.

He went over to collect his kit, shouldering the rifle.

"What are you doing here?"

"Following you," he told her. "Seeing what you're up to."

She was trying to get the blood flowing in her fingers. "I'm just doing my job."

"And I'm doing mine."

"British Army." Her brows lowered, lips pressed tight. "So you're not going to shoot G-man?"

"G-man?" He raised one brow. "As in an FBI agent?"

"The snow leopard." She spoke as if he were dull-witted.

"Snow leopards are a CITES listed endangered species." He threw her a hard look. "It's against international law to kill them." His prey walked on two legs.

She grabbed his elbow. "You're not the person shooting my cats?"

That got his attention. "You have a poacher?"

Her fingers drifted down his arm to his wrist and her eyes softened. Up close they were a deep rich brown edged with ebony, so dark her reactions were hard to read. She'd make a talented operator—assuming she wasn't one already.

Her throat convulsed as she choked up. "Someone's shooting them."

"Tell me what's going on." He disengaged her hand, even though he liked it on him, maybe because he did like it, and urged her to sit on the bare rock.

"I don't have time for this, I have to…" She looked at his widened stance and huffed out a frustrated breath when she realized he was serious. "Look, I get it. British soldier, national security and all that, but this is the Wakhan Corridor and there's no conflict here."

"This," he corrected with considerable patience, "is the Hindu Kush and a regular hangout for Al Qaeda and Taliban

57

fighters." He shot her a look that told her to shut up and start talking.

Her jaw worked as she lowered herself to the ground. "Last fall we collared ten snow leopards, and we have been tracking them remotely from our home base at Montana State University—that's in the US."

He resisted rolling his eyes because she obviously considered him a total moron.

"A few days ago we started seeing signals that were stationary." The line of her throat rippled. "We figured out someone's using the collars to track the cats before shooting them." There was a strain to her voice, a fine pitch of anxiety even though she was trying to control it. "We flew in to try and deal with the problem as quickly as we could."

Dempsey raised his brows. The country was under strict lockdown, so getting here that fast showed a hell of a lot of initiative and some solid contacts.

Bits of intel began to fall into place. The man his squad was hunting was a former communications specialist for Vympel—an elite Spetsnaz unit. Not only that, he'd mapped these mountains for the Russians prior to the Soviet invasion. And though MI6 though him dead—caught in one of his own explosions while trying to destroy the British embassy in Yemen—ten days ago he'd been spotted buying a hunting rifle in Pakistan.

"The pelts are worth a lot of money, right?"

"That's no reason to kill them." Her eyes flashed.

"It's reason enough for someone." Because, unless Dmitri Volkov had developed an irrational hatred of snow leopards during his years in exile, nothing else made sense. The man needed money. Why? Or rather, why now?

"We're trying to trap the cats and release them before this sonofabitch shoots them all. What are *you* doing here? This is way out of the war zone."

The whole fecking planet was a war zone.

When it was clear he wasn't going to answer because name

rank and number were the only information he was allowed to divulge, Axelle Dehn, rose to her feet.

"Anyway, I'm sorry about the gun thing." She stared at his pocket as if she expected him to hand it back—*I don't think so*—before marching off to untie her horse. "I don't have time to sit around chatting." Something about her demeanor suggested she never sat around chatting. It was ironic because as a Special Forces soldier he spent much of his time sitting around, waiting, and chatting.

But she was a woman of action. Seemingly fearless.

What was she scared of? What was her weakness?

The sun had started to dip in the sky but if they headed back now they might make camp before dark. He pulled his pack on his back and watched Axelle retrieve her receiver and antenna from where she'd stashed it before she'd ambushed him.

That's right, Dr. Dehn. Mount up. Move out. Let's go home.

She didn't even look around as she led the horse up the hill after the leopard.

He sighed, scanned the ridgelines and exhaled a resigned breath. He had his first real clue in the hunt for one of the world's most notorious terrorists. The only obstacle was hiking along the path ahead of him, hips swaying with a grace no man could feign. He didn't kid himself it was for his benefit. Axelle Dehn looked like she'd rather be staked out naked in sub-zero temperatures than touch a flesh-and-blood soldier like him. He stuffed down his impatience and trudged after her. Thank God she wasn't his type. She was arrogant, quick-tempered and rash.

A pain in the arse.

He caught himself watching those long legs in those baggy gray pants and remembering how she'd looked in the shower. He settled his breathing and pulse rate and put his wandering thoughts down to the effects of altitude. He needed this woman's cooperation because he didn't have time to chase his target all over the Hindu Kush, but it wasn't going to be easy.

The SAS believed that winning hearts and minds was the key

to winning any conflict. Axelle Dehn's heart, mind, and entire existence appeared ruled by her obsession with these cats. They were her Achilles' heel and his biggest asset in hoping to track down a killer. He'd already figured a way to set a trap for the world's most elusive Russian terrorist, but no matter the justification, he had a feeling Dr. Axelle Dehn wasn't going to like it.

――――

St. James's Park, London

Jonathon Boyle sat on a bench near the bandstand enjoying a copy of *The Times* in the sunshine. The theft of a laptop belonging to a high-ranking RAF officer had been reported—along with that of an encryption key needed to unlock its secrets. A real coup for him and lesson to those complacent pricks in the MOD, not to be lax with Top Secret information. He was doing them a favor although they were such total asses they never learned.

He folded the newspaper and placed it neatly to one side. In this world of electronic communication he often went the old-fashioned route to transfer information. He did, however, have a burst transmitter he could flash a signal from if he was ever in any real danger, but he generally mailed packages of relevant information to PO boxes, then emailed coded PO information to his handler. His codes and ciphers were almost unbreakable, and he never reused the exact same method. He applied the same diligence as a serial killer to not leave forensic evidence, and only a handful of people very high up in The Centre even knew his real identity. Over the years, his spy name had changed numerous times from Vera to Valentina, Nero to Milo. He'd never revealed his communist sympathies or Russian affiliation to anyone and kept his nose clean during the spy scandals of the sixties when he was just getting started. Working for the Foreign Office rather than MI6 had been a bonus. Now, after all these years, he was the highest-placed, longest-serving agent left. That he knew of, anyway. Secrecy was the name of this game and that was the way he liked it.

There were always new spies being sown and cultivated but he'd been at this his entire life and it wasn't over yet. A swell of pride filled his chest that he'd gone undetected for so long, and yet his greatest victory might still be ahead of him.

The preliminary meeting with the people from Aldermaston had confirmed something Jonathon had long suspected. Britain's scientists were developing many new weapon technologies. Everything from military stun guns to grenades that also delivered precision bursts of electromagnetic energy that disabled enemy communication systems but left their own intact, bullets made from recycled material—was that really considered *green*?—and a radar-cloaking device they'd whispered about for years. There was a new division that had made him sit up and salivate. A division so secret that they'd refused to reveal anything about it, not even the name. But they had hinted it was part of the new Anglo-French venture—or *timeshare* as the GRU officials had laughingly put it.

The mystery had his spidey senses tingling.

The committee, comprising himself, two MPs, a peer of the realm, an army general and rear admirals from both the Navy and RAF, plus a high-ranking official from the Home Office—*total wanker*—were under the supposed authority of some spotty youth from the MOD. The kid, who looked like he knew more about videogames than warfare, had told them they had to wait for additional security clearance before any of them would be allowed inside the restricted access areas of Aldermaston. The others had been pissed off. Jonathon had been grudgingly impressed.

What could it be? Something nuclear? That was France's strength and Aldermaston's primary business. Or something chemical or biological? Both strictly prohibited under international law, but everyone did it anyway. How else were you going to keep ahead of the terrorists and crazy-ass dictators?

The clods in the MOD understood little except furthering their own careers and making sure budget cuts didn't touch their desks, but the scientists at Aldermaston—despite their spotty countenances—were the real deal. It was the home of Britain's Atomic Weapons Establishment, a place where Spitfires had been manufactured during World War II and where the Campaign for Nuclear Disarmament had protested most loudly during the Eighties. His palms were damp from heat and excitement. This was one of the most thrilling opportunities of his life and he'd thought his glory days were over. Now he had the inside track on Britain's future defenses and budding military strengths—all because a ghost from his past had resurrected himself from the dead.

The irony.

The bench creaked as a man sat beside him. The sight of the pockmarked face brought a shiver of repulsion over Jonathon's skin. With a gusty sigh the gentleman set another copy of *The Times* on the bench between them.

The Russian Ambassador's Chief of Security smiled, showing off straight new teeth. His eyes narrowed with enough enjoyment to stir the embers of unease inside Jonathon's chest. It had been a long time since Valisky had played errand boy.

He waited for him to get to the point. A long beat of silence insulated them from the throngs of tourists and lunching City workers. "I hear an old friend of yours turned up in Pakistan."

"What of it?" Jonathon allowed his outrage to show. A true, blue-blooded Brit being accosted by a nasty communist.

"Do you think he realizes who the new prime minister is?" Valisky's eyes didn't alter when he smiled. "Or rather, who his father *was*?"

The first sliver of fear slipped under Jonathon's skin. "How could he?"

"Less than a month after Sebastian Allworth's son gets voted into power and the wolf shows his face again?"

"Coincidence." Jonathon unclenched his fists and rested his hands along his thighs.

"Well, if he is alive, I bet he remembers *you*, Mr. Boyle. He did try to kill you in Yemen."

Jonathon did not trust Valisky. He didn't trust anyone. Nevertheless, this was an old game they'd been playing since they'd been small boys in a Russian orphanage and there was too much at stake to risk exposure. "Dmitri Volkov is a fool. We all thought he was dead."

"That's what he wanted you to think, so maybe he isn't quite the fool we all wanted to believe."

Rage flickered over his vision in a haze of patriotic red. "What does he want?" Jonathon could think of no reason for Volkov to return to the limelight when all he'd achieve was a quick and violent death.

"Revenge?" Valisky's expression was sly. "To destroy the man who destroyed him?"

"Men," Jonathon corrected with bite. "The *men* who destroyed him."

"You asked for my help. I helped." Valisky shrugged, then looked away—perhaps remembering exactly how he'd brought Volkov down. "His family disappeared." Those shrewd black eyes looked back at him. "He has to be up to something."

Jonathon closed his eyes and raised his face to the heat of the sun. "The SAS are after him."

"So are Spetsnaz."

"And what happens if British and Russian Special Forces meet?" Despite the sunshine, Jonathon's skin felt clammy. *Why this? Why now?*

The big man shifted, his shoulders moving heavily beneath the jacket he wore to conceal his weapons. Valisky never went anywhere unarmed. "That part of the world is a dangerous place,

Mr. Boyle. Full of drug dealers and bandits." He laughed. "Denial is everything, and these days no one wants open war."

Jonathon didn't have time to deal with shadows from the past. He had important things to do. A bright shiny new goal. A way to prove he was the greatest spy who'd ever lived. "You'll have to excuse me, Mr. Valisky. I have important business to attend to this week. Something that cannot be put at risk. Especially by someone who should have been taken care of years ago." His tone was quiet but harsh.

Valisky's brows rose in cold assessment. "I heard a rumor you'd cancelled your retirement party."

Jonathon climbed to his feet, grimacing at his stiff joints. "*Do svidaniya*, Mr. Valisky."

"Comrade."

Jonathon wandered blindly in the direction of Horse Guards. The sun glared but it had lost its warmth. A bead of perspiration trickled down the channel of his spine and soaked into his starched white shirt as he passed through the shadows of White-hall. The clock had begun to tick but the jackpot was bigger than ever. Dmitri Volkov had to die. Before he revealed secrets he didn't even realize he knew.

CHAPTER
FIVE

THE SOLDIER WAS WATCHING HER. Not that he looked like a real soldier with his mismatched gear, and he was alone. She frowned. Soldiers never traveled alone. But the weapons and vest he wore were menacingly authentic.

A mercenary?

His gaze probed a spot right between her shoulder blades, making it itch. What was the British Army doing in the Wakhan Corridor? She didn't want soldiers here. *Soldiers*…she swallowed hard and forced the memories away.

This wasn't about her past. It was about saving one of the world's most endangered species. There was no time to waste.

Maybe he was the poacher, playing his own little game of cat and mouse with her. Maybe she was going to get her throat cut when she least expected it. She raised her hand to her neck.

Thinking logically, he'd had the chance to hurt her earlier and hadn't taken it. Sure, she was dusty and a little sore from being pushed face-first in the dirt and hogtied, but he'd gone out of his way to defend himself rather than attack her. And she'd held a gun on him so she was lucky he hadn't put a bullet in her. He hadn't raped her or shot G-man, so she had to assume he was who he said he was and had his own reasons for sneaking around the Hindu Kush—reasons she didn't want to know.

Snow and ice outlined the peaks, and a frigid wind tore down the valley, slicing through her clothes like splintered glass. Right now she had little choice except to follow the leopard she was convinced was injured. She'd deal with the soldier later—if she had to. She checked the radio signal and adjusted her course.

The air smelled clean and sharp, the landscape rising aggressively before her even though she was far from the summits. The sky was fading to gray and she was losing the light. Damn. She urged the horse faster, got to a narrow ravine and dismounted to make her way down a path hardly wide enough for a goat. The horse's nostrils flared. Hot breath flowed against her cheek as the animal's hooves slipped and dug in.

"Steady." Axelle turned to soothe him, smoothing her hand over his equine nose. "It's okay." If she didn't find G-man soon she was going to have to camp out with the wolves, because the terrain was too rocky and treacherous to travel by horseback in darkness. That pissed her off. She didn't want to be away from camp, not knowing what was going on with her project overnight. Not to mention being in the company of a gun-toting stranger.

Spooked, the gelding jerked his head and rolled his eyes. He'd scented something dangerous. Axelle's scalp prickled. She looked up, and even though she knew he was there from the signal, she had a hard time picking out the leopard until his teeth flashed in a snarl. He was still some distance away and growing more indistinct with each slip of the sun.

Her heart tapped against her ribs. She slid her hand into her saddlebag, pulled out one of the tranquilizer cartridges. Slowly she eased the rifle free of its case and inserted the cartridge. Cocked the gun. She raised the rifle and sighted the leopard. Deliberate footsteps snagged her attention. The soldier—Dempsey.

Why the hell is he following me?

She didn't need a damn babysitter.

He stopped by her side, relaxed and loose-limbed. Despite being on foot, carrying all that heavy gear, he wasn't even out of breath. He stared from the leopard to her as though he was her instructor, assessing her performance and finding her wanting. Her jaw clenched as his sleeve brushed hers. A purposeful contact that made her take a step away into the horse. Weakness he was sure to notice.

She resettled the rifle against her shoulder but felt his stare. She flicked a glance at him. "What?"

Eyes of startling blue met hers, weighing and measuring every piece of information with razor-sharp intelligence. She hadn't noticed how shrewd those eyes were when he'd been tying her up and sitting on her. She should have.

"Can you make the shot?" The Irish was clear in his voice now.

Axelle pursed her lips. She was at the limit of the range of the rifle, light was fading and although she was an okay shot, she wasn't a brilliant marksman. She could miss. The thought made her pause. Then she'd have to spend the rest of tonight and probably all tomorrow trying to get near the injured creature again, a creature who might succumb to infection if the poacher didn't find him—and her—first.

She lowered the rifle. "I need to get closer." She took a step forward, but the soldier put a hand on her arm, pulling her to a stop.

"Give it to me."

"Are *you* good enough?" Her gaze skimmed his gear. He had some sort of mean-looking rifle strapped over his shoulder and a handgun holstered to his thigh. He wore them with the same ease she wore boots.

Of course he's good enough. She handed him the gun. She had nothing to lose.

"Are the sights set properly?"

She nodded. "Josef set them up."

"Who's Josef?" He paused for a second and looked at her through the corner of one eye.

Impatience made her muscles tense. "My research assistant." She shifted her weight from one foot to the other. "He used to be in the Danish Army before he started studying for a Ph.D."

The rifle settled into the hollow of the guy's shoulder. "This Josef thought it was a sane idea for you to come here on your own even though there's a hunter killing your leopards?"

"I'm his boss; he does what he's told." *Unlike some people.* Axelle stared pointedly at G-man. "Take the shot or give me back the rifle."

The hint of a smile curved the corner of his mouth. "I bet poor old Josef didn't stand a chance." He slowly squeezed the trigger.

She flinched as the leopard jerked to his feet, his long tail whipping in a tight circle, looking for his attacker. He'd been hit.

"Good job." She searched the saddlebags for the sutures, antibiotics, antidote, along with a blanket. She thrust the reins at Dempsey before pulling her headlamp onto her head. "Hold the horse while I do this, okay."

There wasn't time to wait for a response. She headed up the hillside, scrambling over rocks that kept giving way under her feet. It wasn't high, but the last bit was a rocky, difficult climb, the slippery talus hampering her progress. By the time she got to him, G-man was flat-out snoring.

She covered him, then examined the wound on his hind leg. A four-inch gash that could have come from getting clipped by a bullet or from an altercation with another cat. It wasn't deep, just dirty and bloody. She cleaned out the wound with alcohol swabs, injected antibiotics and ripped open the suture packet with her teeth. First, she held the torn muscle together and stitched them with dissolvable thread. Then she did another row to repair the outer layer of skin. The thick purple stitches looked unnatural on a wild animal but hopefully they'd be enough to let the wound heal and not turn septic. Three-legged snow leopards didn't survive this brutal terrain.

She started work on the collar but the electronic mechanism seemed to have malfunctioned. Dammit. She pulled out her knife and inserted it into the lock to try to pry it open. All of a sudden she realized the gentle rhythmic breathing of the leopard had altered, and muscles that had been slack and lax beneath her fingers were now rigid.

The cat was coming around. She fought frantically with the collar only to freeze when G-man's eyes opened and fixed on her with an enraged gaze. Frantically, she hacked at the jammed mechanism. Suddenly the cat whirled, lightning fast. She fell back and hit her head on the ground, white light blazing behind her lids followed by a sharp searing pain as inch-long claws sank in to her skin. She cried out and grabbed the animal's small ears, holding the feline head away from her throat where his gleaming white teeth were aiming for her jugular. There was pain and confusion in his eyes, and a healthy dose of pissed-off alpha male.

The sound of falling rocks alerted her to the fact she wasn't alone.

"Don't hurt him!" she yelled at Dempsey, whose silhouette she could just make out looming toward her in the dusk.

The man cursed as he put away his pistol. G-man rolled his eyes at the soldier but kept both front paws hooked into her flesh and those ice-white canines bearing down on her neck. Her arms shook with the effort of holding him off.

"We've got to get the collar off him before we chase him away." She was trembling from pain and fatigue but if they didn't get the collar off, every scratch would be for nothing. And it hurt too much to waste.

"You are fucking nuts, lady." Dempsey grabbed the blanket and threw it over the cat. G-man retracted his claws—*thank, God*— and turned to face this new threat. Dempsey got the blanket wrapped around the cat's body, but not before the leopard raked his arm. He used his weight to pin the cat down, the same way he'd pinned her down earlier. Then he leaned back to avoid the claws and that treacherous mouth full of razor-sharp teeth. Once he had the blanket secure, Axelle climbed shakily to her feet.

Pain stabbed her body. Each scratch stinging like a row of angry barbs. "Wow. I'm actually glad you're here."

"Damned by faint praise but I knew I'd grow on you eventually." He flashed her a grin that transformed his face into handsome. "You *are* going to tranquilize him, right?" He looked suddenly nervous and the muscles in his arms were taut with strain.

She spotted her horse trotting over the crest of the ridge, clearly on his way home. "Oh, shit. There goes the horse."

"It was the horse or you, lady. Did I make the wrong choice?"

Axelle's knees wobbled as she dropped to the ground beside the soldier. "Hold him still while I get this collar off."

"I *am* holding him still." His voice was low and tight, revealing the enormous physical effort he was putting into immobilizing the leopard.

It took another minute, by which time the soldier was grunting and cursing. Axelle concentrated hard until the lock finally popped and dropped away.

"Get behind me so I can let this bastard go." The soldier's voice was rough in her ear. She hadn't registered they were pressed tight against one another on the small ledge, and suddenly she was aware of every square inch of body contact.

Dempsey kept hold of the blanket as they both jumped back. G-man hissed and snarled. The soldier's right hand slipped to the butt of his pistol and Axelle stepped forward and waved her hands at the leopard, who seemed frozen in place, confused from either anesthetic or shock.

"Go on. Get out of here." She thrust her arms high over her head and made herself as tall as possible, yelling at the stressed-out creature. G-man shot off up the cliff, into the twilight. Her throat ached. "I want him scared of humans," she murmured as the leopard bounded up and over the ridge and was gone. "Not thinking we might be good to eat. Otherwise we'll never get locals to support our conservation efforts."

"Never mind the poor sod who ends up as dinner."

She huffed out a weary breath. "They don't attack people."

Dempsey raised one brow and touched one of the rips on her clothes. She shrugged away from him. She was cold now. Very cold.

"That wasn't his fault." She picked up the collar and ran the tough fabric through her fingers. Frustration ate at her. She hated sabotaging her most important research project because of someone else's greed.

But she should be ecstatic. Despite everything, with the help of this soldier, she'd treated and released G-man. He should be safe from the most imminent threat to his survival. But it was a long walk home, and she still had other leopards to save. The weight of responsibility pressed down upon her, made her feel small, insignificant, worthless.

And the soldier watched her.

With shaking hands she gathered her supplies and pulled the blanket over her shoulders to try to get warm. The cold had seeped into the marrow of her bones, and the fierce breeze had developed a wicked edge. Adrenaline evaporated, leaving every one of her scratches singing in pain.

Dempsey followed her as she climbed awkwardly down the hillside. She got to the bottom of the path and shivered, knowing she was only going to get colder at this altitude. Her breath condensed and her toes had begun to tingle, more from shock than cold. If she stayed out here, high in the Hindu Kush with only a blanket, she'd be lucky to keep all her fingers. She needed the soldier's help to survive and didn't know how to ask for it. She'd once spent thirty hours screaming for help and it had got her nowhere.

"You think this poacher is following your animals using these collars, right?" Dempsey reached out and took the radio/GPS collar from her hand, examining it thoroughly in the light of her headlamp.

"Yeah. We don't know for sure, but we think he's killed two, possibly three of our leopards." Anguish tightened the muscles in her throat. "They're almost impossible to find normally. He has to be using the signals." The light of her head torch bobbed as she spoke. He reached up. She flinched but he fumbled around in her hair and found the Off button. It took a moment for her eyes to adjust to the darkness and she swayed. He held her by the shoulders as if anticipating her disorientation. It was disconcerting to realize she liked the feel of his strong hands holding her up.

"Give it a minute and your night vision will kick in." His fingers were warm through her shirt. Then he moved them up and down like someone reassuring a child, and she yelped in pain as he caught some of her wounds.

"Shit. Sorry. I forgot he nailed you back there." His grip loosened but he didn't let her go. Just as well because she'd have fallen flat on her face. Her knees were shaking as the aftereffects of the encounter finally began to sink in.

"I heard two shots in close succession this morning." He paused, clearly turning thoughts over in his mind. "But the poacher didn't chase after the leopard we just caught even though it was injured."

"Maybe you scared him away?" Her teeth chattered.

"I'd have spotted him." His confidence was tangible even in the twilight. Not cocky. Just sure of his abilities. "Is it possible two leopards could be in the same place at the same time—or close enough that he could have taken pot shots at both cats at the same time?"

Mating season happened in winter so it was too late for that. She frowned. "We've found some evidence the leopards follow one another around. Generally males, checking on rival males." There had only been one collar in the valley when G-man had been shot this morning, but an uncollared cat could have been there too. Her brain was moving lethargically, fatigue slowing her down. "If he spotted an uncollared leopard or maybe a markhor—they're worth a lot of money too—he'd have gone for them first, knowing he can track the collared animal later.

"Does he know you're trying to release your leopards?"

"He knows we've established camp—he left two young cubs there when he slaughtered the mother. I doubt he's realized we're uncollaring individuals yet." And he'd be pissed. She pulled the blanket tighter around her shoulders. "For all I know, he could be a local man who knows our every move." She grimaced. "I don't think so though, and we haven't spoken about releasing the cats on the radio. Not even the Trust knows what we're doing…" She trailed off. She was jabbering. She didn't jabber.

There was a power to silence—one her father had taught her from the cradle. One she usually used to her advantage. But her eyes kept trying to close no matter how hard she worked to keep them open. She wanted to lay down on the bare earth and go to sleep. Suddenly her eyes sprang wide. "We could set a trap." She whirled to face him. "Stake out this collar and wait for the poacher to show." She caught the flash of white teeth in the darkness and knew that he'd already thought of it. He was waiting for her to catch up. And she'd thought she was the smart one.

"It's risky," he said. "You'll be tipping him off that you're on to him."

"How are we going to do this?" Axelle sniffed against the deepening cold and dug in her pocket for a tissue. "Why are you helping me?"

"We'll pick an exposed position to place the collar. Say the entrance of a shallow cave on the side of a cliff. I'll contact my squad—"

"There are more of you? What the hell are you doing here?" It would be a disaster if conflict moved into this impoverished region—the people and wildlife already lived on a knife-edge of survival.

"We'll set up some observation posts and hopefully your problem will be solved by this time tomorrow."

"If you radio your buddies, he might intercept your transmissions."

"I've got a sat phone."

"What if he's using the satellite signal to track the cats?"

"He won't pick up our signal. Trust me."

Trust me? *I don't think so.* Her night vision was sharp enough now to pick out the crease in his cheek when he smiled. No way was she trusting him, or that attractive smile.

"He's the reason you're here. Isn't he?"

"We're looking for someone," he admitted, less smiley now. "It might be the same guy. I may as well check it out and perhaps help you out while I'm at it."

"Okay, let's go do this—"

"We need to clean your wounds first."

"No. We'll do that later." She started marching away but when she turned around he was still kneeling beside his pack, not going anywhere. "What are you waiting for?"

"You. Wounds. Sit." He pointed to a rock. "Now."

Even though Axelle couldn't see his expression from where she stood, she recognized stubborn when she saw it. As tired as she was, she couldn't out-stubborn him right now. Not when she needed him. Her boots crunched deadweight back down the path. "Fine. But we're wasting time."

"Getting an infection in a place this remote would be wasting time." He cleaned the cuts on his arm with an alcohol swab and smeared antibiotic cream over his skin.

"I'm not going to get a goddamn infection." She sat on the boulder with more force than necessary and refused to wince as her butt connected with solid rock.

She was being childish. She knew it but everything she cared about was in danger and she didn't know how to get control back.

"Well, you look like shit."

She glared. "Maybe I always look like shit."

"Take off your shirt."

The terse order made her laugh.

He reached forward and whipped her headlamp off her head. Pulled it over his own short-cropped blond hair as she eased out of her jerkin, fleece, and shredded shirt. Now she'd stopped moving, it *hurt*. She tried not to wince, but her stiff movements probably gave away how sore she felt. He snapped on the light and she squeezed her eyes closed and turned her head away from the glare.

He knelt in front of her and stared from beneath lowered brows, eyes intent on her face. Something about the way he stared made her think he'd be intense about whatever he was doing. A tremor rippled through her flesh that had nothing to do with cold —it was an awareness she hadn't felt in years. He kept his expression neutral except for those eyes, which even in the dim light glowed with unspoken emotions before he made them go resolutely flat.

She looked away. Soldiers were off-limits. Period.

It was freezing, sitting there in her tank top. She grabbed the blanket and draped it over her shoulders. The smell of leopard reminded her exactly what was at stake. This wasn't about her, or the soldier. It wasn't about memories or fleeting moments of desire.

The wind swept down from the mighty heights above them and funneled through the narrow canyon. The scent of snow tainted the air, reminding her humans were vulnerable and puny among these vast peaks.

She watched him work, the light from the headlamp casting a yellow glow to his features. A warrior's face trapped in frozen darkness. Handsome enough if you liked sharp planes and blunt features. She didn't. She frowned, trying to remember what she did like. He wasn't her type at all, but he reminded her she'd once had a type, and that was a first in a long time.

———

Dempsey tore open alcohol swabs and sucked in a breath as he took in the six-inch gashes that raked her skin. Blood streaked her body. Though the injuries were superficial, they must sting like hell.

He concentrated on her shoulders first, moving the blanket, cleaning each scratch thoroughly, as clinical and professional as an ER doc. He'd done a stint in an ER once. The nurses deserved medals for dealing with all the pinheads that came in. Axelle Dehn wasn't being a pinhead. She wasn't making a sound of complaint now he'd finally got her to cooperate. He had to move her bra strap to treat one scratch, and his thumb brushed the petal-soft skin of her collarbone.

He ignored the pleasure that simple touch gave him. Cleared his throat. "That cat shredded your hide."

Some of it would scar. He had the feeling she wouldn't give a flying fuck about scars.

He pressed the gauze harder to a welt, and she sucked in a breath.

"Hold still." He used his firmest voice, the one that told his soldiers the joking was over and it was time to get down to work. Even half-dazed, she raised a fine brow that told him she wasn't used to taking orders. He hid a smile.

One of the cuts on her shoulders was still bleeding. He put on a plaster and continued to clean her up, pretending she was one of the guys and he'd never seen her naked. He smeared antibiotic cream over the cuts.

"Ouch."

"Sorry." He didn't want to linger over that smooth skin. Maybe he shouldn't be bothering at all, but he needed this woman on his side. Plus, he liked her. Not in a let's-get-married-and-have-babies sort of way. But he liked her determination, her grit. You needed a barrel load of both to get in the Regiment. More to stay in it. Her job was as demanding as his, and who could fail to admire someone who dedicated their life to protecting wildlife?

Who could fail to be moved by the passion she obviously felt for her snow leopards?

He shifted position. Passion wasn't what he should be thinking about with her bare skin beneath his fingers, but it had been a while since he'd touched a woman.

Back home there were a lot of women who wanted to get off with Special Forces soldiers. SAS groupies who hung around the local bars, getting turned on by the mere whisper of Who Dares Wins. But he hadn't gone for that type of woman in a long time. He preferred women who weren't looking to add him as a notch to their bedposts, before they compared notes on his performance with their BFFs. He'd rather face enemy fire than a bunch of drunken women on a hen night back home in Hereford.

Done with treating Axelle Dehn's shoulders, he went through his pack, thrust a thermal shirt at her, followed by her fleece and jerkin. When she'd pulled them on, he settled the blanket back around her shoulders.

Nothing for it. He took a half step back. "Drop your trousers."

She didn't hesitate, and he blinked.

Something about this woman reminded him of a soldier. Her utilitarian nature. The set of her shoulders, *shit*, even the way her long, shiny hair was pulled back in that practical ponytail. She pushed the trousers down and he knelt at her side feeling like a perv because he was rapidly revising the way he liked her. The woman had *legs*. She shouldn't have looked sexy with her trousers slouched around her ankles. But she did.

His skin prickled as his body reacted. Who was he trying to kid? He was attracted to every inch of her whether he wanted to be or not.

A row of five-inch long gashes stood out on her thigh, reminding him she was probably in shock and pain. He was dirt. Dog meat.

But the situation was achingly intimate as his hair brushed her thigh. She jumped. *Jesus.* He forced himself to concentrate on the rivulets of blood that ran down her legs, rather than the black cotton panties and elusive feminine scent. He shook his head, disgusted with himself. Nice. She was injured and vulnerable. And he was getting turned on.

You're a stellar human being, Tyrone Dempsey. His mother would be proud. Except she wouldn't. Ever.

He grabbed the tube of antibiotic cream and smoothed it over her skin with clinical precision. Applied butterfly bandages on two cuts.

Abruptly he stood and turned away. "All done." He handed her an extra pair of pants to pull over the shredded canvas of hers and added a pair of thick wool socks for her boots. At least they were clean. Which was a frickin' miracle under the circumstances.

He shoved his supplies furiously into his pack and turned to find her staring at him with an odd expression on her face, parted lips and high color burning across her brow. He didn't kid himself that she was feeling lust for his manly body. *Fever*? He felt her forehead and dug out some Paracetamol and handed them to her along with her canteen.

"Thank you."

He grunted in response.

She climbed to her feet and eased her other arm into her jerkin and pulled her hat lower over her ears. It was starting to dip from a wee bit nippy to holy-fuck freezing. He found his night-vision goggles, pulled off her headlamp, turning it off before handing it back to her. He took the bits and pieces she'd been carrying and stuffed them in his bergen. He stood, shouldering the weight with ease after years of practice.

Through his NVGs she had a green tinge and a worried edge. He stuck out his left hand, leaving his right free for his pistol. "The easiest way of doing this is to hold hands."

She snorted, then realized he was serious. He watched her hesitate before reaching to take his hand. She didn't ask for promises to keep her safe. Her long, smooth fingers slid over his palm and then gripped him firmly. She trusted him because she had to. But at least she trusted him.

This was about survival and the mission. And for this mission to be successful they needed one another. There was a man out there with a hunting scope and the training to use it.

Dempsey's target was one of the most ruthless terrorists in the world, a man who'd taught explosives to extremists, knowing exactly the sort of death and mayhem he was going to inspire. Hatred drove these men—hatred and vengeance. Dempsey had a personal relationship with both, and had spent every day since his sister had been murdered trying to make up for the atrocities committed by his father. Catching this old Russian bastard might finally even the score.

———

Wakhan Corridor, Afghanistan, May 1980

"*Kapitán.*"

Dmitri was already slipping stockinged feet into his boots when the young soldier stuck his head through the tent flap. The fire had gone out and the temperature easily matched a Siberian winter. He shrugged into his greatcoat and pulled his bearskin hat over his burning ears.

"What is it, *Serzhánt?*" he asked. He'd been stuck in this valley for four weeks while his Spetsnaz unit protected key facilities from the mujahedeen further west in Badakhshan Province. He'd been in Ishkashim, helping protect a bridge vital to the Soviet supply line, when the former commanding officer of this remote outpost blew himself to pieces playing with what he thought was a dysfunctional butterfly mine. *Mudak.*

Dmitri was the only officer who could be spared and that was because he was supposed to be on leave.

"Your replacement has arrived, *Kapitán.*"

"Thank God." He wasn't trained for this slow attrition of the enemy. He was used to hitting them hard and fast, and moving on to the next target. Killing women and children was not his idea of warfare. It was cowardice and he'd made sure everyone on this outpost knew it. He pushed out the door and squinted at the pink rays of dawn as he looked around their fortified position. "Where?"

"At the lookout."

Dmitri was pleased. The man was keen to get on with the job, which meant he'd be free to rejoin his unit, might even be granted the leave as originally promised. He jogged the narrow path and through the tunnel they'd constructed through this part of the mountain to give their men safe passage. He had to duck his head and nodded greetings to sentries who regarded him with wariness. He was used to it. Maybe even proud. Spetsnaz had an almost mystical reputation and Vympel were the premier unit within Spetsnaz.

Dmitri had discovered years ago that reputation was often enough to win a fight without firing a single shot, which was fine by him.

He saw a group of *serzhánts* clustered around an impatient-looking man. He saw the large single star on the man's field uniform and slowed his step. "*Mayór.*" He saluted.

Slowly the man turned and Dmitri felt the first hint of alarm pierce the dawn. The man's eyes were small and round, a gleam of malice sparking from their black depths.

"Ah, you must be our famous *Vympel Kapitán*, Dmitri Volkov, graciously taking care of our infantry."

Dmitri ignored the jibe and bowed his head. "No doubt you will do a much better job of it than I, *Mayór.*" He just wanted to get back to his unit or his wife.

The *mayór* eyed him without blinking. Dmitri kept his head bowed. He might be Special Forces but he knew how pissing contests ended in the military.

The *mayór* nodded approvingly. Egomaniac. "I am *Mayór* Valisky. Come with me."

Frowning, Dmitri followed the man down the slope of the hill toward the sniper positions dug into the hillside. The man hunched over and cowered from possible enemy bullets. Dmitri walked tall. They were out of range, and death did not scare him.

He followed the *mayór* inside one of the bunkers and his eyes widened when the man took one of the long rifles from the *starshiná*. The major nodded in the direction of the other rifleman. "I hear you are a crack shot? One of the best in Russia?"

He inclined his head slowly. "I once had that honor but—"

"Come then, *Kapitán*." The major's voice boomed into the clear quiet dawn. "We will have ourselves a little shooting competition."

Dmitri could just make out figures on the opposite side of the Panj River, dark points against the bleak snow. Tiny, they snaked their way down the mountain carrying pots and pans.

"You have not killed a single mujahedeen rat since you took over the camp."

Revulsion moved through Dmitri as the other man sat and sighted his rifle.

"I've captured plenty."

"Captured." Valisky spat. "So now we have to feed the vermin. What kind of soldier are you?"

Dmitri stood a little straighter and kept his eyes on the wall above the man's head. "They are only children, *Mayór*."

The man turned to him with indignation. "They are the rats who feed the enemy, who then shoot down our helicopters and kill our troops."

Dmitri met his superior's gaze. "They are children. I will not kill them."

"Would you shoot them if they were English spies?"

Dmitri blinked with sudden understanding.

A look of satisfaction settled on the *mayór*'s features. "I'm thinking you're not such an impressive marksman, eh? Not such an impressive patriot?"

A core of anger started to burn in Dmitri's chest. "I serve

Mother Russia, *Mayór*, and no man has ever dared say otherwise." He stared hard at this man who wanted to grind him into the dirt for no reason.

Except he knew the reason. The blond cherub of a man he'd captured in the Wakhan last summer had told him he'd make him pay for his humiliation. Dmitri wished he'd put a bullet in the swine before he'd known they were on the same side. Now the bastard was dancing in the shadows and showing Dmitri exactly how much he liked to call the tune.

"As your superior officer I command you to prove your loyalty by destroying the enemy, otherwise I will have you court-martialed and shot," Valisky threatened.

The idea of killing children in cold blood repulsed him. "According to the Geneva Convention"—Dmitri pointed his finger at the valley floor—"they are not soldiers and therefore *not* the enemy." Dmitri couldn't believe what was happening. He'd gone from having a dream about making love to his wife to being fucked by a commanding officer in the space of five minutes.

The *mayór's* cheeks suffused with the color of wrath. "*Starshiná!* Arrest this man for insubordination and cowardice."

No one moved.

Perhaps they'd felt the wave of fury that moved through Dmitri at the suggestion of cowardice. From this little pig of a man.

"You have no authority over me." Even so, Dmitri took the rifle. He had no choice.

The *mayór's* lips peeled back. "You are not leaving this camp until you have shot ten of the little bastards, *Kapitán*. Or my order for arrest will stand."

Ten? His heart imploded. Crumpled to dust and disappeared. Dmitri wanted to close his eyes and howl, but he was a professional soldier and he knew how to do his duty. He knew how to kill.

This was his punishment for capturing the spy, for spitting on him and making him reveal his true identity. This was his punishment for being better at his job that the other *mudak*.

These children meant nothing to *Mayór* Valisky or the spy. And now they had to mean nothing to him.

He settled into position. Cleared his mind of the man and became the machine. He no longer saw the big eyes of children who struggled every day to carry a heavy load of water up the steep slope to their starving mothers and siblings. He no longer saw their pitiful rags, which failed to disguise the shivering of their gaunt limbs.

One—he started shooting—two—faster as they began to scatter behind boulders—three—and run back up the path toward a slow death by starvation. Four, five, six. Scarlet sprayed the pristine snow. He was doing them a favor by putting them out of their misery. Seven, eight, nine…and the last child couldn't have been more than five years old with bone-thin legs and hollowed-out cheeks. She stopped running and turned toward him. Tears running down her cheeks, she raised her hands to the sky in prayer.

Ten.

He swore he saw his soul flying to Heaven along with hers.

———

British Embassy, Rabat, Morocco. May 1988

"Come away from there, Axelle. Quickly now."

Axelle knew better than to argue with her mother, but she flashed her a disgruntled look before leaving the fountain in the middle of the heat-baked courtyard. She shook off the water and then wiped her hands on her pink cotton dress. *Ugh. Pink. Vomit.*

She'd almost rebelled at wearing it, but her mom had promised her a new book if she did. And finding new children's books written in English wasn't easy in Morocco—not when Axelle read a book a day and still had time left over to get in trouble. She winced. Trouble was a bit of a specialty of hers, much to her father's disapproval, although she was pretty sure her mother liked it when she made her father angry.

That fact upset her more than her father's shouting.

Axelle was scared her parents were going to get a divorce. A tight pain constricted in her chest. She didn't want them to split up. And she was doing her best to remember not to be naughty anymore.

Palm trees rustled in the wind that came off the ocean but didn't alleviate the hot stickiness of the day. She eyed the nearby pool with a sigh of envy and rolled her eyes for good measure as she followed her mother inside the pale square building that was the British embassy in Rabat. *God.* She huffed out a frustrated breath and kicked the doorway on the way inside.

When her mother had suggested she skip school that morning, the idea had sounded fun. But it soon became clear that rather than spending the day at the beach as she'd been promised, her mother just didn't want to be alone on her various errands around the city.

Axelle would rather be listening to her grade-five teacher read *Charlotte's Web* aloud, than sit down with boring grownups. She yawned and felt her jaw crack. Maybe there'd be cookies—or biscuits as her mother called them. Her stomach rumbled as she remembered she'd missed snack time.

She ran and caught up to her mother, catching hold of her fingers. "I'm hungry. Why didn't Daddy come with us?"

Her mom paused and hefted her leather satchel higher on her shoulder. "Your father was busy." She pursed her lips, which Axelle recognized as a sign to drop the subject. She hadn't seen her father for more than a minute all week.

Axelle gnawed her lip as they climbed the stone stairs. She was tired and hungry and *bored*. "When are we going to the beach?"

"Soon." Her mother smiled and Axelle was struck as always by how beautiful she was. Long, straight, shiny brown hair; light hazel eyes that looked exotic with their black eyeliner; lips deep red from the lipstick she always wore. And when her mom smiled at her like that, Axelle would promise her anything—even to sit quietly in a stuffy room when she could have been at the beach.

"I have a little surprise I didn't tell you about." Her mom's eyes sparkled from some secret mischief.

Excitement raced. What could it be? A pony maybe? She'd been begging for a pony for months. Axelle grinned back and tightened her grip on her mother's fingers. Even though today had been boring, she loved spending time with her mom.

Maybe there was a TV she could go watch while her mom talked. "Can I have candy?"

"Remember what the dentist said last time you saw him?"

"No." Axelle pulled a face.

"He said you ate too much candy."

Axelle hung her head to hide her mutinous expression. She hadn't enjoyed having a filling but she still liked candy.

Their footsteps echoed down the long cool corridors. There was hardly anyone around. Well, only the usual boring men in their dull boring suits. One passed them and eyed her mother like *she* was candy. Axelle's held tighter to her mother's hand. Her mom shot her a grin and they swept on by.

They paused in front of a huge set of wooden doors. Her mom knocked, opened it, and looked inside. Her shoulders sagged. "Oh, he isn't here yet. We should probably wait outside."

"Who?" Axelle snuck beneath her arm and peeked. Only faint light filtered through the window shutters, but even so she spied a tray of fresh cream cakes and a pitcher of ice-cold water. She let go of her mother's hand and slipped inside the room.

"Oh, I suppose we can wait in here." Her mom looked at the Swatch watch Axelle had given her for Christmas. "How ironic that I'm actually early for once." She laughed but it didn't sound happy.

Anxiety worked its way through Axelle's body and made her uneasy.

Her dad was always complaining that her mom tried to make him late on purpose. Last time, he'd left his wife behind in a huff and they'd later had a huge row. Axelle didn't want to think about it.

Her tummy rumbled. She was starving. "Can I have a cake, mommy? Please?" There were bright couches and paintings on the wall, but the only thing that spoke to her were the cakes on the tray. They looked delicious and her stomach growled noisily.

"You can have a drink of water until your surprise arrives." Her mom walked over to the tray and poured Axelle a long tall glass of water. Axelle drank the whole thing in one gulp, her eyes never leaving the cakes on their pretty three-tiered platter.

Suddenly there was a powerful vibration in the air, and the room seemed to shimmer like a desert mirage. Then a massive *boom* that hurt Axelle's eardrums. The floor shifted and she screamed, but she couldn't hear anything except that *boom* and *roar* that scared her so bad she thought she was going to pee her pants. The ceiling cracked, and huge chunks of plaster started to fall. She lunged for her mother's hand as the floor disappeared beneath them and they were both falling.

She landed awkwardly on her back with a jarring thud. Letting go of her mom's hand to curl up into a tiny ball, she threw her hands in front of her face to protect herself from the dust and plaster and concrete that rained down. Her whole body shook with terror. Dust clogged her throat and she started coughing and retching, her heartbeat so loud it drummed through her ears.

It took a moment to realize the noise had stopped. Axelle tried to blink the grit out of her eyes and see where they were. Where had the sun gone? It was dark, really dark—like nighttime. Then she saw a weak beam of light pierce the stone.

What had happened? Had the world exploded?

"Mommy?" Her ears still rang and she didn't know if she'd

said it loudly enough for her mom to hear. "Mommy!" she shouted and it echoed strangely.

But when the echo died away only eerie silence remained. Panic welled. She couldn't catch her breath and she gulped air, panting as a wave of dizziness hit her. A noise behind her made her spin, and her heart lodged in her mouth. A long block of concrete had fallen and seemed to be resting on a huge solid piece of wood that creaked and groaned under the weight. The thought of it crushing her had her scrambling away from it, but there was nowhere to go.

She couldn't breathe, couldn't think. More plaster and timber trickled down, burying her. She clawed at it, trying to shift it to get to where her mother should be, and away from the groaning wood that was going to collapse at any moment. Sweat ran down her face as the heat built inside the dark suffocating prison. Her hands were cut and bleeding but she didn't stop digging.

Somehow she made a tiny hole just big enough to wriggle through. Jagged edges ripped her dress and scraped her legs, and moments later she heard the wood shatter in her wake. Her lungs pumped, her mouth dropping open in shock.

She'd almost been killed.

"Mommy?" she whispered into the darkness. Away from the shifting concrete, she made herself stay still and listen. After a moment, the dust resettled and her eyes adjusted. She made out the dust-covered figure of her mom lying half buried in the rubble. She crawled closer. "Mom?"

Why wasn't she moving?

Axelle frowned in confusion and touched her hand, squeezing her mother's fingers and waiting for that answering response. But her mother never moved. She peered at her mother's pretty face, touched a finger to her powdery lips. Nothing. She didn't react. Wasn't breathing.

A huge terrifying fear invaded Axelle's body and drove away all thought and reason. She shook her mother's arm and started screaming. "Mommy, wake up! Wake up! Mommy, Mommy!"

When she had no voice left, when her throat was raw and her lips covered in the same dust that coated her mother's body, she quieted. It was useless. Her mother wouldn't wake up. Hot tears scalded her cheeks as she huddled in the dark.

Loneliness pressed in on her, and her heart started pounding again as panic bit once more. She didn't want to die. Her hands throbbed from cuts and bruises; whimpering sounds echoed in the darkness and it took a moment to realize it was her making those noises. Finally, finally, the faraway wail of sirens broke the silence, and Axelle started screaming all over again.

CHAPTER
SIX

HOW MANY YEARS had it been since she'd held hands with a guy? A soldier? A shiver brushed over her skin like a ghost from the past.

It felt strange. As if she'd been transported back in time. And yet, here she was, relying on the strength of those long, strong, foreign fingers to guide her safely through the night. Adjusting her footing in response to subtle pressure changes, tuning her body to match his. Trusting a man she'd just met. Relying on a man, period.

It wasn't something she did.

It wasn't who she was.

She believed in saving things, in using data to make her point, not violence. But data wasn't going to save her leopards from their current predicament. Her fingers tightened involuntarily and he slowed to match her pace. The guy was fit, not even breathing heavily, despite everything they'd been through and how many miles they'd walked. She was fit too, she ran and worked out, but exhaustion was making her feet scuff and her vision blur. Not that she was about to admit weakness to this newcomer.

The clouds had disappeared and a thin moon shone clear and

bright. "Tell me about the man you're after," she said, trying to force herself awake.

"It's classified."

"Oh, for the love of God," she snapped. "I need to know who I might be dealing with."

"Keep the volume down," he said calmly. "*You* don't have to deal with anyone. You have to stay hidden until we catch this bastard."

"Yeah, that's gonna happen," she whispered caustically. "Soldiers aren't immortal." Her voice cracked with buried pain. "I need to know what's going on in case you're not around to handle it."

"I'll be around, don't worry about that." His fingers tensed around hers.

She didn't believe in those sorts of promises. She'd heard them before. "Who are you really? How many men do you have?" The moonlight was bright enough to watch his expression turn grim. He shook his head, walking faster.

"Tyrone Dempsey. Sergeant. 2350045."

"Ha-ha." Her scratches stung but the fatigue helped numb the constant ache. "How long before we set up the trap?"

He stopped and said in a low voice that bristled with impatience. "Keep the noise down. Sound carries for miles in these hills and we've no idea where he might be."

Axelle grimaced. "Sorry." She wasn't used to a cloak-and-dagger existence. She left people alone and they usually returned the favor.

He started forward again. "We'll stop over this ridge and assess the area."

She looked around and recognized her surroundings. "Wait, there's a shallow cave in that hillside over there." She pointed along the narrow gorge they were traveling through.

The team had set up a hide there the first summer they'd come to this region. Dempsey looked at the ground, then at the surrounding hillside. There was a faint dusting of snow. He nodded as if trusting her decision. "We'll climb up via the ridge and I'll circle back along the top and down into the cave to try and not leave tracks." He looked at the dusting of snow. "Although that's almost impossible under these conditions. We better hope for more snow or enough wind to sweep them away."

She started the steep climb out of the valley. "I assume this person is a terrorist?" She noted the way he tensed even though he didn't answer. "Figures. How'd you know he's in this region?"

"Do you *ever* stop asking questions?" Still the conservation was barely above a whisper.

Out of breath, Axelle used a hand on her knee to help her climb. "Sure—"

"When you're asleep?"

She grunted. It wasn't attractive but she didn't care. The guy had already seen her at her worst. "Asking questions is what scientists do."

A soft huff of air told her he was laughing. He let go of her hand. The sudden feeling of separation caught her off guard. He pointed along the faint trail. "Keep moving carefully along the path, I'll go plant the collar and catch you up." Suddenly he was gone, leaving her alone in the frigid landscape.

"Don't be foolish," she whispered. Alone was fine. She *liked* alone. She wasn't scared of the dark. Just of caves and enclosed spaces the same way any sane human would be if they'd been trapped beneath tons of rubble that could shift at any moment... She put the brakes on that train of thought.

If she concentrated hard she could make out the snake and curl of the trail in the glimmer of moonlight. Ice coated some of the rocks, and each footstep was treacherous. She hoped her horse was safe but in her experience animals were smarter at finding their way home than humans. He'd have gone back to camp for the warm mash he knew was waiting. Josef and Anji would worry but there was nothing she could do about that.

The world was absolutely silent except for her breath puffing in and out of her lungs and her footfalls scratching the brittle earth. Dempsey materialized at her side like a specter and she jumped. He caught her elbow. "Come on. I planted the collar and spotted a decent place to lay up. We'll embed and call the lads for backup."

Excitement tripped through her veins at the thought of taking this fight to the poacher. Although why Dempsey thought her poacher and his terrorist were the same person she couldn't fathom. Didn't matter. She'd take any help she could get in the effort to save her leopards.

They worked their way up the opposite side of the valley. Wind blew the dusting of snow across the trail, obliterating their tracks.

It was getting much steeper.

She jolted when Dempsey maneuvered her in front of him and put both hands on her hips to hold her in place. A frisson of sexual awareness shot through her.

"The cave is just above this boulder." His hands burned imprints through her clothes and into her skin and she was suddenly, for the first time in what seemed like decades, aware of herself as a woman. "I'm going to give you a boost, which probably means putting my hands on your arse." His voice was husky, his breath brushed against her ear as he tried to keep the volume as inaudible as possible. "If you have a problem with that, I'll figure out some other way. But this is the quickest and easiest method to get where we need to be."

The idea of his hands on her ass stirred long-repressed erotic memories, which bothered her a lot. Her heart pounded and her mouth went dry. But there was another problem. A bigger problem. "I'm not real big on caves."

He took that as affirmation and boosted her up. She reached for the lip of rock and tried to find purchase with her feet. Two big hands found her butt and gave her a forceful shove that allowed her to crawl over the top. She didn't know what the hell she was feeling and didn't have time to think about it as his backpack bobbed in front of her. She caught the straps and the damn thing nearly pulled her back over the edge. It was heavier than she was.

She hung on and leaned back, pulling the thing with every ounce of strength. Then he was beside her and yanking the pack beside him with what looked like ease.

"You need a lesson in traveling light." Her breath came in shallow pants.

"Yeah, well my horse was busy and at least *I* have my comms and sleeping bag with me. If you're lucky I might share." He winked.

She smiled for the first time in days. She'd almost forgotten the art of banter, but right now it eased the tension and untied the knot that constricted her throat. "We've held hands and you've copped a feel, I guess now we *have* to sleep together."

Mischief danced in the sparkle of his eyes. "I'd heard American girls were easy." He held out his hand and pulled her along behind him.

"I'd heard Englishmen were charming." She deliberately got his nationality wrong. "I guess we were both wrong."

He clutched his chest and pretended to stagger. "English?" He shuddered. "I'd rather be stabbed through the heart with a toothbrush."

He was kidding with her. Something about him was so relaxed and familiar it almost hurt. Axelle felt comfortable in his presence and yet wired by the unexpected attraction. It was as if they'd known each other for years. As if they trusted one another.

She followed him, still holding his hand.

Don't think about the cave.

She looked out at the valley instead. It was almost dawn now, the soft glow of the newborn sun edging along the tips of the distant peaks.

They stopped in front of some straggly scrub. He held back a bush, and the fragrant aroma of sage filled the air.

She looked at the entrance of the cave and her skin prickled. It was more of a crevice than a cave. About two feet high and four feet wide, deep enough for them to crawl inside. More of a crack than a real cave. Her pulse hammered in her ears. Whenever possible, she had her students do anything that involved over-hanging rock, but this was all on her.

She stared up at the cliff face. She could almost feel the pressure of all that stone pressing down of her. *Oh, shit.* Memories tried to crowd her and her hands shook. The moisture in her mouth evaporated. Dempsey crouched, exploring the space with a stick to make sure nothing nasty lurked in the recesses.

Tremors struck her body. She couldn't do this. She retreated a half step and he reached out to catch her arm.

"Easy. That's a steep fall back there."

She glanced behind her and saw the dizzying drop. Jesus, she'd almost stepped off a cliff because she was freaked out by a simple hole in the mountain—an indentation—not even a real cave.

He slipped his sleeping bag out of his pack and unzipped it, spreading it out on the rough stone. "Right then. In you go."

She opened her mouth but nothing came out. He caught her expression and went still. "Or"—he drew the word out as his eyes catalogued her features—"we can abort this idea and head back to camp and make a new plan."

Because she couldn't cope with lying beneath a rock.

"Give me a minute." She dropped to her haunches.

"The main thing about this sort of observation work is keeping still. We've got enough cover around the entrance to keep us hidden and enough dust over our skin that shine isn't going to give us away. But movement draws the eye and that's where covert surveillance fails."

He pulled out the satellite phone and called his team members and HQ. She heard them exchanging a few details.

Another problem rose to the forefront of her mind. "How long will we be staying here?"

He looked over at her like she'd grown horns. "Until he turns up or the situation changes."

She fidgeted and pressed her legs together but it didn't help. "I need to go to the bathroom."

Lines cut around his lips as he smiled. There was even a dimple. "Ah."

They looked out at the barren surroundings. He peered past her shoulders. "There's a boulder along there."

"What about your men?"

His expression was serious but she could tell he was trying hard not to laugh. "They won't be here for a while. Satellite images are good but they aren't that good so hopefully everyone at HQ won't see your..." He coughed and hid a laugh. "I'll look the other way. Watch the drop-off," he warned.

She crept along the ledge, a little worried her bodily functions might be broadcast to the entire British Army but resigned anyway. It wasn't exactly easy, trying to pee on a cliff face, but nothing about this situation was easy.

When she came back, Dempsey was stretched out inside the cave. She swallowed the lump of dread that solidified in her throat. Locking her jaw, she crawled down beside him, aware of every inch of his body—and hers. He felt good. Really good. Breathing steadily, she concentrated on him rather than the thought of all that rock above her head.

She'd almost forgotten how enjoyable it could feel to press against a hard male body. Certainly no one had elicited this sort of response since Gideon. She squeezed her eyes shut, wishing she wasn't so chicken. She hated being afraid of anything and this was so...stupid. Wishing there was room to edge away from Dempsey, she fidgeted, which made her even more aware of him and his scent and shape.

Why did she have to be even vaguely aware of this guy as a male? After Gideon had been killed, she'd vowed never to go through that kind of pain again. She'd never get involved again, period. She thrust away the memories.

It took her a moment to realize she'd been so busy thinking

about men that she'd forgotten her fear of caves. She didn't know which she'd rather deal with.

She kept her eyes on the horizon, wriggled for another minute. Shifted her hips. Scratched her arm. Pushed her hair behind her ears. Shifted her hips again. She felt the weight of eyes on her and turned to meet a pair of the bluest, most-intense irises she'd ever seen.

"What?" she asked.

He cocked a brow. "Movement, remember?"

His eyes were even bluer close up and she found herself cataloguing his features. Straight, flat nose. Full lower lip. Sandy blond stubble gracing a lean jaw. Sun-bleached brows and lashes that looked white against his tanned skin and high, Slavic cheekbones.

"What?" he murmured.

For a moment she held her breath and then broke away from his gaze. "You've got big ears," she said.

"All the better to hear you with." His lips twitched. "I've got big hands too."

She blinked at his hands and swallowed hard. Heat crept up her cheeks. She watched him out of the corner of her eye and decided to change the subject before she embarrassed herself. "What made you become a soldier?"

"I like guns."

She rolled her eyes. "You should come live in Montana."

He smiled without looking at her. "Why are you scared of caves, Dr. Dehn?"

It wasn't a secret. Hell, it was on Wikipedia, although generally she didn't talk about it.

But for some reason she felt compelled to answer him. Maybe it was the trust thing, which relied on a certain amount of honesty and this was old history. "I was trapped under a collapsed building for two days."

"Holy fucking hell."

"Yeah, it was." A shiver of cold slid down her back and she

inched closer to him. After a quarter of a century the memories generally didn't hurt anymore, instead they'd coalesced into this childish terror of small, dark spaces. But right now she was remembering all the fear and all the terror and all the endless hours of waiting, trapped beside her dead mother. Her lungs hurt. Panic snatched her breath. Once. Twice.

His fingers found hers. Hot. Smooth, and reassuring. He squeezed and she held on.

"How old were you?" His deep murmur calmed her raw nerves.

"Ten, but I don't remember much of it." She'd blocked it. She'd almost died from dehydration and she'd blocked it. A freak rain-storm had kept her alive, enabling her to suck moisture from the rubble. She'd blocked that too.

"I'm sorry."

"Yeah." After another moment. "It's Axelle. Not Dr. Dehn."

"After the lead singer of Guns N' Roses?"

"Yeah." She rolled her eyes. "Mom was a big fan."

He'd let go of her hand and had been staring down the scope of that mean-looking rifle with his trademark intensity. He looked back at her, and the smile that lit his face turned him from hand-some to hot in a heartbeat.

She swallowed and shifted a little bit away from him but then felt cold again. She sighed with misery. She didn't want to be attracted to anyone, hadn't had this problem in over a decade. Being attracted to a soldier felt fundamentally *wrong*. The fact she was having these thoughts when some sadist was shooting her leopards made her feel like a loser on every level. But this man was helping her. Perhaps that was why she felt the attraction. It was nothing more than misplaced gratitude.

She laid her chin on her hands. "It's French—means 'father of peace.' We lived there when I was born. When I went to school in DC I always wished they'd chosen something ordinary—like Karen or Julie or Susan—but no, we had to have something sophisticated and unusual...according to my father."

"Is your dad still alive?"

She nodded.

"Brothers or sisters?"

She shook her head. "What about you?"

"Tyrone Dempsey. Sergeant. 2350045."

After her confessions his impersonal answer felt like a slap in the face. "You're a pain in the ass, Sergeant Tyrone Dempsey. 2350045."

"Copy that, ma'am. Try and get some sleep. And, for the record? So are you."

———

Time was running out. Desperation drove him onward, barely letting him sleep because with every footstep he imagined the life running out of his grandson's frail body. He'd trudged through the night using the Soviet-era night vision goggles he'd bought in Gilgit. Now dawn was exposing the land in shades of gray. The jagged peaks were eerily silent, except for the giant's breath of wind that pulsed and robbed his own.

Yesterday he'd been gifted with the sighting of a snow leopard and a markhor together in the same valley. It was God's blessing on his quest. He'd taken down the shaggy goat with the magnificent twisted horns but had only clipped the predator.

The signal was gaining in strength. He was closing in on the wounded leopard so he tied his yak to a stunted tree and stealthily slid the rifle from its case and over his shoulder. The receiver and antenna were bulky but he could carry all three items over short distances. He wasn't the man he'd once been—had spent too many years wallowing in self-pity and trying to drown his mistakes in hard liquor.

He felt ancient. But death was a mercy he didn't deserve.

The wind came off the mountain, taking his scent with him.

He climbed the ridge silently, peering furtively into the next valley. He didn't want to spook his prey. There was more snow in the clouds, he could smell it. As long as it didn't block the road to his hideout, it didn't matter. Then he spotted it…a footprint. Human? And another. Two people. The biologists? Or someone else?

He listened, used the scope on his rifle to scan the opposite side of the valley. A faint trail in the light snow led to a small cave. The awareness that had kept him alive for so long prickled over his scalp and he narrowed his gaze. The biologists had set a trap. Fury welled inside. His grandson was dying and they set him a trap? He started to slither backwards, but froze as a man, swarthy as an Arab, with the bearing of a soldier, faded into position. He'd never seen him before but he immediately knew the game had changed.

Dmitri slipped out of sight and jogged to the pack animal.

Hurry.

Anger filled him, anger and fear. Fear that he would be too late, that they would stop him. *Magdalena*…the name came out of nowhere, ripping through him with a tidal wave of yearning.

Snow started to drift out of the sky again, swirling around him in an endless crystal ballet. He headed in the opposite direction to his yak, circling around, searching for signs that anyone else was here. But the snow obliterated the earth now as surely as it cloaked him.

Dmitri took the rope and led the animal into the swirling flurries. He'd kill a thousand snow leopards, shoot the last tiger on earth to save one precious child.

They hadn't found him yet. He intended to make sure they never did.

———

The midday sun beat harshly on this patch of barren rock, melting the inch of snow that had fallen during the morning. The woman beside him had finally stopped wriggling and fallen asleep a couple of hours ago. His team was in position and they'd been on stag duty while he caught a quick nap. Now he was wide awake and refreshed, but so far, nothing, *nada, nyet*.

What had made Dmitri Volkov turn his back on his former homeland? What made him defect to fight on the side of people who got their kicks out of brutalizing innocent civilians?

Dempsey understood terrorists better than anyone this side of a suicide vest. He'd grown up with them, would probably have become one himself if not for the tragic death of his sister. That was the family business, right alongside farming. Being immersed in that indoctrinated shit from a young age meant he understood how people born into it found it hard to break free. It was so ingrained, so fecking *normal*. Talk about brainwashed. His sister's death had severed all connections with that life. Obliterated everything that had come before it. But this guy, this old Red Army soldier, and many like him, had actually opted to join forces with the nutters.

Silence pressed down on him. False. Unnatural. He lay absolutely still but he was starting to get one of those feelings.

He keyed his comms. "Report."

"Nothing."

"Clear."

"Not a fucking thing."

He frowned. Wishing he didn't trust his intuition more than he trusted his men. "Taz, take a look around."

"Copy that."

The silence held the essence of expectation. Like everyone was waiting for something to happen.

Axelle woke and bashed her head on the rock. He automatically cupped his palm over her hair, which felt like warm silk and had red-gold streaks in the morning light. A look flashed between them. A nameless connection though he'd done his best to keep his distance. Usually he was skilled at distance and, judging from the wary expression on her face, so was she.

"Report," he ordered Taz.

"No sign of anyone or anything along the rim of the valley," said Taz.

Cullen and Baxter both checked in.

Axelle pulled out her radio receiver and turned it on.

"What have you got?"

She frantically scanned the frequencies and frowned. "There's something about a mile west of here."

"One of your collars?"

"I don't think so." She shook her head. "It's on the same frequency but…"

Dempsey slipped out of the cave. "I'll check it out."

"I'm coming with you." She scrambled out.

"You won't be able to keep up."

Her chin jutted. "Try me."

"You'll make too much noise."

"These are my leopards. You can't stop me." She was whispering but her voice still dared him to try.

He couldn't exactly knock her out. Well, he could, but he didn't want to. "Fine. But you do what I tell you, when I tell you." He grabbed his stuff because he wanted to be able to keep after this bastard if it was indeed the Russian. And leaving your pack behind unguarded was a stupid way to die.

"Baxter—you and Cullen stay here with this collar. Taz, you and I—"

"And me."

"—are going to check out another transmitter signal a mile due west."

"Roger that."

He set off fast down the cliff but had to slow when Axelle refused to hand over the receiver to allow him to follow the signal. Probably better this way even though he seethed with impatience. He joined up with Taz at the head of the valley. The trooper had his map out and Dempsey checked the radio receiver and noted the GPS position and marked it on the map.

Taz's black eyes gleamed as they took in Axelle. "You seem to have rescued a damsel in distress, Irish."

Dempsey grunted.

She gave him a feral glare.

There were several steep interlocking gullies in their way. Taz took the lead, moving fast. Dempsey ran, making as little noise as possible—all his kit taped down so it didn't rattle. Axelle managed to keep on his heels and though she was breathing hard, she didn't utter a single murmur of complaint. Soldiers in the Regiment weren't just fit, they were run-up-and-down-a-mountain-in-full-kit-and-then-do-it-again-for-fun fit. After half a mile he slowed and she caught them. He didn't want her left alone in these mountains with this character around.

Taz looked over his shoulder and gave him the signal to slow down. They couldn't afford to run into an ambush or booby trap. As far as they knew the Russian was alone, but they had no real intelligence or sightings of the sly sonofabitch, so they couldn't take anything for granted, especially this close to the Afghan-Pakistan border.

"Check the signal but keep the volume down. We don't want to spook the bastard if he's here," he instructed Axelle quietly.

Her cheeks pulsed a vivid red and her chest pumped air at a rapid pace. He did his best not to notice.

The signal hadn't moved. Her lips pressed together in a tight line as she showed him. They started forward again, Dempsey with his rifle to his shoulder. He'd given the Glock back to Axelle earlier but he was grateful she kept it concealed. They worked their way over one ridge, then the next, staying below the horizon line. When he figured the collar was over the next ridge they found an area of dense shrubs and army-crawled until they could see into the basin below.

Axelle gasped and his stomach turned.

Below them, staked into the bare earth, was the glistening red carcass of an animal—some makeshift collar attached to the body of the slain creature. There was no doubt a message had been sent. Axelle stuffed her fist in her mouth to stifle a sob.

Shit.

The fine hair on his nape prickled with super-awareness. He grabbed Axelle's arm and pulled them both behind a boulder. He looked at Taz. "You think he spotted us?"

Taz nodded. "And left us a little fuck-off present."

Dempsey nodded. "Given his expertise"—he flicked a glance at Axelle, but she was staring at the corpse as if she could resurrect the dead if she just tried hard enough—"I wouldn't be surprised if he left us more than that."

It was a grotesque display with the skinned face of the animal —probably a goat—almost smiling at them. He felt the tremors that started to pass through Axelle's body. He called the others on the radio. "Gig's up. He knows we're in the area. Get up here. Strong chance he's set up some booby traps in the area. Go careful."

He nodded to Taz to go ahead of him. "Let's work our way around the valley before we go down. You stay here," he told Axelle. He might as well have saved his breath because she stood and followed him. The glint in her eyes told him she wasn't sitting around waiting for anyone.

"Fine." He caught her flat stare. "Stay behind me. It's possible he set mines or tripwires. Keep your eyes open."

They scouted the entire rim, Taz using the thermal imaging scope on his C8 to search for any heat sources before they headed to the base of the valley floor—the least popular spot for any soldier. Drag marks were visible over the eastern ridge. Flies filled the air, swarming over the dead flesh in a feasting mass. He ignored them but Axelle started swatting at them. He touched her arm but she jerked away from him. This must be her idea of hell.

Her being blown to smithereens was his.

He caught her arm. "Put your feet where I put my feet, but stay back a little, just in case…"

Her gaze swung to his and her mouth opened as she finally registered what he was saying. *Just in case he stepped on a landmine.* It wasn't an image anyone wanted in their heads but this offering posed a tempting trap, so why wouldn't the Russian leave them a little surprise? A few dead soldiers would be a nice bonus after a hard morning's work.

They got within a few feet of the animal and he held Axelle back when she went to run forward. He only relaxed his grip when she stopped struggling. "Let's make sure he didn't conceal any surprises before we check out this collar." His skin felt like it was stretched taut over an electrified body, every sense hyper-aware. Taz was the designated demolition expert in their squad although they all had training, Dempsey more than most. Axelle jerked out of his arms but stood quietly beside him.

Taz knelt beside the dead animal and inspected the mouth and body cavity for explosives. With meticulous care he moved dirt and stones from beside the animal. After five sweat-drenching minutes, he looked up. "Nothing."

Dempsey kept scanning the surrounding area feeling like he was about to get hit by the world's biggest ambush.

"I want to bury it," said Axelle.

"No."

"I can do what I damn well want."

"Normally, you can." He didn't take his eyes off the hills. "But I've never felt so exposed in my whole bloody life so I am not going to let you. Grab the collar and let's go back to your camp and figure this thing out."

"Or?" Her eyes glittered. He'd have smiled if he hadn't wanted to strangle her.

"Or I knock you unconscious and carry you out."

Taz watched them with interest.

He could practically hear her jaw breaking, she clenched it so tight. "I never figured you were the sort of thug to hit a woman."

"I'm an equal-opportunity thug, so don't push it."

Baxter and Cullen radioed him from the ridge, but he didn't

drop his weapon. He felt like the devil had skated over his grave. He whirled. Was the Russian here? He sure as hell couldn't see him. He nodded to Taz who pulled out the infrared scope again and started scanning.

"Even though you're totally bloody barmy, Dr. Dehn." He was pushing her buttons but they were both pissed so who cared. "I'd like to make sure you don't die on my watch. Or is that too fucking macho for you?"

She bent down and detached the fake collar. He spared her a glance. Her expression had become flat, her lips pale, knuckles bone-white. She was barely holding it together.

This collar was fashioned from a long strip of gray cloth with a small transmitter sewn to one end. Axelle stood, then opened her mouth in shock. He caught her arm as she swayed and was about to swing her up into his arms before she fainted when she fought off his grip.

"Look." She flattened the material. On the inside there was a message printed in black ink.

Now I kill them all.

Oh, shit.

"He knew we set that trap." Her skin turned ashen. "This is my fault." Her hands shook.

He nodded to Taz to lead the way out. The boys would cover them. He put his hands on Axelle's shoulders, felt her tension beneath his fingers and wished for some of that closeness they'd shared earlier. "This guy is manipulating you, making you feel like you're the one to blame, but you aren't. He's the sonofabitch who shot these creatures. If he's the guy I think he is, he'd put a bullet between your eyes and not feel a moment of regret."

Huge brown eyes met his. But they weren't soft. They were angry with a hard gleam. "And what sort of man are you, Sergeant Dempsey? Aren't you manipulating me? Are you any different to him? You've shot people. Killed them. Did you feel regret?"

CHAPTER
SEVEN

FOR FUCK'S SAKE. He spat in the dirt. Great. He'd spent his whole life fighting against scumbag terrorists and what happened? He ended up accused of being exactly the same sort of nutcase by someone he was trying to help. It stung. He wasn't about to let her know that.

"That's right, love. That's why they pay me the big bucks, so let's move it." He maneuvered her in front of him. "Step where the trooper steps if you want to keep your legs." He let her walk a few paces ahead and spoke into his comms. "Baxter and Cullen, keep a low profile as we head back to the RV. See if this bastard's hiding somewhere and decides to follow us."

They both acknowledged with radio clicks and he followed Axelle through the bush and along the rocky path. The old guy must be damn good or damn lucky to have spotted them near that other collar. He must have night vision equipment to move so swiftly at night too. Or he had insider information.

Dempsey moved closer to Axelle. "What can you tell me about the locals in this area?"

She shot him a glare from beneath fine black brows but refused to answer him. Great. He'd managed to alienate her when he was supposed to be winning hearts and minds. Though taking a bullet or getting blown up wasn't conducive to positive relations either, and he swore he felt eyes all over him.

They tramped silently over the ridge. They were only about three miles from her camp but it was three miles up and down, and she was done and too stubborn to let him help. He knew all about stubborn. The sun was sliding down the western slopes when they finally approached the yurts.

A headache began to pound his temples, and he knew Axelle was holding on to her temper and composure by the thinnest of strands.

As the three of them crested the last ridge, he saw the tall redheaded man from the camp, riding toward them. The guy— Josef, he remembered—carried the AK-47 and the look in his eyes was both fierce and determined.

"Don't shoot. Don't shoot!" Axelle yelled. At whom he wasn't sure but they all tensed.

The man pulled the horse to a halt in a cloud of dust and leveled the gun in their direction. Dempsey and Taz shouldered their weapons.

"Step away from the woman."

"Josef, it's okay—" Axelle went to take a step forward but Dempsey gripped her arm. He didn't want her in the firing line if things went south.

"Let her go. Get behind me, Axelle. Now." Josef yelled.

Shit. This guy was in a state.

Every sense sharpened. Dempsey stood ready to defend his unit and Axelle. He'd started to include her in his list of responsibilities, which was a mistake because he might be gone by morning. And she wasn't exactly the sort of woman you looked after.

She moved in front of him again and raised her hands to try to calm down her student. Dempsey put his rifle down. He needed more hands to deal with Axelle Dehn.

"You don't understand, Josef. These men helped me catch and release G-man yesterday. They're going to help us find the poacher."

Assuming the poacher was the same guy they were after. Dempsey winced and the student spotted it. No choice, he wrapped his arm around Axelle's waist and brought her firmly against his body. Her muscles stiffened in shock. This could rapidly turn into a shoot-first-ask-questions-later interlude, and he wanted to get control of the situation before it deteriorated further. He drew his SIG which had an extended 20-round magazine, and Taz kept his carbine trained on the big guy.

"Relax," he breathed in her ear. "Trust me." He shifted her until he had her sideways to Josef—who could be in league with the Russian for all he knew—and tried to shield her with his body. "Drop the weapon, Josef." He could feel the pounding of Axelle's pulse against his wrist. "And we'll tell you what's going on."

Josef's eyes narrowed into thin slits. "If I do that you'll kill us both."

"No, I won't. I'm not about to kill anyone but I need you to drop the rifle so I can explain who I am without worrying you're going to nail us."

Axelle pushed hard against his arm.

His pistol did not waver from the other man's chest, and at this distance he would not miss. "Put the rifle down and get off the horse or you're a dead man."

"Axelle?" Her student asked with a nervous swallow.

He could feel her body heat through the layers of clothes. She took a deep breath. He could almost hear her thinking. Surely she'd figured out that if he'd wanted to hurt her, he'd have done it in the mountains where no one would have found her body.

This was the moment of truth. Did she trust him? He'd helped her beloved leopards. They'd walked hand-in-hand down a mountainside. They'd slept side by side in a shallow cave. She'd confessed her fear of enclosed spaces. But he hadn't given her anything in return except name, rank and number.

Silence stretched taut through the air. He watched a bead of sweat drip down the side of Josef's face. Maybe Axelle did believe he was nothing but a cold-blooded killer…

"Put the rifle down, Josef," she said finally.

"Aye, laddie." A voice came out of the ether. "We're not here for you or the woman. You need to put the rifle down, and at least give us the chance to say our piece."

Axelle turned her head to whisper in Dempsey's ear. "He's one of yours, right?"

He nodded. His aim never wavered.

"Let me go. Josef isn't going to shoot anyone." Her fingers were no longer pushing against his arm. They gripped him tight as if in reassurance. God, he liked that feeling.

"Are you sure?" He glanced hesitantly at the big man atop the horse. He looked as fierce as a mamma bear protecting her cubs. Perhaps his feelings were deeper than that of a student for his supervisor.

She nodded and he let her go. Trust went both ways. He even lowered his SIG but he wasn't about to holster it until the AK was slung across the guy's back.

Slowly the big guy dropped the rifle's muzzle toward the ground. His shoulders heaved as he seemed to realize they weren't about to murder him on the spot.

He climbed off the horse and came toward the woman. Dempsey had to force himself not to react.

"Where the hell have you been?" Josef asked. "I've been worried sick since the horse came back without you, but one of the traps was sprung and I knew you'd want me to deal with that first..." His eyes pleaded for understanding.

Axelle nodded and Dempsey realized these cats meant everything to this woman. More than her own survival. "Did you release a leopard?" Hope lifted her voice.

Josef shook his head. "The trap was empty when I got there."

There was a stretch of silence and she finally remembered he was there.

"Sergeant Dempsey here"—she held his gaze for a brief moment—"helped me release G-man, who had a wounded back leg." She fisted her fingers around the fabric of the fake collar,

"Then we tried staking out G-man's collar in case the poacher came for him." Her voice broke and Dempsey had to force himself not to take her in his arms to try to comfort her. Especially when the Dane glared at him with more than a professional light in his eyes. *Oh yeah*, the guy had feelings for Axelle all right, but she was oblivious.

A spark lit his bloodstream. She hadn't been oblivious to him. No, there had been definite hints of attraction even though she'd tried to conceal it. Of course, that was before she'd called him a manipulative cold-blooded killer.

"The poacher didn't fall for it," Dempsey told the Dane. "Instead we found a skinned goat staked out with this fake collar attached." He watched Axelle struggle to regain control.

Her eyes hardened. "I don't know if this sonofabitch found out about the soldiers being here or about us uncollaring the leopards, but either way he wants to punish us." Her jaw firmed. "So we better find our last five cats and release them before this bastard finds them."

"Er…there's a problem with that." Josef spoke hesitantly.

"What do you mean?"

"The Trust emailed us back."

Dempsey exchanged a look with Taz.

"And?" There was a quiver in Axelle's tone.

Josef cleared his throat. Whatever he was going to say he knew his boss was going to be furious. "Under no circumstances are we to remove the collars or try and track this hunter ourselves."

"You have got to be kidding me? Do they know what's at stake?" Axelle closed her eyes as she raised her face to the sky. Her skin was like marble—pale and flawless.

"They said the head of the Trust is going to visit Afghanistan's Interior Ministry ASAP to try deal with this, but it could take a week."

"By which time the leopards will be dead." Axelle planted her fists on her hips.

Dempsey took a step forward as he holstered his handgun "It

looks to me like you need us as much as we need you." He watched her face. Thoughts rapid-fired inside that brain of hers, and her lips thinned when she reached her conclusion.

The frost in her gaze turned to flint. "You want to use the leopards as bait."

"My plan is to capture a man responsible for taking hundreds, if not thousands, of innocent lives."

"And you intend to use one of the world's most endangered species to bait the trap." She got in his face. "Don't you, Sergeant?"

"He's already after them. You should be grateful for our presence rather than bitching at me about it." Dempsey bit the inside of his cheek to stop from losing his temper even more. They'd had a rough night. She was upset. He got it. "Your snow leopards are getting some of the best soldiers in the world as bodyguards. You should be thanking me, Axelle."

He deliberately used her first name, reminding her they'd moved beyond this pissing-contest stage to what he'd thought was approaching friendship.

"I should, should I?" She tried to stare him down, but he didn't look away. She took a step closer and they were almost nose to nose. "I *am* uncollaring those leopards as soon as I catch them. They will not be used as bait by anyone, especially not *the best soldiers in the world*." A whirlwind of emotions cascaded through her dark eyes. But it wasn't the anger or determination that clamped down on his tongue. It was the pain.

He looked over at Taz, breaking eye contact. Letting her win. Because winning didn't matter when it came to staring contests. It only mattered in life and death, and football. "Even though your bosses have ordered you not to?"

"The survival of a species is more important than bureaucratic red tape."

"You could lose your job." He looked back at her then. Gauged her reaction.

"I don't need the Conservation Trust to dictate terms to me

when it comes to international law." Her eyes glittered. "I'm still the person in charge of this project on the ground. Don't you forget that." She stabbed him in the chest with her finger even though he wore body armor. It probably hurt but she didn't seem to notice.

"Even if they give you a direct order?" he asked quietly. Things weren't going according to plan for either of them.

She leaned close again and he could feel her breath on his lips. "No one orders me around when it comes to the survival of my animals, Sergeant. You'll use those leopards over my dead body."

That was what he was afraid of.

She turned and started marching back toward the camp. Her student followed with the horse like an overgrown sheepdog coming to heel.

The troop came together.

"She's a firecracker." Scottish, belligerent and proud, Craig Cullen eyed Axelle with a wild glint in his eye.

"She's a bloody pain in the arse." Dempsey pulled up his sleeve to check the scratches, which were starting to itch. Even though he'd helped her he'd got nothing in return but blind hostility, and that was despite the stirring of attraction between them. He frowned. Maybe it was because of it.

His wounds were healing. He tried not to wonder about hers.

"Bloody hell." Baxter walked up behind him. "You look like you had sex with a tigress."

Dempsey's temper flashed and he was thankful he could hold his tongue. It must have shown in his eyes though, even in the dim shadows of twilight. Dempsey met Taz's gaze and some silent understanding passed between them. He might have called Axelle a pain in the backside, but it didn't mean he didn't care about her. Taz accurately read the nature of his feelings for a woman he'd only just met.

"It was one of her bloody snow leopards," Dempsey told them.

"You wrestled a snow leopard? For fun?" Taz asked.

A reluctant grin tugged his lips. "It *was* fun. Anyway, it turns out Dr. Axelle Dehn is the lead biologist on this snow leopard project. Our target appears to be hunting leopard. Did you see anything while I was gone yesterday?"

"Not much." Cullen scouted ahead as they headed toward the camp. "The big guy spent most of the day on the ridge listening to the radio transmitter. When did you figure out they were biologists?"

Dempsey grunted out a laugh. "When I found tranquilizer darts in her saddlebag a fraction of a second before she got behind me and shoved a Glock up my arse."

Cullen grinned. "You're getting old."

"I can still beat you in a footrace." But he felt old. As old as the mountains. He'd seen so much death throughout his lifetime he sometimes wondered why they bothered. To protect innocents, he reminded himself. That was what he'd dedicated his life to and he'd quit when he was dead or Returned To Unit. Same thing.

"We'll contact HQ but I think our best bet right now is sticking with the biologists and staking out the leopards. When our man shows we'll make sure he has nowhere to go."

"Corner him like the rat he is," Cullen agreed. "The orders were dead or alive but this guy must have fuckloads of information..."

"Let's try for alive unless he's a threat. Then all bets are off. We'll stay out of sight until we receive orders. Maybe the old fecker doesn't know we're here. He might have realized the biologists were uncollaring the leopards and got pissed off."

"It might not even be him," Cullen put in.

Dempsey nodded and trudged down the valley to the yurts. If only he could forget the fierce flash of betrayal in Axelle's eyes the moment she'd worked it all out. Because, yes, he'd always intended to use her leopards as bait. He was a soldier and he had a job to do—he was still planning on getting rid of her poacher, which would ultimately save her cats. *But maybe too late...*

He reined in his runaway thoughts and concentrated on the

barren landscape. It didn't matter what Axelle Dehn thought of him. With any luck he'd be gone before daybreak and she'd never cross his path again.

———

Axelle shoved back the yurt flap. Anji flung up his hands in surprise and gave a nervous laugh. "You're back. You scared me."

"There's a lot of that going around."

He smiled at her, brown eyes twinkling. "Josef was worried when the horse came back without you, but I told him you be okay."

Anji had more faith in her than she did. He returned to whatever he was doing with the cubs.

She strode to the computer and opened her email and read the message. Christ, the Trust really had forbidden her to release the animals. She inhaled deeply and tried to calm the rage that continued to burn inside. They thought she was overreacting and had no proof, and in the next sentence they told her it was too dangerous for her and Josef to go after a guy with a gun. Josef came slowly into the tent. She didn't know if he was scared or angry. He had a right to be both.

"Did you reply to this email?" She was vibrating with emotion. Moisture filmed her eyes but it wasn't tears.

"No." He stood behind her.

"Did they ask for confirmation of receipt?"

"No." He frowned.

She pressed delete. "Then it never arrived." She held his gaze. "Are you okay with that?"

His blue eyes flicked to the computer screen and back. He nodded.

"Good. I'll resend the original email again after we get a few hours sleep."

"What about those men?"

"What about them?" She wanted to pretend they didn't exist, that she'd never met Dempsey or exposed some of her darkest secrets in the shadow of the mountain. She should have known he was buttering her up so he could use her. It was all about the mission. That was what made a man a soldier.

She went and stood before the fire because she had no new answers and was so tired and wrung out she could barely see straight. She needed a few hours' sleep before she got back to releasing collars. Surely the man hunting the leopards was also tired? Surely he needed sleep? She helped herself to salted yak's milk tea and flatbread. Grimaced. You might acquire a taste for local food but it didn't mean you didn't miss Starbucks.

The cubs clambered over Anji's legs and drew a smile from her lips. "How are they doing?"

"They eat plenty." He looked up and smiled. "They survive and get fat, *Inshallah*."

The ice around her heart cracked a little. "Good."

"I fix other fire in your yurt."

"Thanks." Propriety demanded she sleep separate to the men but for the first time in years she didn't want to be alone.

She hugged herself with little comfort. The memories of Gideon had been brief but searing. She didn't let herself think about him often and that brought its own guilt. He'd been a wonderful man. An honorable man. She'd loved him fiercely. He'd joined the Marines because his best friend had died fighting for his country and he'd been compelled to do the same. Pity he hadn't asked his wife's opinion first.

She didn't think about him because it hurt too damn much.

"Did that guy really help you release G-man?" Josef broke into her thoughts.

She nodded. Some of her anger cooled. Dempsey *had* helped her; in fact she might not have caught G-man at all if he hadn't been there.

A man hunting terrorists would use any means available, and

she'd do the same to save her cats. She squeezed her temples with her thumb and index finger. She needed to apologize to him but at the same time she hoped she never saw him again. "He said he's British Army but he's not wearing a uniform."

"Special Forces." Josef's eyes gleamed. "Probably SAS. Some of the most respected soldiers in the world. Dangerous men."

He'd exuded danger and skill. But, except for that first heart-stopping moment when he'd disarmed her—easily disarmed her, now she thought about it—she hadn't been scared of him at all. Not even when he'd grabbed her in front of Josef.

"Why? Why are they even here?" She dragged her fingers through her bedraggled hair.

"Do you trust them?" he asked.

Wearily she shrugged. "I don't know. I guess if they'd wanted us dead we'd be dead." Maybe that was the only truth that mattered. Her eyelids started to droop. She needed sleep. "I'll see you at dawn." She went outside and the air was clean and fresh. Pink seeped along the edges of twilight. She could barely drag one foot in front of the other as she headed to her tent. She glanced at the surrounding hills and wondered where Dempsey was. They'd spent the night together and somehow forged a bond. What it meant, she didn't know.

Her scratches were sore and her bones ached. But there was also this weird sense of loneliness that she hadn't felt in years. She half expected Dempsey to be sitting on her bed, waiting to chew her out for yelling at him earlier. That thought tangled in her brain and slowed her feet because she wasn't sure what she'd do if she found him there.

She threw back the flap but her tent was empty. The quick stab of disappointment was shoved into the furthest corners of her mind. She lit the fire, shook out her bedclothes and took off her boots. Then she lay down and slept like the dead.

Dempsey sat and watched as Josef started the dirt bike and headed to the top of the ridge with the radio receiver. Why hadn't Dmitri Volkov booby-trapped that carcass? Why hadn't he planted mines or explosives to take them out? The questions nagged him constantly.

He didn't know.

All he knew was catching Dmitri Volkov alive would provide valuable intel and save lives. Sergeant Ty Dempsey wasn't here to save leopards or babysit biologists. He was here to catch a traitor. The Russian knew things. He had connections. He was dangerous.

Yet these biologists were directly in the line of fire...

"I think we need a change of plan." Dempsey spoke into his radio so the whole squad could hear. He and Baxter had already packed their kit. They started trudging down the slope.

"What are you thinking, Irish?" Taz's voice was calm and even.

"Come on down, bring the gear." He stared at the thin blue sky. "I think we're about to become field biologists." There was a high chance the Russian knew there were soldiers in the area. Dempsey had spoken to HQ and they were sending in more troopers.

When they got to the camp Dempsey's eyes flashed up to Josef on the ridge. "Keep your eye on the big man."

Baxter nodded and sat on the sunny side of the yurt.

Inside the main tent a local man, Wakhi from the look of his features, was brewing tea and jiggling something gray and furry in his arms. It took a moment for Dempsey to realize it was a snow leopard cub, and there was another one, who began to squawk from the bottom of a large box.

"Where's Axelle?" he asked quietly.

The Wakhi man pointed east. "Next yurt." Dempsey took a step away but the little man shook his finger wildly in a "no" action. He thrust the squalling kitten at him and Dempsey took it, followed by a bottle of warm milk. "Go feed cub. Leave Axelle sleep," the man scolded.

Dempsey raised his brows and did as he was told. He assumed feeding a baby leopard was much like feeding a baby human, and as he had a huge family, with enough cousins to take on the Regiment, he did have some experience feeding babies. But it had been a long time.

He stuffed the teat into the eager pink mouth and realized he'd missed this. He'd missed feeding his nieces and nephews. He'd missed seeing them grow up. He missed the connection, the roots. His stand for a peaceful future for the Province of Northern Ireland, for an end to sectarian violence, had led to the total destruction of his place within his family. The irony wasn't lost on him that he was the one with the weapons now. He hoped he had the sense and skill to know when to use them, as opposed to bombing innocents in market towns or kneecapping informers.

Dempsey held the warm body in the crook of his arm and went to peek at Axelle despite the hissing protestations of her bodyguard. Sheesh where was this guy when she'd been out in the wilds all alone?

She lay snuggled deep in her sleeping bag. The bag lifted and fell steadily, and her cheeks flushed with rosy heat. He didn't have the heart to wake her. He went back outside, careful of the cub suckling greedily. He walked over to Baxter who stroked the cub's tummy.

He heard the dirt bike start up and saw Josef coming back down the hill. He rolled up beside them and started past them into the yurt without a word.

Dempsey stopped him. "What's going on, mate?"

There was no anger in Josef's gaze today. Acceptance. A reluctant interest. "No snares were tripped in the night. I'm going to check the collar coordinates and see where our cats are."

Taz joined them and looked at Josef with pensive brown eyes. "Do you get many poachers here?"

"Not like this. Who are you looking for anyway?" Josef's eyes sharpened. Axelle would have told him they were soldiers. "A terrorist?"

Dempsey weighed his options about what he could say. "Someone the British government wants to talk to."

"You're going to stop this poacher from killing our leopards?"

"That's the plan."

"Good."

Dempsey looked at the seemingly endless spread of the Hindu Kush and across the valley to the Pamirs in the north. He passed the satisfied kitten to Baxter, who was eyeing it with a look usually reserved for beautiful women.

"We can help each other," said Josef.

Dempsey nodded. He should be feeling satisfied too. He should have been feeling bloody marvelous but these people were not the sort of partners he wanted when hunting one of the world's most notorious terrorists. So what if GCHQ thought the guy had been inactive—presumed dead—for a decade? To Dempsey that spelled some seriously dodgy connections. And an even more sinister reason for coming out of hiding now.

Axelle was a liability. Rash, brash and female—a powder-keg of trouble in a country like Afghanistan. Maybe he should hogtie her, release the horses, dismantle the computer, take the mother-board and Sat Link with him. But the Russian had come to them; they hadn't gone searching for the Russian. They were already involved in this mess, and something about the determined set of Axelle's jaw told him he'd have a fight on his hands if he tried to shut them down. As fun as that might be under normal circumstances, he couldn't afford the distraction when this mission might cost lives. He had to work with her. And he had the feeling it was going to cost him more than swallowing a bit of false pride.

———

When she woke she was staring straight into the startling cobalt eyes of Sergeant Tyrone Dempsey. He looked like he'd wait all day for her to wake up.

"I must be dreaming," she croaked.

He held out a mug of black tea.

"Definitely dreaming." She sat up, took it, and sipped. The warm liquid eased her dry throat. "Thanks. What time is it?"

"0600." His voice rolled over her. She blinked groggily. There was enough of a burr in his accent to make his voice very sexy and she figured he was laying on the charm this morning.

His face was scrubbed and clean-shaven. She found herself studying his features. The vivid eyes shaded by thick brows, the cheeks scraped smooth, the jaw firm and obstinate, his nose too flat to be conventionally handsome. Yet the combination stirred up her insides like hot coals. She fought the urge to run her fingers through his short blond hair. He was tall and lean and he looked really, really good.

She did not like the whip of attraction that shot through her veins when those blue eyes twinkled. Damn. She needed distance, not attraction. "I was a bitch yesterday."

"Is that an apology?"

"More of a reminder." Reluctantly one side of her mouth curled. "But it's probably as close as you're going to get to an apology." She squinted at him. The lines around his eyes were cut deeper today. Had he slept? Or had he been up all night searching for the man he was chasing? The same man killing her leopards.

"My CO has been in contact with your bosses at the Trust. I've been ordered to use any means possible to apprehend this individual."

Fury engulfed her, but he moved into her space, sitting down on the edge of the bunk and trapping her in her sleeping bag. "So I'd like to propose a compromise." His expression remained even but lines around his eyes creased as she tried to spit out words. He reached out and removed the mug from her hand. "I'm going to put this over here in case you get any ideas."

The brush of his fingers against hers caused all sorts of fireworks to explode inside her that had nothing to do with anger. The man knocked her off-balance, made her crazy. *More crazy*, she conceded as she forced herself to get a grip. "What sort of compromise?"

"I've called for more men and equipment so we can start tracking our target properly. In the meantime, we'll split up and stake out the cats using the signals and"—he raised his voice as she tried to cut in—"we will help you release any animals you snare."

The sudden silence pulsed against the walls of the tent. "You'll let me uncollar them?"

"Yes."

They held each other's gaze for a long silent moment. "Why? Why not force me to leave them collared until you catch this guy?"

One side of his mouth dragged back in a wry smile before he answered. "You're not the only person in the world who gives a damn about endangered species, Dr. Dehn. *However*, capturing this man is my mission and the mission is my priority. Otherwise I wouldn't be a very good soldier"—his eyebrows rose—"now, would I?"

He stood and walked to the door of her yurt.

She was back to being Dr. Dehn, she registered. "And that's really important to you. Being a good soldier?"

He paused inside the tent with his hand on the felt. "Maybe it's all I've got."

"Sergeant..." A slice of pain at saying the military rank out loud made her suck in a breath. "*Dempsey*," she said urgently to stop him from leaving.

He looked over his shoulder, the sun coating his silhouette with gold.

"Thank you." She held his gaze, willing him to understand what his gesture meant to her.

He grinned, blue eyes flashing as they swept over her

121

disheveled form, reminding her that while he might be a soldier he was most definitely a guy. "You can thank me when this is over." Then he was gone.

————

A beep told Axelle she'd got email. When she checked the message every other thought fled as she realized she had a download from one of her camera traps.

"Dempsey!" she yelled.

There were six hidden cameras set up in three pairs around the mountains. Placed in obscure valleys and passes to try to avoid people, and more important in this region, goats, from triggering them. No one wanted five hundred pictures of goats. The camera images automatically uploaded to satellites whenever the data storage units were full and then were emailed to her server in the States. Dempsey came inside and walked over to her side. She clicked on the first image and they watched as, pixel by pixel, a photograph of a white-haired man leading a yak downloaded to the screen. He was dressed as a local. The pants, the jerkin, the pakol hat. His build was tall, slim, broad at the shoulder, but his facial features were not Asian or Arabian. He looked fair-skinned, his beard as red as Josef's, his eyes iced with lines of bitterness.

She sat stunned, her eyes taking in every detail of the man's face, looking for some whisper of compassion in the deep rugged lines on his face. Strapped over the back of the yak was a rolled-up pelt with a trimming of dappled fur, over his shoulder was a high-powered hunting rifle. Fear and fury swirled in the depths of her stomach. This was the hunter. To put a face on this monster made everything more real, more dangerous. "Sonofabitch," she whispered. "Is this who you're looking for?"

Dempsey leaned over her, trapping her between his arms as his fingers typed furiously. He pulled up some sort of secure website and uploaded the image into the database. She could feel his breath on her neck, his lips close to her ear. She shivered. He smelled of clean warm skin and the Ivory soap that they kept in their improvised shower cubicle. His hands were square, the fingers long and tapered. Small hairs shone white gold on his wrist and forearms. Every cell in her body was acutely aware of this man.

He finished, cleared the history, shut down the web browser, and went perfectly still as if he suddenly realized his arms were around her. Or maybe he could tell the effect he was having on her nervous system. His breathing changed and heat began to build in Axelle's veins. She turned her head a fraction and found her lips an inch from his. They held each other's gaze warily, a wave of something startling shooting through her body. Dempsey's gaze dropped to her mouth and her lips parted. He started to lean toward her, but a noise outside made him break away, leaving her to grab a breath she hadn't realized she'd been holding.

"I'll get the guys ready to go." His voice was gruff and he avoided looking at her.

She nodded. She couldn't have formed words for three wishes and a genie.

CHAPTER
EIGHT

HE SPLIT them into three groups.

"Can't I go with the doc?" Cullen moaned. He might have the reputation of being the ladies' man of A-Squadron's Mountain Troop, but after what Dempsey had been thinking five minutes earlier while trying not to kiss Axelle Dehn's lips, legs, and everything in between, maybe he was a frickin' ladies' man too.

He wanted her and he'd let his eyes tell her exactly how much he wanted her.

What was he thinking? There was a time and a place for that sort of thing and this wasn't it.

"No." He kept his voice light. None of them were here to get laid. "You're with Taz. Baxter you go with the Great Dane. I'm with the doc." He gave them a firm smile that told them this wasn't up for debate. "We'll get the biologists to give us a demo how to tranq and release the cats before we head out. I want hourly radio checks." He nodded to the men. "It might be a couple of days until the other guys get here. I'm still waiting on a rendezvous time. In the meantime, we watch the leopards and hope we capture our target while he's trying to poach the cats."

"Cool," Taz said.

Baxter was beaming.

Protecting snow leopards was a plum assignment, as long as they didn't forget the very real threat out there—someone who knew his way around explosives the same way the boys knew their own dicks.

"Keep your eyes peeled." He turned as Axelle came out of her yurt. She'd braided her hair and wore clean clothes—olive pants, stone-colored fleece. Except for her scrubbed-clean pink cheeks and dark eyes, she blended right into the landscape.

She looked at them and they all stared right back at her.

"You've eaten?" She raised her voice across the dusty arena. She looked as if she didn't want to approach them, as if by keeping her distance all her problems would disappear.

If only.

Each man nodded. He could tell she'd captured their interest the same way she'd captured his. They rarely dealt with women in their jobs. He liked it. Figured they did too.

She ducked back into the bigger tent. Josef came out a second later with the two cubs in his arms. The guys went over and started playing with the balls of fluff, pulling out their cameras to take photos. He held back a smile. Three of the toughest soldiers on earth, turning into big softies because of a couple of pussy cats.

"We need a demo of how you tranquilize the leopards and detach the collars," he said when the student stood.

The Dane nodded. Not exactly friendly. Not exactly hostile.

Axelle came out of the tent and headed over to the horses. Dempsey saw a change in the student's expression. A microsecond of yearning burned across the man's features before he masked it again. Josef caught his eye and the two men regarded each other with absolute understanding.

"You're with Baxter—the short ugly bugger, rolling around on the floor."

The Dane huffed out a gruff laugh. "You're with Axelle, I suppose?"

Dempsey nodded.

"Keep her safe. And keep your hands off her."

Cullen glanced at him. Dempsey swore with impatience. He wasn't on a Club Med vacation. He was on a mission. "Look, Josef. She can barely stand the sight of me. I don't think you've got much to worry about, right, pal?"

Hell, he'd be gone in a day or two and that pissed him off. For the first time he wanted this mission to last longer. Maybe a few weeks would give him the chance to get to know Axelle Dehn better. A *lot* better. But she didn't want to know him at all. She just wanted to save her leopards.

Josef scratched his neck. "You remind her of her husband."

"Husband?" Dempsey had to work hard not to choke. *She's married?*

Josef nodded. "He was a soldier. Died in Iraq years ago."

Relief mixed with guilt. *Poor bugger.* It explained her antipathy toward soldiers. Maybe she blamed the military as a whole for her loss. Or maybe, like any sane person, she hated war.

They watched her lead two horses across the dusty ground and stop a few feet away. A tiny frown marred her forehead as if she sensed they'd been talking about her.

"Who's coming with me?" she asked.

"I am." Dempsey took a step closer and her gaze flicked over him. He felt his cheeks burn and knew the lads noticed it, too. Why the hell had he wanted to stick close to the woman? Because he thought he could handle her? It'd be easier to handle a live grenade.

She thrust a pair of reins at Josef. Then she handed out sheets of paper to everyone, which made him grin. "We only have two receivers and one always stays in base camp." He and Cullen exchanged a quick glance. *Yeah. Right.* She pointed to the markings she'd made on the maps she'd printed out. "These are the coordinates of the snares Josef and I set up."

There were several crosses on the map, some close together. All in valleys.

"You and your partner take this zone to the northwest." She gestured to Cullen, who gave her his film-star grin. Dempsey stood behind Axelle and cocked a brow at the soldier. "The next group takes the snares east. Dempsey and I will head southeast again. I'll show you how the collars work and how to tranquilize the animals without harming them. Radio in if something unexpected occurs. Any questions?" She stared them each in the eye like the Commander of the Regiment and it was all he could do not to salute.

"No, ma'am."

Dempsey saw the suppressed grins and knew they were all thinking the same thing—she was something else. He stopped listening and just watched her demonstrate the tranqs as the cubs played with her bootlaces. He already knew how they worked. He and Josef held the horses, the lads watching her every move.

"Does she have this effect on everyone?" he murmured to the Dane.

Josef nodded and tightened the horse's saddle girth. "Pretty much." He looked resigned.

"She's young to be in charge of a project this big," Dempsey noted. Although the setup looked basic, this sort of operation inside a theatre of war would cost a fortune.

The big man shrugged. "She's the top researcher in her field. Had a featured article on her in *National Geographic* a couple of months ago."

Dempsey raised his brows. "I guess that explains why she's so bossy." Just then she turned to face him.

"Are you ready to go yet, or do you need to fix your makeup?" he asked.

The lads grinned.

A hint of scarlet brushed her cheek as her eyes narrowed dangerously. She knew he was baiting her. Thankfully she just huffed out a breath. "They need to know this stuff."

He tapped his watch. "We need to get moving."

She looked at her newest recruits. "Is he always such a jerk?"

"Yes, ma'am." They all nodded in unison, the pride of the British Army. "He's a total fucking jerk."

And they'd die for him. He just hoped they didn't have to.

———

Axelle spent the next few hours boiling under the concealment of a desert tarp in a narrow valley, far enough from the snares not to be spotted by terrorists or wildlife, but close enough to see everything that was going on, which was nothing. It should have been boring but she was so tense from this forced proximity to Dempsey, she couldn't relax. He'd switched back to professional friendly and she wondered if she'd imagined the heat in his eyes this morning.

It scared her.

Not him.

But the fact he'd awoken this edgy sexual energy inside her freaked her out. So, for a change, she'd been cranky with him. It was a wonder he hadn't put a bullet in her.

"Josef said you lost your husband in Iraq."

Her chin jerked up and she swallowed the unexpected punch of grief. "Josef talks too much." She blinked rapidly, sideswiped by the memories and the feeling of betrayal her response to this man evoked. Yet it was so long ago—should it still hurt this much?

Since Gideon died, she'd dedicated her life to helping endangered species with no time or emotional energy for human complications. She wasn't sure how to act or how to feel now that someone had finally worked their way past her guard. Especially someone who'd probably leave in a day or two. Especially another soldier who might die.

He didn't even look like Gideon and that felt like a double betrayal. How could she lust after someone so different from the man she'd loved? They'd been teenage sweethearts, and with their matching brown eyes and hair, she and Gideon could have passed as siblings. They'd loved each other from the moment they'd met. He wasn't supposed to enlist. She'd never agreed to be an army wife.

God, how they'd fought about that.

It was the only time they'd truly argued and it had been vicious. And then he'd been killed.

She pressed her lips together. Even now, after so many years, she still hadn't let go of the anger or the grief. Maybe she never would.

She turned on the receiver and checked the signals from this high elevation.

"Still the same?" His eyes were as blue as the brightest sky.

"Yes." She looked away.

"The good news is there were no gunshots today." Dempsey was trying to make her feel better, which made her feel worse. "Maybe we should head back and see if I can raise HQ for more intel."

She swatted at a fly. "Okay."

Dust rose as they packed the gear, trying to do it as quietly and surreptitiously as possible. Her eyes were drawn to the tanned muscles of his arms as he shoved things into his pack.

"I was so angry when he joined up." The words came out of nowhere.

"Your husband? He didn't talk to you about it first?"

She shook her head. "I was in graduate school. He was a computer programmer and his best friend was killed by an IED. He signed up the next day. Came home and told me." Even now, more than a decade later, the feelings from that moment threatened to choke her. He'd chosen to leave her. Chosen to go to war. It had scraped her to the bone.

Why was she telling him this? She never discussed it. Never. "He promised he wasn't going to die." She felt his hands on her shoulders and gritted her teeth, fighting her anger and her shame.

"Axelle." He sighed. "I've been a soldier for a long time. I've lost a lot of friends—especially over the last decade. Some died heroes, others died because of shoddy equipment and because penny pinchers in the MOD know sweet Fanny Adams about warfare. But none of them died on purpose."

"What about the people you leave behind? Don't you even care about them?" Her vision swam but she needed an answer to the questions that haunted her.

"You'll need to ask someone else." His expression flattened out into an impassive mask. "I don't have anyone who gives a rat's ass whether I live or die."

"You're an orphan?" Her eyes sought and found his, pushing for answers.

"I wish."

"Your family would care—"

"I'm dead to them." His eyes grew detached, his voice hard.

She grabbed his fingers. Held on even when he tried to pull away. His jaw tightened and his eyes narrowed. He could fight her off if he wanted to. They both knew it.

"Why?" she pressed.

Unexpectedly, he pulled her against his chest and she caught her breath as his lips hovered an inch from hers. He didn't kiss her. She wrapped her arms around him in a way she hadn't allowed herself to touch a man in years. Maybe not since her husband had been deployed.

It felt good to hold him, to feel warm supple muscles flex beneath her fingers. His Adam's apple rippled in his throat. He smelled strong and warm.

"My story isn't going to tell you what your husband was thinking when he died. It won't teach you forgiveness."

She closed her eyes and buried her nose in the crook of his neck. Some of the awful tension she'd been carrying for years leached from her marrow. Even though she wasn't a woman who needed anyone, it was cathartic and reassuring to be held by such physical strength, by such emotional surety.

"He shouldn't have joined up without talking to you about it." His hand brushed over her hair.

No, Gideon shouldn't have enlisted without talking to her first, but hating him for it served no purpose. She had to let go of the past.

"Although I doubt it would have changed anything in the end."

She pressed her lips tighter together.

He held her away from him and she forced herself to look into that perceptive gaze.

"He needed to fight." One side of his lips pulled into a crooked smile. "Some of us need to fight for our country, the same way you fight for wildlife." With a final squeeze he let her go and stepped away. Busied himself folding the tarp.

"Are you married?" She suddenly needed to know.

"No." He was bent over but he lifted his gaze to meet hers. "Are you proposing?" A glint of humor lit his eyes.

"No." Somehow she was both relieved and intimidated and she didn't bother to fake a smile. "It just might have been easier if you were."

Their gazes collided and a million sparks ignited the air between them. Heat rose to press against her skin because she didn't want this and she could tell from his expression neither did he. "You remind me of everything I lost."

"I'm just an ordinary soldier." His voice was low and fervent. "There are thousands of us, trying to protect civilians by doing the dangerous, ugly jobs most people don't want to think about. It doesn't always go to plan." There was a faraway look in his eyes. "But that's what we try to do. Kill the bad guys. Save the innocents. And although I never knew your husband, I'd bet my ass that's why he went to war—to protect the people he loved. To protect you."

A hawk cried overhead and her head pounded with an incoming headache.

"If you can accept *that* then maybe you can begin to forgive him, and yourself."

"Maybe I don't deserve forgiveness." *Damn*. Her epiphany

didn't seem to surprise him, but it shocked the hell out of her.

He tied the tarp carefully to his pack. "Then become a Catholic because then it doesn't matter what sins you commit. Christ the Lord will welcome you to Heaven with open arms as long as you repent and go to Mass." Bitterness made his voice sharp. "Bloody fucking religion. Let's go."

She'd roused some inner demon. *Terrific job, Axelle.* Although pissing him off kept distance between them and right now she needed that distance, because when he'd held her she'd never wanted to let go. This man wasn't sticking around, she reminded herself. He went where he was ordered, when he was ordered.

It took them an hour to get back to camp, but neither said a word. Dempsey walked while she rode. He was unstoppable, seemingly tireless. When they got back Anji was standing outside the main yurt, wringing his hands.

"Dr. Dehn. Thank goodness you're here. Josef radioed, he's been trying to reach you. They think they spotted the poacher's tracks near their snare."

"Shit. Are they sure?" Dempsey answered.

"No. Not sure." Anji replied with a hint of fear. "Nobody sure of anything."

Dempsey eyed their Russian van. "Would that thing make it to their position?"

Axelle thought about it. "Pretty much. It might get stuck in the stream though," she warned.

"Can I borrow it?" Dempsey asked her.

"Sure." This would give her the chance to break the effect he was having on her. She slid from the horse's back, her muscles feeling like she'd been kick-boxing an iron giant. "Keys are in it. Take Anji with you," she suggested. The poor guy had been stuck here for the past few days doing nothing except feed kittens. Although that was more than she'd achieved today.

Dempsey frowned.

"He's training to be a ranger. It'll be valuable experience for him and he knows the area better than anyone. I'll look after the cubs."

Dempsey stared at the man and finally nodded. "Okay. Be good." He winked at her, and a half smile lit his face before he and Anji climbed in the van and trundled away into the dusty brown vista.

"I'm always good," she whispered. That was the problem.

She checked on the cubs, who were snoozing in the wooden crate Anji had procured for them. She headed over to the shower area and had a quick wash to remove the worst of the grime. Tired, she decided to grab a nap before sorting through her email. She pushed into her tent and bent to take off her boots. The next moment, a hand clamped over her nose and mouth, and a prick of pain shot through her thigh. Panic blasted away her exhaustion but even as she fought and struggled, strong hands muffled her screams so they died like whimpers in her throat. Then she slammed into darkness.

They'd followed the spoor for two hours but ground sign was disappearing as dust swirled in the wind. Dempsey was torn. Did he keep following the unknown originator of these tracks or go back to base camp and regroup. Base camp was calling his name but he wasn't sure whether that was because Axelle had destroyed his objectivity or because it was the smartest thing to do.

Hell, right now he was going in circles.

"Let's mark this GPS position and head back," he said to Taz quietly. The sound of horses hooves drumming against solid earth made him glance in the direction of the biologists' camp. The student—Josef—came flying into view, coat open and flapping in time to the rhythm of the horse.

"What the feck?" They'd all rendezvoused at the snare where the tracks had been spotted, but he'd sent Josef and the local man back to camp on horseback an hour ago. He hadn't liked the idea of Axelle being alone, although she'd managed without him all these years, so she could probably cope for an afternoon.

Josef started yelling, which made Dempsey shake his head and climb slowly to his feet. Any hope of a clandestine patrol had been eliminated, although with all the general commotion he didn't know why he bothered.

The big man stopped in a shower of gravel. "Is Axelle here?"

Dempsey frowned as he grabbed the horse's reins. "What do you mean? Isn't she back at camp?"

The big man's cheeks were red and his breath puffed out of his lungs in short bursts. He shook his head.

"Maybe she went out to check the traps?" Cullen suggested, walking up behind them.

Josef shook his head. "None of them have been sprung, and even if they had she'd never leave without one of the receivers." Cullen looked guiltily away—he had the second one, which he'd filched from camp. Josef was still trying to catch his breath. "The shortwave radio is smashed. Otherwise I wouldn't have ridden all this way. I'd have called."

Dempsey pulled Josef from the horse and swung into the saddle. Something was wrong. He could feel it. As the sun was dropping in the sky he kicked the horse into full gallop. Panic squeezed his chest. Where the hell had she wandered off to? Why did he feel like someone had fucked him over?

At full gallop, Dempsey felt a rush of adrenaline as the raw breeze lashed his skin. He let the animal have its head. It seemed to take forever but the horse knew exactly where it was going and was surefooted as any goat. Finally, he could see the pale outline of the camp ahead. Anji was standing outside the main yurt, a look of confusion stamped on his features. Dempsey was beginning to suspect that was his default expression. He pulled the horse to a stop and leapt down. He went inside Axelle's yurt, noted the bedroll neatly laid out and the undented pillow. Unlit fire. He pushed his way back outside and turned to look in the corral, but the yaks and camel weren't telling him anything.

He stalked to the main tent and headed straight to the laptop, which was already running. He needed to talk to his CO but wasn't quite sure where they were in the hunt—aside from the obvious lack of one of the most wanted terrorists on the face of the earth.

Anji came to stand behind him, his fingers dancing agitatedly across his chest. "We checked as soon as we got back but she wasn't here."

Dempsey glanced at a box that bumped and moved beside the fire. "The cubs are okay?"

"I fed them. They were hungry. Axelle hadn't fed them the way she said she would. That isn't like her." The Wakhi man reached down and pulled out a fluffy mass of fur.

It reminded Dempsey that the poacher had known about the biologists' camp all along. They suspected the Russian was using the collars to track the leopards, leaving no doubt he knew about this operation. He was a bold, smart, slippery sonofabitch.

Where the hell was Axelle?

White-hot fear stabbed down his spine. He had the feeling he'd missed something—that he'd been looking straight ahead while someone sideswiped him. That was usually the Regiment's job.

He frowned. Maybe he was asking the wrong questions. Not *where* was Axelle, but *who* was Axelle Dehn?

He googled her name and came up first with her webpage for MSU. Then clicked the link to the snow leopard project that was funded by The Conservation Trust. He scanned the short biography, and clicked another link to the *National Geographic* article Josef had mentioned.

"Bloody fucking hell."

The Wakhi man flinched.

"When do Axelle and Josef normally arrive to start tracking the leopards?"

"In summer when she's done teaching. Josef was supposed to have come earlier than her this year, but—"

"It says here she's the daughter of the US Ambassador to Great Britain?" It said a hell of a lot more too. Shit. She had more potential enemies than he did, and her name and face and summer location had been broadcast to the whole world. Incredible.

The Wakhi man shrugged nervously. "I don't know anything about that. She doesn't talk about anything personal."

Dempsey jolted. *She talked to me.*

Anji shifted nervously, placed the cub back in the box.

Dempsey strode outside, grabbed a smoldering torch and carefully examined the ground. Josef's massive boot prints and Axelle's much narrower ones. The Wakhi man wore small boots with narrow pointed toes. Dempsey knelt. There was another track, no tread marks on the sole—almost indistinct. He scanned the area, following the indents to Axelle's yurt, then the deeper indents that exited and arrowed behind the yurts. There were hoof prints here. A jumbled mess that suggested the animal had been tied up. He looked at the corral again and noted they were one yak short. *Shit.*

He carried on, scanning the ground. It was hard to track over dust and rock, almost impossible at night. Subtle changes in the color of the surface meant he was pretty confident he was following someone carrying something heavy.

Shit. Shit. Double fucking shit.

They'd been conned.

The boys arrived, bumping wildly over the rocky terrain in the van. Cullen leapt out and ran to his side, concern in his eyes. "What's going on?"

"I think we've been looking at this situation from the wrong angle."

Cullen's face remained impassive.

"We were going to use the snow leopards as bait, right?"

Dempsey watched the hills, trying to pick movement out of the darkness.

Josef grunted in disgust.

Dempsey ignored him. "I think our poacher was killing them for the same reason."

Cullen pressed his lips together, silently following the faint trail of human and animal spoor in the dirt at their feet. "You think he was after Axelle all along?"

Josef's eyes flared and his fists clenched as he started to run forward. Dempsey stuck out his leg and toppled the giant. "Don't destroy the tracks by doing something foolish," he told him.

Josef spat dirt from his mouth. "You know what could happen to a woman like Axelle, alone with this man?"

Anger stirred his temper. "I know *exactly* what could happen." He'd seen it more times than he wanted to think about. "Running after her unprepared isn't going to rescue her. You'll get yourself killed. Leave it to people who know what they're doing."

Josef climbed heavily to his feet. "What happens if it becomes a choice between completing your mission and saving Axelle's life?"

Dempsey stared dispassionately at the Dane, and Cullen answered for him.

"Dempsey's never failed in a mission yet."

He flinched. That wasn't the answer he'd expected. "I'll get her back." There was an unfamiliar quiver in his stomach. The stakes had been raised. Axelle was in danger and he was responsible.

"Should we call her father?" Josef asked suddenly.

"Her father?" Cullen questioned.

Dempsey laughed. "It turns out her dad's an ambassador."

Cullen rolled his eyes. "No shit."

"Yeah. Exactly." Dempsey grabbed his backpack, cognizant the whole camp could have been booby-trapped now that the Russian had Axelle in his grasp—assuming it was the Russian. It explained why he hadn't set any mines or explosives earlier. He'd wanted the woman alive.

Moving slowly, keeping his eyes open, he grabbed the tired horse he'd ridden and swung back in the saddle. "If this turns into a hostage situation, the ambassador's going to find out soon enough anyway."

"Not that the US negotiates with terrorists. And not that he can reach this place before the sonofabitch…" Cullen stopped talking. Nobody wanted to think about what the Russian and his extremist buddies might do to a Western white woman connected to a powerful diplomat.

"You get through to HQ, tell them what's going on, and find out where the fuck the backup troops are." Dempsey gathered his reins. "The kidnapper's got a few hours' lead on us but he might not travel in darkness and I've got NVGs." But the bastard knew these mountains like the wiring on a bomb. He was proving a wilier adversary than Dempsey had ever imagined.

"I want to come with you." Josef grabbed the reins.

Dempsey assessed the big man, understanding the need, knowing he'd only hold him back when he needed to move fast. "You travel with Cullen, Taz and Baxter. Axelle said you'd had military training?"

Josef nodded.

"Right, then you get to carry a gun."

"Dempsey's the best tracker in the Regiment," Cullen assured the Dane. Josef nodded again but looked sick with worry.

"I'll take the lead in the search and make sure there're plenty of tracks for you to follow, plus Cullen can see my GPS signal. Let's maintain radio silence as much as possible in case the old feck is listening in. See if HQ has intel we can use for a change."

"What do we tell them about Axelle?"

Dempsey's mouth went dry. Was this the man's plan all along or had he taken advantage of Axelle being left alone? What if the man had just wanted a female for a few hours' entertainment? The thought twisted his gut. "Tell HQ we believe he's taken a female hostage. Don't mention her name yet—he might not know it. It might not even be the Russian." Although instinctively he knew it was. He'd set an elaborate trap in motion.

The Wakhi man watched them from the door of the yurt.

"Check the camp for explosives while you're waiting for confirmation from HQ."

Cullen nodded. "Don't do anything stupid, Sergeant."

He wound a scarf around his head to keep off the worst of the cold. "Roger that. I'll wait for the cavalry—unless she's in immediate danger. Then all bets are off."

"Does he know we're here, do you think?" Cullen asked, halting the horse with a grip on the reins.

Dempsey nodded. "He created a diversion and we fell for it. Maybe he's been setting them up all along, hoping to get Axelle alone."

"But you kept getting in the way. What do you think he wants?"

Dempsey bent his lips into a smile that wanted to rip something apart. "That's what we're going to find out."

———

Axelle came awake slowly. Painfully. A sharp ache pulsed inside her head and made her wince as she tried to open her eyes. *What?* She was facedown over an animal, no saddle. The animal's spine dug into her hips and stomach.

Her hands were bound. The lack of blood flow and frigid temps meant they were like ice blocks on the ends of her arms. Dammit, what if she had frostbite and was too far gone to even know it? She wriggled her fingers, and the returning blood made her gasp. She kept moving, tried to wriggle her legs but they were also bound. The struggle shifted her center of gravity until she was in danger of toppling upside-down beneath the animal and being trampled. Hell. Who'd done this to her? What did they want?

The smell of musty fur was overpowering, making her throat heave as her stomach rebelled.

"I'm going to be sick." The contents of her stomach splashed against the gray talus that the horse was working hard to cross. Despite her situation they didn't stop moving. She spat the residue of bile out of her mouth, grateful she hadn't eaten in hours. A dull dawn seeped along the edges of the mountains. She tried to look ahead but her view was blocked by a fold of the blanket. Behind them, desolate foothills stretched in a shadowy silence as they climbed higher along a narrow mountain pass.

Had members of the Taliban captured her?

Fear made every muscle clench. There must be a misunderstanding, although exactly what kind of misunderstanding led to being hogtied over a horse didn't compute. She had to escape, had to get back to the camp and figure out why the whole goddamned world had gone mad.

The horse reached the end of the loose shale and the sound of the hooves changed as they clambered onto hard-packed dirt.

"Please, I need to stop. I need a bathroom break." Her head pounded and her vision swirled. Aftereffects of drugs, combined with dehydration and altitude.

To her surprise the caravan came to a halt. She heard the slide of cloth against leather as a heavy weight dropped to the ground. She braced herself, expecting a black-bearded Arab to approach her. Her eyes widened in recognition of the tall, ragged-looking man with white hair poking from his pakol hat and plenty of ginger among his whiskers. The man from the camera trap images. The man killing her leopards.

"You? What do you want with me?" She pushed the words through her raw throat.

He said nothing as he reached beneath the horse's belly to undo the bindings on her hands and feet. Her legs swung over her head, and she rolled forward and landed with a solid whack on her back. If he'd gone around the other side to release her she would have given him a taste of her boot. Maybe he knew that. She crawled inelegantly away from the unshod hooves. Her legs were numb and she struggled to stand.

"You need to piss?" He raised a brow, all matter-of-fact. "Piss." He pointed to the ground.

"Here?" Axelle asked incensed. "Aren't you going to turn around?"

"You have nothing that I haven't seen before—"

"You haven't freakin' seen mine!" Anger choked her. She did not want to be a hostage to anyone, and in this part of the world being taken captive was often a death sentence. Assault. Beatings. Rape. Torture. Decapitation. *Damn.* She couldn't even think about it.

With a grunt he turned his back.

Quickly, she undid her trousers and squatted because she was afraid that if she didn't she wouldn't get another chance. But her hand found a large rock, and as she pulled up her trousers one-handed, she swallowed her hesitation and smashed the rock into the back of the man's head.

He lurched forward and missed the worst of her attack.

She tried to grab the horse but the man caught the reins and held on tight even as he stumbled to his knees. She planted her boot on his ass and shoved. The horse danced out of reach, so she took off like a markhor down the loose shale, slipping and sliding, lungs sucking air so frantically she thought they might collapse. She held up her pants with one hand. There was nowhere to hide, but she didn't stop.

The mechanical slide of a rifle being loaded made her sprint even faster as dread sliced through her. He was going to kill her.

Run, run, run.

He called out, his voice echoing calmly off the bare rock. "If you don't stop, I will shoot you. First in the arm"—she automatically tucked her arm in front of her body and a shot whizzed past and blasted the ground ahead—"and next in the ankle, meaning you will never walk again." A bullet spat dirt at her feet.

"Last chance."

She slowed as she heard the awful finality in the next ratchet of the rifle. There was a vast plane of nothingness ahead, nothing but dirt and rock. She staggered to a halt, lungs pumping madly in the cold air. Turned around. "What do you want from me?" Her cry echoed off the mountains emphasizing their isolation.

"A blood debt." His eyes were dispassionate. "A debt paid. A life saved. That is all I ask."

She wanted to run. She wanted to fight. She did not want to die. She set her teeth and fastened her pants zipper. Then she walked back to her captor, head held high. "I don't owe you any debt."

He watched her silently as she marched to within a foot of his rifle. She didn't shy away from the barrel. She wasn't cowering from a spineless killer.

"Your blood owes me."

"My blood?" She frowned, suddenly unsure. "My family? I don't understand."

He spun her around and tied her hands behind her back. "You don't have to understand, you just have to endure."

She rolled her eyes. The bonds hurt but she wasn't about to let the sonofabitch know it. Her gaze swept ahead to the yak packed with goods and her heart jammed for a moment. There were furs rolled upon its back and she recognized the regal hue of a snow leopard pelt.

"Did you kill the leopards for money?" She kicked out behind her and connected with a sharp shinbone. He jerked her arms high up her back. Sweat poured down her brow as she bit back a scream of pain.

"No." He leaned close, until she could smell his sour breath and count each whisker sprouting from his leathery face. "I killed them for you."

CHAPTER
NINE

GUNFIRE. No corpse.

So far. So good.

The guys were a couple hours behind Dempsey. No worries there. He'd catch up with his target, establish an OP, settle in and wait for reinforcements.

Mist steamed from his mouth as his lungs strained for oxygen. He'd found where the abductor had tethered pack animals outside camp and marked the spot. Traveling through the night meant he'd gained some ground, but he'd seen no evidence the other man had stopped to rest so he hadn't caught them yet.

Why take Axelle hostage? Did he know she was the U.S. ambassador's daughter? Shit, Dempsey wasn't even sure it was the Russian who'd kidnapped her as opposed to some white slave-trader just passing through.

Whoever it was, they were about to get a taste of SAS justice.

Women often got caught in the crossfire. Bullets and bombs didn't differentiate between the innocent, guilty, men, women or children. Shit, that's why he was here. He'd get Axelle out of danger and hopefully sew up this mission while he was at it. Then he could go home and forget about the difficult prickly female and her fierce dedication to her cause.

And if the kidnapper wasn't his target? They would have saved a civilian who happened to be an American diplomat's daughter. Win-win.

He constantly checked the ground for sign. The way the rocks were pushed around showed definite evidence of having been trodden on recently by man or beast or both. He checked the sky. A bank of storm clouds bore down on him from the east. The scumbag up ahead would be thinking about making camp soon. Dempsey passed a patch of damp earth where an animal—or human, he realized, checking the ground for prints—had relieved themselves. He noticed the stones were disturbed for about a hundred meters in a straight line down into the valley.

He followed the tracks and saw where bullets had scored the earth—that explained the shots he'd heard a half-hour earlier. Axelle had made a break for it. He shook his head, not knowing whether to be impressed with her spirit or terrified she was going to annoy the gunman so badly he'd shoot her. Something brassy caught his eye and he jumped off the horse and pocketed a spent bullet. The trail dead-ended, suggesting she hadn't got away.

Dempsey started back up the hillside.

The tracks were fresher now, the edges of the kidnapper's boots more sharply defined, less eroded by the elements. Dempsey remounted. He daren't go faster than a walk because sound carried along these narrow canyons. He dismounted again before climbing over the ridgeline and scanned the next valley for sign of his quarry.

Cresting the ridge in the distance was a small caravan of pack animals, and Dempsey would bet his service medals that the black shape tied to that last animal was a woman with bottomless brown eyes and a stubborn jaw.

The clouds billowed like angry sails in the sky. "You can run, you nasty old bastard, but you can't hide." Not from him. Not for long.

Dmitri knocked the woman out with another dose of tranquilizer he'd stolen from a doctor's surgery in Pakistan, and hoisted her limp body across his shoulder before propping her against the wall of the cave. He left her bound. Magdalena wouldn't have approved of his rough handling of the girl, but then there were many things Magdalena wouldn't have approved of over the years.

Not that it mattered. Not anymore. Thoughts of his wife brought the usual swift pain that resonated and amplified over time. He'd told her to forget him. To move on. But he'd never looked at another woman the way he'd looked at her. Never wanted another woman in all the years since.

She'd asked him to find a way to save their grandchild. This was the only way he knew how.

Dmitri hobbled the animals inside the wide open cavern. The entrance was narrow and the cavern tapered into a maze of tunnels behind him. The roof was decorated with beautiful stalactites and mineral deposits that glittered in his torch beam.

He'd first found these caves more than thirty years ago. The fact he'd never recorded them on any official Soviet map said more about the swiftness of his fall from grace than the sloppiness of his cartography. He had no doubt who was behind the destruction of his once-exalted career in Vympel. He took a satellite phone from his pack and went to the entrance of the cave.

Dmitri had honed his grievances over the years, used them to teach others how best to fight back against the crushing might of the USSR, but he hadn't been able to control who those people targeted once the Soviets left. He'd paid a price worse than death for his petty revenge, and regret had long since morphed into bitterness.

For long years he hadn't known the real name of the Englishman. The irony of how many people had died because he hadn't put a bullet in the man before he'd opened his mouth was not lost on Dmitri. Such a small humanitarian mistake had been catastrophic.

If he could reverse time, he'd go back and kill him twice.

After several years of searching, he'd lost hope of ever seeing the man again. Then, in the late 80s, he'd been watching a news report on a bombing of the British Embassy in Rabat and he'd spotted the *mudak* being interviewed. He'd been stunned at first, and then his anger had simmered. Revenge *was*, after all, a dish best served cold.

By the time Dmitri had tracked him down and set his plans in motion, twelve more years had passed. He looked at the stubby digit on his left hand, a constant reminder of his failure. Killing the Englishman was supposed to have been his last act of violence. He was sick of death. Sick of killing. He'd sacrificed his finger as both a way of claiming the death of that bastard and of retiring.

It hadn't worked.

After 9/11, and the death of the son he'd never laid eyes on, he'd retired to a remote region of China, trying to drink himself to death.

That hadn't worked either.

He sat huddled in a blanket, looking out at the snowstorm that had snaked unexpectedly out of the Himalayas. Holing up in these caves was part of his plan, so it didn't matter—in fact, the storm would hinder any pursuit. He dialed the number and listened to the echoing ring while looking at the savage beauty of the mountains rapidly disappearing behind a veil of snow.

The connection crackled and there was a time delay.

"Yes?" The snap of impatience in the man's voice ripped the scab off Dmitri's heart and made him bleed afresh. "Who is this?"

He cleared his throat. Spoke in Russian. "I wonder if you remember me?"

"Volkov?" The voice sounded tinny, strained.

"I am flattered."

There was silence. Dmitri's heart squeezed painfully. He could never trust this man, and yet he had to ask him to save the thing he loved the most in the world. It all came down to who had the most to lose. "I found the daughter of an American diplomat in the Wakhan Valley. You need to check your email." He'd arranged for it to send automatically at a certain time from the woman's computer. He heard a strangled breath. Knew he wasn't the only one suffering now. *Good.* "I sent instructions about what you need to do. Obey them and I'll release her—alive."

"Britain does not negotiate with terrorists." The spy grasped at that futile worn-out line. Perhaps his phones were tapped? All the more reason for the spy to cooperate quickly.

"So noble to toe the British line. What a loyal subject you are. Luckily, I don't need your British connections; I need your Russian ones. Otherwise I'd have already called the Americans."

"What do you want?"

He heard the calculation in the man's voice. He glanced over to where the woman slept. He'd given her enough drugs to knock out a horse—for her own benefit.

"Follow the instructions you receive. Get my family out of Russia, get my grandson a new liver, give them new, better lives in Europe or America. I'll keep your dirty secret."

There was a long pause followed by a snort. "That's it?"

That was *everything.* "You only have forty-eight hours. If you fail in this I've arranged a dramatic...news event...that will ensure I have the world's attention when I tell my story about two *British* spies I encountered years ago in Afghanistan."

"How do I know you'll keep your word after I get your wretched family out of Russia?"

"I've kept it for this long, *mudak.* Unlike you, I am a man of honor." A rustle brought him around, his finger tightened on the trigger of his rifle. The woman was awake. She met his gaze with keen brown eyes that looked sharp enough to pick the secrets out of his soul.

He turned away. His secrets were the only thing he had left.

———

Jonathon Boyle sipped brandy in the Vauxhall Cross offices of the Chief of MI6. He tapped his fingers impatiently on the glass. Everything was falling apart. Just as he was about to pull off the biggest coup since the Cold War, this phantom rose from the grave and threatened *everything*. He needed to stall Dmitri's "event" until after he'd visited Aldermaston's top-secret division—a few days at most. Agents were scouring Russia for what remained of Volkov's offspring and they would find them. Once Volkov was dead he'd make sure every one of them followed the same path. In the meantime, he had to at least look like he was toeing the line. A lifetime of toeing the line was starting to grate on Jonathon's elderly nerves.

"You're telling me that in 1979, Dmitri Volkov shot Sebastian Allworth in cold blood while you and he were distributing anti-Soviet material in Afghanistan?" Christopher Gleeson's eyes gleamed as he fingered the typewritten pages of the old file one of his lackeys had finally unearthed in the murky depths of the building. "What were you doing while he was getting shot?"

Jonathon put down his glass and tented his hands meekly over crossed knees. "Running for dear life, old boy." He gave an exaggerated shudder. "I was lucky. I made it to the ridge and caught up with the local guides who had the horses."

"You outran a squad of Vympel soldiers?" The director's eyes narrowed a fraction.

"It *was* thirty years ago." Jonathon pointed to his thinning pate. "Don't let the gray hair and short legs fool you—show me a gun and I'd still be able to outstrip you in the hundred-yard dash."

Gleeson grunted.

"There was a rock fall. It caused enough of a distraction to let me get away." Jonathon shuddered. "Poor Sebastian wasn't so lucky."

"Our new PM thinks his father died in a plane crash over Kashmir."

Jonathon nodded and sipped his drink slowly, trying to savor the smoothness of expensive brandy, ignoring the heartburn he knew would follow. Old age wasn't for wimps. Maybe Sebastian was the lucky one.

"And now Volkov has surfaced again only weeks after David Allworth is elected Prime Minister? It does seem like an odd coincidence." Gleeson pursed his lips. "You know, of course, that there are people searching for him?"

Jonathon lifted one lazy lid. "They don't know the threat he poses to Britain's national security."

"Do you know where he is?" Gleeson watched him closely.

His nostrils flared. "If I knew where he was, I wouldn't need you," he retorted.

Gleeson laughed. "Still got connections with some of the more unseemly side of the Foreign Office?"

Jonathon's smile thinned. "Don't pretend those in SIS are all law-abiding citizens, Director." His eyes narrowed. "We're both too long in the tooth to bother with such a preposterous two-step."

Gleeson held his gaze. "Why didn't you work here rather than for the diplomatic corps?"

Jonathon swirled the golden liquid in the heavy crystal glass. "I admit I prefer life's creature comforts—plus, I had a family at the time." His brow plummeted. "The point is if the SAS do capture this Russian alive and we end up putting the bastard on trial, it puts our PM in an extremely awkward position."

"Whereas if he's dead no one can accuse the PM of acting out some personal vendetta."

"Exactly, because no one will know there's cause for a vendetta." Jonathon nodded. "As long as Allworth remains ignorant of how his father died, then he can maintain his righteous indignation because we both know…"

"Allworth can't act worth a damn." Gleeson chuckled.

"How he ever became Prime Minister I'll never know. The man is far too honest." Jonathon swilled back the rest of his liquor and stood. David Allworth was a soft-hearted idealist. Would that change if he discovered his father had been shot in the back? Always interesting to force people up against their principles.

Gleeson leaned back in his leather chair and rubbed a jaw that needed the kiss of a razor. "I'm not sure the SAS will go for an assassination assignment."

"Don't they take orders from you?"

Gleeson looked down at his desk. "I wish."

Jonathon knew the man had E Squadron to use if he wished. Plausible deniability. Black Ops. It was a question of whether he'd pit them against their own operational SAS soldiers and risk a friendly-fire incident.

Morals were a bitch.

Jonathon had dedicated his whole life to Moscow. *He* wouldn't waver just because no one else knew how to make a sacrifice. "What about those weaponized drones?"

"Even *if* we knew where he was for sure, we have more important targets to focus on." Gleeson arched a brow.

"More important than the man who killed our Prime Minister's father and taught Islamic militants the fine art of explosives?" Jonathon gave him a sardonic smile. "If you think so." He pulled on his jacket. "Anyway, I've done my duty. I'll leave the decision in your capable hands as the whole incident is still covered by the Official Secrets Act."

Gleeson inclined his head and Jonathon strode out of the building wishing, not for the first time, he'd been born less of a ruddy patriot.

The blizzard smashed him in the face like a C-130 transport. He stopped and pulled on more layers of clothes, including his white snow gear. He held tight to the horse because it was spooked now the wind had started to bay. Tracks were obscured and he knew his squad would need to find cover or hunker down.

It was so cold the air sank into his lungs and burned soft tissue. Dempsey pushed on, needing to get himself and the horse out of the elements and into some shelter before they fell off the side of a cliff. He shielded his face against the onslaught and stilled as he saw a movement off to his right. For a split second there was a mirage of the tall spare-framed man they'd been chasing for days. A sweep of horizontal flakes obscured his vision before clearing again and the figure was gone. He stared harder through the whiteout. There was a narrow fissure in the side of the mountain—a fissure where someone had stood moments before.

Holy fuck. He pulled out his GPS unit and entered the coordinates of where he stood, along with an estimate of the position of the cave, then he pulled the horse onward, grateful for the gelding's smoky coloring that faded into the blizzard, and the howling gale that blew their trail into oblivion. He rounded a craggy boulder, his boots slipping over the slick surface, and spotted another opening in the side of the mountain big enough for himself and the horse to squeeze into. His boot crunched and he looked down to see pale bone shards scattered about the floor. The horse's nostrils flared.

"Easy, buddy, relax." Dempsey rubbed his hand over the animal's soft nose until he settled. In the dimness he saw more bones and scraps of fur. The irony of ending up in the lair of a snow leopard wasn't lost on him.

He kicked the bones out of the way and walked a little further into the cave, letting his eyes adjust to the murk. There was an empty, unused feel to the den. Maybe it belonged to one of the poor bastards the Russian had shot.

He undid the horse's girth, sliding the saddle free from the animal's back and taking it to the opening of the cave where the blizzard battered his face and made his ears hurt. He dumped the saddle and his bergen on the floor and pulled out the satellite phone. He tried the PRR first but got nothing but static. The rest of the team was miles behind, possibly days away in these conditions. He was on his own.

His thoughts turned to Axelle. Was she hurt? Of course she was hurt. Shit, she was in a cave, which was her worst nightmare —not to mention having been kidnapped. Anger squeezed him inside and he forced himself not to think about her. He'd get her out of there. He'd save her and catch the old bastard who'd been running them in circles for days.

He dialed HQ in London and was surprised to be patched straight through to the CO of the Regiment.

"You've got a definite sighting on your target, Alpha Alpha One Nine?"

"Yes, sir, holed up in a cave a few hundred feet from this position. We've been hit by a massive snowstorm." He relayed the coordinates of the cave and his present position.

"He's likely to stay put for a couple of hours?"

"With a female hostage, sir." The freezing air that whipped into the cavern didn't cool his anger. "He'll be stuck here as long as the blizzard continues and maybe some time after that, depending on how much snow gets dumped."

"Good job, Alpha Alpha One Nine. Stand by for orders. Out."

Shit.

Dempsey stared at the phone. He was stuck in a cave mere meters from his target and had no idea whether Axelle was being raped and tortured or even if she was still alive. He didn't like those images in his brain.

But he had no clue how many people were involved or how big the cave system was. If he acted alone he might get them both killed faster. What if Volkov got away from him again?

It could take weeks if not months to find one man in this staggeringly difficult terrain. Time Dempsey didn't want to spend away from the men in his troop. Time terrorists could use to blow up marketplaces and schools. The image of his sister, her hand tightly clasped in his, flashed through his mind. Siobhan Dempsey would have been a beautiful woman if she'd lived. She'd have championed the peace process, maybe even persuaded his family to abandon their deeply rooted hatred.

Dempsey pushed the images out of his head. Memories of his sister always stirred when he was in the mountains. Maybe he was closer to her God up here. Or maybe the lack of oxygen affected his brain.

He was done with the God and religion that had torn apart generations of people. He was done with family who murdered and blamed the authorities for bloodshed and violence. He was done with everything except trying to prevent the same thing happening to someone else's sister or daughter—people like Axelle who tried to help snow leopards.

He put the phone away and explored the back of this cave but found a dead end. His fingers were too cold to grip his rifle so he blew on them. He braced his carbine against the wall and started a series of jumping-jacks and running in place, getting the blood flowing as he planned his next move. He gave the horse a drink and fed him a bit of flat bread he had in his pack. Next he pulled out some rations and took a swig of water before he started stuffing flash-bangs and spare ammo into his webbing.

Presumably the Russian wanted Axelle for a reason and would keep her alive until he'd attained that objective. It didn't mean she wouldn't be hurt. *Shit*. Dempsey swallowed and eyed the entrance. The Provos always claimed they wanted to end British rule and occupation, but his father had been driven by hatred, pure and simple. Dempsey didn't know what had motivated an elite Russian soldier to defect and join the jihadists. Money? Revenge? Social conscience? Some said he'd betrayed his homeland and his family... The parallel with Dempsey's own life gave him a jolt, but there the similarities ended. Dempsey wasn't a soulless destroyer. Sure, he shot bad guys. You pick up a gun, you become fair game. But civilians? Children? Young women in the first flush of love? No way. No fucking way.

But things were never black and white, and no one knew that better than him.

His father had lost three fingers and killed more than two hundred people with his so-called skills. Yet Dempsey remembered some of the best moments of his life making sandcastles with that same man on the beaches near Wicklow. He'd grown up with Semtex and ArmaLite rifles in the pantry, and as a little kid had been thrilled with the idea of fighting the British. As he'd grown older he'd seen his father's hatred twist the lives of his older brothers.

After his sister's death he'd turned his back on his family and taken revenge by joining the most despised group of soldiers in the Province. He'd never gone home again. Never spoken to his relatives. He'd seen his brother Declan once while on patrol in Crossmaglen. The hatred blazing from his brother's eyes had told him there'd be no forgiveness. Decimate shoppers on a busy market day—fine. Join the enemy? You were better off dead.

Dempsey was fine with that. Absolutely fucking fine. He'd do whatever it took to stop the violence using as much force as necessary on whoever got in his way.

He stopped exercising as heat started to bloom and he braced his hand against the wall. Bottom line—it was the least he could do to even the score for his shitty relatives.

He shook himself out of the past. Thinking about it didn't get the job done. He was here for Dmitri Volkov who had taken a woman Dempsey could care about, from right under his nose.

The Russian had fallen off the terrorist map after 9/11 but that didn't mean he didn't have friends in low places. The next cave over could be milling with Al Qaeda and Taliban fighters. Dempsey checked the chamber of his carbine. Decided it was time for a little reconnaissance work.

She opened her eyes slowly, her lids crusted and sore. Her tongue swept the inside of her mouth, searching for moisture, instead finding fur. She made out the cavernous roof above her head and the huge dome of rock, and her bones shook and sweat drenched every inch of her skin. Memories filtered back. The roar of the explosion, the massive force of the blast, shaking walls as the building started to collapse. There'd been no chance of escape.

She squeezed her eyes closed and wished she'd never woken. Except then she'd be dead and the evil old man would have won. She forced her eyes open again and searched for him. There—a shadow in the corner, hunched over a small fire.

A sharp ache scored a line between her shoulders, and a shallow pounding settled deep inside her skull. She swallowed her fear. She wasn't going to lose it in front of this mean sono-fabitch. She shoved the terror and immobilizing panic to a small corner of her brain and concentrated on how the hell to get out of there. Her wrists and ankles were bound. Her fingers burned with cold, and she kept the blood flowing by flexing her fingers and toes every few seconds.

He glanced over, then stood.

A fierce gust of wind blew a swathe of snow inside the cave and she realized they'd been hit by a blizzard. They might be stuck here for days. The thought grew talons which latched onto her insides like retractable claws.

From what she'd overheard when she'd woken briefly from her drugged stupor, the man was trying to blackmail someone, presumably her father. But the chance of her being released before she was abused and her body dumped was as remote as this wilderness. She couldn't hope for rescue from Dempsey's soldiers because who knew when they'd returned to camp—and in this blizzard, they wouldn't find any trace of where she'd been taken.

She was on her own.

The ache of despair solidified into determination. She tensed as he came toward her carrying a tin mug and a handful of jerky, which he tossed on the ground beside her.

"I can't eat unless you untie me." She hid the anger by keeping her eyes downcast.

He laughed. "You don't *have* to eat." He held the mug to her lips and forced her to take a swallow of salted green tea. Then, with his dirty fingers, he held a piece of jerky to her lips.

His eyes met hers in challenge and his brows lifted. Did she want to live? What would she do to survive? The thump of her heart sounded overloud in her ears. This sonofabitch had killed her leopards and kidnapped her.

Hatred stirred as she held his gaze. His eyes were bleak. Not just cold—empty. She opened her mouth and he fed her, slowly, patiently. Like she was livestock.

She chewed and swallowed and inside she smiled. This wasn't his victory, it was hers. She needed sustenance to escape. Giving up wasn't an option. *Don't think about the thousands of tons of rock suspended over her head or the disgusting, despicable old man. Think about getting away.*

After he fed her two pieces of dried meat, he gave a satisfied nod and walked away.

She glanced around, still mechanically chewing the tough jerky. The cave entrance cut through the mountain as if it had been slashed by a knife. At least there was light. She didn't think she could sit here without screaming if there hadn't been some light.

The man started feeding the pack animals. Steam came off their backs, which helped warm the dank cave. Her body was conflicted by panic on the inside and frigid temperatures on the outside. Fear opened her pores and sweat heated her back, but still she shivered from the icy blast of the blizzard. She was being torn apart. She watched the man from beneath her lids, flexing her hands to try to keep the blood circulating. The sat phone was near the entrance. How could she get it? He caught the direction of her gaze and strode across the cavern and grabbed it and plunked it down beside the yak. Hostility bled into her gaze.

The man stretched to his full height and smiled. "Now you begin to understand."

Bitterness wrapped itself around her bones. She understood all right.

"Who are you?" she rasped.

He chewed his meat and spat gristle on the floor. "My name is Dmitri Volkov."

"You're Russian?"

He nodded.

"Why did you shoot the snow leopards?" Her grief over the leopards had gained another dimension. They'd died because of her.

"I already tell you."

"Tell me again," she yelled. "Because I'd have been back in the summer anyway. You didn't have to kill them."

"I couldn't wait that long."

"Why not—"

"Quiet."

She'd never been a big fan of being told what to do and figured she was dead anyway. "Fuck you." The incentive to cooperate evaporated. She pushed back against the wall and climbed unsteadily to her feet. Pins and needles attacked her and she ignored the pain.

The Russian glared at her. "Sit down."

"Why? Are you afraid I'm going to run off into the storm?" she said in disgust. "I'm not an idiot."

"All Americans are crazy."

"And you're not?"

He grunted and turned his back on her, fiddling with the packs.

"You're going to sell the pelts, aren't you?" This wasn't just about her. It was about money and this man's greed. The realization lessened some of the guilt. But the cats were still dead.

She picked at her bonds, loosening the knots as she strove for warmth and constant motion. She lost her balance and landed on her chin. The Russian smirked.

Bastard. She curled onto her side, started rubbing her arms up and down her legs, surreptitiously working on the rope that tied her ankles, loosening the knot with each small movement.

"Are you going to tell me what you're after?" she asked.

His eyes flashed from benign to remorseless. Then the light died. He sagged. "I am trying to get my grandson out of Russia because he is seriously ill."

Yeah, right. "Most people try charity before they resort to kidnapping."

"Not the people I know." His laugh was like a cold lash of air. His gaze like an icicle through her heart. She didn't think she'd ever defrost.

"What's wrong with him?" It was important to form a relationship with your captors. She'd learned that in Lessons for Children-of-Diplomats 101.

"His liver doesn't work." His fingers stopped their work. "No one would help my kin, not after what I've done." He sounded disgusted with himself. "My family is innocent but I am not."

"Didn't you think of them when you started all this?" She didn't even know what his crimes were. She'd assumed he was a terrorist because the soldiers were after him, but he could be a serial killer for all she knew. That thought brought fresh chills crawling over her skin.

"You are too young to know how one simple decision can shape your life."

"You mistake age for experience." She tilted her chin and forced back the tears that suddenly threatened. She knew exactly how small decisions could change your life. Her husband was dead. Her mother was dead. Her father estranged. Her life's work rolled up on the back of his fucking yak. She knew exactly how one decision could impact every aspect of your life.

He studied her expression. "Perhaps you do know." He turned

away, fiddling with something on the floor. "I was naive enough to think I was helping people liberate themselves from their oppressors. It turns out I was only teaching people better ways to kill."

"Why did you do it?" She craned her neck to see what he was doing.

His eyes crinkled in a cross between pain and amusement. "You wouldn't understand."

"Try me."

"I was angry. Angry men make mistakes."

"I think you've made another one by kidnapping me."

"Some things cannot be changed, others…" He shrugged. With the movement of his shoulder she finally got a look at what he was doing and terror raced up her body and grabbed her by the esophagus. Packs of plastic explosives were laid out neatly and he was carefully sliding them into the pockets of some sort of vest. She started to shake so hard her teeth clacked. *No.*

Her knees grazed the dirt as she crawled. Rock took skin from flesh but she didn't stop wriggling across the barren cavern floor.

He put the barrel of her own Glock next to her forehead.

"Believe it or not, I do not want to kill you." His breath moved her hair. "But if anyone is going to die, it is only fitting that it is you."

Why? Axelle wanted to slap the gun away. But she knew he would kill her. One more evil act wouldn't burden his conscience too greatly.

Primal fear washed down her back and she fought hard to keep the tears at bay. "You're a monster."

The light in his eyes was flat as a sheet of ice, his regret as ancient as a glacier. "Yes. Yes, I am."

———

Soviet Union, September 1979

Dmitri rolled over and stared at the ceiling of their farmhouse bedroom. His wife ran her hand up the warm muscles of his stomach, over the smooth planes of his chest.

"Don't go back, Dmitri."

He laughed and kissed the back of her hand. "And be shot for deserting? You wouldn't want that, would you, *moya golubushka*?" His eyes danced as she lifted her head from the bedcovers.

"I would if it meant you staying here, with me," she mumbled. She burrowed closer, pressed her cheek to his heart, her long legs twining with his in silent plea. "We might have made another baby." She nipped his earlobe and he felt himself wanting her again. Needing her again.

He tipped her onto her back and entered her in one smooth thrust. He rested on his elbows as he swept the hair back from her face. Saw burning passion edged with worry in the depths of her eyes. He thrust deeper and watched her eyes change. He didn't want her to worry. He wanted her to feel cherished and safe. He rolled them so she was on top, her dark hair falling like strands of silk across her shoulders, curling over the pink tips of her breasts.

"You are so beautiful," he whispered, cupping her cheek in his calloused palm.

"Stay with me," she pleaded.

Tears blurred his vision. His voice trembled. "I can't." He splayed his hands across her tummy. "I pray you are pregnant and that this time—"

"Shush." She pressed her finger to his lips. "This time it will be okay. This time we will have a fine son to raise, who will be handsome and brave like his papa." She slipped her finger between his teeth and rubbed it over his tongue. He groaned.

Fire and passion burned through his veins. Dark eyes, almost black, held his as she took him up and over the edge. His wife. His lover. His heart. Still he waited for her to cry out before he let himself join her. Magdalena. His personal star. His reason for breathing.

How had he ever got to be so lucky?

"You are my heart, my blood, the reason I breathe."

"Don't forget to come home to me." Her eyes grew sad again.

"I'm always with you, Magdalena." He pressed his hand to the beat of her heart. "Always."

CHAPTER
TEN

THE SATELLITE PHONE CRACKLED.

"Alpha Alpha One Nine, come in."

He snatched up the handset "Alpha Alpha One Nine, over."

"You need to make your way to a safe zone, over."

Dempsey frowned. "There is a civilian hostage in the area—"

"Your orders are for immediate evac of the area, Alpha Alpha One Nine. Over."

He grabbed his pack, saddled the horse and led the animal to the entrance of the cave. The snow was lighter but still coming down in a hoary veil. He had to get the hell out because those orders meant certain death was winging its way north. He looked in the direction of the cave.

Axelle was going to die.

She might already be dead.

He swallowed the image. *Get on the horse and ride away.* He wasn't paid to make the big decisions. Men with his genetic heritage couldn't afford to disobey orders without the risk of serious consequences. Men like him did as they were told or they got RTU'd. He put his foot in the stirrup. Looked into the gray overcast sky as the first hint of an engine throbbed in the distance.

Fuck that.

Letting the horse go, he jogged through the waist-high drifts. Heat surged through his muscles as he struggled through the incapacitating powder. He scrambled and slid over the uneven surfaces, throwing himself over boulders and praying he didn't set off an avalanche in his rush. No time to check snow conditions, the drone of the engines had grown louder.

He turned the corner and saw the narrow slit of the cave entrance. So much for stealth and guile. He approached from the side but had to slog through the snow with the subtlety of a four-year-old discovering snow angels. His breath puffed out in white clouds and his lungs hurt. He pulled out two flash-bangs, pulled the lever and tossed them in. He gripped his Diemaco and went through the entrance of the cave in a low crouch, eyes watering from the acrid smoke. Horses danced around the cave and one bolted, almost flattening him. The yak circled in confusion. There was no crowd of militant fighters. Just one lone enemy fighter. The Russian brought his rifle around but Dempsey shot his hand and put two more into the man's torso.

One of the world's most wanted terrorists fell unmoving to the floor.

No time to check if he was dead but he grabbed the Russian's rifle as he ran over to where Axelle was propped against the cave wall, gagged, and covered in a blanket. Her eyes were so wide with fear he could see white all around her irises. Her usually pretty hair was slick with sweat. He pulled away the blanket.

His jaw dropped.

This he didn't need.

He undid her wrist and ankle bindings as he visually checked the explosive vest. Normally he'd call in the bomb squad to deal with this shit but this wasn't normal. He dragged her to her feet where she wobbled unsteadily. He checked the duct tape on her lips for booby-trap wires before ripping it away.

"You okay?" Stupid question but she nodded anyway. He turned her around to check out the vest.

She trembled like an earthquake beneath his fingers.

"Did he booby-trap this?" Dempsey asked.

"He told me it would explode if I tried to take it off."

That was what he'd have told her to control her without having to watch her every single instant. There was no way of knowing if it was true without examining the wiring in detail and he did not have fecking time.

"We've got to go." He grabbed her arm to pull her with him but she dug in her heels.

"Get this thing *off* me!"

"There's no time."

But she wouldn't budge even though she hated caves. Dempsey ran his eyes quickly around the simple setup. Okay. He took a settling breath. Shit, he'd grown up knowing this stuff—it wasn't that complicated. Were there anti-tampering measures? He didn't see any and it didn't make sense for the old guy to bother when he, presumably, still had to move her through the mountains to whatever destination he'd planned out.

Dempsey pulled his multi-tool and was about to snip the wire when she grabbed his hand with shaking fingers.

"Do you know what you're doing?"

She still thought he was an idiot. Now would be a fantastic time to prove her wrong.

"I guess we're about to find out." He leaned forward, watched her eyes flash with something other than terror as he kissed her on the lips—just in case this was his last moment on earth. Her lips were rough and dry from cold, and oh so sweet. After a moment of surprise they softened under his. He held her gaze and a connection passed between them that had nothing to do with the situation they faced. It was a connection filled with possibility and wonder and the blinding knowledge that if they were about to die—it wouldn't be such a bad way to go.

He snipped the wire. Nothing happened and they both blew out a sigh of relief as he quickly helped her out of the vest. Then the ground shook and rest of the animals bolted out the front of the entrance.

Axelle shrieked as the first bomb missed the target but brought down a rain of stone on their heads. Her fingers grabbed a handful of his shirt. "What the hell is that?"

"My guess is a Spectre gunship."

"Oh, my God." Her skin bleached chalk-white as more bombs started to strike closer. There was no way they were getting out the front of this cave. It had never really been an option.

"Come on." He dragged her toward the back of the cave and they started running through the dust-choked air. The Russian was gone, along with his pack.

Not as dead as he'd hoped then. Old bastard must be wearing a bulletproof vest.

"No, no, no!" She pulled against his grip every step of the way, but he didn't let go. This was her greatest fear—being buried alive —and it was about to come true. And he was propelling her toward her destiny as fast as he could whether she liked it or not.

They had one chance and a slim one at that. As he ran, he pulled a flashlight from one of his many pockets and made out two passages ahead. He shone his beam across the floor; a blood trail led one way. He followed it—because the Russian was still his mission and he hadn't failed a mission yet. This crafty old bastard wasn't about to outfox him.

He forced Axelle to move, knowing the chance of them making it out of this hellhole alive was about as likely as Al Qaeda becoming pacifists. The roof above them groaned. Stones shifted and showered down in a rush. Giant slabs of rock torqued and heaved as the mountain buckled under the bombs.

This wasn't how he'd expected to die. His fingers tightened over Axelle's slim hand, half apology, half encouragement, all desperation. A God almighty explosion brought the roof of the cavern down behind them, and they were thrown forward by the percussion. His head hit a rock and blackness washed over him.

Axelle opened her eyes but she was blind. *Omigod. Omigod.* Her chest heaved like broken bellows. Dust filled the air and she couldn't breathe. Blood pounded her ears, the pressure so intense it rammed her brain and made every nerve in her body fry as she lay there in the darkness with only the sound of her own mortality for company. Thousands of tons of rock blocked the cave entrance, and they would never get out. The bombs had stopped, but the absolute silence was solid and terrifying. They were buried. In a crypt. In a tomb.

Rock was like a malevolent living creature, squeezing her airway, licking her skin. Sweat ran freely down her brow and beneath her armpits and heat radiated from her body even though the air was frigid. She wasn't hurt beyond the bruises and scratches she'd been carrying for days and yet she lay on the ground, paralyzed by sheer terror and piteous weakness, unable to move. She wished she was dead.

She drew in ever shallower gulps of air, the rational part of her brain understanding she was hyperventilating and would pass out if she couldn't control the panic.

Unconscious sounded pretty damned tempting right about now.

Roll over and die while you're at it.

Her fingers groped around her and she touched something soft and warm—a sleeve, a hand.

Dempsey?

God, please don't be dead.

She cupped her hands over her mouth and nose, and willed herself to take slower, deeper breaths. He'd risked his life to save her. She had to help him or he might die. *Assuming he's not already dead.*

She reached out again and found his wrist. His skin was warm and there was a faint but crucial flutter beneath her fingers. She rolled onto her knees, moving slowly and using her hands to check for jagged rock overhead. Her stomach roiled. Fear threatened. But none of that would save her from this nightmare. Nor would tears. Nor would screaming for her mommy for thirty hours straight. She snapped out of the memory. She was here with Dempsey, whether she liked it or not, and she had to deal. She pushed the fear into some other part of her brain and refused to think about it.

Through touch, she worked her way up Dempsey's body until she found his face. She placed her palm near his lips and felt a puff of air against her skin. He was still breathing. She closed her eyes and let out a breath. She shook him gently but he didn't stir.

What if he was seriously injured? How could she help him? "Dempsey?" Her words echoed in the thick darkness and she almost lost it. The idea of being alone down here was enough to drive her insane if she let herself think about it.

Don't think about it.

She ran shaky hands over him, searching for sticky blood, bending each limb, looking for obvious sign of injury. She was sweeping her hands up his torso again when he grabbed her wrists. She lost her balance and fell against him and he huffed out a groan.

"I'd let you keep doing that but this is too dark to be heaven." His voice was hoarse. Such a bolt of relief shot through her system she couldn't speak.

"I take it we're still alive and kicking?" he said.

She gripped his shirt with both hands, forced emotion into bite-sized chunks that she could talk around. "Not sure we're at the kicking stage yet, but we're alive—thanks to you." This man, this soldier, had run into a cave that he'd known was about to be bombed, to save her. How did you thank someone for doing that? What could you say to a man like that?

He eased out a breath and tried to sit up.

"Are you hurt?" She went to grab his arm to help but connected with a body part a damn sight more personal.

"Jesus," he hissed and groaned. "Woman, I'm in no condition for that kind of thing."

She heard laughter in his voice. *Laughter*?

They were buried inside a mountain with no way of knowing if they'd ever get out, and he was amused? Was he crazy? She felt herself retreating, the walls closing in on her again, the reality of their predicament drilling holes through her reason.

He swore in obvious pain and reached out a hand that brushed her thigh before finding her fingers curled into tense knots against her body. "Are *you* okay? Did that old fecker hurt you?"

Shaking her head, she raised blind eyes to the ceiling. "He didn't rape me, if that's what you're asking. Didn't beat me either." Her throat felt raw with the effort to talk when she was enveloped in terror. "Physically, I'm fine"—her voice cracked—"but I'm so scared I can barely breathe..." She swallowed repeatedly, feeling her throat shrink with every inhalation. Admitting weakness went against everything in her nature, but she owed this man complete honesty. "If you weren't here with me, my heart would already have exploded."

They knelt together in the void. "No one in their right mind would be happy about this situation. The important thing is"—he ran his hands down her arms—"that we work together. We don't panic because panic is what gets you killed."

Tears burned but she refused to let them fall. She would cry when they got out of this hellhole. She would bawl her eyes out and sob like a baby for twenty-four hours straight, but not until then. She hadn't reached breaking point yet, because this man was at her side and she trusted him. She wouldn't let him down.

"I'm going to need your help." She couldn't do this alone.

"That's what I'm here for."

A sudden rush of alarm swamped all the calm that had started to settle her blood. "We're going to die, aren't we?" She gripped his arms and shook him.

"Christ. It's a good job I don't have a big ego, lady, because you crushed it the first day we met and have been stomping on it ever since." Laughter swam around her even as strong hands squeezed her shoulders.

God, she was such a witch. "I'm sorry."

"Pardon?" She felt his breath on her face as he leaned closer. "I didn't quite catch that?"

She gritted her teeth because he was teasing her and she wasn't comfortable being teased. "You heard."

He snorted and her temper spiked and she tried to pull away. She hated everything about this situation. Hated being helpless. Dependent. So damn scared she couldn't think.

"Relax." He smoothed a warm hand down her back and, despite everything, it felt good. "You're funny." Her anger dissolved when he kissed her knuckles. "Now help me stand and we'll figure a way out of this fucking shithole."

She eased him upright and put her shoulder under his arm, trying to avoid being poked and prodded by various pieces of his equipment. "You swear like a trooper, you know that?"

"Here I've been trying to watch my language around the ladies." There was more amusement in his voice. He was working at keeping her mind off their situation and her incapacitating fear.

She forced herself to make the effort, to push past the horror. "How's that working out for you?"

"Like a total pile of wank." There was a click of a flashlight and suddenly she could see his face, the crinkles around the blue eyes, the slight twist of his full lower lip, blood trickling from a gash on his forehead.

"You're hurt." She raised her fingers to the swelling but he captured her hands.

"It's nothing." His voice grew serious. They stared at one another in the beam of the flashlight as if they'd never seen one another before. His deep piercing eyes didn't judge her fear or insecurity. Instead they promised her hope. When had she ever been that generous of spirit?

She constantly pushed people away because being alone was

easier than dealing with heartbreak. But to survive this, to not lose her mind, she needed Dempsey.

"We'll find a way out of here, don't worry."

To her horror, hot tears flooded her eyes and a sob filled the air. Dempsey pulled her to him and pressed her face against his chest.

"We'll get out of this mess and you can plead my case at my court-martial." He rubbed his chin in her hair and she gripped him as if she was hanging over a precipice.

"What do you mean, court-martial?" She hiccupped.

He drew away. "Let's start moving before this rock decides to shift—"

"Don't scare me any more than I am already and don't try to distract me." She took his chin in her hand and made him look at her even though his expression went carefully blank. "What court-martial? How did you find me?"

"I tracked you from camp."

Her eyes lit up. Did that mean the other soldiers knew they were here?

He shook his head, reading her mind. "I left before the others. They were at least an hour behind when the storm struck. Josef was with them." His lips tightened. "If I'd played by the rules and stayed with the others, *this* would never have happened."

"No," she said softly, "I'd still be sitting in a cave wearing a vest packed with explosives, and the chances of you ever finding me would be zero." Dust shimmered in the air between them. Dust and something else. Something sweeter. "They'd court-martial you for leaving your men behind?"

He grimaced and her thumb brushed his lips. His eyes flared with heat that found an echo inside her. She pulled away. Now wasn't the time for anything except survival.

He released her to check his gear. "A couple of hours ago I caught a glimpse of the Russian in the entrance of this cave. I found another cave around the corner and called in the position to HQ. Next thing I know I'm ordered to get the hell out of the area because they were going to bomb the bastard to smithereens."

"But…" *What about me?* The mute question must have shown in her eyes. He lifted a hand and stroked it across her cheek in a move that sent a ripple of sensation clear down to her toes. She didn't back away. If she could find any courage at all, it would be in facing up to her attraction to this man.

"They knew he had a hostage but they didn't know your name or your fancy relations." His voice was gentle. "It wasn't personal. They've been after this guy for decades because he's been teaching bomb-making to the masses. No way they'd risk him escaping during a hostage rescue mission."

And once again her death would have been deemed acceptable collateral damage. That was when she figured out exactly why he'd get court-martialed. "You came for me anyway."

"It's my job." But he was lying. He took a step back, obviously uncomfortable talking about what he'd done. His job was to follow orders, *not* to save her.

"Come on." He hoisted his pack more securely. "I might have shot the old bugger—he must be wearing Kevlar under his shirt— but the old wolf is still a threat."

He held out his hand. She could almost stand straight, but he had to bend his head to avoid the top of the tunnel. She squeezed his fingers in simple thanks, was grateful to be squeezed back by such a capable human being.

She was capable—but not under these circumstances. She could barely walk and talk, let alone make a constructive plan to escape this nightmare.

Their footsteps competed with the occasional drip of water from the rock above their heads. The air smelled dank and stale and there was something surreal about following this man into the unknown—into her darkest fear. The walls sparkled in the faint beam of light and were generally worn smooth.

"Who made these tunnels?" she asked.

"They could be natural." Dempsey kicked some of the loose

debris out of his way. "But they were probably expanded by humans at some point." He turned to her, impossibly handsome as a smile cut deeply into one cheek. "Could have been Marco Polo for all we know."

They carried on through passages that seemed to lead deep into the mountain like some dark maw. Part of her wanted to panic, to curl into a pathetic ball and stay there forever. But Dempsey held onto her, and she would not fall apart in his presence. No matter how much she wanted to.

They trudged onward. She followed him closely, using his broad back as her lifeline at the same time refusing to think about the situation they were in. They came across a rope ladder that someone had cut down, proving humans had used these caves at some point in history. It didn't take Dempsey long to scale the rock face and rig a rope for her to climb. He moved quietly but fast, stopped regularly, listening to something she couldn't distinguish over the treble of her heart.

Everything hurt—her muscles ached, her head throbbed and she was tired and thirsty. Having this soldier here inspired her to keep on moving. She didn't whine that they were going to die because it wouldn't help. She didn't want to be the damsel in distress, even though that was exactly what she had been when he'd found her wearing that explosive vest. She couldn't begin to describe that sensation. Being scared on such a primitive, cellular level.

Dempsey had saved her life even though he'd been ordered not to.

Yesterday, he'd told her he tried to save innocent lives. She might not have truly believed him, but she'd never doubt him again. He was a hero. A goddamned hero.

What about her meager existence? Even though she'd worked her ass off, she wouldn't leave much of a legacy. It turned her stomach to think she might become more famous for getting animals killed than for rescuing them.

Her stomach growled and without a word he handed her

some dried rations which actually tasted pretty yummy. They didn't stop to eat. Just kept walking through the maze of tunnels.

"Did you ever see *Lord of the Rings*?" she whispered at last, trying not to think about the implacable rock balanced above their heads and the absolutely no chance of rescue should it collapse.

"About a million times," he whispered back. "Are you keeping an eye out for trolls?"

"And the Balrog." She stepped in a blood drop that had smeared across the stone and shuddered. The Russian was still alive. "You think he knows a way out?"

"I'm betting on it." Dempsey nodded. "I only hope he doesn't bleed to death before he gets there."

She was quiet again, concentrating on placing her feet without tripping. Her breath was hoarse and she was starting to shiver despite the physical exertion. She stumbled for the third time and Dempsey turned. His eyes narrowed with concern. He glanced at his watch.

"Let's take a break and get a few hours sleep." There was a relatively flat area tucked between two rocky outcrops.

"I'm sorry. I can't keep up."

"Two apologies in one day? This must be one for the record books."

The gentle teasing in his voice made her let go of her natural tension. He was trying to keep the mood upbeat and she appreciated the effort in this nightmarish situation. "Am I that bad?"

He considered his answer as he slipped out of his pack and started unpacking some supplies. "You're driven. Stubborn."

She nodded. "That I can admit to." She held up her palm when he opened his mouth to add more. "Please. I promise to be a better person if we get out of here."

"*When*," he corrected. "Not *if*."

She braced herself against a boulder as she started to sway. "I don't know what's wrong with me." She bowed her head and tried to blink away her exhaustion. "Maybe I'm not stubborn enough."

"Yeah, you're a real lightweight." He took a step toward her and she registered how attractive he was. She hadn't thought so when she'd first met him. He'd scared her to death because she'd thought he was killing her leopards. All the while it had been her fault. "In case you've forgotten, you've had barely any sleep for days."

She opened her mouth to argue that he'd been awake too.

"You've been mauled by a leopard, kidnapped, hauled for miles on the back of a horse, bombed and trapped underground."

"You haven't had it any easier."

"It's what I train for every day." He rested his hands on her shoulders, the pressure reassuring. "It's why they pay me the big bucks."

She rolled her eyes. Money had nothing to do with why he did what he did. He passed her the canteen and didn't have to tell her to ration water. It was all they had. She caught the drip on her chin and sucked it off her finger, memories from her time as a child fresh in her mind.

"At least your leopards are safe," he said.

A pain shot through her chest. "If it wasn't for me they wouldn't have been in danger in the first place. Volkov killed them to lure me here."

He pressed his lips together. "What did he want? Did he say?"

She shook her head. "He called and threatened someone about me—I'm assuming it was my father but I don't know for sure. He drugged me. I think he said something about wanting his family out of Russia?" If he'd called her father, why had the military bombed the place? Her father was a top US official with a lot of political clout. He wouldn't have stood by while his countrymen murdered his daughter. They hadn't been real close recently but she didn't think he hated her that much.

A chasm cracked open in her chest. She hadn't even spoken to him in months. He'd disapproved of her career choice and she'd disapproved of his new wife. It seemed childish now. She loved him. She should have told him she loved him. They both knew life could be cut short in an instant.

Dempsey spread a sleeping bag out on the uneven ground. "If you want to stay warm you're going to have to cuddle up next to me." He held up his flashlight. "I need to turn this off to conserve battery life."

She wasn't adverse to sharing body heat or stealing some comfort, but she didn't want to think about the dark. She lay beside him, the floor uneven and hard. He spread a silver emergency blanket over them both. She shifted uncomfortably, grateful when he passed a T-shirt to use as a pillow.

He spooned himself around her and she sank back into a cocoon of heat. His holding her didn't seem awkward. After years of sleeping alone, she thought it would take time to adjust, but being next to him felt natural. They fit. Her body relaxed. After everything they'd been through she trusted him. And she didn't trust easy. He hooked his arm around her waist and held her tight.

"Get some sleep." His breath ruffled her hair.

Fatigue was already dragging her lids down, but she was relieved to be holding onto something strong and vital when the light went off.

CHAPTER
ELEVEN

DEMPSEY WOKE SURROUNDED by the scent of warm female. It was pitch-black but his other senses were making up for loss of vision and his imagination supplied the rest. His nose was in Axelle's hair, and every inch of the front of his body was plastered to the back of hers. He realized his fingers were curled under her arm and clamped possessively over her breast. Her nipple pebbled against his palm—from cold, not desire, though his body couldn't tell the difference.

He tried to ignore his dick's pathetically predictable reaction to waking up holding a beautiful woman and think about the next course of action instead.

Follow the blood trail, checking for booby traps along the way. He shifted his knee, accidentally nudging her thigh forward and bringing his erection into direct contact with her arse—her very fine arse. He *had* seen her naked, and every glorious detail tortured him now.

Most people—let alone someone who'd suffered what she'd been through—would have freaked out by now. The number of ways they could die was staggering. He'd taken on that risk when he'd signed up for active duty. She hadn't.

He made himself shuffle back, creating a space between them.

She wasn't his lover. She depended on him and that wasn't a position he intended to exploit, no matter how his body was crying out for some basic human contact. Very basic. Lots of contact.

She'd been through hell.

She was exhausted, tired and scared.

Who knew how long they were going to be trapped together. This cave network might not go anywhere except down. The bombing raid could have blasted shut every exit, and if it hadn't, the Russian could still do the job for them. He needed to catch up with the old bastard but couldn't risk losing Axelle in the warren of tunnels.

He listened to her deep even breathing while he lay there stubbornly aroused, his skin prickling with hyperawareness and desire. He tried to distract himself with things that weren't making sense. Like *if* her father had been contacted, why would the Brits—assuming it was the Brits—order the bombing of the cave when he was in position to at least chance a rescue? Why waste an opportunity to catch this old fecker and extract as much intel from him as possible?

Why try to blitz the old goat into oblivion?

Axelle edged toward him in sleep and now he was trapped against the wall and couldn't move away without waking her. He lay there gritting his teeth as she wriggled against him. A long strand of hair tickled his nose and he smoothed it gently away. She stirred.

He heard the panic enter her breathing and she whipped toward him in the dark.

"Shush," he whispered. "Everything's okay. Go back to sleep."

"Dempsey?" She gave an audible swallow of relief, but she was still shaking with fear.

"I think you can call me, Ty, now you've slept with me twice."

Her fingers sank into his shirt, searching for some sort of anchor in the dense sea of blackness. "Funny."

"Thank you. How're you feeling?"

"I haven't bathed in days and I'm in danger of throwing up

every time I remember where I am." She laughed nervously. The silence grew and he felt her staring at him. "Every time I think about where we are—"

"So don't think about it." He smoothed hair off her brow.

She captured his fingers. "Then distract me." That gave his small brain a jolt. "Tell me something about yourself that isn't name, rank and number. Tell me why you joined the army."

Lingering thoughts of sex and arousal evaporated.

Normally, he'd have lied. But he could feel her nervous breath against his neck, knew her panic was right on the periphery. And, for once, he didn't want to lie. It was a big part of what made him who he was and he wanted her to know. To know him. "My sister was killed by a terrorist bomb when I was seventeen." Faded memories of his sister's smiling face and deep laughter rang through his mind, and immediately he was catapulted back to the day they'd put her in the ground.

Rain dripped down from the sky like God himself was weeping. But Tyrone doubted the deity his family prayed to would have enough pity in his heart for a bunch of murdering feckers like the ones who stood before him.

Not that they saw themselves that way. Oh, no. *They were heroes of the revolution. Heroic fighters in a guerilla war that had lasted decades. It was him they blamed. He could see it in their eyes.*

The priest droned on and on. Finally, as one, they made the sign of the cross. It was a wonder they weren't struck down dead on the spot for hypocrisy. If Tyrone had been looking for a sign that religion was bogus he'd have just found it. But he'd stopped believing three days ago when his little sister had been caught in the bomb his dad had built and his brothers had planted.

Prayers ended. Rage simmered.

The priest moved away for the mourners to pay their private respects. His father stood by the grave and looked down at the shiny white coffin for a long moment before turning away, deliberately pushing past Tyrone as he went. He fell back a step, shaking so hard from trying to rein the fury all in, that it was consuming him, cell by cell. His brothers stared at him stonily.

"What are you looking at?" he jeered.

"Shut your hole," his father snarled.

"Or what? You'll fecking kill me too?"

The patriarch of the family's lips firmed. "Don't think I'm not tempted," he murmured.

Then his mother was in his face, wearing her old wool coat and a black scarf that she'd tied over her rampant curly hair. The whites of her eyes were red, skin blotchy. "Hush, love. Give your da some time and space."

"I hope he gets all he needs in his own fucking cell in H-block."

She slapped him. Hard. But her betrayal struck him harder. "That's enough of that talk, Tyrone Dempsey."

He rubbed his cheek. He should be used to it by now, but it always came as a shock.

"That's your father you're talking about. Show some respect."

He almost choked. "Catch yourself on, Ma. He's a fucking stone cold killer and you let him in your bed every night." His voice had grown louder, accent thicker. Too loud for a churchyard full of mourners. Too loud for secrets this volatile. His dad turned to face him, his expression a cold mask of loathing.

Hatred welled up inside Tyrone. He hadn't known what his father and brothers were planning to do, but he'd known they were planning to do something.

He stabbed his finger toward his da and raised his voice. "It was him! Paddy Dempsey who laid that bomb that killed twenty-seven people last Saturday, and the only reason you lot give a fuck is because he got Siobhan too." His voice broke but he was done with this shit. He was done with living in the land of bigotry and misery. He looked at his ma. "How can you not see how wrong this is?"

His mother flinched and two of his brothers came over to give him some. God, he was ready. He'd never hurt a fly in his life but he was desperate to pound something or someone into the ground.

"You're the one who was supposed to watch her. It was a fucking

Orange parade." Ronan grabbed him around the back of the neck and leaned so close their faces were touching. Tears drenched his brother's cheeks. "And keep yer fucking voice down—the Brits'll be watching."

Tyrone pushed him away. "It was market day, you ignorant shite, or are you too stupid to understand women and children go to market on the weekend to get their fucking groceries even when the Orange men are marching?"

"You were told to watch her." Declan—the brother closest to him in age—shoved him hard. Twenty pounds heavier, he'd always liked throwing his weight around. Tyrone didn't give a shit. He welcomed a pounding almost as much as he wanted to dish one out. It might numb the pain of losing his sister. If only for a few brief moments.

"I was in the fucking kitchen listening to the fucking radio the way you told me. She snuck out of the bedroom window. I didn't know she'd gone to town to meet Rory until you came home looking like the cat who'd got the fucking cream." He shoved his brother, who fell back a step. Surprise widened Declan's eyes before they narrowed with malice. Tyrone sneered. "You're not enjoying the victory quite so much now, are you, Declan?"

Declan's skin went bright white. "It wasn't supposed to go off until later. Until the shops were closed and the fucking Brits were doing their rounds."

"Jaysus, will you listen to yourself? You fucking loved the carnage, the wreckage. You strutted around that kitchen like a rooster in a cock-fight, right up until we found out she was gone." Dead. Siobhan was dead. She'd never grin at him again. Never tug his hair or tease his gentle nature when surrounded by all these killers. Dead, dead, dead.

They were right. Siobhan was dead because of him. Not because he'd failed to keep her locked up in her bedroom like an animal, but because he'd let his father and brothers ply their deadly trade and never said a word. Never fought back.

His vision blurred, or maybe it was just the rain. It didn't matter. He looked at his da who was staring at him like he wanted to put a bullet in his brain. Well, he knew the fucking feeling. He pointed again. "You killed her. And I'll never forgive you for it."

He turned his back on them and started walking. Things were about to change, and there'd never be any going back.

The touch of a hand on his face snapped him back to the present. Axelle. The cave. Russian terrorist. There wasn't much left of the boy he'd once been and sometimes he missed the naivety and innocence. He was shaking, and grateful for the darkness.

"I'm sorry," she said. He could hear her thinking, heard the hesitant probing in her voice. "You told me you were dead to your family—did you have something to do with her death? Is that why you try so hard to save people now?"

He'd forgotten the sharpness of her brain.

"No. I didn't kill her. They did." He didn't want to reveal all his deep dark secrets. Not yet. Maybe not ever. "We may as well cover some ground if we're both awake. Let's go."

An hour later, the batteries in the torch began to fade. Not good. They were making progress but without light they were going to struggle to cover much ground. The spots of blood had disappeared, suggesting the Russian had managed to patch himself up and keep moving. Dogged, determined, old bugger.

They got to a divide in the tunnel.

Down one Dempsey could clearly hear the rumble of fast-flowing water. He hesitated.

"I feel a breeze." Axelle went to take a step forward but he stopped her and pulled her close, whispering in her ear.

"This is where I'd set a trap."

She moved back around the corner to give them more cover. Dempsey dropped his pack and stripped off his body armor.

"What are you doing?" Her expression was outraged as he tried to hand it to her.

"I only have one vest. I want you to wear it."

She folded her arms, her eyes glinted but she kept her voice low. "Why are you here, Sergeant Tyrone Dempsey?"

Use of his full name and title gave him pause. "To catch a known Russian terrorist."

"This is your job. Right? Your mission." He nodded. "And they provide you with body armor to do your job, right?"

"It's personal now." After another look at her determined face he pressed his lips together and nodded. "It's my job, yes. That doesn't mean—"

She held up her hand. "I appreciate you rescuing me—I do." Her eyes flashed with unexpected fervor. "Because I couldn't have survived in here alone. But no way in hell am I wearing your bulletproof vest when you're the one he'll be shooting at."

"Axelle—"

"No."

"Axelle—"

"No. We can argue about it all day." She was someone who was used to giving orders not taking them. At least she was getting some of her mettle back, but damn, he'd rather it happened a little later in the operation. "I'm not changing my mind." She stood in the wide stance he used when he was determined to get his own way.

He pulled the vest back over his head. Damn stubborn woman. "Why did you become a wildlife biologist?" It was suddenly important he knew what made her tick.

She frowned at the change in topic. "Because animals need people who care enough to fight for them."

It wasn't so different to why he'd become a soldier. To stand up for those who couldn't stand up for themselves. He stared at her as their light faded. For some crazy reason he slipped his arm around her waist and pulled her tight against him. Hip to hip. Her eyes widened before her gaze dropped to his lips, and he slowly lowered his mouth and kissed her—half expecting a kick in the balls for his audacity. Instead she wrapped her arms around his neck, leaning in as she kissed him back.

Her body felt amazing. Lean and strong, but soft in all the right places. Her mouth like hot wet silk. She probed the seam of his lips and he deepened the kiss, holding her hard against him so she could feel his arousal, feel how much she turned him on. He didn't know the last time he'd wanted a woman like this. Like his brain was going to explode if he didn't have her, right here, right now.

It was a heart-pounding, skin-scorching, soul-blasting kiss, and he didn't want it to end.

Breathing hard, he released her mouth and rested his forehead against hers. He stared into her dark eyes, wondering if his held the same mixture of insecurity, curiosity, and need swirling in their depths. They should, because that was exactly what he was feeling.

He let her go.

No time to enjoy the moment. No time to get distracted.

He pulled NVGs from his pack and slid them over her head. He left his kit against a rock and gripped his carbine. He turned on the night scope.

"You'll be able to see through the NVGs if there's any ambient light at all." He folded her fingers over his pistol. "It's loaded, so shoot any bastard who looks like he wants to kill you. But I'd appreciate if you didn't nail me when I come back."

"What if you don't come back?" her whisper was gruff.

"I'm coming back." Her mutinous expression told him she'd heard that promise before. Her eyes rolled toward the ceiling.

"Hey, don't think about the past," he ordered. He leaned down and kissed her again, hard and fast. His heart rate jacked up to full speed in a split second. And suddenly he wanted to do a whole lot more than kiss her, so he backed away. "I'll be back, if only to see if you're good at anything beside kissing."

Her eyes narrowed. "I wasn't going to shoot you before—"

He grinned at the crispness of her tone.

"—but now I might."

"Be safe, *muirnín*." Then he took off.

Right fork in the tunnel went toward the thundering rumble of water, which spelled trouble if they had rain—one reason to be thankful for the frigid temps outside. To the left was another dark abyss but the air seemed to move slightly against his skin with the barest hint of a breeze.

He didn't trust the other guy. This is where he'd set up an ambush if he were the one being chased. He was definitely getting light through the scope as he moved along the tunnel as fast as he could while still checking for tripwires.

Dempsey frowned. The Russian could have set mines and trip-wires that would have slowed down soldiers and possibly killed them. Why hadn't he? A lot of the intel they had didn't make any sense.

The floor of the tunnel was surprisingly smooth. He suspected the reason for that rumbled forcefully down a nearby chasm. Piles of boulders had been dumped and he had to crawl up and over them. He was careful about where he put his hands and feet. That was why he'd left Axelle behind. He didn't want to risk her life by walking down what could be suicide alley. There was no visible danger but the absolute quiet had the hairs on the back of his neck vibrating. He rounded the corner and saw the dim sparkle of stars blinking through an opening ahead.

Thank bloody Christ.

He thought about going back and getting Axelle, or maybe trying the communication systems. But he wasn't home free yet and she was safer back there, especially with the exit so close.

His boots made a gentle scrape against the rock and he swore he heard the mountain itself draw in a deep breath. He could see no one. Hear nothing. The wind brushed his skin with fresh air he was grateful for after the stale atmosphere beneath ground. But he'd swear on everything he held holy that he was not alone.

He crouched and kept scanning the ground, the opening. He made it out to the face of the mountain and cautiously peered around. Row upon row of spectacular peaks surrounded his position. No trees. Snow, ice, rock and sky. Then above him he spotted the mottled coat of an animal disappearing over the shoulder of the mountain. He gave it a salute, knowing that despite Volkov, these creatures would endure in the high inhospitable peaks.

A deep furrow snaked through the snow, heading over the nearest ridge and out of sight.

The Russian? Who else?

Maybe the old feck hadn't had any more explosives with him? Maybe they'd all been in Axelle's vest, which had helped bring down the cave earlier? Or maybe the old man couldn't risk injuring Axelle until his demands were met. Which meant she was still in danger.

The sound of a footfall behind him had him wheeling, his finger already hugging the trigger. Axelle. *Holy shit.* Her eyes widened but she said nothing. The stubborn woman had also carried his pack, which weighed over seventy pounds. She dropped it to the floor and took in huge deep breaths of fresh air and freedom. He lowered the gun and went and grabbed the satellite phone that was about to save their sorry asses.

"Who you gonna call first?"

"HQ."

"Let's hope they don't send a rescue mission like the last one." She crossed her arms against the frigid temperature.

"That could have been the Americans…"

Her arms tightened. "I know."

"What sort of relationship do you and your father have?" He pressed the on button but nothing happened. *Crap.* He started fiddling with the device.

"He hasn't tried to kill me before, if that's what you're asking."

"I spoke to the Regimental CO, which isn't exactly normal." He locked his teeth in frustration as he played with the phone. "Something tells me someone high up is more interested in seeing Dmitri dead than alive."

"No matter the consequences for others?"

"Collateral damage is accepted within a war zone."

She flinched. "Not by me."

He straightened. "I'm not a big fan either." His eyes held hers and she lost the suspicious look that pinched her features. Who could blame her for being pissed? No one wanted to be sacrificed for someone else's political machinations. Enough of his fellow troopers had already died because shitheads in the MOD had failed to take their equipment requests seriously. Like this piece of shit sat phone. He tried it again.

"I'll be lucky to keep my position at the Trust after this fiasco." Which meant she wouldn't get to work with her precious snow leopards anymore. She met his gaze—her expression defiant. "Josef knows what he's doing, though, and someone else can take over as his supervisor. I've got plenty of work to do in other countries."

The Dane wouldn't be happy about that but Dempsey wasn't gonna tell her Josef's feelings weren't strictly professional. He wasn't a hypocrite.

He tried the phone again with a growing sense of frustration. Swore and wanted to throw it down the mountainside. "It's fucked."

"Let me have a look." She held out her hand.

He hesitated. The problem with Axelle was she needed to be in charge and so did he. They were basically incompatible because they were too similar. "The battery is dead." He'd managed to dismantle the back.

"Lemme see." She gestured. He gave up and handed it over. "The battery is damaged." She passed it back with a grin.

"No shit." He tried his PRR radio. "Alpha Alpha One Nine, over. Come in, over." He waited for a moment but there was nothing but dead air.

"We'd do better yelling," Axelle said quietly. She shaded her eyes, the strain around her mouth evident. "Except then Volkov would know we'd made it out of that nightmare alive."

Her hair stuck up and her eyes were dark with turbulent knowledge and residual fear. Too vulnerable, too innocent to be swept into this kind of deadly situation. But she was coping well, considering what they'd been through.

Taz had the shortwave radio, so despite all the advances in modern technology he and Axelle were incommunicado. At least his GPS signal should have reappeared on the main system by now—assuming *that* wasn't broken.

"What do you reckon? Do we stay here and wait for rescue or climb down the mountain and try to hook up with the squad?" he asked.

She stamped her feet and blew clouds of mist into her hands. "I don't want to stay here."

"You're sure? Because it could be a difficult descent."

"Hell, yes, I'm sure."

He dug into his pack for his fingerless gloves and handed them over. "You want to borrow these? Only the ends are bulletproof."

"Funny ha-ha." She pulled them on and nosed over his shoulder for what else he had in there. He had a fleece. She was already wearing two of his T-shirts and his other pair of socks. He pulled out some dried rations and threw them to her.

"They taste like dog biscuits, but should keep you going."

"Thanks." She tore into them and they shared a drink of water from his canteen. He packed it with clean snow and slipped it inside his shirt.

He took a good look around. They weren't out of danger yet. "Okay. Let's go."

────

Axelle trudged in Dempsey's footsteps, so grateful to be out from the belly of that mountain she wanted to hug him until he couldn't stand up. The past week was her idea of hell, and she'd got through it because Tyrone Dempsey had been at her side. For a woman who had an aversion to being taken care of, he'd done a heck of a job of saving her life.

He'd kissed her.

Her fingers rose to her lips.

She'd been shocked by her own physical response. Now she found herself watching the way he moved, all those lean muscles exerting themselves to make her path easier. And wondering if they'd ever get the chance to take things further than a kiss. Did she want to? Damn, it had been so long she didn't even know what a man felt like anymore. She shook her head and watched her breath freeze. This wasn't the time to think about it. Although, Christ, she didn't want to think about anything else in her life right now either.

Sex would be damn good.

Axelle had never been shy and retiring. Her dad had taught her early you didn't get anywhere with "walk all over me" plastered to your forehead.

If she regretted anything in her life it was that she'd pushed her father away when he'd tried to help. She'd needed to prove she didn't need anyone, she could do everything alone. She'd cut herself off emotionally from everyone. Falling in love with Gideon had been like a rebirth, and his death had hit her doubly hard and sent her so far in the opposite direction, she'd been impossible for anyone to reach.

Did her father know she was being bombed in this narrow finger of land that she'd boldly declared peaceful? Had he condoned it? Ordered it? Was he consumed with worry, already convinced she was dead? She'd never seen him truly grieve. Even when her mother had died she'd seen more anger than sadness. That's how the Dehns dealt with loss. Anger and rage, burning away the softer emotions that might reveal their weakness.

So she'd avoided getting emotionally involved with anyone, concentrating on the needs of helpless animals instead. Dempsey had somehow penetrated her defenses. She should be grateful he wasn't going to be around long enough to break her heart.

Her muscles screamed as she lifted her leg up and out of the snow. Angelina Jolie had nothing on Axelle Dehn—except beauty, a bunch of kids, loads of money and Brad Pitt. She grinned with fierce determination as she put one foot in front of the other. She refused to think of the pain or exhaustion. She was going to think about what Ty Dempsey might look like with his shirt off and how she'd whip Angelina Jolie's skinny butt in a real fight.

The gunfire came out of nowhere and spat snow around them.

Dempsey spun around, grabbing his deadly-looking rifle and returning fire, shoving her behind him as they stumbled over a ridge.

"How did he get behind us?" She ran as fast as she could, stumbling in the snow, bracing for death as shots rang out. Dempsey hauled her up, still firing, still running.

"That isn't Volkov." He didn't take his gaze off the attackers. He reloaded as they ran across another short, sheer face. "Shit, this snow is about ready to drop."

Panic wedged itself tight into Axelle's throat. The thought of an avalanche was as scary as facing a bullet, but they were more than halfway across the face now so she forced herself to move steadily through Dempsey's tracks and prayed.

"Why don't you think it's Volkov?" She huffed out of breath. The altitude drained her energy.

Dempsey grabbed her arm and propelled her faster. A burst of bullets added extra incentive. They threw themselves over another small lip and Dempsey pulled her down behind a large overhang while shrugging out of his backpack. "Volkov lost his rifle when the cave came down, and these guys are firing AK-47s."

"Are they Americans or Brits?" She crouched into a ball as bullets flew over their heads. "Perhaps they don't know we're friendly."

"Perhaps." Dempsey didn't sound convinced. "They didn't exactly ask, did they?"

"Why are we stopping?" Her legs felt like jelly but she was ready to sprint.

"We can't outrun them." He popped his head up and let out a

burst of fire. Dawn started to paint the horizon crimson. She could make out the flicker of flames coming from the barrels of those weapons.

He put his pistol in her hand and curled her fingers around the grip. It was a damn site heavier than her Glock. "Keep firing at them, but keep your head down."

He removed the magazine of his rifle and reloaded it with different bullets.

"We can't just sit here." She pointed the gun over the rock and squeezed the trigger three times.

"I'm waiting for them to begin crossing this face."

The implications slowly locked into place. "Oh, God."

"Here they come. Four of them." He hunkered down to avoid a spray of bullets that splattered them in snow crystals. He took the SIG back and began rapid firing, spraying the hillside with a long volley. "Take cover. Armor-piercing round." He raised his rifle and blasted a round into the slope above the heads of their attackers and hunkered back down. The boom was incredible and bounced off every peak.

An unhurried creak, as if huge fingernails were being drawn slowly over a chalkboard, made her freeze. Then it felt like the whole mountain began to shift.

"Holy shite!" Dempsey swore and the men screamed.

She eyed the snow above them and a wave of terror rushed through her. The entire snow load on the mountain had started to move. She grabbed Dempsey and pulled him beneath the over-hang that sheltered them. He pressed against her and wrapped his arms around her so tight she couldn't breathe. They clung to each other as snow rained over their heads and all around. It seemed to last for hours—a long massive snarl of nature's fury that sent dread screaming along her nerves. When the noise finally stopped, agonizingly long seconds later, she opened her eyes and found herself staring into Dempsey's intense blue gaze.

They were still alive.

There was utter silence around them, as if the world held its breath. Snow buried them in a thick shroud. Axelle felt a familiar panic but she'd already faced her biggest fear. She wasn't about to let a new one paralyze her. Dempsey's arms were shaking from the effort of pushing back against the snow at his back. They were shoved close together against the rock face, bodies flush, legs entangled, but nothing even remotely romantic about the situation.

Dempsey started clawing his way upwards, exertion obvious in his labored breathing. Axelle was helpless. She was trapped beneath the weight of his body and the snow above them. Her lungs felt squeezed. She wriggled her feet to try to loosen the snow's tight grip. Grunting with effort, Dempsey worked until he created enough space for her to get free of him and help dig. The tightness in her chest eased and she could finally breathe more easily.

Snow melted as it touched her bare skin, drenching her cheeks in false tears. She was cold, but the effort of digging heated her muscles, and it wasn't long before she was perspiring.

A small patch of sky appeared and she almost choked on a suppressed sob as Dempsey made it wider.

She hadn't panicked, but that was only because of the man now searching the snow above their heads for his pack and weapons. She didn't know what she'd have done without him, and it wasn't just because he'd saved her life too many times to count. He felt like a part of her—like an extension of herself. Her best friend.

She struggled upright, shoving more snow aside. Dempsey hoisted himself up and crawled to look over the ridge. She followed cautiously, testing the snow's depth with each foot. With the exception of their overhang, the whole face had been swept clean, leaving nothing but a thin coating on the rock behind it.

She swallowed the lump of granite that lodged in her throat. "Are they dead?"

He peered toward the base of the mountain. "Hopefully."

"You don't care?"

His face was expressionless. Eyes scarily cold. "If someone shoots at me and I kill them—I win. I don't waste my energy feeling sorry for the bastards. It was them or us. Thankfully, this time, it was them." He scanned the face of the mountain. "Next time we might not be so lucky. Let's get out of here, but carefully." He raised his hand to indicate they take it slowly, down the mountain rather than across it.

She followed him, at times clutching bare rock as he helped her place her boots into decent footholds. He tied them together at one particular steep point. *Christ*. Her hands shook so badly she could barely hold on.

Fear and fatigue and icy cold continued to wear her down. She was completely out of her element and yet Dempsey seemed to be at ease with their predicament. He didn't panic or sit around wailing. Not that she was the wailing type, but she understood the need. He stayed in the moment and dealt with what needed to be done. It humbled her. Made her realize she was a control freak who didn't do well with the unexpected. She was a planner. Maybe that was why she'd been so pissed when Gideon joined the Marines. She'd no longer been in control of their lives together. When she'd lost him to the chaos of war, it had cemented her need to plan and organize and prepare.

She couldn't plan, organize or prepare for men kidnapping her, getting buried alive or being shot at.

Survival of the fittest was one of the basic tenets of ecology and evolution. In nature the strong ruled and the weak were culled. She'd been in enough war-torn countries growing up to know that without soldiers like Dempsey the world would be a dark and anarchic place, but she was still idealistic enough to wish it wasn't so.

It took nearly an hour to gingerly climb down the roughhewn face with them sliding the last five hundred feet as if they were on a toboggan run. For the first time in what felt like days, maybe years, exhilaration filled her as the wind whipped her cheeks. Laughter burst out as she slid, out of control, relieved to be finally off Death Mountain. The humor was punched out of her system when she spotted an arm sticking out of the snow a yard from where she landed. She rolled over and retched in the snow.

Dempsey had already seen the man. He began scooping snow away from the body.

"What are you doing?"

"I want to know who's shooting at us."

Axelle helped then, digging frantically around the corpse. It took forever. They uncovered him slowly. Black hair. Brown eyes. He looked mid-forties, clean-shaven, neck at exactly the wrong sort of angle.

"At least it was quick," Dempsey pressed his lips tight together.

Axelle swallowed her horror and helped him pull back more snow. They cleared a hole to the man's waist, and Dempsey started searching through his pockets.

"No rank or insignia or uniform. No labels on the clothes." He held out some rounds which meant nothing to her. "Generic." He paused and looked up. "His comms are gone. The writing on the MRE packs is Russian." He stuffed one in his pocket. He got a camera out of his pack and took a photograph of the man's face and a tattoo on his arm.

"Who were they?"

He caught her hand and searched the area, then took off downhill toward a pass heading northwest. Back toward the Wakhan Corridor. "They're either nonmilitary"—*mercenaries*—"Russian Special Forces, or some sort of Black Ops."

Her eyes widened. She looked at him as he helped drag her through the snow. "Josef said *you* were Special Forces."

He looked at her with bright blue eyes and said nothing.

What sort of military units traveled in small packs far from backup? The secretive deadly kind. Axelle wasn't surprised Dempsey hadn't answered her questions. His silence confirmed her beliefs. He *was* British Special Forces.

"We need to get you to safety and I need a radio to try to find out what the hell is going on. Find out where Dmitri Volkov is and how we can bring him in." He let go of her arm and checked his own rifle as they marched onward.

"Are we still following Volkov?" She shuddered. She wanted to get back to her leopards but until Volkov was stopped she couldn't be sure he wouldn't start taking potshots at her animals again.

Dempsey nodded toward a broken snow trial off to the right. "He's going the same way we are. What's the nearest settlement to here?"

She thought for a moment. She'd been tied up and unconscious for much of her ordeal yesterday but she had a general sense they'd been moving east. "There's a small Kyrgyz settlement, south of Bozai Gumbaz. I'm guessing that's the closest."

They traipsed onward through the snow, which was melting under the now midday sun. The mountain had finally fought off the enveloping cloud. A few straggly dwarf shrubs and bushes started to appear and Axelle let out a sigh of relief as she spotted a swathe of green on the valley floor ahead. The snowstorm had only been in the mountains. If this was a trial of endurance, her quivering muscles told her she was just about done.

Birds darted all around and she spotted some goats on the hillside, which meant there was a goatherd not far away.

She stumbled and Dempsey stopped and supported her with an arm around her waist, helping her to keep moving when she was so exhausted she literally wanted to fall on the ground and close her eyes.

"If we could risk a fire I'd stop and build a shelter."

It sounded wonderful.

"Why can't we build a fire?" Her brain cells were sluggish. Excited by nothing except the thought of sleep.

"In case there are more gunmen out here. Or Dmitri Volkov isn't as wounded as I hope. He's clearing a hell of a lot of ground for a man with a gunshot wound."

"You must have only clipped him."

"He wore body armor, otherwise he'd be dead." Dempsey's lips were hard. Soldier mode. "He's gone to a lot of trouble to get his hands on you. Something tells me he isn't going to run away because he had a setback."

"It was a hell of a setback." She scanned the hillsides, but could see nothing moving through the valley. Her skin suddenly prickled and she pressed closer to Dempsey because he was the one thing that made her feel safe in this new world of bombs, bullets and death.

CHAPTER
TWELVE

FROM THE SHELTER of a group of boulders on the western side of the track, Dmitri lay prone on the ground and followed the man and woman's progress through a gap in the rocks. His hand throbbed from where the soldier had shot him. The bullet had gone straight through his palm but all his fingers worked so Dmitri counted that as a miss. His chest was badly bruised but for once he was grateful he wasn't dead.

He was glad the soldier and the woman had survived. He admired their tenacity. But it did not change his plans. All the sacrifices and degradation his family had endured, not because he'd sinned, but because someone else had...

Sergei's boy was dying and needed immediate hospital care. The pelts were lost. He had to change his plan. He still needed money, still needed to get his family out of Russia. Thankfully he still had something of extreme value in his sights. And Magdalena was counting on him.

His grandson would be saved no matter who else had to die to achieve it, but the bombing complicated things. Who ordered it? Russians via their spy? Or the US and British via the soldier? The man was impressive, Dmitri conceded. More impressive than he'd anticipated. Reminded him of himself from a long time ago.

Dmitri had made all the wrong choices in his life, trusted all the wrong people. He was paying for those mistakes now, but it broke his heart that his grandson was bearing the brunt of his grandfather's legacy. If Dmitri hadn't defected, if he hadn't taught a young mujahedeen captain how to fight, he wouldn't be wanted in half the nations of the world and his son would still be alive today. Dmitri had been painted a monster, but he'd never believed in collateral damage or civilian casualties. Women and children should be kept out of war. The mistake he'd made, over and over, was not realizing others had no such qualms.

He turned to the wide-eyed boy who sat beside him cross-legged on the rocky ground. "Tell your father to give them food and shelter. Tell him to put this into the soldier's tea before he retires for the night." He handed him a small capsule. A useful drug for those who had lost the power to sleep. "I need supplies and another horse and yak. Tell him I will pay him soon." Just not yet.

The young boy adjusted his hat, nodded his elfin face, and stood to gather his goats.

"Be careful."

The child scooted off and Dmitri turned back to watch the man and woman move out of sight. Another time, another place and he'd have let them go. Not this time.

———

The sun was sliding down the western horizon and she was still walking, although she was almost blind with exhaustion. Dempsey stopped and eyed her critically. "Do the people here know you?"

She looked toward the village and nodded. "Some do. We met the elders in Sarhad for a meeting when we started the project."

"Then you and I just got married."

Her eyes popped. "We did?"

"Otherwise we'll be split up when we get to their village and I don't trust Volkov not to pull another stunt."

She frowned. It wasn't the idea of pretending he was her husband that bothered her. It was the curious pang at the thought of being separated.

"Then we're newlyweds because last summer I was single." She'd had offers; one man had even stretched to a camel.

He took her hand as they approached the squat clay structures. "Let me do the talking."

"As long as I like what you're saying, you can do the talking."

"Stubborn doesn't even begin to describe you, Dr. Dehn. My GPS signal should have kicked in by now. Volkov's trail veered east about half a mile south of here. I'll go after him as soon as the squad catches up with me. You'll be back in your camp by tomorrow morning watching out for your cats." His fingers squeezed tight.

She had to clear her throat to speak. She didn't know why she was feeling so sad at the thought of rescue. "How do we explain the rest of your guys when they turn up? Bachelor party?"

"Students?" His grin was devilish.

"Too many guns." Her smile faded. She wasn't okay with people dying. They could have family. Wives… Who were those other soldiers anyway? She assumed the target was Dempsey, but getting caught in the crossfire wasn't her idea of fun. The thought of Dempsey being killed settled like an onerous burden on her chest and she found it hard to inhale. The force of her reaction startled her.

"Let's rest for a few hours. I'll contact the CO from the village and worry about the details later." They approached a group of squat buildings that seemed to be made of clay. Tiny puffs of smoke rose from holes in the roofs.

A group of children ran toward them dressed in brightly colored garments and smiling gap-toothed smiles.

"Hello." Dempsey smiled and tucked her hand into the crook of his elbow. "What language do they speak?" he asked her.

"Probably a mix of Wakhi and Kyrgyz."

He grunted, which suggested his skills didn't include those two obscure languages.

"Some of them speak English," she added.

They marched into the center of the tiny village and a little man came to the door of his house and smiled at them widely. He wore two jackets and a knitted cap, his features those of ancient Mongolia. The others wore an eclectic mixture of clothes from the traditional to a soccer jersey pulled tight over several layers of sweaters. The man in the doorway, clearly the chief elder, chattered at them in his own language. Axelle pulled her hat more firmly over her hair until it was covered. The people here were moderate in their religious beliefs but she didn't want to offend.

Dempsey said, "I need a telephone, and my wife and I need somewhere to rest." He put his hands together and leaned his head to the side, mimicking sleep.

She swallowed the knot that formed in her throat at the words. The man was nodding and trying to drag Dempsey into his house for tea while the women urged her to follow them.

"Go," she said. "I doubt the guy would take on the whole village." She could barely keep her eyes open anyway.

"I'll be there as soon as I've radioed HQ."

She nodded gratefully. She knew he'd check on Anji and Josef too. And her leopards. The weight of guilt wanted to crush her— so many had died so that Dmitri Volkov could lure her here a few months early. Who *had* he been talking to on the sat phone? Her father? Or someone else?

The women showed her into a hut. Before she went inside she noticed Dempsey watching her from the doorway of the other hut. He smiled then turned away. Her heart hurt. She could hear him asking for a radio or telephone. The women ushered her inside and she asked to use the facilities, which were as basic as she'd expected. After she'd cleaned up, they gave her some clean clothes but she was too tired to get undressed. She pulled back the heavy cloth curtain to reveal a rich red blanket spread on top of a roughly constructed platform. It was as close to a real bed as she was likely to get in this place and she wanted to kiss the ground in relief. She nodded her thanks and, as soon as they left her alone, she fell face-first onto the bed and was asleep in seconds.

———

Reports were Volkov survived the bombing raid.

Jonathon stepped from his car outside Lucinda Allworth's Suffolk home and ran his fingers through his hair. Security was subtle but thorough and he had to show ID to a protection officer before he was even allowed to knock on the door. He hadn't called ahead. Didn't want to give her the opportunity to refuse to see him. He knew that if he turned up on the doorstep she was English enough to invite him in for a cup of tea.

"Jonathon?" She opened the door, looking thin and delicate in a pretty cotton dress covered with summer flowers. "Come in." She smiled and waved to her security detail before stepping away from the door and ushering him inside.

He leaned forward to kiss her cheek and she blushed. She'd always been an oddly shy creature. Pretty, but almost embarrassed about it.

"You look beautiful, Lucinda, but then again you always did." He let his gaze warm as his eyes swept over her. His skin prickled with unexpected desire. This wasn't going to be a chore at all. He was old. He wasn't dead.

"Oh." She touched her cheek and blushed. He contained a smile. She always acted so…surprised when he gave her compliments. You'd think he'd never kissed her or seen her naked.

"How are you, my dear? Coping with the circus?" He closed the door and followed her through to the kitchen. She was always baking, and the smell of scones scented the air. No wonder Sebastian had needed to lose a few pounds. Maybe if he hadn't been so fat he could have escaped that bullet. Maybe not. Jonathon pursed his lips.

It was Volkov's fault. All of it.

"I would have brought you champagne to celebrate David's victory, but I remembered you don't drink."

"It was all rather super, Jonathon." Her eyes sparkled at him. "I did actually have a few glasses the night of the election." And was probably dragged out of the hall and stuffed in a taxi before she'd ended up on the breakfast news, nissed as a pewt.

He touched her arm. A calculated move. Comfort and interest. Enough of both to gauge her reaction to him—to *them*. "Sebastian would have been proud, my dear. You've done a wonderful job with your son."

She smiled sadly and touched his hand. "Not many people remember Sebastian anymore." She chewed on her bottom lip, then met his gaze. "Sometimes I think you and I are the only people who knew he existed."

Jonathon moved closer, saw her eyes flicker with sudden awareness.

"I'll never forget him, Lucy. I loved him. He's with me every single day." He touched his heart, then tipped her chin and slowly leaned closer. "I tried to forget *you*, but after I saw you on the news I had to come." He kissed her gently. Eased her into the idea of heat and passion. She kissed him back, this hollow little woman in her pretty dress in her sweet country kitchen. She kissed him back and he was going to reward her by making slow sweet love to her and then, in the dark depth of night, he'd confess his deepest darkest secret—that Sebastian hadn't died in a plane crash at all. Instead he'd been killed by the same monster who'd tried to blow him to smithereens in Yemen. A monster who'd risen from the grave.

He sank his hand into her hair and nipped gently at her mouth and started backing her up the stairs toward the same bedroom she'd once shared with her husband. And this sweet little woman was going to grasp wholeheartedly onto the idea of revenge for her husband's killer because she'd be feeling guilty about the pleasure Jonathon was about to give her in ways fat old Sebastian had only ever dreamed of.

Well, maybe they both deserved a little fun in their dotage.

And once she found out this new truth, she'd run to her son, the Prime Minister, and he'd stop at nothing to avenge his late father. And they could all live happily ever after. Except Dmitri, because he'd be dead.

———

Dempsey walked up to the small hut they'd been given for the night, gritting his teeth with frustration. The village's Soviet-era radio wasn't working and there were no satellite phones to call HQ. As far as the Regiment was concerned he might as well be dead. He assumed his GPS was still sending out a signal, but with a mysterious hit squad after them that signal was as likely to kill them as save them. Still, there were other troopers in the Wakhan Corridor and it wouldn't be long before some of them caught up to him. Then they could pursue the subject—a sixty-three-year-old demon with a bullet hole somewhere in his hide—who'd so far managed to kick Dempsey's ass.

They were a different breed, that generation, pure gristle and spite. Like his da. The only time he'd ever seen his old man break was when he'd found out Siobhan was dead, and that hadn't lasted long.

He yawned, his jaw cracking. Except for a snatched hour here and there, he hadn't slept properly in days and he was starting to drag. When adrenalin was pumping you didn't need much sleep. In the relative safety of the village, he figured he had little choice but to finally drop his guard and get a few hours' kip.

He pushed in through the thick curtain that formed the door and strode to the drape that divided the room. The paraffin lantern the village elder had given him created an intimate atmosphere. He exhaled a long slow breath when he saw Axelle fast asleep on the bed. To the consternation of his hosts he'd sat with a view of the hut the whole time he ate. Volkov was the wiliest bastard he'd come up against in years and he worried about Axelle's safety.

But she was okay. She was more than okay.

He didn't remember the last time a woman had affected him like this. Maybe never. He put the tea they'd given him beside the bed. Smiled at the vision she made asleep. Like any old combat veteran she slept with her boots and hat on. He dropped down to the bed and rubbed his eyes.

She stirred.

"Sorry. Didn't mean to wake you," he said.

She blinked awake and pushed into a sitting position, pulled off her hat and dragged her mussed hair over one shoulder. She suddenly looked young. Not kickass and capable. Dark circles smudged tired eyes. The set of her chin looked uncertain for once, not ready to take on every adversary.

"There's no working radio or satellite dish within twenty miles." He sounded as disgusted as he felt.

"These people have next to nothing."

He handed her his canteen of water and she took a drink. They were way beyond the social niceties.

"How they survive here is beyond me," she said.

"I was going to ask *why* the hell do they stay here but having visited the rest of Afghanistan, this place has some advantages."

"It used to." Her dark eyes haunted him. "Maybe not so much anymore."

He shrugged out of his backpack, which felt like it had been welded to his back. "The military only want Volkov. They won't stay unless there's a reason."

"It doesn't bother you?" Her eyes drifted away from his.

"What?"

"Being sent on a mission to kill someone."

"I wasn't sent on a mission to kill anyone. I was sent to capture him." He closed his mouth, pissed he'd admitted that much.

She smiled. Knew she'd got him. "Dead or alive though, right?"

He rubbed his hands over his eyes then rested his elbows on his knees. "Axelle, you're a smart woman. You know there are times when we can't all hold hands and sing 'Kumbaya.'" He decided to tell her the truth because he wanted her armed with real knowledge in case she had to face this bastard again—especially if he wasn't there to help her. The thought tore at his guts. "Volkov went AWOL from the Red Army and joined the mujahedeen in late 1980. When that fight was over, he was still so full of bloodlust he sought out Islamic militants and taught them the basics of bomb-making, which they're now using to terrorize governments and civilians around the globe. I don't care what his reasons were. Perhaps he's misunderstood, but I don't give a rat's arse. I spent my life protecting people and he's spent his trying to destroy them. There is no redemption for a man like that, no matter the circumstances."

She sat staring at him, her eyes wide with understanding rather than the horror of killing she'd expressed earlier. He'd said more than he should but after being kidnapped she was due some sort of explanation. Not that the bosses would see it that way.

"Are we staying here overnight or are we leaving?" Her eyes were still bleary, but she was clearly ready to go if they needed to. But, Christ, he was toast.

"Let's get a few hours' sleep, and we'll slip out before dawn." He wasn't sure they'd find a safer spot than this anywhere close by. He felt exposed but there was only one of him—he couldn't stay awake indefinitely.

He undid the laces on her boots and pulled off one, then the other. He rubbed her feet and she groaned, and he tried to ignore what the sound did to him deep in the pit of his belly.

"Go back to sleep. I've got a few things to do before I get any rest."

He checked each of his weapons and made sure they were clean and loaded and within arm's reach. He went outside and did a quick perimeter check of the village, seeing what everyone was up to and if anything seemed out of place. He didn't know if the people here were fooled by the cover story he'd given them—that he and his wife were on a hiking trip from her camp for their honeymoon. Hell, he didn't even know whether they'd understood any of his words, but they'd eyeballed his weapons with a healthy dose of respect and Dempsey figured they recognized the gear of a professional soldier when they saw it.

Though he'd never told them he *wasn't* a soldier. He'd just said he was Axelle's husband—something he didn't want to dwell on. Back in the hut he bent down and undid his boots. Slipped them off with his socks. Drank a sip of his lukewarm tea. Unstrapped his body armor and placed it on the floor beside his other stuff. Damn, he was tired. He figured he'd better keep his T-shirt and trousers on, else his reflex reaction to Axelle might scare the shit out of her if she woke and found him pressed against her like some horny git.

He turned back to the bed expecting her to be asleep. She wasn't. She lay watching him with an expression that made his heart stand still for three hopeful beats.

"You ever been married before?" Her voice was soft and a little bit husky.

He cleared his throat. "No. The army doesn't go well with marriage and I've never met anyone…" He stopped, disconcerted. "Is this difficult for you, pretending to be married to a man like me?" He'd known it might be but had ignored it. He needed to keep her safe, whatever the cost.

A sad smile curved her lips. "We were only actually married for a year and he was gone for half of that." The pain was there though, beneath the surface.

He sat and didn't break eye contact. "I'm sorry."

She nodded. There was nothing he could say that would make up for what she'd lost. Shit happened. People died every day. They died crossing the road, eating unwashed vegetables and sneaking off to the market to meet boyfriends they weren't supposed to have.

He lay down and closed his eyes. He could feel her beside him. Her breath soft against his arm. Her knees brushing his as she curled toward him. Trusting him because of what they'd been through together.

Somehow—inconceivably—he'd bonded with this fiercely independent woman. They'd become partners in survival, and those feelings merged with desire in his head to create something mind-blowingly complex and yet utterly simple. Her hand crept down to meet his and their fingers entwined and locked.

"Dempsey." Her voice was soft in his ear.

She was driving him crazy and she didn't even know it. "I'm trying to sleep."

"I haven't thanked you, for everything you've done since we met."

His heart banged like a teenage boy having his first wet dream. "I'm just doing my job."

He felt her nod then he felt her hand on his stomach and his heart about stopped.

"It's more than that." Her hand rested lightly on his shirt. *She's trying to get warm, idiot.* Then her hand traveled south and he didn't have to second-guess her intentions any longer.

"Axelle…" He groaned as she touched him. He'd dreamed about her stroking him there, like that. He lay, afraid to move because he might already be asleep and this could be a hell of a dream, except dreams didn't feel this hot, and dreams didn't smell like an exotic mix of honey and silk. Her hand slipped to the waistband of his trousers, and she started undoing buckles and buttons.

Oh, fuck. Put a gun in his hands, he was fine. Give him this woman and he was lost. Blood pumped. Flesh burned. He was too scared to move. He wanted her so badly, lust crawled over his skin and licked its way over his body in a wanton feast. Her fingers unsnapped his pants and suddenly she was touching him without any barriers, and his eyes flashed open. He grabbed her wrist and twisted her flat onto her back. He drilled his gaze into hers. "You don't owe me this sort of thanks."

"What if I want you?" She blinked away a sudden sparkle of moisture from her eyes. "What if, for the first time since my husband died, I actually want a man?" Her lips trembled as she fought with emotions.

He couldn't stand to see the anguish in her gaze. He already knew what she'd lost. And he felt the echo of that loss because it was something he'd never have. He lowered his lips to hers, tracing the outline, memorizing the texture and taste.

Her lips parted on a sigh. "We don't need promises or rings. Give me something good to remember."

There was no way he could deny her. Who was he kidding? He didn't want to try.

"I almost died today and can't even remember what it feels like to have an orgasm."

"Really?" His voice broke. So much for Mr. Macho. She was kissing him, those soft pink lips nibbling his skin, and he was remembering how amazing she'd looked naked through the scope of his rifle. How desperately he wanted to touch her skin. Giving her an orgasm would be his pleasure.

"Do you have a condom?" she asked.

He reached into one of his zippered pockets and pulled out a foil package. "They're standard issue." He would have explained the 101 uses of condoms but she took it from his fingers. She was going too fast and at the same time not fast enough. He wanted to be inside her, but he also wanted this to last more than five seconds.

She was about to rip it open when he stopped her. "Wait." Hungry for the sight of her bare skin he started peeling off her shirt and pushed aside the material only to be confounded by another T-shirt.

"Good God, woman, how many layers are you wearing?" He pushed the shirt off her shoulders, then lifted the T-shirt over her head.

She sat in the lamplight in her plain black sports bra and baggy trousers. He watched the swell of her breasts rise and fall. Heard the catch in her throat as he touched her smooth skin with his calloused finger—so soft. Her nipples pressed against the cotton and he lowered his head to taste her.

The press of beaded nipple against his tongue had lust ripping through him. His hands molding her body, he pulled her closer, tasting every inch of skin he could find. She tugged at his shirt, trying to drag it over his back but he wasn't helping, he was too busy unclipping the fastenings of her bra, his heart pounding like a machinegun.

This was a mistake.

He was letting down his guard at a time when he should be on high alert. And his brain felt like he'd been dipped in anesthetic because he was so tired.

But it might be the best mistake he'd ever made.

Somehow she wriggled out of her trousers and panties at the same time, and he swallowed as she sat naked in the middle of the bed. He ran his hands reverently over the dusky pink of her nipples, watched fascinated as they budded with his touch. Her lips parted, her eyes black with desire. Need scrambled along his veins. Somehow she'd managed to tug his T-shirt over his head where it got tangled and he threw it off. He clenched his fists. He should say no. This wasn't a sensible time for her to be making these sorts of decisions, and having sex definitely wasn't part of his orders.

But holy shit, how could he say no?

He'd wanted her from the moment he'd seen her and done his damnedest to keep his hands off her and stay professional. She'd made this decision. She liked to be in charge. Now it was his turn.

He eased her down on the bed and crawled between long smooth legs. She cried out in surprise.

"I don't think this is a real good"—he widened her thighs as he sank his mouth over her and nuzzled and licked until she bucked in his arms—"idea."

She tasted sweet and salty. Her fingers clutched the blanket, and her skin was covered with a damp sheen of perspiration. His hands roamed higher and discovered her breasts, plucking and teasing her nipples until she writhed and twisted. Her long hair came loose of its braid and unraveled at the same moment she did. She came in a rush of high-pitched little groans, both of them mindful to keep the noise down.

But tasting her release made his own body strain to be inside her.

She lay panting for a moment and he admired the view, so aroused just by the sight of her he didn't want to move. Not yet. She hooked him with her foot and flipped him onto his back. He laughed, so surprised he lay still for a whole second. Long enough for her to curl her fingers around him and rip open the condom package. Yeah, he was fighting it all right.

"I want the whole deal, Dempsey. Not a pity party. If this is my quota of sex for this decade, I want you deep inside me."

A weird thrill shot through him as he prepared himself to be dominated, but he wanted this to last. He gripped her thighs as she straddled him, but it just sank her hot wet core closer against him and she rode the ridge of his erection for a few heart-stopping beats. Desire scorched his skin. Blood heated in his veins.

It somehow seemed *wrong*, like it should mean more than this —that *they* should mean more than a quick fuck in a dirt hut. But God help him, he couldn't stop now. He gripped her hips as he slid slowly inside her. Her back arched, thrusting out those small perfect breasts, her head falling back so that her soft hair brushed his knees. The sensation was so incredible he did it again. And again. Framing her hips with his big hands to hold her exactly where he wanted her, even as she rode him at her own pace—

sometimes fast, sometimes slow, but always with that knowing glint in her eyes. He smiled grimly when she raised her hands over her head and twisted her hips and came with a satisfied groan.

He held on to his own release by a gossamer thread of control, giving her a long moment to enjoy her pleasure. Then it was his turn to flip her onto her back and hook her knee over his elbow and drive back into her slick velvet heat. She cried out, but not in pain. He gripped her hands as he thrust hilt-deep into the cradle of her thighs, so deep his balls ached.

"Is this what you want?" His voice was guttural. She'd destroyed him. Reduced him to an animal with only one thought in mind. Lust tore through him, and he wanted to take her hard and fast, slow and leisurely, as many different ways as she'd let him.

Her eyes were laughing as she met each thrust with one of her own. "I'd forgotten how good it could be, but"—she gasped on a thrust and he felt a quiver in his heart—"this is exactly what I want."

They held the connection as they both slammed into one another, building to a climax that ripped his world apart. His vision went white and this time Axelle screamed so loud he started laughing and couldn't stop even as the orgasm rolled through his body and into hers in endless, shuddering ecstasy. When it was over, he collapsed on top of her and she wrapped her legs and arms tight around him, as if savoring the moment. He eased onto his elbows and squeezed her tight, unrecognizable emotions bursting inside him. He didn't want to let go. He didn't want to ever let go.

Christ. That was a problem.

It took an eternity to find the strength to crawl off her and even then he didn't want to withdraw. She lay there sprawled against the blankets. Eyes closed. Silent. And he wanted to do it all over again, so they didn't have to talk, didn't have to think about never doing it again.

But things were never that simple, and sacrifice was part of the job.

He got rid of the condom and pulled on his trousers and T-shirt, finished his cold tea to try to ease the ache in his throat. She got dressed too, her amazing body disappearing from sight, and he knew chances of getting her naked again were close to zero. Frustrated, he pressed his lips together. *Get used to that feeling, pal.* He was on a mission, for fuck's sake—he shouldn't have been having sex in the first place. Especially not incendiary sex that had blown his head off.

With the exception of their boots they were now both ready to go. Her eyes reflected his sadness. Damn. He hadn't meant to make her feel sad. He pulled her against him and dragged the blanket across them, feigning self-assurance he was far from feeling. "*Now* can I go sleep?"

She elbowed him in the gut, which was answer enough.

———

Nuristan Province, Afghanistan-Pakistan border, October 1980

A car approached the barren, dusty outpost. The first in two days. Winter was fast approaching and Dmitri wrapped his greatcoat tighter around his waist. The clouds overhead were a bruised angry white that promised imminent snowfall. Only a desperate man would try to cross the Hindu Kush in the face of a winter blizzard, but this was Afghanistan and everybody here was desperate.

He stood, stretched out his muscles, and walked to the barrier next to a guard box that straddled the road to the Pakistani border in eastern Nuristan province.

The middle of nowhere.

Grinding monotony.

Silent ridicule.

This was his meteoric fall from grace.

It didn't matter. Nothing mattered except obediently doing his time and getting back to Magdalena and their young son, Sergei. He had no pride left. No loyalty to the motherland he'd once loved. Bide his time, get out of the Red Army, and settle back on the farm his parents had worked before him. That was all he wanted now.

The sound of jackboots hit the ground. "Someone must be in a hurry to leave this shithole to risk crossing this late in the year, huh, Dmitri?"

"*Ya, Serzhánt,*" Dmitri checked his weapon. A decrepit Kalashnikov that he'd stripped and cleaned and repaired until it was finally reliable. Dmitri's skill with weapons more than compensated for the gun's lack of accuracy.

The car approached, the exhaust rattling like a tin can beneath it. A young man, maybe seventeen, was driving. Dmitri watched the vehicle carefully. A dark head bobbed in the backseat. He stood in the middle of the dusty road and held his weapon on the car as it rolled to a bumpy stop ten feet away. The traveling companion was a woman. A girl. Dmitri took a step forward, but his superior office stopped him with a hand on his arm.

"I'll deal with this, *Yefréytor.*"

From a *kapitán* in Russia's premier army division to a common soldier in less than twelve months. The bitterness had diluted. The sourness had receded. He did not care. Not anymore. They couldn't take anything else from him except his family. He would not risk them for anything.

Dmitri walked away and leaned against the hut, waiting in case his asshole boss needed help carrying the cash he was about to steal from these poor unfortunates. He lit a cigarette and made toe prints in the dirt.

"Papers," the man snapped. The sound of paper rustled in the wind and Dmitri heard them ripped away by a strong gust. Dmitri walked slowly over to where the documents had pressed themselves tight against a rock. He picked them up and straightened.

There was a reason his companion was manning an almost deserted border outpost. A reason that did not involve the injured ego of a Russian spy.

"Get out of the car," the *serzhánt* barked at the young man.

Dmitri stood at his boss's shoulder and handed back the paperwork.

"Take him and search him." He snatched the documents and threw them into the car. His eyes flashed with malice. "Search him properly."

Dmitri hid his distaste but took the youth by the shoulders and pushed him roughly against the side of the hut and started a slow and thorough investigation of the man's clothes and hidden crevices. It wasn't dignified but Dmitri didn't have much use for dignity. Not anymore.

He heard the girl scream as she was hauled out of the car, heard the smack of a fist on flesh, felt the young man go rigid beneath his hands. Dmitri pinned him firmly against the wall. For his own sake.

"My sister. Please, don't hurt my sister. She's pregnant," the young man pleaded. Dmitri tensed even though he kept searching for weapons and drugs and other illegal paraphernalia on the youngster. "We are making our way to her husband's village in Pakistan so she can have her baby in safety."

"I don't care," he grated into the young man's ears. The young woman was screaming louder and louder. *Don't look, Dmitri. Don't fucking look.* A quick glance told him what was about to happen. That and the terror in the girl's black eyes—as black as Magdalena's—as she met his gaze from where she was splayed on the bonnet of the car.

His illustrious *serzhánt* punched the girl in the mouth again, then held her by the throat as he shoved her skirt over her swollen belly and wedged her thighs apart with his own. The young man bolted away from his grasp and Dmitri grabbed him before he'd gone four paces and slammed the butt of his rifle into his temple to stop him getting killed.

"Good. You can have the little whore next," the *serzhánt* said with a sneer. "If she's any good I won't shoot her brother."

Her eyes flashed and Dmitri watched a terrified smile try to form on her lips. Because a young woman about to be violated should smile at her attacker.

"That's better, *devotchka*. I'll even let you lick me clean when we are done." The *serzhánt* undid his pants, penis jutting, red and ugly in the wind.

Bile burned along Dmitri's throat, acid and disgusting. Patriotic pride withered and died. He was completely ashamed to be Russian.

The *serzhánt* ripped her blouse and clamped his hand to her full breast. It hurt her. Dmitri could tell. His heart shriveled as he watched the animal spread her legs wider and open her woman's flesh with his thick fingers—flesh only a husband or a doctor should see or touch. The *serzhánt* spat on his fingers and forced them inside her, excitement blazing a fierce blush against his cheekbones. "See? She is already wet for me."

Dmitri squeezed the trigger of his gun and the man fell dead in the dirt.

The woman stared at him with shocked eyes and swallowed a huge sob of air. He took a step closer and pulled her skirt down. "Move. You must leave. Now. Hurry."

She ran to her brother, who was out cold. Dmitri lifted him—childlike in his arms—and threw him into the back seat. Then he went through the *serzhánt's* pockets and removed all the money and cigarettes and ammo he could find.

"You can drive?" he asked the girl.

Her eyes wouldn't leave him. "What will happen to you?"

"They'll probably shoot me." Magdalena would have wanted him to save the girl. He knew it, even though it meant he'd never see her again.

"Come with us."

"What?" he asked.

She hesitated as if gauging the strength of her trust. "Come with us. My brother and I are going to join relatives in Pakistan. Amir is going to fight with the mujahedeen. You'll be safe with us."

"A Russian safe in Pakistan? You're crazy." Despite everything, he almost laughed.

"Please. I need you. I don't know how to drive. Amir is unconscious." She gripped his sleeve with small, strong fingers. "Our family is rich. We can protect you. You will be a hero in my town."

The word "hero" bit him like a bullet in the chest. He'd wanted to be a hero once. Now he'd lost everything and the words meant nothing to him anymore. His career, his wife, the son he'd never met, even the cold callous bitch of his homeland were stripped from him now. He opened the passenger door and helped the girl inside.

What did he have to lose?

CHAPTER
THIRTEEN

AXELLE WOKE with a start and her eyes widened as Dmitri Volkov stood with a matte-black pistol pointed straight at Dempsey. Dempsey was thankfully fast asleep. She closed her eyes and opened them again, but it wasn't her imagination playing tricks. The man actually stood there, tired, grim, and resolved. She blew out a silent breath. He was a determined sono-fabitch, that was for sure. Volkov pressed his finger to his lips, pointed his finger at her, then jerked his thumb in the direction of the door.

Dammit.

Not only was the man not done with her, odds were he'd shoot Dempsey if he woke up and tried to stop them. She couldn't let that happen. She'd started to care deeply about this man and no one knew the danger of getting involved more than she did. She edged out of bed slowly, moving carefully away from the man she'd made love to, keeping her body between the Russian and the soldier. Volkov held her boots and jerked his head to the curtained doorway. If she made a wrong move, all the Russian had to do was squeeze that trigger and Dempsey was dead. She nodded, silently snagging her fleece and jerkin on the way out, and getting outside as fast as she could to try to draw Dmitri's attention to her rather than Dempsey.

Two horses waited in the darkness. Dmitri stood behind her as she put on her boots.

"What's the point in taking me again?" she asked quietly. "My family has already proven they won't meet your demands." Her throat went dry as she recalled the vest of explosives he'd made her wear and the terrible cascade of rocks that had been the West's response to her capture. She couldn't cope with that again. She gazed around in desperation but there was no one outside. Everyone was asleep.

He stuffed a rag in her mouth and tied a stinking oily cloth around her lower face to keep it in place. She tried not to gag, strove for calm as her heart pounded. He pulled her wrists behind her back and bound them tight enough her arms screamed in protest. He was punishing her for her escape—although it hadn't exactly been her fault. She forced herself to breathe calmly through her nose. She would not panic. This insane old man was not going to destroy her. But she knew that if she struggled, if she made noise and alerted help, someone might get shot. Better to go with him and figure out another way to escape when they were far from the village.

Dempsey would find her.

She blinked back emotion because somewhere over the past few days she'd learned not only to trust the soldier, but to rely on him. She didn't want him to die because of her. She could survive pretty much anything—even being buried underground—as long as he was around. But she could not survive his death.

He might not be hers to keep, but she didn't want him to die. Not now. Not ever. But he had the skills to find her and he would help her.

Axelle squared her shoulders as they started walking. Dmitri nudged her forward and caught the lead rein of the horses. She straightened her back and raised her chin. They went quietly around a low-slung house, and something flew over her head and smacked into the Russian like a wrecking ball. The whirling mass of arms and legs was nothing but a blur in the darkness. For a second she stood there like a fool, then she started running back to the village. A man rose out of the ground like a phantom, and she froze as he pointed his gun straight at her heart. Two shots later his head exploded. Blood sprayed her face and she was struggling not to choke as he crumpled in front of her.

Suddenly gunfire rang out from every direction, muzzle flashes lighting the darkness. She threw herself to the hard ground and rolled toward the nearest building as bullets flew overhead. Screams rang out from the terrified villagers, who found themselves in the middle of a raging gun battle. Crap. She couldn't help anyone until she got rid of the gag and bonds, but no matter how she wriggled she couldn't dislodge either. Finally the shooting stopped and she looked around not knowing what the hell was going on. Or who'd won the fight.

Someone touched her shoulder and she startled. It was the soldier, Cullen. "Where's Dempsey?" he asked, pulling off her gag and helping her to her feet.

She twisted so he could untie her wrists. "I left him asleep in that hut." Her mouth parched with sudden dread. "He didn't come out when you started shooting?"

The man she knew as Taz limped toward her.

"Where's Volkov?" Cullen asked him.

"The bugger slipped away once the firefight broke out."

"You okay?" Cullen eyed his limp.

Taz nodded. "I twisted my ankle when I brought him down. It'll be all right in a minute."

Axelle threw off her bonds and raced across the dusty ground toward the hut she'd shared with Dempsey. Had he already been dead when Volkov kidnapped her? Had the old man tricked her? Her heart vibrated in an unsteady rhythm of dread. She sprinted through the door, the other soldiers on her heels, thrust open the curtain and ran to the bedside. She touched her hand to his chest but he was breathing steadily. Fast asleep.

Cullen poked him and he still didn't stir.

Taz leaned closer and lifted his eyelids. "Drugged."

Her hand shot to her mouth as her thoughts whirled. "We ate separately."

"The villagers were helping Volkov. I saw one of them meet with him to the east of the town and the guy gave him horses," Cullen told her.

Baxter stuck his head through the door. "Four armed men dead. No identifying insignia."

Taz was checking Dempsey's vitals and Axelle tried to slow her breathing, but the fear she'd felt for him made her hands shake. This was crazy. Getting involved with a man who did this sort of thing on a daily basis was emotional suicide. Feeling this much reminded her of how desperately it hurt when it all went wrong.

To do something useful she gathered their few scattered belongings and stuffed them in Dempsey's pack.

"Is he okay?" Her voice wavered.

Cullen narrowed his gaze at her. "Any idea who the shooters were?"

Axelle shook her head. Cold to the bone. "No, but there were more of them in the mountains. Dempsey set off an avalanche and killed another four men." She caught Cullen's blue-eyed gaze. "We dug one guy out of the snow, but there was no identification on him either. Dempsey took a photo."

The soldiers looked at one another, Baxter keeping watch from the front door.

"What's going on?" A shiver rippled over her flesh as she realized how close she'd come to kidnap and death—again. She didn't want any of this. She wanted to be left alone with her cats, but Dempsey was lying unconscious on the bed.

Taz sat on the bed. "Why does Volkov want you so badly?"

She frowned. "I don't know." She huddled into her fleece, reached out a hand to touch Dempsey to reassure herself he was still alive. He felt solid and warm and immovable. "He saved me. I don't want anything to happen to him."

"We thought you were both dead," The controlled tone of Cullen's voice betrayed him. "We sent Josef back to camp while we came on, looking for bodies. Then Dempsey's GPS signal started pinging again and we busted a gut running here. Arrived in time to see Volkov leading you out the door."

"I woke up to him holding a gun on me. I figured if I left quietly, there was less chance of Dempsey getting hurt."

Cullen grinned. "You do know he's the one supposed to be protecting you, right? Not the other way around."

She hooked her hair behind her ear. "He already saved my life more times than I can count."

Taz lifted Dempsey's arm and let it flop back down. "He's out for the count."

Cullen frowned at his friend. "At least he's got a smile on his face." He waggled his brows at Axelle.

She pushed past him impatiently. "We need to talk to the elders."

Cullen grabbed her arm. "We will, but you're staying here."

She wrenched out of his grasp. "Why?"

She noted a glance flicker between the three men. Uncertainty. She crossed her arms. "You don't trust me?"

"That isn't it exactly." Cullen shrugged. "We need to protect you and Dempsey, and the easiest way to do that is by keeping you contained."

She narrowed her eyes to thin slits and stared him down.

"Me and Taz will talk to the locals. Baxter will be your look-out." The way his eyes strayed over Dempsey, she knew they'd all be watching her to make sure she didn't hurt Dempsey either. Which made no sense, but then none of this made any sense.

She walked forward until she was nose to nose with the pretty-boy soldier and gave him a shove. "That man on the bed rescued me from a sadistic bastard who'd kidnapped me and put me in an explosive vest. Dempsey led me through tunnels in the mountains—my own personal version of hell—and brought me out alive on the other side. I would *kill* for this man." She poked him in the chest again. "And if you think I'd hurt him in any way"—she had to pause for a moment to swallow her rage—"then you're more stupid than you look."

His eyes softened a notch and he held her by her upper arms, his grip gentle. "I found him in bed, drugged. I have no idea where you've both been for the past twenty-four hours. You were walking away with one of the world's most wanted terrorists when heavily armed men pop out of nowhere and try to kill you. Not just the terrorist. *You*. Now, I might not be a scientist and I may look pretty stupid, but don't let the handsome face fool you." He let her go. "Something fishy is going on and until I figure it out, or until Dempsey wakes up and tells me you are Mother-fucking Theresa, I'm being cautious. Is that okay with you?" With a nod he left her to Baxter's watchful eye. She sat on the bed beside Dempsey. Closed her eyes and wished them all to Hell.

————

Holy mother of God, his head ached like he'd downed ten pints of bitter and finished the night off with a bottle of Famous Grouse. Dempsey tried to open an eye but it hurt too much. He gave it five beats, then forced his lids apart, forced himself upright on the bed and waited for the world to settle. He scrubbed a hand over his face to try to wake himself up, but he felt like he had glue in his veins and it was all he could do not to throw up.

Baxter watched him from the door. Flashing a grin, the soldier walked toward him and handed him a canteen of water. Axelle lay asleep beside him, her mahogany hair fanning out against the red covers, her lips slightly parted. He took a swallow and washed away some of the sourness that coated his tongue. His memories were a little fuzzy but he was pretty sure he and Axelle had…*Christ*.

Exactly *when* had Baxter arrived?

He wiped his mouth with the back of his hand and forced himself to his feet. Sunlight shafted through the tiny windows. He walked to the front doorway—not that there was an actual door—and stepped outside. He peered at three local men digging graves in the hard-packed earth.

"What happened?" His voice sounded as though he was a forty-a-day smoker.

"You slept through the party." Baxter filled him in. Anger mounted up inside, but Dempsey held it back until Baxter finished.

"We were worried Dr. Dehn might be involved in some way."

"No. Axelle's an innocent in all this." Dempsey shook his head, trying to clear his thoughts. "We ate separately. They probably put something in that tea that tastes like piss anyway." His stomach churned. "Any idea what they gave me?"

Baxter shook his head. "I figure Taz and Cullen will get it out of the chief there."

Dempsey nodded. "Volkov is trying to use Axelle as leverage for something. I just don't know what it is."

Who were these other shooters? Snake eaters? Why try to kill Axelle—unless they just didn't want any witnesses? Shit. He didn't know.

"Watch her," he said then strode across the dusty square and walked straight into the chief's abode. He nodded to Cullen, who was sitting talking to the leathery faced old sod.

Cullen grinned.

The old man's eyes swept over him and widened. He stood stiffly, bent with age, and bowed from the waist. "I must apologize. I do not know how drugs got into your body. Your soldier assures me it must have happened while you were here in my home, and I am deeply shamed."

Dempsey ignored the old man. He'd once watched his father

feed a couple of squaddies tea and biscuits in their farmhouse kitchen, all full of chat and smiles. Half an hour later, they'd bombed the army checkpoint where one of the lads had been on duty. He'd been sent home in a box and never made it past his teens.

This man's wife and daughters stared at him from what he assumed was the kitchen. They averted their eyes but not before he saw fear in the old woman's eyes. These people had seen a lifetime of war and treachery. Damn, he didn't want to add to it, but shit… He looked away.

Old photographs were propped in various places of honor on an antique wooden cupboard. He scanned them. Plucked one grainy black-and-white image from the pile.

"This man." He held the photo beneath the elder's nose. "You were friends?"

The old man shook his head.

"You're lying." The photo showed a much younger Dmitri Volkov. "This man is a known terrorist who taught Islamic extremists everything they needed to know so they could vaporize innocent civilians."

The old man's jaw looked thin and fragile but it firmed up. "You are mistaken. The man in that photograph saved this village from the Soviets when they were shooting anything that moved and burning everything you could eat." The unfocused eyes sharpened. "That man in that photograph died many years ago."

Dempsey held his tongue and rifled through the other photos in the man's collection. Most of them were black and white or sepia. He didn't know what he was looking for and slammed them down in frustration. Nothing made sense. Then he collected all the photographs and slid them into a pocket. The old man looked stricken. "I'll make sure you get these back." He looked at Cullen. "Did you radio HQ?"

Cullen nodded and they went outside to talk. "We'll have another two four-man squads in a couple of hours. You sure Axelle Dehn isn't involved in any of this?"

Dempsey might have blacked out after he'd made love to Axelle, but he remembered everything that had happened in the run-up to that perfect, glorious moment.

"I'm sure. Volkov's trying to use her but her father isn't falling for the bait. I'm surprised the Americans haven't turned up yet."

They looked at one another.

"You don't think...?" Cullen looked toward the four corpses, neatly wrapped and ready for burial.

"I fucking hope not because there's another four on the mountain who won't defrost until spring. Do you know which way he went?" he asked, meaning Volkov.

Cullen pointed south to the Boroghill Pass. "He's running scared."

Maybe.

They had to follow him ASAP but they couldn't take Axelle with them and he wouldn't risk leaving her behind with these people. "Get HQ on the blower. I want a helo here, ASAP, dropping off reinforcements and getting Axelle to safety." He had a job to do. His heart battered his ribs when she appeared in the doorway of their hut and looked his way. Her eyes were narrowed, mouth pinched, and yet he'd never seen a more beautiful sight in his life.

He didn't want to leave her but he needed her safe.

A subtle vibration lit the air. As one, the troopers cocked their heads and held their weapons higher. The villagers ran back to their huts. He jogged over the dirt courtyard and caught Axelle's hand and dragged her back inside. Helicopters. If they were friendly, bloody great. If they were foe, unless one of the boys had found an old Stinger missile lying around, they were in for the fight of their lives.

———

Axelle stared at the soldiers who stepped out of the helicopter and felt the tangible release of tension from the four men around her. Dempsey ran out to talk to the man on the door of the chopper. Then he jogged back to her, the expression on his face freezing the words she wanted to say to him. He took her arm and pulled her into the bedroom they'd shared. The room where they'd made love a few short hours ago. She pushed the memories aside. It was done. Finished. A moment of happiness in a lifetime of loneliness.

"The pilot agreed to give you a ride back to base camp. You should head back to the States as soon as you can, until it's safe to return."

She started shaking. Whatever she'd expected it hadn't been this abrupt departure, and she couldn't explain the feelings that ripped through her at the thought of leaving him. He was a soldier on a mission. Not a holiday romance. He had to go. More important, *she* had to go. There was work to do.

"You're going after Volkov?" she asked. Her teeth chattered, but neither of them mistook it for cold.

His vivid blue eyes stared hard into hers. A muscle ticked in his jaw. All the years of doing everything by herself crowded inside her. All that experience of pushing people away surged up in an unstoppable wave. She raised her hand to stop him when he started to speak.

"Good, because I need to get back and see how the leopards are doing. Reevaluate the project. See if the cubs are okay." Her voice cracked. Why was this so hard? She wrapped her arms tight around herself and took a step away. She felt colder than she had during that blizzard. Colder than jumping into a frozen lake. She didn't want Dempsey to go. She didn't want to be alone anymore. But he was a soldier—this was what he did.

And this awful aching heartbreak was exactly why she didn't get involved.

"Axelle—"

"Please...don't say goodbye." Her plea turned into a sob as he took a step closer. "The last time I said goodbye to a soldier he died. I can't go through that again."

He said nothing but his eyes spoke volumes. *This* was his reality. He might not come home. Even if he did survive, the chance of them ever seeing each other again was nonexistent. This was goodbye.

She needed to tell him things. Important things. Meaningful things. She opened her mouth and nothing came out. She reached out and took his hand. "I don't know how to thank you for everything."

The memory of them coming together last night flashed through her mind and she saw it reflected in his expression. He squeezed his eyes shut and raised his face to the ceiling. She watched his Adam's apple bob as he swallowed whatever words he wanted to say. There was no way out of this. This was the end for them.

She raised herself on tiptoes and kissed his cheek though he didn't move and didn't look at her. "So, thank you for everything, Sergeant."

His fingers tightened on her arms for a moment and then he let her go.

She ran out of the hut, forcing a smile and wave for Dempsey's men and blinking away the sudden onslaught of tears that wanted to drown her in misery. She had promised herself a crying jag once she escaped the mountain; she just needed to hold it together for a few minutes longer. She jogged across the hard-packed earth, bending instinctively away from the threat of the rotors. One of the crew pulled her on board, and like that they were airborne, her heart falling out of her chest as the ground dropped away. She watched Dempsey as he stood in the village square, staring after her.

Some things weren't meant to be.

Maybe she was meant to be alone. But there was this physical pain at the thought she'd never see him again. A sickness that wanted to take a bite out of her soul.

A crewman offered her water and she shook herself out of her melancholy. She yanked her gaze from the man on the ground because he'd been a short interlude and now it was time to get back to reality. Her leopards should hopefully be safe again. Now she had to get back to camp and decide the way forward for the project. For the first time ever the thought didn't excite her. She slumped against the unforgiving metal sides of the chopper.

Maybe she was just tired.

She closed her eyes against the majesty of the mountains and a sky that reminded her of one man's eyes. One man she needed to forget. One man she was terrified she'd never get over.

CHAPTER
FOURTEEN

DEMPSEY ORGANIZED the men into groups and they pored over maps—ironically Russian-made and probably by Dmitri Volkov—and checked gear and comms. He did not think about the sadness of Axelle's mouth, or the tumult of emotions washing through her eyes. He didn't think about how it had gone against every instinct inside him to send her away. He just did his job, followed orders the way he had for the past two decades, ignoring the unsettled turmoil going on inside him.

"Same squads as before then?" Captain Robert Prentice was the requisite officer on the op. The team had worked out a new plan together, based on their knowledge of the situation, with eyes in the sky and boots on the ground, taking into account someone else was also looking for Dmitri Volkov.

Dempsey nodded. "One team tracks him directly, the rest circle and flank. Pretty sure he's lost all his communication equipment so we should be okay to talk over the PRR and secure radio."

"We've discovered his grandson is sick and needs a liver transplant," said Captain Prentice.

Dempsey drew in a tight breath. That was why he'd reappeared after a decade as a ghost. "He was trying to use Dr. Dehn as some sort of leverage to get his grandson treatment?" He couldn't help it, it changed his outlook a little. No one knew better than him that bombers and terrorists were flesh-and-blood people with families, lives and hopes. And shedloads of regrets.

"Seems that way. The Russians have had tight restrictions on the family leaving the country for years." The captain laughed. "Ironically, the last time one of them left it was Dmitri's son, Sergei. He was part of a trade delegation to New York in September 2001."

Dempsey reared back. "He died in 9/11?"

The captain nodded.

"That's not irony, that's bloody tragedy." Dempsey ground his teeth together.

"The irony is Volkov helped these bastards in the first place. Now everyone and his ruddy cat is looking for the man's dying grandson in the hopes of controlling the old bastard and finding out everything he knows."

"I don't like the idea of using kids as pawns." Dempsey planted his boot on a rock.

"The boy is the grandson of one of the world's worst terrorists. Shit happens." The officer tried to look down his Sandhurst nose at Dempsey but he had to tilt his head too far back to get there.

"You can't make the kid pay for the crimes of the father." Dempsey held the naive gaze of the young officer.

Captain Prentice frowned uncertainly, unsure what had happened, but knowing he'd somehow upset the most experienced man on his team. There was an unwritten rule in the SAS: Don't fuck with the NCOs if you wanted to make it out of an op still breathing.

His own service record spoke for itself. He had more years in than anyone else here, and yet he still felt the need to prove himself every fucking day because of mentalities like this guy's. "At least the poor little bugger probably has a better chance of survival if we pick him up, rather than the Russians."

They'd used facial recognition on the dead men. Spetsnaz. The Russians wanted Dmitri dead. No surprise there.

Dempsey got his head out of his ass and got ready to move out. "Watch out for this fecker. He's a sniper, plus he could set mines, tripwires, and he moves like a bloody greyhound. He knows all the hidey holes not marked on this map. Plus, he has friends here in this valley, people who'll help him." He let his eyes stray over the locals. They'd leave behind a squad here and use the position as their forward operating center, see if they could build some positive rapport by the medics treating any health issues in the village.

Hearts and minds.

But somehow Dmitri Volkov had already beaten them in the race for hearts and minds. They were playing catch-up in a place very few people cared about.

Dempsey tapped the photos in his breast pocket, scanned the crowd and felt the dull thump of his pulse as he realized he was looking for Axelle. He looked at the sky and blinked hard. Axelle was gone.

She'd forget about him the moment she got back to her leopards.

The sun burned his eyes, and his throat felt like someone had stripped it with turpentine. He gripped his carbine and jerked his chin. "Time to move out."

———

A chauffeur-driven limo pulled up outside Jonathon's Fulham home and he locked his front door behind him. He'd bought this terraced home in the late Fifties before the area got trendy. After his wife and daughter died, he'd had it divided into three flats, and made enough money from the rental to buy a property near the coast, plus a smart little yacht.

The chauffeur opened the car door for him and Jonathon climbed in.

"Good morning," he said to Rear Admiral Walter Jenkins. *Arrogant old sot.* The driver shut the door and climbed into his seat, nosed out into rush-hour traffic.

"Finally see what these people think is so ruddy Top Secret, huh?" Walter grumbled, helping himself to coffee.

"Some James Bond space weapon, I'm sure." Jonathon replied drolly, then opened his paper. He yawned. It had been a late night. An operational success, not to mention physically pleasurable. Just as well he'd waited until afterwards to tell Lucinda his secret though. Poor woman had turned into a blithering wreck when he'd told her beloved Sebastian had been shot in the back by a Soviet traitor. How long would it take her to tell her son, he wondered, glancing at his watch. Had she phoned him straightaway? No, she'd brood for a few hours. Have a shower and try to pretend she hadn't spent the night shagging her husband's best friend before she phoned David. He checked his watch again. He should have plenty of time.

"They probably got the idea from Ian Fleming." The admiral laughed at his own wit.

"Art mimicking life mimicking art?" Jonathon raised a brow and crossed his legs. The admiral looked uneasy at the effeminate gesture and inched back, nursing his coffee as the driver weaved through the commuter lanes. Jonathon smiled.

"I see Warwick were all out for fifty-five." Jonathon knew the other man supported Yorkshire. The man preened and Jonathon told him the rest of the cricket scores. He'd always been fascinated by the loyalty people had to their place of birth.

They stopped off to pick up the next member of the committee. He hid a smile but excitement made his chest hum. Dmitri Volkov was being hunted by some of the most deadly forces in existence. No way would he get the chance to open his disloyal mouth before they put pretty little bullet holes in his hide. And as soon as

Jonathon found the rest of the Volkov clan, he was looking forward to wiping them out too. One rat at a time.

———

Axelle stared in disbelief as Sir Ian Turner, OBE, Chairman of the Conservation Trust, threw back the flap of her tent and walked out. She thanked the helicopter crew for the ride. They'd wanted to take her to a military base, but hadn't balked too much when she'd explained she had to pack up her equipment and would get the next available flight out. *Yeah. Right.*

She jumped down. Josef and Anji both ran toward her and she was engulfed in Josef's giant hug.

"I thought you were dead," he shouted over the noise of the departing chopper. Emotion was stark on the big man's face and he grabbed her for another hug. "Oh my God. I thought you were dead."

Anji hopped on his heels. "You safe. You safe."

Axelle clasped Josef for a moment and smiled at Anji. She waved at the departing chopper, watching until it disappeared over the next bluff, and used the time to contemplate why the big boss was here.

"I got trapped inside a mountain." She let herself shudder. Dempsey had taught her it was okay to show weakness. It didn't actually make you weak.

"You're okay? The soldier? He found you? He's alive?" Anxiety was clear in Josef's gaze.

A surge of pain hit. Fresh. Devastating. He wasn't dead. He was just gone. "He saved my life, but they didn't catch the poacher yet. That man is still on the run and the soldiers are tracking him." She held her boss's gaze. "What are you doing here, Ian?"

He looked uncertain for a moment. "We should talk inside."

"No. You can speak in front of Josef and Anji. They deserve to know what's going on." She braced her arms across her chest and widened her stance. She had the feeling whatever he had to say, the others would find out soon enough anyway.

He shifted his feet. Took a breath. "I'm afraid I'm going to have to relieve you of your position as project head."

"What are you talking about?" Her voice dropped low but the guy didn't catch on to the danger.

He stretched his brows high and wide, looking both obsequious and dismissive. "You've willfully disregarded the Trust's orders and have been responsible for the death of several leopards and the removal of three radio collars against clear instruction. We've lost at least half of the sample size—"

"I saved the lives of as many leopards as I could from a ruthless poacher."

"From what I understand he wasn't after the leopards at all." He swatted a fly. "He was after you, which makes you unfit for this position."

Her fingers curved into fists. Axelle looked at the ground. She could argue the point, but that was the reality of what had happened. "Who's taking over?" Her bones felt like they'd crumbled. Leopards were dead and it was her fault.

He pressed his lips together, clearly surprised by her lack of opposition. Josef looked like he'd been pole-axed.

"Myself for now." He was an asshole administrator but had once been an adequate wildlife biologist. "Until we can bring someone else out here for the long term."

There would be plenty of volunteers for such an exciting and illustrious position.

"What about Josef?"

Turner looked uneasy. "He's going to have to transfer supervisor if he hopes to continue—"

Josef stirred his mountainous frame. "Dr. Dehn is the best in the world at what she does but you make me work with someone else?"

"I'm not making you do anything," Turner snapped. "You can quit any time you want. Dr Dehn has set this project back decades. Do you know how much bad publicity hurts an organization like ours?"

"Don't yell at Josef. He didn't do anything wrong." God, she was tired. She could barely stand, let alone argue, but she walked over to Turner. "You find Josef a decent supervisor or I'll sue both you *and* the Trust for unfair dismissal. I was kidnapped and nearly died during the rescue and the first thing you do is *fire* me? Oh, yeah, that's gonna look real good in the press. And given who my father is, believe me there is gonna be press." She shoved past the man and into the main yurt. She booted her laptop and Sat Link.

Anji came and stood beside her. "I am sorry, Dr. Dehn." He wrung his fingers together.

Axelle forced herself to take a steadying breath and give him a smile. "You are the most important person here." He would train more rangers. Protect more leopards than she could ever hope to reach. "I'm relying on you, Anji. Don't let me down." The way she'd let everyone down.

She felt numb. Dead inside. It was a sensation she recognized and no longer felt comfortable with. Her adventures with Tyrone Dempsey had changed her life; it was time to try to find a new normal.

Turner came inside, but she ignored him, busy checking her email and packing things away. "Where are the cubs?" she asked Anji.

"I sent them to Kabul," Turner answered instead. "They will be raised in the zoo there. A symbol of hope for the future of Afghanistan."

Everything inside her stilled. A hot rage engulfed her body. "A symbol of hope? I asked you to send someone out here to try and keep them habilitated to the wild. *That* would have been a symbol of hope, not a goddamned cage."

"It wasn't feasible—"

"You never even tried!" she yelled. "You could have done something revolutionary, something extraordinary, but you didn't even try." Fury burned through her, melting her fatigue, her misery. She'd almost died and this pompous ass hadn't even broken a sweat in his efforts to save the leopards from a fucking concrete zoo. The director of Kabul Zoo himself had said endangered species had no place in his zoo. It was too volatile. Too open to attack.

"You've said enough, Dr. Dehn. Pack your belongings and leave immediately. There's a flight that you can catch this afternoon."

She jerked out the leads to the laptop and Sat Link.

"What do you think you're doing?" Turner took a step forward and put his hands on her elbow.

She faced him and made sure he understood exactly what would happen if he touched her again. "This is *my* equipment, and as I'm no longer wanted here, I assume you remembered to bring your own?" It was small. It was childish. It felt magnificent. "The van's mine too. Josef and Anji can use it, but *you* do *not* have permission." She carefully placed each piece of equipment in its case and pictured him on the dirt bike or one of the horses, which did belong to the Trust.

"You can't do this. It'll take at least ten days to replace this stuff." He put his hand on her arm and she thought about breaking his fingers. "Think of the animals—"

She pushed him away. "The animals are all I ever think about, you jerk. You can collect scat and hair samples until the new equipment gets here. Now get out of my way."

She went to her yurt and saw that Turner had already made himself comfortable. The mourning period had been brief. She stripped the room of everything that belonged to her, including the sheets and pillow on the hard cot.

"I can come with you." Josef spoke quietly from the doorway.

"Stay here. Help Anji." Emotion threatened to make her knees crumple but she couldn't afford that weakness. "At least someone who knows what they're doing should be here for our cats."

He caught her hand and held her gaze. In his eyes she read feelings that had nothing to do snow leopards. How had she missed all the signals?

Because she'd been dead inside. Until Dempsey she'd been an emotional black hole regarding anything except her animals. She touched his dear face. "I can't be anything other than your friend and supporter, Josef. Even if I wasn't your supervisor…"

He took in a deep breath and closed his eyes. "I know." He pressed his lips together. "I'll stay here for now. See what you can do once you get back to Montana. I want to work for you, not that asshole. Not because…" He cleared his throat, then forged on. "Not because of my feelings, but because you're the best conservation biologist in the world and the Trust is treating you like shit. And I called them in."

"You had to, Josef. You thought I was dead, remember? Give me a week. I'll fix this."

She wasn't going back to Montana. Not yet. She needed to see her father, a man she hadn't spoken to in months. She needed to know if he'd ordered an airstrike even though she might die in it.

"Take care of our cats, Josef." She held his bloodshot gaze, tried not to pity him the same way she hoped Dempsey wouldn't pity her. At the door Anji shifted nervously from one foot to the other. "Now which one of you is giving me a ride to Kurut?"

She smiled when they both hopped in the van. In the rearview, Turner paced uselessly around camp. His visit reminded her why she hated politics and would rather live in a tent in the wilderness than deal with bloodsuckers like him. But this was her new reality and she was going to have to deal with it, whether she liked it or not.

Dempsey's patrol had been dropped by helo deep into the Hindu Kush. The ground was soft as most of the fresh snow had melted over the past twenty-four hours. They had a sighting of their prey over the next ridge, heading straight toward them. The old man wasn't slowing down. It was as if he was possessed. Dempsey used hand signals and Cullen and Baxter faded east. He and Taz hunkered down behind a boulder the size of a small car.

He wanted this bastard. He wanted him so badly he was drowning in it. He waited. Calmed his breathing, felt Taz doing the same thing beside him. They couldn't afford to give themselves away. The Russian was running from the team on his tail and Dempsey didn't want this to turn into a firefight or standoff. Nor did he want Spetsnaz turning up and starting WW III.

He'd been ordered to kill the man.

The bosses hadn't couched it in exactly those terms, but "terminating the threat" seemed pretty unambiguous to him. He remembered the look of terror on Axelle's face when he'd found her wearing that suicide vest. Oh, yeah, he could kill the old fucker for that alone.

There, finally, the lean shape of his quarry ran toward them with his head down, clutching his side and dragging his left foot. Still he moved doggedly and determinedly. Dempsey couldn't see any weapons, but the old guy could have a handgun in his pocket. Or a grenade.

When he got thirty feet away Dempsey stood, sighted the gun, and the old man stumbled to the ground, mud splattering in his wake.

Dempsey walked toward the old man as he lay there panting. "Hands up. Let me see them empty, Volkov, else your grandson will never get the help he needs."

Dmitri lifted his head and stretched his hands slowly into the air. "My grandson? You have heard from my grandson?"

Dempsey stepped closer. "I know he's sick. I know he shouldn't be punished for your crimes. The same way you shouldn't have hurt an innocent woman to try and force your demands."

"I didn't hurt her. I could have blown you all up a thousand times but I didn't." Dmitri struggled to his knees, keeping his hands nice and wide. Dempsey did not trust this wily old bastard, but he had a point. He hadn't set any booby traps and he'd saved the cubs' lives.

These were not the acts of a completely vicious man.

"I did what I had to do to get my grandson out of Russia. Now what?" The old man's eyes narrowed and he smiled. "I bet they told you to kill me, didn't they?" He laughed. "Getting an English soldier to shoot me here in this valley seems like the perfect irony."

Orders *had* changed. Why? There were a lot of questions about what was going on here that only this man could answer. Who wanted him dead? More important, why?

Taz raised a questioning brow at him. They were soldiers. They weren't cold-blooded killers even though some people couldn't tell the difference. There were rules of engagement. But there were also direct orders.

Dempsey had never failed on a mission and always followed orders...except for rescuing Axelle out of that cave.

He wasn't paid to make the big decisions. He was a soldier. He was a damn good sergeant, and proud to be part of the best regiment on earth. He took another step and watched the light in the old man's eyes change from defiant to pleading. Volkov raised his chin. "I don't care about me, but please help my grandson."

Dempsey nodded. "You have my word." Then he pulled the trigger.

———

There had been a delay. The demonstration the scientists had organized hadn't happened. They'd toured the facilities—nothing new or exciting to report there. And now they'd been stuffed into the nearest hotel and left to twiddle their thumbs overnight. Still, this kept him conveniently out of the way if Lucinda let slip how she'd come by the information about Sebastian's death to her overprotective son.

He didn't want his lights punched out.

Jonathon sipped a nice Bordeaux. Maybe he should pursue Lucinda on a more public level… He mulled the idea over. It had merit. An inside track to the PM. Prestige. Regular sex. It was an interesting thought. He pushed his lips out as he contemplated the pros and cons. Trouble was if Dmitri's little surprise did occur, then Jonathon could be arrested and charged with treason. He wasn't about to spend the last years of his life in some little cell when he could receive a hero's welcome back in Moscow. No. As soon as he discovered what secrets Aldermaston was hiding he was going home. Finally.

In the meantime, he savored his roast beef dinner. He might as well enjoy himself at the British taxpayers' expense.

Really, it was what he did best.

———

"You're sure he's dead?" Captain Prentice asked for the fifth time.

"You can dig him up if you like," Dempsey told the younger man.

Baxter tossed down the spade, making it clear he wasn't digging up what he'd just put in the ground. It was hot. Too fucking hot for digging graves in this thin shallow soil.

Dempsey handed the officer a bloody shirt and a photograph of the dead Dmitri Volkov. "That should match the DNA we have on file and, if it doesn't, then what we have on file is bollocks." He held the man's gaze. "He's dead."

Dempsey wanted no mistakes here. No doubt. He was not a man who'd ever let his bosses down. With his background he couldn't afford to.

The chopper hovered over the hill and the captain jogged off. Mission accomplished.

Thank Christ for that. Dempsey sat tight for another ten minutes waiting for the next bird. They needed to get back to Hereford ASAP. They needed to debrief inside RAF Credenhill. Frustration squeezed his chest because he wanted to talk to Axelle. Desperately wanted to tell her all the things that had stuck in his throat earlier because he hadn't known how to deal with everything he was feeling and wanted—and yes, he wanted.

She didn't exactly work down the road from him even when he was stationed in Britain. Although distance seemed like the least of the obstacles to their relationship.

Crap.

Fuck.

Relationship?

He rolled his eyes skyward. She wasn't interested in a relationship. But there had been something in her eyes when they said goodbye…something that connected them on a fundamental level. He'd never felt that sort of connection before and he wanted to explore it. It was time to see if it actually meant something. Time to take a chance on something beside the military.

He'd email her, although what the hell he'd say he had no clue. Email wouldn't look at him the way she did. Email wouldn't let him touch her soft skin or smell her hair. *Shit*. Now was not the time to be mooning over a woman.

When he heard the rotors growing louder he nodded to Taz, who stood and pulled away a filthy desert tarp that had hidden the gaunt, bleeding old man who now staggered stiffly to his feet. Time to go. They pulled a camouflage smock over the Russian's head and gave him a hat. They had to get the man to the hangar where they could stow him with the gear. It wouldn't be a comfortable ride back to Blighty but it beat a 9 mm round to the temple.

Time to see what the hell was happening and hope he wasn't about to lose his career because of an unwelcome epiphany. He was a soldier, not a killer. Although it wasn't the Geneva Convention he'd been thinking about when he hadn't murdered Volkov in cold blood. It had been his humanity.

CHAPTER FIFTEEN

ON THE FLIGHT TO Heathrow Axelle ignored the man next to her, who alternated between trying to hit on her and angling to stare down the front of her top.

Kabul airport had looked more like a war zone than a commercial airport. She flexed her fingers. Somewhere in that city of ruin and desperation, two tiny cubs tumbled around a dirty broken cage to be prodded and stared at like spectacles in a circus.

It sickened her that the organization that should have been moving heaven and earth to care for them in their natural habitat had buckled under the pressure of sensational headlines and political fallout.

Now she was on a flight out of Pakistan, and the hours of mindless travel had given her time to think about what the Trust had done and her anger kept growing. She'd been trapped under a damn mountain. They had to have assumed she was dead. Rather than celebrate her survival, they'd got pissy because she'd done what she had to do to try to save the leopards.

She turned her head and the man next to her lifted his glance from her nonexistent breasts. Sandy-haired, square-faced, he wore a dark green suit jacket that had a sheen from overuse. His pants were brown cord and his shoes were slip-ons that looked at least a decade old. Axelle wasn't into appearances, but he was hitting on her in a crowded aircraft and all she could think was he was no Tyrone Dempsey.

"You on vacation?" he asked. The lines on his face put him over forty, possibly over fifty. He had one of those completely forgettable, nondescript faces.

"Do I look like I'm on vacation?" Her clothes were dusty with travel grime, stained with various unknown substances. She hadn't showered in more days than she cared to remember but the guy didn't seem to care. He must be into grunge.

His eyes slid down her face, and he gave her a semi-hopeful smile. Jeez, the man must be simple, or desperate. She eyed him with the sort of expression that made stones squirm. Nothing worked.

"You look like you've been on a backpacking adventure."

She huffed out an exasperated laugh. Understatement. Some of what she'd been through hit her and she turned away and stared out the window. Her fingers clutched each other in her lap. Every time she closed her eyes, she saw Dempsey's smile and felt his lips on hers. They hadn't talked. Not properly. He'd shoved her on an aircraft, and she'd gone because she'd been too dazed and too proud to do anything else.

Her fellow traveler turned on a movie and she ignored him for the rest of the trip; she wasn't in the mood for idle conversation. Three of her precious cats had died and it was her fault. Volkov had said her family owed him a blood debt but she didn't understand. Her mother had been killed by a terrorist bomb. Dmitri's bomb? Or someone else's? She didn't know but maybe her father did.

Finally they were almost in the UK. The sky over London was the sort of solar blue that made you believe in global warming.

"Where are you staying? In London?" The guy next to her asked.

She turned her head to pin him with her gaze. He didn't flinch. He was goddamn persistent, though obviously not very bright, despite the handsome enough face and modulated English accent.

She buttoned her olive green shirt over her tank top, all the way to her throat.

"Do you have a number I could call you on?"

"My cell doesn't work in the UK." A lie. She wasn't naturally a cruel person. Or maybe she was. Hell, she didn't even know anymore. But she wasn't interested in him.

The plane landed with a minor bump. She collected her laptop and bag from the overhead locker and headed for the exit. Seconds later she was striding away along the epic walkways, her legs outstripping most people who were struggling with fatigue and excess baggage.

Agitation swirled. She hadn't told her father she was coming. She'd wanted to surprise him, but a tiny part of her admitted she was slightly scared of arriving unannounced. He was a busy man. Austere and powerful, his loyalty was always first to his country and second to his family.

She wanted to catch him off his formidable guard. See his reaction when he saw her and she told him about being buried alive—again—and see if he'd had anything to do with it.

The urge to see if she could track down Dempsey was strong, but chances were he was still in the Wakhan chasing that insane old Russian. If she tried to find him she'd probably end up being arrested or something. She bit her lip to stop herself thinking about him. She couldn't afford the angst of daydreaming about a man she couldn't have. Why would she even be attracted to a soldier who might die any day? A man who dealt in bullets the way she dealt in academic timetables and GPS coordinates?

It was crazy. After losing Gideon to war, she'd be damned if she'd go down that route again. She knew better than to open herself up to anyone. Getting close led to vulnerability. Vulnerability led to pain. Better to stay alone, then she wouldn't get hurt.

Except alone felt goddamn lonely.

She hit customs and stood in line, a little disconcerted to see the man who'd sat beside her on the plane, ahead of her in the enormous snaking queue. He hadn't looked like he could move that fast. She inched forward, a mother and her toddler in a stroller ahead of her. The little girl had hair that stuck up on end and enough food encrusted on her clothes to ensure that she'd survive for days in an emergency. Axelle smiled and the child started to cry.

She rolled her eyes. Story of her life.

She got to the customs agent and handed over her passport.

"Reason for your visit?"

"I'm visiting my father."

"Do you have an address where you'll be staying?"

Axelle shook her head. "I'm going to pick up a hotel room in the city. My father is the United States Ambassador."

The man's eyes looked completely unimpressed. "Wait here." He disappeared while Axelle sagged against the counter. She didn't usually try to strong-arm her way into a country using her connections, but she was tired and just wanted this journey over with. She scrubbed her hand over her face, trying to wake herself up. She should have known it would backfire.

"Follow me." The guard was back and leading her across the thin gray carpet to a side door. Armed men were stationed throughout the massive room. Nerves tingled despite her weariness and exhaustion. She followed the man and entered another series of corridors. Finally she found herself in a small interview room. Sitting at the table was the man she'd spent the past eight hours ignoring.

"What do they want with you?" she asked.

Those soft eyes and nondescript features sharpened and hardened into something surprisingly ruthless. A quick zip of her heart rate confirmed her error. She'd been set up.

"I'm the one doing the questioning, Dr. Dehn. You can begin by telling me what you were doing associating with a known terrorist in northern Afghanistan."

Associating? "I was kidnapped."

245

"The British and American embassies were never informed of any kidnapping."

She took a step toward him, wavering between falling over and smacking him in the jaw. "There wasn't time to tell the authorities and, anyway, do you think it was up to *me* to alert the authorities when I was the one bound hand and foot?"

"Sit down, Dr. Dehn."

She snorted. "So you can stare down my top again?"

His smile chilled her. "Not that I don't appreciate the perks of my job, but no. I want to know everything that happened between you and Dmitri Volkov. Everything he did. Everything he said. Sit. Now."

She hesitated but the message in the man's eyes was clear. She wasn't going anywhere until they had this conversation, and maybe not even then.

———

Dempsey closed his eyes and rested his head against the shell of the aircraft. Two dozen scruffy men dressed just like him were stretched out in sleep or sitting in groups, playing cards. His mouth felt dry. He had a feeling he'd just screwed himself over. Taz shot him a glance. Chances were he'd screwed them all over. He stared at the large flight cases and hoped the old bugger was still alive. Otherwise they'd be burying a corpse in the Welsh hills come midnight.

God help them if anyone ever dug him up.

As the plane landed in Brize Norton, he waited for most of the men to head back to base in the waiting minibuses before he motioned to his captain that he needed a word.

"What is it Dempsey?" The man's shoulders were slouched with tiredness.

He wasn't a bad officer. Just inexperienced.

"I've got a little confession to make, Captain." Dempsey stood to attention. "And I need you to know it was my decision and my troop was not in any way responsible—"

"We didn't kill the Russian," Cullen piped up.

Taz shook his head. "Though we did shoot him so he'd bleed—"

"All over that shirt you have in your plastic bag, boss," Baxter finished.

The captain's impressive jaw dropped and his skin blanched. "You did what?"

"We didn't kill him."

"You've got to be kidding me."

"No, sir!" the three stooges shouted.

His mates. His family.

Dempsey shook his head with an internal sigh. Tapped a crate with his toe. "We brought him back with us."

The box started talking. "Get me out of this box, stupid *mudak*. You are torturing me!"

Blood drained away from the captain's cheeks as he stared at the talking box. His hands started to shake. "You disobeyed orders—"

"I followed the rules of engagement—"

"You've got to be kidding." The captain backed away a step.

Dempsey grabbed his arm and stared him dead in the eye. "Something is going on. Something that doesn't make any sense. I'm almost blown to shit. The American ambassador's daughter is almost blown to shit. Russian Spetsnaz forces are doing their best to start a war over this guy. He's been inactive for years and yet we're ordered to kill the old fecker, rather than apprehend? Why? I mean, he isn't Bin Laden. No one is going to rally to his war cry. Hardly anyone even knows he exists." Dempsey could see the cogs turning in the officer's mind. He kept his voice low and fervent. "He knows stuff that could help in the war on terror. Save lives."

"I'm not telling you anything until you find my grandson and get him a liver transplant." Volkov yelled from the box. "Get me out of here."

The captain looked around to see what everyone else was thinking. Realized belatedly it was just the five of them and the captured Russian.

"The Firm is up to something." Taz stood by his side.

"Civil serpents," said Cullen.

Dempsey put his not inconsiderable frame in front of the ranking officer. "I didn't mention it before now because I didn't want to be diverted to a black camp or shot down on the way home." The captain's eyes flashed. "Because whatever they're all scared of is worth more than a plane full of soldiers."

"You really think the Russians would start a war over this guy? Why?"

"That's what we need to find out." Although to be fair, he hadn't said it would be the Russians shooting them out of the sky. "Did you leave your Jeep here?"

The captain nodded. Dempsey tilted his head toward Taz, Cullen and Baxter. "Grab the luggage, lads." He tossed an extra kitbag to the captain who staggered under the weight. "We'll bring the rest."

———

"What the hell were you thinking, Sergeant? You've put the Regiment in an untenable position."

Apparently, getting a new asshole did hurt. Funny that.

"I was put in an untenable position when I was ordered to shoot an unarmed man, sir." Dempsey stood at ease but didn't drop his guard. "The Geneva Convention—"

"I am well aware of the Geneva fucking Convention, Sergeant." Flinty eyes of the Regiment's CO stared him down.

"Sir." Dempsey lowered his voice. "You know something

weird is going on here. GCHQ bomb the fucker. The Russians sending Special Forces after him."

"He's a deserter; they have a right to him. More than we do."

"He deserted more than thirty years ago, but they still want him dead. The Yanks want him dead too."

"He's a terrorist! Everyone wants him dead. The change in orders from capture to kill came direct from the PM, and you disobeyed." A court-martial offense. The CO pulled on his lower lip, thinking. It was no secret the CO was a true-blue Tory, but no soldier liked politicians messing with their army. Recent cuts and bad military decisions had deepened the growing divide.

"Why is this old soldier worth so much to so many?"

The CO remained quiet for a moment, then added, "I had a report the Volkov family managed to sneak out of Russia and walked into the American Embassy in Paris, claiming asylum. There are rumors the Aga Khan had a hand in whisking them away from under the nose of the Russian authorities. They have a boy with them who is in desperate need of medical treatment."

Which confirmed Volkov's story. "Can they get him sorted?"

"The Americans can probably keep him alive long enough to receive the operation he needs, as long as someone is willing to pay their price."

"The price is?"

"Volkov." From the look on the CO's face, this wasn't good news.

"They know he's alive?"

"They suspect. Someone was watching that satellite feed *very* carefully." Dempsey had been afraid of that. Still it had bought them enough time to get home. That was something.

"Any reason we can't hand him over to the Yanks?"

The CO spat out a laugh. "Yes. Our esteemed new PM won't allow it. Seems he has some sort of personal grudge against Volkov that he'll even risk the old 'special relationship' for."

Sweat broke out over Dempsey's brow. He'd promised the old man he'd get the boy the treatment he needed. He didn't fancy breaking into the American Embassy in Paris to keep his word. On top of everything he had this driving need to talk to Axelle, to make sure she was okay back in her quaint little yurt. Because there was this feeling in the pit of his stomach that they'd somehow stoked a hornets' nest, and she was the most likely to get stung. She'd become important to him. Very important.

"I put the Regiment in a difficult position, sir. I'm sorry. I didn't mean to do that. I was concerned we were being played by spooks and God knows who." He resisted fidgeting. He still didn't know if he'd fucked up or not, but at least he hadn't executed an unarmed old man. He could live with that. After twenty-two years in the army, he'd finally made peace with his past. He'd finally done enough to forgive himself his heritage and could live with his choices even if he got kicked out of the Regiment. Axelle had a hand in that.

"You're a good soldier, Dempsey. As far as you're concerned you were following *my* personal orders, got it?"

Dempsey blinked in surprise. The man was saving his ass, possibly at his own expense. "Why? Why would you go to bat for a man like me, sir?"

"A man like you?" Keen gray eyes assessed him. "You know way back when you applied for selection?"

Dempsey nodded.

"I was there, son. No one ever intended for you to get in to the Regiment."

His eyes widened.

"Trouble was, no matter what we threw at you, you never gave up. You never stopped fighting. You never quit. The DSs started looking at one another and shrugging as if to say, 'I'm not going to axe the best guy here.' The hypocrisy was too great. We kept waiting for you to fail. To not make the cut, but you just kept coming." The man smiled and Dempsey felt emotion expanding in his chest so much he couldn't speak. "Then the Regimental CO at the time called a meeting and said something that stuck in my mind ever since. That you were probably one of the few soldiers who really understood what we were fighting for in Northern Ireland. Having lost your sister to your father's bomb, *you* understood the stakes better than any of us. So you passed and have been a great asset to the Regiment ever since."

Dempsey's mouth felt as dry as the Gobi.

"Now I need to make some phone calls. You keep Volkov secure before the various factions arrive to start a tug-o-war over him."

"And the grandson?" Dempsey grated out.

"Not in my remit, Sergeant. Not in yours either."

No, but making a pawn out of a child's life didn't sit well. Didn't sit well at all.

———

"Do you deny you spent a day in Dmitri Volkov's company?"

Axelle didn't bother trying to hide her utter disbelief. She leaned across a small square table and told herself not to hit the sonofabitch. They'd been over this ten times already. He was trying to rile her. "He kidnapped me, twice, shot at me, and strapped me into an explosive vest. It was hardly frickin' date night."

"So you say."

Whoa, the guy's eyes contained the same emotion as a bullet, but a bullet was warmer.

She tapped a foot. "I don't get why you're even interviewing me."

"Because you spent time with—"

"I get that." She raised her voice. "It doesn't make any sense."

His brows crunched together.

"I was kidnapped and you guys sent in a freakin' airplane's worth of bombs to blow us both to smithereens. The only reason

I'm alive is a soldier saved my ass and found us a way out of the mountain."

His face remained impassive. "What did you talk about with the Russian? Did he tell you what he wanted?"

She felt trapped and wanted to pace up and down like some caged animal. She sank her fingers into her hair, trying to remember everything so they'd let her go. She had nothing to hide. "He told me my family owed him. That it was a blood debt and it didn't matter if I died because my family deserved it. Something like that anyway."

The man in the green jacket wrote it all down. "What else did he say?"

"Nothing."

"What about the soldier? Sergeant Dempsey? What did you talk to him about?"

Axelle stilled. Inside everything stopped rattling. "What do you mean?"

"What did you tell the soldier? What did you and Sergeant Dempsey talk about when you were escaping the mountain?"

She could hear her blood rushing through her ears. She didn't want Dempsey in trouble. She didn't want her time with him dissected. "We were too busy trying to survive to talk much. We didn't exactly have a lot in common." She stood and walked to the one-way mirror. Tapped the glass. "I'm done here. Unless you're planning on breaking out the cling film and buckets of water, I suggest you get my father on the phone."

Her interrogator shrugged one shoulder as if to say "I'm just doing my job."

But she knew better. She narrowed her eyes at him. "Who do you work for?"

His smile stopped. "You can go. It must be nice to have contacts in high places."

If her family flipped burgers for a living she had a feeling that she wouldn't be sitting here being grilled like a piece of meat.

Axelle snatched up her bags—which had been thoroughly searched—and left. Before he changed his mind.

———

Dempsey refused to let Dmitri Volkov out of his sight. He even showered with the guy, with Taz and Baxter guarding the door. Not his finest moment but if the old man escaped in this country and killed anyone, he'd never forgive himself. Now Volkov lay on an uncomfortable couch in a small coffee room in a building they used for lectures and debriefs. The *News at Ten* was on. Taz stood at the door, Baxter and Cullen slept in a side room. They had perimeter guards too. On base in Credenhill they were secure. If anyone attacked the SAS on their home ground, they'd not live to regret it.

But Dempsey felt unsettled. Nervous. He had a laptop out and was trying to track down Axelle.

Pointless.

They'd hooked up, that was all. Parted ways. So why couldn't he stop thinking about her?

Because he was worried. Because he had that horrible feeling he'd done something stupid like fallen in love with her. All these years trying to prove himself to the army and suddenly he couldn't stop thinking about a woman.

He'd emailed the address on her MSU website and received no reply. Yet his senses were tingling. He'd tracked down her cell number and left her a message there too. He felt foolish. He also felt like he'd missed something. Again.

"Why did you kidnap Axelle, Dmitri?" *Keep working the hearts and minds angle and don't beat the old bugger to a pulp.*

Volkov turned his head. They'd found him some old jeans, olive green socks and a West Ham United T-shirt no one dared claim. He was cuffed, secured to the base of the couch. With his

253

straggly hair and long beard he looked like a lot of former soldiers —a panhandler.

Dempsey didn't like staring into this man's eyes because the more he saw him, the more he became aware of the similarities between them. They'd both betrayed their roots for a seemingly better cause that hadn't turned out exactly as they'd expected. He'd dedicated his life to saving innocents, but people had died too. People always died and it wasn't always the bad guys.

Shit happened.

The Russian shrugged. "I wanted to get someone's attention."

"Well, it worked." Dempsey narrowed his gaze. Maybe they weren't so similar. He'd never have done that to an innocent woman.

"Who is *that*?" The Russian pointed at an image of the new PM on the telly.

"David Allworth, the new British PM. Why?" Dempsey sat straighter. Volkov had gone whiter than a June bride. "What?"

"He looks like a man I captured in the Wakhan many years ago."

"Captured?"

Dmitri clammed up but Dempsey could see the cogs turning. He googled information on the Allworth family. He turned the computer screen toward the man who was now leaning toward him with bright alert eyes.

"It says here Allworth's father died in a plane crash in Kashmir in 1979." He showed him a picture of Sebastian Allworth.

Dmitri nodded. "He died in '79, but it was not in a plane crash." A crafty grin spread over his face but his eyes hardened to stone. "Get my grandson a new liver and I'll tell the prime minister exactly how his father died."

"The Americans have your grandson and will only get him treatment once we hand you over."

"Then hand me over." The man's tone got imperious and he shifted against his bonds. "What are you waiting for?"

"They're waiting for me." David Allworth, the British PM, walked into the room flanked by the CO of the regiment and his own personal bodyguards. Dempsey recognized then because he'd trained them. He climbed to his feet.

"Sergeant Tyrone Dempsey." Allworth looked him over, then held out his hand. Dempsey was aware of his less than stellar pedigree when shaking the hand of the leader of his country. "I've heard a lot about you."

"Sir." He nodded to the PM but didn't shift his defensive position in front of Volkov. The Russian had hurt a woman he was halfway in love with. More than halfway. The old goat had helped extremists murder thousands of innocent people over the years. Why the hell did he care what happened to Volkov?

The PM vibrated with tension as he peered at Volkov. "*You murdered my father.*"

Volkov's smile was neither bitter nor surprised. He looked resigned to whatever treatment they decided to dish out. "I will not talk to you until my grandson is in surgery, getting the new liver he needs. Then I will tell you everything."

"You shot my father in the back." A pulse throbbed in Allworth's temple.

"If I did, it was standard practice for both our countries." Dmitri's eyes burned with bitterness. "He was a spy, spreading anti-Soviet propaganda." He eyed each of the weapon-carrying men in the room. No one said a word but they all knew the truth of his words. "Why would I lie? What difference would one more crime make to a man like me?"

Allworth stepped forward and raised his hand as if to strike. "My father wasn't a spy."

"Sir." Dempsey shifted a half step and the PM's guards closed in exactly the way they were supposed to. Dempsey didn't back down. "You need to hear him out," he said quietly. "After that, you can make your decision on what to do with him. But if we can get him talking and help save a child's life, even his grandson's"

—brown eyes rose to meet his—"don't you think that's something your dad would have been proud of?"

Allworth's jaw flexed as he tried to rein in his fury. "My father worked as an interpreter for the Foreign Office. His best friend told my mother exactly what happened, and he said this animal tortured my father, and then shot him in the back."

"That is *not* what happened." A pained smile touched the edge of the Volkov's lips. "Give me to the Americans and I will give you the name of the man who shot your father."

Allworth clenched and unclenched his fists. "Tell me the name or I'll send you somewhere no one will ever find you."

"I have nothing left to lose except my grandson." The eyes were ancient and as emotionless as stone. "If you want the information about who killed your father, hand me over to the Americans. I won't tell you otherwise." The Russian turned and looked Dempsey straight in the eye. The hair on the nape of Dempsey's neck stood erect. "If you really love someone you need to protect them."

———

In the back of the limo on their way back to London, Jonathon hid a fake yawn behind his half-finished *Times* crossword. His heart hadn't stopped doing a jig for the past eight hours.

"Damned exciting goings-on. I'd assumed it would be more of the same over-engineered, overpriced rubbish we've had for years, but this time they actually look like they're on to something." Rear Admiral Jenkins puffed out his barrel chest.

They did indeed. Moscow would be both terrified and thrilled.

"We can't discuss it off the base," Jonathon admonished the naval officer, who looked a little startled to be chastised. Jonathon rolled his eyes. Seriously, how the Brits ever won any war when they were led by such imbeciles was beyond him. "Top Secret. Eyes and ears and all that." He tapped his nose.

"Of course, of course." The admiral crossed his arms.

Not a weapon *per se*. But something that would give the Brits a new dominion of power nonetheless. He had to get this information to Moscow, and he had to leave ASAP to return to a hero's welcome finally acknowledging the brilliance of his long and illustrious career. The perfect spy. The most successful spy in history. There would be books written about him—he might even write his memoirs. He tried hard not to grin like an idiot.

The car pulled to a stop outside his Fulham home.

"Good night." He climbed out without the driver having to get the door for him. He stood and gave them a wave, sauntered to the big front door and slowly went into the house he'd lived in for almost fifty years. Volkov's spawn had turned up at the American Embassy—Jonathon had seen it on the news in the limo. Even though his sources told him the man was dead, he couldn't risk that he'd left some sort of evidence to be sent to the media in the event of his death. Hell, the Volkovs could be selling him out right now as he climbed his creaking stairs. But he couldn't rush this. He had to act as though this was an ordinary day, especially after what he'd seen earlier. It was imperative for him to get this information to Moscow.

In this day and age it was all about satellite communication.

The Brits had sent a device into space that could control and disable any satellite of their choosing. It was a way of blinding and deafening the opposition. Simple, yet brilliant. Moscow needed to find a way to neutralize this threat if they were to stay in the game.

His feet paused on the stairs. The cotton he'd left on his doorknob was gone. Of course it was a crude and flawed early-warning system, but he also had other monitoring systems in place inside his apartment, and state-of-the-art locks and electronics defenses on his windows even though he was on the top floor. No alarm had been tripped.

He eased down a step when he heard a voice coming from within his apartment and his heart beat faster. *No…*

The door was flung open and there was his granddaughter on the telephone. The only person in the world who had the code to his alarm system. "Oh, there you are. I just left a message on your cell."

Shocked to his core he touched his pocket. He'd thought she was dead. He'd mourned her loss deeply as a necessary sacrifice. His voice was gruff. "I had to leave my phone in the car when I had a meeting, and forgot to turn it back on again."

He opened his arms. Was his cover blown? "I won't ask what you are doing here. I'll simply enjoy my precious girl and thank God you finally came to visit. It has been too long."

———

Axelle sat back on the couch while her grandfather puttered about the kitchen. After clearing customs at Heathrow she'd dithered about going to see her father. She couldn't get over the coincidence of his position and everything that had happened to her over the years. The more she thought about it, the more she'd started to wonder if her father couldn't have been behind the bombing in Rabat as a way of getting rid of his wife and child.

That was too twisted, right?

Twisted or not, she'd decided to stall dealing with her father by visiting her grandfather instead. She needed to see them both anyway.

"So, I thought you'd retired?" She had a key her grandfather had given her years ago. When she'd arrived to find no one home, she'd changed out of the clothes that had offered to walk back to the States on their own, showered, and caught an hour's sleep on the couch.

"I was about to hang up my boots when the new PM decided I

was the man to do him a favor." Her grandfather's eyes twinkled when he came into the room carrying a tray of pasta and a glass of white wine. "Excuse the lack of dining facilities. I usually dine out or on my lap while watching the telly." He handed her the tray.

"After the week I've had, this is luxury," she assured him.

He fetched his own tray through.

"What have you been up to, and why aren't you staying with your father?" His lips pinched perceptively. There was no love lost between Franklin Dehn and Jonathon Boyle. The only thing they'd ever had in common had been her mother, and now her.

She waved her fork. "Oh, I almost forgot. A lady called Lucinda left a message earlier. I thought it might be you calling me back so I picked up. Sorry."

Her grandfather tried to look innocent but she wasn't fooled.

"She said she needed to talk to you about the other night." Axelle kept her face straight.

"Right." Her grandfather pulled a face and grinned. "Well, I'm old darling, not dead."

"Obviously." She raised a glass to him and he shook his head and gave her a smile.

"If you must know she's a dear friend I've known for many years. And it isn't any of your business, madam. I repeat, why aren't you staying with your father? Have you had another fight?"

Axelle scooped another forkful of delicious pasta into her mouth and shook her head. "Is it a crime to visit my grandpa? I haven't seen you in ages."

"No." He ate delicately, dabbing his lips with his napkin between bites. "But I'm pretty sure your father has something to say about you being here and not there…"

"If he knew."

He raised one silver brow. "He doesn't know you're in the country?"

Axelle took a slug of wine, hoping to drown a rash of bad memories and one really good one. "I haven't told him." He might have been keeping tabs on her, which was what she was afraid of. She was wrecked, her body so strung out from the kidnapping, jetlag and trauma, she'd decided to take another day before she confronted the man. Their relationship was already rocky. She didn't want to burn all her bridges by accusing him of trying to blow her up, then having her interrogated. Not without thinking everything through anyway.

They ate the rest of their meal as she told him about some of her recent adventures with her snow leopards and the poacher.

"And those bastards in the Trust dismissed you? Bloody cheek after all you've done for them."

Axelle nodded although she was hoping she could talk the board of directors around when things calmed down. "I know. I should sue them." She smiled because she knew what he'd say to that.

He rolled his eyes. "Bloody litigious society you Americans live in. Can't sneeze without someone suing someone for damages."

"We're not stiff-upper-lip, like you, Gramps. We like to hit back where it hurts—in the wallet."

He smiled and shook his head at her Yankee nickname for him. "I supposed you'll want to stay here tonight?"

"I can sleep on the couch, assuming I'm not cramping your style with lucky Lucinda."

"There's a spare room, wench. Get in there and get to sleep. We'll talk in the morning."

She was going to argue when a massive yawn almost dislocated her jaw. She nodded as she covered her mouth. "Sorry." She leaned down to kiss his brow. "Don't forget to call Lucinda."

He patted her hand. "You're a good girl, Axelle. Just like your mother."

CHAPTER
SIXTEEN

A COUPLE OF HOURS LATER, Axelle was propped up in bed, checking her email. A ridiculous thrill zipped along her nerves when she saw Dempsey had contacted her through her web account. There was an unfamiliar stirring of excitement; she missed him so much it was crazy. She didn't remember feeling like this before—not even with Gideon.

She generally held people at arm's length.

Not Gideon though.

Not Dempsey either.

Seemed some people had a way of forcing themselves into your life. And ripping you apart when they left, she reminded herself as she started to write back. She closed her email instead.

There was a noise out in the hallway—probably her grandfather. He'd aged significantly since she'd last come for a visit. There was a web of lines around his eyes, and his hair seemed almost pure white now. Still he was charming and handsome. It was no surprise the ladies still found him attractive.

She yawned but couldn't sleep. Her body clock was out of whack and she'd been on edge since her "interview" at Heathrow. Couldn't shake the idea she'd become entangled in something complicated and messy, when all she wanted to do was be left alone to help wildlife. She stood and went to the door. Edged it open and saw someone going out the front door. Her grandfather?

It was no business of hers where he went, but she pulled on a pair of jeans and a T-shirt and shoved her bare feet into trainers. She was in the hallway when the door opened again.

"Oh, excellent, you're awake. I was putting my suitcase in the car. I have a meeting with the builders at the cottage in the morning. Can't delay else the roof will fall in before they actually start work. I'll be back tomorrow night? We'll go out to dinner?"

She paused.

"Or…come with me. There's a railway station in the village if you need to come back and face your father." He smiled, knowing her weakness where her father was concerned.

Still she hesitated. She wanted to talk to Dempsey but she hadn't been to her grandfather's cottage since she was a teenager, and the hankering to see it again, to revisit some of the photographs of her mother as a child, was strong. Generally, she tried not to remember her mother because it hurt too much, but now… Now she wanted to honor her memory.

"You can sleep in the car on the drive down."

"Okay."

He grinned. "Grab your stuff. I'll meet you downstairs in five minutes."

———

Wakhan Corridor, Afghanistan, July 1979

Dmitri's steps dragged as he walked back to where the men lay bleeding on the ground. "Cut his bonds."

The blond cherub's lips curled in a show of bloody condescension. Dmitri knew he'd made a dangerous enemy.

"What's going on, Jonathon?" the brown-haired man asked.

He twisted onto his side and stared into Dmitri's eyes. "You realized you made a mistake, didn't you? You checked our permits?" The brown eyes were earnest. Dmitri went with the easy explanation.

"Yes, comrade. I need to apologize for my attack on your caravan. My country has reprimanded me for the death of your guide and his family will be compensated."

"And I'll personally make sure you pay." The blond man was brushing himself down with short sharp swipes that spelled fury. He bent to pick up his belongings.

Dmitri understood the need for spies, but he didn't respect them. They dealt in lies, betrayal, double-crossings and deception. They lived shady, underhand lives with no real honor.

The *starshiná* dragged the larger man to his feet and undid the ropes that tied his wrists and ankles.

"Well then." The big man, Sebastian, looked nervously around. "Do we just walk back the way we came?"

Dmitri almost pitied his naivety. "There is a village five miles east. Or you might try to catch your guides on the Pakistani border." Dmitri pointed south.

Sebastian took two steps in that direction. "Right then. Are you coming, Jonathon?"

"Yes. Of course." Laser blue eyes narrowed as the dark-haired man nodded with relief and began walking away. Dmitri flinched even though he'd expected the gunshot.

The blond spy turned to him and Dmitri read the threat in his malefic gaze. If the Englishman could have gotten away with it, he too, would be wearing a bullet in his back.

"*Do svidaniya*, comrade," Dmitri said bitterly.

They both served Mother Russia but this man felt like his enemy. The spy touched his revolver to his forehead and marched away, not even glancing at the body of his dead friend. "Until we meet again, comrade."

———

What did that mean?

Dempsey turned the words over and over. Volkov had seemed to have been speaking directly to him. *If you really love someone you need to protect them.*

What the hell did that mean?

He shifted and turned to face the tired, wrinkled face of the most wanted man on the planet. They were sitting in a Land Rover trundling toward Brize Norton, the PM's crew creating the sort of motorcade that usually screamed "presidential visit to hostile nation." It was the early hours of the morning. Traffic was almost nonexistent. And he was on a razor's edge of tension.

"What did you mean?" He held the man's gaze and saw the first flicker of uncertainty. "If you've got something to say about Axelle, you need to spill it before the Yanks whisk you away to Guantanamo."

Dmitri flicked his eyes to the side, licked his lips. "The reason I chose Dr. Dehn…"

"Because her father is the American ambassador to Britain."

"But who was her mother?" Ancient eyes drilled him.

Jesus. "If anything happens to her, I'll…" Dempsey dialed Cullen, who'd been assigned to sorting kit after their recent adventures in Afghanistan. "Get on the Internet."

He told the guy what to look for, who to search for. They were about to enter the gates of the base. Thirty seconds later, Cullen said, "Iris Boyle. Daughter of Jonathon Boyle, who's a veteran of the Foreign Office. He has Top Secret security clearance. There's a photo. I'm sending it to your phone now."

He looked Dmitri in the eye and said, "Jonathon Boyle." The man's eyes flared.

Cullen kept talking in his ear. "Iris died in the bombing of the British Embassy in Rabat."

"It was you who killed Axelle's mother and trapped a little girl in the rubble—because you were after that guy, Boyle?"

Dmitri shook his head. "No. No. I didn't plant that bomb. I was blamed, of course. I'm always blamed, but that one wasn't me." Dmitri swallowed and for the first time Dempsey saw real emotion cross the man's features. "I did try to bomb Boyle in Yemen but the device failed."

"The trouble with bombs is they don't discriminate." Dread scraped along Dempsey's nerves. "Why were you after him?"

"I want my grandson to have a chance to live his life. Is that too much to ask?" Tears glittered in the man's eyes.

"What about all the kids you've been responsible for killing over the years?" Dempsey sneered. "Did you give a fuck about them?"

Dmitri's skin bleached whiter than bone.

Dempsey's phone beeped and he opened the image. The guy, this Jonathon Boyle, looked vaguely familiar and he had no idea why. He squinted, then pulled the photographs he'd taken from that elder's hut in the Wakhan Corridor out of his top pocket, and bingo. There was their man looking bright and shiny, standing next to a man who he now knew to be Sebastian Allworth. "Jonathon Boyle shot the PM's dad," he said with sudden intuition. It was the only thing that made sense and brought every piece of the puzzle together.

"I'm saying nothing." Dmitri turned away from him. "But..." He hesitated. "*If* that were true, the GRU won't let Axelle Dehn live. They won't risk that I told her the name of their most beloved spy."

Cold flooded Dempsey. He grabbed the man by the throat and squeezed. "Are you telling me Axelle's grandfather is a Russian spy?"

Dmitri was turning blue beneath his hands. The car had stopped. Someone was hauling him out and trying to force him to release the bastard, but he wouldn't let go. "Tell me why she's in danger."

"Yes! Yes. He's a spy. Jonathon Boyle is the man who shot Sebastian Allworth in the back and who ruined my life." Tears filled the man's eyes as Dempsey finally let himself be pried loose. "They won't let her live. It's too late." The Russian lay there on the asphalt gasping for breath.

The British PM stood right beside him. His hands shook as if he wanted to finish the job Dempsey had started.

"That can't be true." Allworth's eyes bounced off all the people standing there. "He's lying, I've known Jonathon Boyle all my life. I just put him on a committee monitoring weapons development for British Forces." There was a sudden air-sucking silence. He pulled out his phone, no doubt calling the Firm and the Met. Damage control.

Dempsey rolled his eyes. He almost felt sorry for the guy—except the idiot might have helped compromise British Forces for generations to come, which meant men and women like him might die. The old boy network should have been abolished years ago.

Dempsey pulled out his cell. "Cullen, get Signals to put a trace on Axelle Dehn's cell phone and do it now. I need to know exactly where she is so we can get her into some sort of protective custody."

Dmitri Volkov lay there with his face buried in his hands. A broken old man who'd caused more death and destruction than the entire regiment. Dempsey looked up as a Jeep full of soldiers in American BDUs screamed toward them.

Two tall men in a dark suits emerged from the mass of camo and heavy weapons. One had CIA written all over him, the other bore a remarkable resemblance to a woman he'd fallen in love with. Dempsey took a step forward, only to realize he was nothing to this guy. Nobody. Not his daughter's lover. Not his future son-in-law.

He intercepted the ambassador while the spook went over to Dmitri.

"Do you know where your daughter is, Ambassador?"

"You are?" Eyes like winter questioned him.

Dempsey didn't blink. "A friend." More than a friend. "I met her in Afghanistan a few days ago." A lifetime ago.

"She's in Afghanistan?"

"You didn't even know that?"

"Last time I spoke to her she wasn't due to go back until summer." The man shook his head, pressed his lips together, tense. "She's all right?"

Dempsey watched him carefully. He wanted to know if this man would sacrifice his own daughter for some unknown political agenda. "Has no one informed you of her kidnapping, sir?"

"Kidnapping?" The ambassador stared at Dempsey as though he were seeing him for the first time. His voice sounded strained. "*Volkov* kidnapped her?"

"Yes, but she was unharmed when we left the Wakhan."

The ambassador seemed to physically collect himself as he looked at the Russian lying on the tarmac. "I expected one of the most notorious men on the planet to look a little more threatening and a little less pathetic."

The guy wasn't listening to him and *pathetic* wasn't how Dempsey would have described the person he'd chased through the Hindu Kush.

"I told her it wasn't safe, but she never listens to me." The American's expression hardened.

Dempsey braced his feet even though he could see some of the Yanks wanting to physically sweep him out of the way. They could damn well try. "With all due respect, this isn't about you, sir. It's about her, living the life she was meant to live. She's got more brains and balls than any person on this base, but I think she might still be in danger, sir."

The ambassador went to push past him, so he got in the guy's face. "I'm talking about your *daughter*, sir, you own flesh and blood. She could be in extreme danger. Dmitri Volkov named Jonathon Boyle as a Russian spy."

"You can't be serious." The American soldiers stepped

forward but Dehn waved them away. Anger narrowed his dark gaze and tightened the set of his jaw. He seemed to realize Dempsey was deadly serious and something enigmatic moved through his eyes. "I see, but I doubt Axelle is in any real danger if she's still in Afghanistan. I saw Jonathon in London a couple of days ago. The man is too"—his lips twisted with distaste—"prissy to get his hands dirty, and he dotes on Axelle. However, I'll make sure she gets a security detail assigned ASAP." The ambassador nodded thoughtfully as if filtering information, then stared after the British PM, who ignored him as he climbed back into his limo to make more phone calls.

The CIA spook motioned two American soldiers over and they hauled Dmitri to his feet.

The Russian refused to meet Dempsey's gaze as he was marched away.

"I never did like Iris's father." The ambassador nodded again to Dempsey, and turned to leave.

That's it? Christ, he hated politicians. "Ambassador Dehn," Dempsey snapped. The man whirled back toward him, obviously unused to being yelled at. "You *are* going to save the man's grandchild, aren't you?"

Dmitri raised his head and shot him a startled look.

It took a moment but the ambassador jerked his head in a firm nod. "We'll get him a new liver, but I can't promise how long he'll survive. I'm not a doctor. I'm certainly not God."

"Thank you." Dmitri Volkov spoke over the heads of his guards, a broken, hunched figure.

Dempsey didn't know if he was talking to him or the diplomat but he held the man's gaze as he was bundled away.

There but for the grace of God…

Dempsey blew out a massive breath as the PM's security detail and US ambassador's mini-army headed in opposite directions, leaving him and his mates sitting on the tarmac like a bunch of delinquents. They looked at one another uncertainly.

The phone rang. It was Cullen. "Got a trace, Irish, but you're not gonna like it. Brace yourself." The uneasy turmoil in his stomach intensified. "She's not in the Wakhan or the States. Her phone is headed south on the M20 in Kent."

What the…?

Dempsey got back in the car. "Taz, put your foot down. Baxter, get on the blower to the CO and tell him what's going on. But I'm not here." He took off his watch which contained his GPS transmitter and left it on the seat. "You can't contact me, right?" They nodded.

If this went pear-shaped, Dempsey didn't want others taking the fall for what he might have to do, because, suddenly, keeping Axelle safe and sound trumped his career and his loyalty to the crown. He would not follow orders if it meant putting her life on the line. Not this time. The thought alone was cause for being RTU'd and a dishonorable discharge.

———

"We're nearly there," Jonathon said as he noticed his granddaughter open her eyes and look at the pink-tinged sky. Fate was a remarkable thing. He'd thought he was going to have to sacrifice this beautiful, brilliant young woman and never see her again. Providence was rewarding him and he'd decided to take Axelle with him.

Why should they both be alone?

She was adroit with languages. It wouldn't take her long to find a job over there, and they'd be good company for one another. She'd never got on with her father anyway, and had been unhappy since she'd lost that young man she'd married.

This was perfect. He grinned at her.

"While you were asleep I got a call from the marina where I berth my yacht. They need me to sail it to another spot down the coast because they're dredging the harbor today." He checked his watch. "We can do that before I need to meet the builders at ten.

"Okay." She yawned and stretched. 'Oh, excuse me, I'm exhausted."

"You've been through a lot. You need proper sleep."

He had all the information about the new defense systems in his head. He was looking forward to his return home and a hero's welcome to a country he hadn't lived in since his early teens. A country he'd missed. His heart tapped lightly against his ribs and he touched his chest. Instinct told him it was time to run, and instinct had been keeping him safe for years.

Another fifteen minutes, and they parked in the secure marina and headed toward his twenty-seven-foot yacht, *Iris*. Named after his daughter, Axelle's mother.

Her lips spread into a wide smile as she admired the sleek craft. "I'd forgotten how beautiful she is."

Jonathon felt a thrill of pride. The boat was his one true indulgence. "All aboard." He swept his hand in a gentlemanly gesture and Axelle hopped across the gangplank. *Iris* was always ready go. He paid a man to run maintenance every day just in case.

Just in case had turned into *just as well.*

"Go put the kettle on, we'll have a cuppa as we motor around the bay."

She leaned over and kissed his cheek. "Thanks, Gramps. This is exactly what I needed." She headed down the stairs as he primed and started the engines.

He cast off. He almost waved goodbye to the familiar coastline where he'd spent enough years for it to feel like home, but he didn't. He hadn't survived this long by taking chances.

———

Axelle found the teakettle and a big unopened bottle of water.

Carefully she filled the kettle and put it on the stove. It was cool near the sea and she rubbed the sudden rush of goose bumps that spread over her flesh. The engine rumbled to life and she felt the boat start moving through the water at a steady chug. She hadn't been sailing in years. Maybe she needed a break, although she'd better get her ass back to MSU before the end of the month to teach the rest of the semester's course else she was in danger of losing that job too. She also needed to sort out Josef's Ph.D., her own future research program, and see if there was any way of continuing her work with the snow leopards with other funding. But she needed this downtime after her ordeal and still needed to talk to her father.

The kettle boiled and she poured the water into a teapot complete with two requisite Tetley teabags.

She glanced around the comfy cabin. It wasn't particularly fancy but it was fastidiously clean and tidy. There were a bunch of photographs tacked to one wall in the galley. She leaned closer, pulling off a photograph of her mother as a teenager and inadvertently knocking another couple loose. She dropped to her hands and knees to gather the pictures and hesitated. There was an old photograph, overexposed and faded, but it looked remarkably like the landscape she'd just left behind. Her grandfather as a young man stood beside a camel. Another much taller man stood on the other side, grinning at the camera. He looked vaguely familiar.

Footsteps sounded on the steps just as Dmitri's words echoed in her ears. *Your blood owes me.*

"Where was this photograph taken, Gramps?"

Her grandfather frowned at her. "Morocco or Yemen maybe? I don't remember."

"It looks like the Wakhan Corridor." She picked up all the photos and rearranged them on the board. "Who's that you're with?"

Her grandfather shrugged and a sense of unease roused inside her. "I don't remember. Some tourist."

Her grandfather had a photographic memory for names and faces. In fact, she didn't think he'd ever forgotten a damn thing. Why was he lying? Or was he simply getting absentminded with age?

She poured the tea and took two mugs up on deck. Passed him one as he steered and she sat on the bench beside him.

The salt-laden breeze grazed her cheeks and her loose hair whipped around her face, blinding her. The enormous cross-channel ferries were coming in and out of port not far away. The white cliffs of Dover gleamed a toothy grin in the background. The sky was pale blue, the sea dark and brooding. She shivered and zipped her windbreaker.

"Do you fancy going on a little jaunt before we head back?" There was an excited light in his eyes. She nodded and he unfurled the sails, the boat surging forward as they caught the breeze. She wasn't big on sailing, but this was his thing and chances were she wouldn't see him again for another couple of years. It wouldn't hurt to spend an extra hour at sea.

She hadn't been a good granddaughter. She hadn't been much of a daughter, either, come to think of it. Ever since Gideon had died she'd closed herself off to everyone except her leopards. It was time to make an effort.

She sipped her tea. Braced against the chrome railings she realized the swell was pretty big, and from what she remembered they were about to enter some of the busiest shipping lanes in the world. After quarter of an hour she checked her watch. "Hey, Gramps, we should probably head back else you'll be late for your meeting with the builders."

He turned his gaze from the horizon. "We're not going back, Axelle."

"What? What do you mean?"

His eyes burned with some inner fire. He seemed to be losing it. "I'm going home, back to Russia."

"Russia?" A frisson of disquiet snaked along her nerves. He'd definitely lost his marbles, which was a bit of a blow because she didn't know how to sail and they were zipping toward Denmark at a scary rate of knots. Damn.

"I was born in a small town outside Leningrad."

"No, Gramps, you were born in Croydon."

He smiled, his cheeks smooth and unlined, unlike the rest of his face. "That's my cover story. You have an entire heritage you know nothing about, and now I'm going to get the chance to share it with you."

Dmitri Volkov's words echoed around her mind again. *Blood debt*. "I don't want to go to Russia. I live in Montana. I have a job that I happen to love in Montana."

"Because you've never been to Russia, never experienced the beauty of the land, the architecture, the people…"

He was serious.

A sense of dread stole through her body. "Gramps, have you ever heard of a man called Dmitri Volkov?"

A tight smile moved over his features. "We've met."

CHAPTER
SEVENTEEN

"WHAT DO you mean you can't isolate it?" She was in trouble. He knew it. The same way he'd known she was in trouble before he'd run into that bloody cave in Afghanistan.

Letting her die was not an option.

"Any luck finding her grandfather, this Boyle character?"

With Dmitri bundled off, probably to some black camp never to be seen again, Dempsey was going to have to rely on his instincts, colleagues, and twenty-plus years of experience fighting bad guys. He didn't know if it would be enough. They had no idea where Jonathon Boyle was or if he *was* a spy, or if Volkov was lying to them. He'd been sent a picture of a handsome white-haired gentleman in a three-piece suit. The Metropolitan Police had raided the man's two homes and put out an alert for his car. So far nothing.

Of all the possible scenarios this was the one he liked least. Jonathon Boyle in the wind—apparently with sensitive MOD information—thank *you*, Prime Minister—and being unable to locate Axelle.

She might not be with her grandfather.

There was also the remote possibility Axelle and Jonathon Boyle were working in collusion and acting against the interests of

Great Britain and the US. Christ, he didn't want to believe it, because the thought she might have lied to him hurt too much. Even though they'd made no promises to one another, it was one betrayal he didn't want to contemplate.

He tried her phone again. It went straight to voicemail. "Hi, Axelle. I'm in the UK." He paused, not wanting to leave a message that gave them away, not wanting to piss her off or scare her away with declarations of undying love or death-do-us-part adoration. "I'd like to see you again. Get in touch ASAP. Please?"

Taz snorted.

He hung up. "Fuck off."

"They're tracking her phone but struggling to pin it down." Taz held up his hand, trying to hear his cell above the growing morning traffic. "Hold it. You're sure? Get off the M25 next exit," Taz told Baxter and closed his cell. "Someone in Signals tracked her cell to the middle of the English Channel. The police are scouring local harbors for Jonathon Boyle's car because it turns out he also owns a boat."

This kept getting worse.

"Coastguard is on alert. If Boyle is a Russian spy with important military secrets then they're not going to let him get away."

His stomach rolled. "We're gonna need gear and a helo."

"They're sending kit down from London."

It wouldn't be fast enough. He knew it wouldn't be fast enough. He looked out the window and spotted a small airfield with signs advertising parachuting lessons.

"Next right, Baxter," he barked. He met the man's eyes in the mirror and the amused glint in his eye as he jumped on board his plan.

———

"Volkov was the man who kidnapped me a few days ago, but

you already knew that, didn't you? He called you." Axelle stared at him as though he'd grown scales.

"I couldn't risk him exposing me after all these years." He slumped forward, abandoning his rigid posture in an effort to appear more contrite. It hadn't been an easy decision, for God's sake, he hadn't taken it lightly. "He said he wanted help for his family, but why now? I couldn't allow him to get in the way of the greater good."

"Whose greater good? Russia's? This is crazy. It doesn't make any sense." She edged away from him. "Did you send the bombing raid?"

"No. No. But…" He shot her a glance. "It's complicated." How to explain? "Before Dmitri Volkov defected to fight with the muja-hedeen, he was a member of Vympel—do you know who they are?" He met her intense brown gaze, which was now focused on him in growing horror.

"They're an elite Russian Spetsnaz sabotage and assassination unit, akin to the SAS and SBS." The morning sun poured over the white sails and shining hull with blinding brilliance. "In 1979 Captain Dmitri Volkov of the Red Army captured me and a man called Sebastian Allworth, in the Hindu Kush. He's the man you asked about in the photograph below deck. Do you know who Allworth is?"

She shook her head. The skin around her mouth was white. The shock would eventually wear off and she'd come to admire the things he'd done. Respect his ingenuity. His guile.

"His son just became the British Prime Minister." He smoothed back his hair with a manicured finger. "The British Government had people on the ground in Afghanistan, stirring up anti-communist sentiment—"

"I thought the Afghan government requested Soviet support?"

"The government did, yes. The people didn't." He hid his irri-tation. He'd warned Moscow to stay out of Afghanistan. He'd tried to sabotage the efforts of the Americans, but they'd insti-gated enough trouble to draw the Soviets into a conflict that had ultimately brought down the USSR. How sweetly ironic that the Americans were now battling it out in those same lands. The lessons were in the history books but people refused to learn.

"It was the height of the Cold War. Tensions between East and West were so fraught the smallest incident could have set off a nuclear war that would have been catastrophic for millions of people." He saw himself as more a peacekeeper than spy. Pity the law wouldn't think of it the same way if they caught him. A bead of sweat formed on his upper lip and he licked away the salty excess. Not far now. He'd activated the flash beacon to say he needed immediate retrieval.

"Volkov caught me in the Wakhan." He gripped his age-spotted hands on the wheel. Axelle was looking at him as though she didn't recognize him. As if she might tackle him, or throw him overboard. But she was a bleeding heart, like her mother. He was her grandfather and old to boot. She'd no more hurt him than he'd change sides.

"Volkov was about to execute me. I had to confess the truth about who I really worked for." Anger warmed him even now, all these years later. "That was the only time I have ever been compromised."

"What happened to Sebastian Allworth?"

"Volkov shot him." Jonathon shrugged and looked away.

She laughed as if she thought him crazy. "So…what are you saying? You're some sort of Russian spy?"

"The fact I fooled my own granddaughter suggests I must be a pretty good Russian spy, don't you think?" He raised a supercilious brow. "I always thought it was a pity to be the greatest spy in history and not ever be able to brag about it."

"My father would have known—"

"Why do you think your mother married a cold fish like Franklin Dehn in the first place?" His shoulders were stiff against the force of the wind. Against the unjust condemnation in this chit's eyes.

"Are you saying Mama was a spy too?"

"No, no. But I maneuvered the two of them together often enough with access to alcohol and privacy, and"—he looked her up and down—"results were as expected."

Her.

Understanding sucked the blood from her cheeks.

Franklin Dehn had been a rising star in diplomatic circles back then. Given the position he'd risen to he'd been an excellent choice. But Iris had died, and the antipathy her father and grandfather had felt toward one another had blossomed into open hostility.

"The bomb that killed her…"

He shrugged. "I don't know who set it. Maybe Volkov, maybe some other nutter. They didn't compromise my identity so I walked away a hero, especially when…" Grief grabbed him around the throat. He tried not to think about his daughter's death. She'd been his princess even though she'd been strong-willed and defiant. He'd never told her the truth about who he truly was, and that had created a barrier between them. That barrier wouldn't exist between him and Axelle. Not anymore. Once she was used to the idea they'd be closer than ever. She could write his biography and get rich on the proceeds.

"I loved your mother. The two of you meant everything to me." He reached out and patted her hand. He could tell she didn't know what to believe.

"Gramps, I'm going to make some more coffee—I need a real caffeine injection after everything you've told me." Land was on the distant horizon now and giant ships inched inexorably by, too far in the distance to be of any real danger to his plans.

He pulled a shiny-looking pistol from beneath the cushion at his side. The metallic click made her chin jerk upwards.

"I'm afraid I don't completely trust you, Axelle. Not yet. Once we're in Russia, maybe, but until then you can't be allowed to ruin my coup d'état. There is too much at stake." Honor and glory. Recognition after a lifetime spent in the shadows. He jerked his head toward the steps.

"You wouldn't shoot me." It sounded more like a question than a statement. He smiled sadly. She stood shakily, almost in a trance as she went down to the cabin. It was only when he got duct tape out of a drawer that she made a run for it, only to be brought short when he grabbed her hair.

She shoved him but he put the gun under her chin. "I will kill you, child, if I have to."

Fear shone in her eyes.

"Hold out your hands," he ordered.

She refused and he sighed.

"Don't make me hurt you. I love you but I don't have time for games."

She suddenly seemed to realize he was deadly serious. She shoved him with all her might and he fell, bruising his hip. Furious, he caught her ankle and she went down hard, her chin slamming into the hardwood. As she lay dazed, he pulled her hands in front of her and circled her wrists with tape. He repeated the duct tape on her ankles. Satisfied she wasn't going anywhere, he swept the hair out of her face and put another strip over her mouth.

"You always were a spirited child." He kissed her on the forehead and went back up the stairs, heading toward fame and glory.

———

They were all locked, loaded, and ready to go. His cell phone rang. He checked the number, hoping it was Axelle, but it was HQ. He ignored it.

Taz's phone rang and he answered.

"Haven't seen him, sir. Yes, sir." He snapped it shut. "We've been officially ordered back to base."

Things were going pear-shaped. He would not risk his friends' careers. Getting into the SAS took more effort and determination than anything else he knew. They didn't need this. "You two drop me off and head back to Hereford."

Taz and Baxter looked at one another.

"I'm not even on duty," Baxter said, glancing at his watch.

"And I need to get some jumps in." Taz nodded to the parachute school. "Might as well start now."

"You could be RTU'd if this blows up in our faces. I'm not worth that sort of sacrifice." But Axelle was. She was worth it to him anyway. Dempsey felt his throat close.

Taz stared at him coolly. "You underestimate yourself, Sergeant."

Baxter screeched to a halt outside a spare looking hangar. "Come on, let's get going, ladies."

Dempsey ran after them. These guys were his family. Not the screwed-up bunch he'd left behind in Ulster. Two minutes of fast talking persuaded the guy in charge of the jump school to do what they wanted—and then he got into it. He already had a plane on runaway. They packed chutes, jumped in and Dempsey called Cullen during takeoff to give them the latest situation report.

"We've finally got eyes on Jonathon Boyle," Cullen told him. "He's got a nice little yacht heading east at a speed of about twenty knots. There is a *lot* of traffic in the Channel today, boys and girls."

Dempsey wrote it on the map they'd borrowed from their pilot and new jumpmaster.

"Any sign of Axelle?" He held his breath. It was possible that Jonathon Boyle had somehow taken Axelle's phone with him. Maybe even accidentally. Maybe Axelle had planted it on him as a tracking device—except where the hell was she?

"No, but thermal imaging suggests there's another person below deck."

Boyle might not know his cover was blown and he might just be out on a jaunt. But he'd have to have heard the report that Volkov's family had requested political asylum in Paris. Dempsey figured the guy would try to leg it with the new specs on Britain's defense systems lodged safely in his head, but he and his squad weren't about to let that happen. Especially if Axelle was in danger.

"We're in position to intercept. Where are the other teams?" Dempsey asked Cullen.

He heard him talking to someone in the background. "Still en route. Nice wings, Sergeant."

Dempsey gave a grim smile. He should have known they'd find him. Hell, he had known it—they still had their cell phones. "Are we going to run into another op if we try to gain access to the target's boat?"

"Negative. They are about thirty minutes behind you. All radio and satellite signals in that area have been blocked, which is creating a frickin' nightmare in the shipping lanes and means I'm going to lose you in the next five minutes. You'll be on your own. They've scrambled jets from RAF Marham, and they will blow his ass out of the water rather than let him make contact with another vessel. They will commit an act of war to stop him if necessary."

His heart stopped for a moment. Tornadoes were armed with Storm Shadow cruise missiles. "Axelle..." Christ, he couldn't even speak.

"Your mission—should you choose to accept it—is to capture the target before he gets to international waters. The Tornadoes are on standby and will only be minutes behind you. Don't fuck this up."

Shit.

Again Axelle's life was being considered acceptable collateral damage, the way all those innocent shoppers had been when his brothers had planted that final bomb. He ground his teeth together. He might have swapped one set of ruthless killers for another, but there was no way on Hell's earth he was letting Axelle get caught in the crossfire this time.

He checked his weapon and harness. Jonathon Boyle could start a war between the UK and Russia, and there was no way the

Yanks would stand back and watch. Dempsey didn't fancy being responsible for World War III.

They were approaching the drop zone, but this plan wasn't going to work. If Boyle had a weapon, and he had to assume the man had a gun, they'd be sitting ducks.

Dempsey scouted the scene below him. Boyle's boat was a speck in the distance. There was a big-ass cruiser about half a mile away. He tapped Taz on the shoulder. "Change of plan." He pointed toward the cruiser, which had enough power to catch the small yacht—assuming the owner didn't mind being hijacked. However, national security trumped most things and, more important, Axelle's life was in danger. He went over to the pilot. "We're going to jump here. I want you to put out a banner and do a few circles ahead in the distance. Then go home." The co-pilot nodded. "I'll be by to pay you for the ride as soon as I get the chance, mate."

They stood at the door, and he felt that instantaneous and instinctive "oh, fuck" feeling shoot through him as he stepped clear of the aircraft. The wind hit him, the fierce roar of air as he fell through the sky, then the savage jerk on the harness as the primary chute deployed. He maneuvered, watched the deck of the cruiser get closer and closer. The captain was craning his neck to watch him, amused at first. Dempsey saw the expression change to horror as he swung the canopy toward the polished wood. He landed on the deck with a gentle hop. Dumped the silk so Taz and Baxter could get on board.

He strode to the pale, scrawny skipper who stood there open-mouthed. "Where are you from?"

"P-P-P-Plymouth."

"Sergeant Dempsey, British Army." Shook his hand. "I need to borrow your boat."

There was a thud, followed by the swish of fabric. Then another thud and a curse as Baxter caught the railing and almost went airborne again. Taz grabbed him and disengaged the chute with a whack.

The captain looked undecided as to whether he should scream for help or jump up and down with excitement. Dempsey went to the steering wheel and opened her up. Jesus this thing could shift. The skip dragged himself to stand next to him at the wheel. "Are you a pirate? Have I been boarded?"

Dempsey grinned. "No, mate. I'm SAS. If we're successful you'll earn yourself a bloody knighthood. We're after a Russian spy." He probably shouldn't be saying anything, but what the hell.

The man collapsed into his plush leather chair. "James Bond." Dempsey raised a brow. "I've landed smack bang in the middle of the boat chase in a Bond movie."

Dempsey nodded. "Only problem is these bullets are real. I hope you've got insurance?"

The man's eyes bugged. "Yes, but I don't know if I'm covered for this sort of thing."

"We need you to come with us," Taz told the skip. They couldn't afford to have an unknown wandering around during an operation. Hopefully they didn't sink the boat and drown the poor bastard as he lay tied up in the stateroom.

"Get me something to wear that doesn't scream *army*, Taz," Dempsey shouted.

Two minutes later Taz came back wearing a yellow flowery shirt that made him look like he should be tanning in the med.

He handed Dempsey a white shirt with red poppies on it. "Christ, it looks like I've already been shot." He slipped into the shirt that barely went over his shoulders. Baxter had gone with a super-tight light blue T-shirt. Dempsey grabbed the hat off the console. A black sailor number. He slipped on his sunglasses, figured they could audition for *Glee* if their soldiering careers didn't pan out.

They checked their ammo. They had carbines and handguns but limited ammo, which was a pain in the ass. They'd been guarding Volkov for the handover, not preparing for an op.

They sped easily past the yacht even though it had all its sails out. Dempsey raised his hand in casual salute as Boyle glared at him because of the wake they were generating. He noted the man slid a hand under the cushion to his right before Dempsey throttled hard on the gas and left the yacht in his wake. No sign of Axelle. "Take over, Baxter."

Dempsey slipped out of the shirt and got into position on the starboard side of the boat. Then, Baxter slid the cruiser in front of the yacht and Dempsey peeled over the side and into the water, disappearing from sight.

———

Axelle lay in the cramped bunk with her hands and ankles tied. Again. En route to Russia like a goddamned sack of corn. She was sick of being treated like a tradable commodity.

Her grandfather had gone nuts, and here she was like some floundering worm trying to get off the hook. Unable to move, unable to talk, unable to make her own decisions. And a man who'd claimed to love her had done this to her.

This wasn't love.

Just because he was related by blood didn't give him the right to tell her what to do.

She was hit by sudden blinding insight. Love didn't give you the right to tell someone else what to do with their lives. Gideon had had every right to go off and join the army and fight for his country. She swallowed emotion because she'd tried to take that right away from him, and they'd been angry with each other at the end, blaming each other for choices they'd made. He'd died with that black emotion swirling between them. No wonder she couldn't forgive herself. She'd been wrong.

And what about Dempsey?

She lay still as her heart jolted. She'd retreated so rapidly from him when he'd told her to get on that chopper, when all she'd really wanted to do was throw herself into his arms and plunge into the unknown. Why had she done that? Why had she run from that wondrous potential?

Because she'd been scared.

Scared of getting involved.

Scared of being hurt, again.

Which made her a yellow-bellied coward.

An image of Ty Dempsey's smile flashed across her mind. It was an impossible relationship to contemplate, but she remembered following him through that mountain. It was as if the sheer terror of that experience wiped her senses clean, rebooted her emotions, and gave her the chance of a do-over. The idea of having a relationship with anyone terrified her; the thought of loving a soldier almost paralyzed her. But she wanted to at least see where it led. Life was too short to not follow your heart.

She'd always considered herself fearless, but she'd been kidding herself. Of course, Dempsey might not be even vaguely interested. The thought made her mouth go dry. She wasn't a good bet. She was going to have to polish her communication skills and try and open up about her feelings. The thought made her nauseous. Then she remembered Dempsey was a guy and grinned. He wasn't big on idle chatter. Maybe they could explore whatever it was between them without having to spill every sordid detail. They could just rip each other's clothes off instead.

She stuck her tongue against the duct tape on her lips. It pulled at the delicate skin and did nothing to get rid of the obstruction. *Dammit*. She wasn't lying here trussed like a stuffed pig, letting her delusional grandfather dictate how she lived her life. She rubbed her face against the rough carpet. At first the smooth tape slid over the fibrous material but then she stuck her tongue in her cheek and worked on loosening one corner. It took a couple of tries to get the first edge loose, but then the material peeled back from her chin and she worked her jaw until it dangled uselessly from one side of her face.

Okay. First obstacle removed.

She used her teeth on the tape on her wrists. It was tough but the key with duct tape was getting it to rip in the right direction. It didn't take long. After that her ankles were a piece of cake, but she kept noise to a minimum and planned her next move. The portholes could be opened but no way would her hips fit through that gap this side of puberty. She glanced at the steps. There was only one way out of here. She drew in a breath that pushed against the sides of her lungs. It involved going past the man who'd lied to her and everyone else who'd known him for his entire life.

Damn, she faced predators every day—she shouldn't be scared, but this was different. This was a man she'd always loved. She spotted her bag and grabbed her cell phone. She turned it on but couldn't access her messages or get a signal. She stared around the room, carefully opened the cupboard beneath the sink and found some kitchen cleaner. Not deadly but a drop in the eye might put his aim off. She swallowed the knot in her throat. He had a pistol and was desperate enough to use it.

Then she spotted a flare gun on the wall and grabbed it. The boat changed direction suddenly and she fell hard against the wall. Crap.

She forced herself to her feet despite the momentum that wanted to push her down and keep her there. She checked the instructions and saw it was a simple device, and braced herself on the bottom of the stairs. She needed a diversion. She aimed at the main sail from the bottom of the stairs and released it with a sharp jerk of her hand. The firework slammed hard into the canvas and it burst into flames. She was already up the stairs and running for the side of the boat when her foot caught on a rope and she pitched headlong to the deck. Her grandfather grabbed her ankle.

"You fool. What have you done?"

Axelle looked up. The fire had gone out almost immediately but the sail hung in damaged strips and clearly wouldn't take them anywhere. However, the boat had a motor so they weren't exactly out of commission. She looked toward the mainland and swallowed. It was a long way. France was closer. She braced herself.

His fingers tightened painfully. "I'm going to give you everything you could ever wish for—don't you understand?"

"I already have everything I want, Gramps. Except my freedom."

He let her go, looked uncertain. "I thought you'd want this…"

"No, you didn't." She rolled onto her back and looked at the old man, compassion moving through her. "You wanted someone to keep you company and applaud your brilliance." She clapped her hands. "No doubt about it, you had everyone fooled."

His eyes slitted and he reached for his gun. "You're making a big mistake."

"No. You are."

The voice came out of nowhere and there stood Tyrone Dempsey, soaking wet and bristling with attitude. His eyes were cold and hard but she knew he'd risked his life for her—again.

She loved this guy.

"Get away from Axelle and put your hands in the air."

Jonathon started to obey when a whoosh of water grabbed all their attention. A submarine surfaced nearby, and a man poked out of the turret holding a big gun. Axelle swung her gaze to Dempsey, mutely asking the question "One of yours?" But he was already launching himself across the deck, picking her up bodily, diving through the air, which was answer enough. Gunfire whipped above their heads as they smacked forcefully into the sea. Frigid cold blasted billions of neurons as they went under. Shock had her sucking in a mouthful of water. A huge wave smashed into them, tearing his fingers from her arms, ripping them apart. Wet clothes clung to her skin, the weight dragging her down. Her movements were awkward and slow. Her lungs squeezed painfully, hungry for oxygen. She twisted in a circle, disorientated. The familiar feeling of panic started to build, stretching her nerves to snapping point.

Dempsey reached down and grabbed her wrist; the expression

on his face showing a cool competence even in this extreme life-or-death situation. Relief swept through her and they kicked to the surface together.

That first guttural breath felt like heaven as her lungs filled. Her throat was raw from swallowing salt water. She coughed and choked as another wave broke over her head.

Dempsey held her tightly, as if he was never going to let her go. Relief was short-lived as bullets sprayed the water—so close they splashed Axelle's face. Her stomach clenched as another wave swept them further away from the deadly salvo.

"Swim!" Dempsey urged.

Her grandfather was shouting. "Comrade, I have the information."

"He's trying to escape to Russia. You can't let him get away." Axelle tried to kick her numb limbs.

"That's a Russian sub with soldiers firing live rounds." Dempsey's hands tightened on her shoulders, his eyes grim. "We need to keep swimming."

More bullets peppered the water in their wake. "But he can't get away—"

"Don't worry. Just swim!"

Axelle's arms ached from the effort of raising them out the water. Shivers wracked her body. They struggled to make progress against the powerful current. Every time a gun fired she flinched, bracing for pain, worried about Dempsey who was trying to shield her with his body. If anything happened to him she'd never be able to live with herself. She dug for courage and energy as she clawed her way through the water.

A huge cruiser nosed slowly toward them. She recognized Taz and Baxter shooting at the sub, drawing fire. Her grandfather began to climb the ladder of the huge gray submersible. No one was firing at them anymore. They seemed to be out of range, but they didn't stop swimming.

"Are you all right?" Dempsey's voice was gruff in her ear.

Her teeth chattered. "I am now. How did you find me?"

Emotion charged through his eyes. "We tracked your cell phone." His face was stark as she started into the crystalline blue eyes of the man she loved. A smile creased his cheek. "I'm sorry I sent you away."

"You didn't have a choice." She spat out a mouthful of salt water, hardly romantic, but possibly more authentic. This was who she was. Not exactly a delicate flower.

Waves bobbed them up and down as the gun battle abruptly ended and the hatch on the submarine slammed shut with a metal clang. The cruiser zipped their way and Taz reached down and hauled her out of the water. In the frigid air she stood shuddering, watching the rapid whoosh of water as the Russian sub started to slide beneath the waves.

"My grandfather can't get away—"

Strong hands pressed her into a plush leather seat as Baxter opened up the throttle and the boat started tearing through the water away from the yacht. The sudden scream of aircraft split the air. First one jet, then another, released missiles headed toward where the sub had gone down. Horror shot through her and her hand went to her mouth. Then the heat and blast of a massive explosion buffeted them. Smoke billowed from the crippled metal wreckage. Splintered pieces of yacht burned across the surface of the water.

The jets looped away with an arrogant flourish. Tears filled her eyes.

Her grandfather had probably just died. Grief welled inside. No matter his treason, he'd always been kind to her. He'd taught her to play chess and had made time for her when her father had been too busy. Perhaps it had been an act, but it had felt real. She'd loved him.

A large gray warship steamed steadily toward them. Baxter shook his head. "That'll be the Navy. Better late than never, huh?"

She stared at Dempsey's face as he stood dripping beside her, his hand on her shoulder. Taz and Baxter busied themselves tidying up. She stood and cupped a palm to Dempsey's cheek and he pulled her to him. She was freezing cold but as soon as his body touched hers, heat began to spread and she didn't want it to stop.

Emotion was expanding inside her. Too much to grab hold of. Nervousness was rapidly beating out hope. "I don't know how we're going to make this thing between us work," she blurted. Who said he even wanted anything more than to save her life?

He dropped his forehead to hers. "We'll find a way, *muirnín*. As long as we believe that we're trying to get back to one another, we'll make it work."

A huge weight lifted off her chest. She finally had the courage to take a risk, and she wanted to shout and celebrate the moment. He kissed her instead, his flavor mixing with that of the sea.

He came up for air. "God, I love you. I never thought I'd say those words to anyone. I never thought I'd want anything that didn't involve the army, but—"

She put her fingers on his lips. "You don't have to give up the army for me."

"I know." His Adam's apple bobbed. "But one of these days I'll have to retire—"

"No rash decisions, okay?"

"Okay." His eyes drilled into hers. "But this doesn't feel like a rash decision. It feels like I've been waiting for you my whole life. I feel like I'm finally getting something right. Like *we're* both finally getting something right."

She nodded and wiped away happy tears. She felt the same way.

He rested his head against hers. "This mess is going to take time to sort out."

She gave him a mirthless smile. "And I need to talk to my father."

"Don't go anywhere without telling me, okay?" He slicked water from his hair, drops sparkling on his skin. With those bold planes and icy features he looked formidable, and yet she knew he'd risked his life and career for her.

How could she not love a man like this?

She squeezed his hand. "That could be difficult because I just realized there's something I need to do back in Afghanistan."

"I'll come with you." His fingers tightened around her arms.

She grinned. "How?" Then her attention swung to a man on the deck of the frigate. It was the same guy who'd sat next to her on the flight to Heathrow. "Who is that?"

"Holy fuck, that's the Chief of MI6. Christopher Gleeson."

Axelle folded her arms and nodded. "Is it now? I wonder if he knows my father because I get the feeling they are about to become acquainted."

The guy saluted her with a wry smile of acknowledgement. When he smiled, he actually looked handsome and not at all slimy.

"Now that's a scary guy," she said.

"Want me to shoot him for you?" Dempsey wrapped his arm proprietarily around her shoulders.

She laughed. "No, but..." A sudden thought occurred to her and she deflated. "You're going to get into serious trouble for this, aren't you?"

He grinned. "For helping contain a suspected Russian spy while rescuing the daughter of the American Ambassador?"

She bobbed her brows. "When you put it like that, you did a damn fine job, Sergeant."

Baxter came up behind them, followed by Taz. "That he did, lass, that he did."

EPILOGUE

TWO WEEKS LATER...

DEMPSEY HEARD the click on his comms to tell him the op was a go, and moved quickly past the concrete bunkers and chain-link fences, avoiding the rudimentary security. One guard. No cameras. No alarm system. Barely any perimeter to speak of. Taz was running surveillance, Baxter in position if things went south. Cullen was driving the getaway car.

Darkness was tinged green by NVGs, the sound of wild beasts juxtaposed against distant traffic.

"This way."

A black silhouette moved through the night, knowing exactly where to go because they'd scoped out the place to decide the best mode of entry earlier that day. The one good thing about a burka was it didn't make his ass look fat.

They moved swiftly through the derelict, often empty enclosures, toward the building where the zoo secretly housed two snow leopard cubs. It was imperative they get the cubs out before their presence was made public. The zoo was struggling to the point of desperation. The administrators were doing their best with limited resources, but the place was a ghost of its former self. They couldn't police the leopards. They could barely feed them.

"You're sure the guy was good with this?" he asked.

"He didn't exactly say 'Go ahead and steal the cubs.' But he did say he was worried about their security if they remained here. Relax."

Relax?

They got to the door and he held the bolt cutters in place, hesitating for one split second. "You're sure the lions aren't loose in here, right?"

"I'm sure. Although if I could think of a way to get them out of this hellhole, I would."

No way was he kidnapping adult lions, but he wasn't about to argue right now. He cut the chain and Axelle slipped inside, Dempsey on her tail, hand on the butt of his pistol even though he figured Axelle would rather lose a leg than let him shoot anything feline.

Life was not going to get boring, that was for damn sure.

The center of the building was empty. He saw the lions watching them from behind a glass wall and walked swiftly to a door opposite. He quickly unlocked it and Axelle rushed inside, scooped up both cubs, and put them each in a separate sack. She handed him one, took the other. "Let's go."

They exfiltrated the same way they'd entered, then headed north to a small wall where they'd agreed on a rendezvous point. He dangled both sacks over the wall and Baxter took them from him. Axelle started climbing and he put both hands on her backside and gave her a boost. A gigantic roar made him pause, the hairs on the back of his neck springing upright in a primitive recognition of danger. The lions.

Sorry, boys.

He vaulted the wall and ducked into the car, which idled at the curb. He wrenched off the NVGs and threw them in the boot of the hatchback with the rest of their gear as Cullen drove calmly away. They headed to a quiet suburb and switched vehicles. Baxter had one cub in the crook of his arm; it had doubled in size since Dempsey had last seen it and it cried hungrily. Axelle passed Baxter a bottle she'd prepared earlier. Taz fed the other cub, a goofy smile on his face.

Dempsey refrained from rolling his eyes because he figured he was an even bigger sap about the woman at his side. She'd used her diplomatic connections to get help with a little wildlife work. It was unethical as hell but after everything that had happened lately, no one was complaining.

They headed to a small airstrip an hour north of the city, loaded the cubs into a crate and, with a salute to his squad, he and Axelle climbed aboard a small twin-prop plane, which immediately taxied along the runway and took off. The boys were headed for parts unknown, and he'd been given a month's leave to do some private security consulting with an outside company.

"Your father came through." He sank into his seat at the back of the aircraft. The pilot turned the lights off as he headed north. No point giving the enemy something to shoot at.

She'd been reinstated by the Trust when the former director had unexpectedly quit.

Axelle smiled and leaned back into his arms. "He did. So did you."

Dempsey covered them both with a blanket and settled back for a long flight.

She nuzzled at his neck and sighed, looking regretfully at the front seat. "Pity about the pilot, otherwise we could…" She whispered things in his ear that did little to settle his blood.

He tucked her closer to his side. She looked like a ninja but smelled like lavender. "We've got four weeks."

Time for things to calm down regarding the Russian spy scandal, as well as to end speculation as to what had been sunk in the English Channel during an RAF training exercise. He was providing Axelle with some close protection in case anything unexpected popped out of the ether in the meantime. He kissed her hard. "We've got plenty of time to continue this later."

Her lips curved into a beautiful smile. She kissed him back for a moment, then pulled away with a gleam in her eye. "Can you imagine what I could do with a whole squad of SAS soldiers?"

"You're thinking about other men when I'm kissing you?" He grinned.

"Only in a purely professional capacity."

"How about you concentrate on what one SAS soldier is going to do to you when we get back to camp." He slid his hand over her breast beneath the blanket, took the lobe of her ear in his teeth and bit gently. Made her groan and writhe until he almost forgot about the damned pilot. He pulled back as a thought struck him. "Josef isn't there, right?"

Her eyes glittered in the darkness. "Because of the sheer number of laws we just broke, it's just you and me while we get the cubs set up with the surrogate. Josef's teaching my course." She laughed and tunneled her fingers through his short hair. "It's a win-win situation. He gets work experience for his résumé. And I get time to try and find a way to raise these cubs in their natural environment."

A few days ago the other tagged female had tragically lost her cubs. Anji had taken their fur, which they would wrap around these cubs and then present them to the pining mother in the den. It was a long shot, but if the mother accepted them it would solve a lot of problems. If it didn't work, Dempsey knew Axelle would figure something out.

She yawned and laid her palm against his heart. He listened to the sound of her breathing get slower and more even as she drifted off to sleep. It had been a helluva day. He kissed the top of her head.

Not long ago the thought about what he was going to do after he quit the army had scared the crap out of him. Now he knew he was going to spend the rest of his life with this woman on her relentless crusade to save wildlife. For years he'd been willing to die for his country but he'd never seriously thought about what he wanted to live for. Finally he'd found it. Axelle Dehn.

A woman who knew everything about him and loved him anyway.

He thought of his sister, who'd died too young. And the young boy who'd two days ago received a life-saving operation in Paris. Life wasn't fair, but Dempsey had done his best to even the score. With Axelle by his side he'd keep trying, keep fighting the bad guys, but also learn to enjoy it. He hugged her closer. Life was too precious to waste.

———

Thank you for reading *The Killing Game*. I hope you enjoyed it. Continue reading the first chapter of my Romantic Thriller, *A Cold Dark Place*.

Lindsey Keeble sang along to the radio, trying to pretend she wasn't freaked out by the dark. It was one in the morning and she hated driving this lonely stretch of highway between Greenville and Boden. Rain was threatening to turn to snow. The wind was gusting so forcefully that the tall trees looming high above her on the ridge made her swerve nervously toward the center line. The back tires slid on the asphalt and she slowed; no way did she want to wreck her precious little car.

She worked evenings at a gas station in Boden. It was quiet enough she usually got some studying done between customers. Tonight everyone and their dog were filling up ahead of a possible early winter storm. You'd think they'd never seen snow before.

A flash of red lights in her rearview had her heart squeezing. *Dammit!*

She hadn't been speeding—she couldn't afford a ticket and never drank alcohol. She signaled to pull over and stopped on the verge. Lindsey lived responsibly because she wanted a life bigger than her parochial hometown. She wasn't some hillbilly. She wanted to travel and see the world—Paris, Greece, maybe the pyramids if the unrest settled down. She peered through the sleet-drenched glass as a black SUV pulled in tight behind her.

A tall dark figure approached her vehicle. A cop's gold shield tapped against the glass. Frigid damp air flooded the interior as she rolled down the window and she huddled into her jacket as rain spat at her.

"License and registration." A low voice rumbled in that authoritative way cops had. He wore a dark slicker over black clothes. The gun on his hip glinted in the headlights of his vehicle. She didn't recognize his face, but then she couldn't really see his features with ice stinging her eyes.

"What's this about?" Her teeth chattered. She found the documents in her glove box and purse, and handed them over. Her hands returned to grip the hard plastic of the steering wheel as she waited. "I wasn't speeding."

"There's an alert out on a stolen red Neon so thought I'd check it out."

"Well, this is *my* car and I've done nothing wrong." She knew her rights. "You've got no reason to stop me."

"You were driving erratically." The voice got deeper and angrier. She winced. *Never piss off a cop.* "Plus, you've got a broken taillight. That gives me a reason."

Lindsey's worry was replaced by annoyance. She snapped off her seat belt and applied the parking brake. She'd been shafted last year when another driver had sideswiped her in a parking lot and then claimed she'd been at fault to the insurers. "It was fine when I left for work this afternoon. I haven't hit anything in the meantime." *Goddamn it.*

"Go take a look." The cop stood back. He had a nice face despite the hard mouth and even harder eyes. Maybe she could sweet talk him out of a ticket, not that she was real good at sweet talk. Her dad could fix the light in the morning but if she had to pay a ticket as well, every hour of work today would have been for nothing.

She pulled the hood of her slicker over her head and climbed out. The headlights of his SUV blinded her as she took a few steps. She shielded her gaze and frowned. "I don't see anything—"

A surge of fire shot through her back. Pain exploded in a shockwave of screeching agony that overwhelmed her from the tips of her ears to the gaps between her toes. She'd never experienced anything like it. Sweat bloomed on her skin, clashing with sleet as she hit the tarmac. Rough hands grabbed her around the middle and hoisted her into the air. She couldn't control her arms or legs. She was shifted onto a hip where something unyielding bit into her stomach. She fought the urge to vomit even as her brain whirled.

It took a moment to make sense of what was happening.

This man wasn't a cop.

Still reeling from the stun gun, she couldn't get enough purchase to kick him, but she flailed at his knees and tried to elbow him in the balls. It didn't make any difference and she found herself dumped into the cold confines of the rear of his SUV. He zapped her again until her fillings felt like they were going to fall out and her bladder released.

The world tilted and she was on her front, face pressed into a dirty rubber mat, arms yanked behind her as something metal bit into one wrist, then the other. Handcuffs. *Oh, God.* She was handcuffed. A sharp pain ripped through her chest—if she didn't calm down she was going to die of a heart attack.

A ripping sound rang out in the darkness. She was shoved onto her back, and a piece of duct tape slapped over her mouth. It tangled with her hair and was gonna hurt like a bitch when it came off.

Something told her that was the least of her worries.

There was no reason for him to kidnap her unless he was going to hurt her. *Or kill her.*

The realization made everything stop. Every movement. Every frantic breath. Her heart raced and bile burned her throat as she stared into those cold, pitiless eyes. With a grunt he slammed the door closed, plunging her into a vast and consuming darkness. Rain beat the metal around her like an ominous drum. She was scared of the dark. Scared of monsters. Humiliated by the cold dampness between her legs. How could this have happened to her? One minute she was driving home, the next…

Where was her phone?

She rolled around, trying to feel it in her pockets. Shit. It was still in her purse in the passenger seat of her car. There was a crashing sound in the trees. She closed her eyes against the escalating panic. He'd gotten rid of her car. An elephant-sized lump threatened to choke her. She'd worked her ass off for that car, but finances and credit ratings were moot if she didn't survive this ordeal. This man was going to hurt her. She wriggled backward so her fingers could scrabble with the lock but there was nothing, and the panel above her head didn't budge even when she kicked it. *How dare he do this to me*? How dare he treat her as if she was nothing? She wanted to fight and rail against the injustice but as the SUV started up, she was immobilized by terror. All her life she'd fought to make things better, fought for a future and this man, this *bastard*, wanted to rip it all away from her. It wasn't fair. There had to be a way out. There had to be a way to survive.

She didn't want to die. She especially didn't want to die in the dark with a stranger who had eyes as cold as death. Tears brimmed. It wasn't fair. This wasn't fair.

A Cold Dark Place (Book #1) available on all retailers.

Sign up for Toni Anderson's newsletter to receive sale information, new release alerts, and bonus scenes.
www.toniandersonauthor.com/newsletter-signup

COLD JUSTICE® WORLD OVERVIEW

ALL BOOKS READ AS STANDALONE
STORIES.

The *Cold Justice* series books are also available as audiobooks narrated by
Eric Dove, and in various box set compilations.

Check out all Toni's books on her website (www.toniandersonauthor.com/books-2)

ACKNOWLEDGMENTS

In 2010, my family and I spent three months living in northwest France. Every day, my husband would take the car and drop the kids at school, leaving me to work in peace and solitude in our tiny rented cottage. I planned to write a category novel, but *this* story just wouldn't leave me alone. Eventually I finished with my snow leopards, and even though it wasn't the standard Romantic Suspense, I loved it. So, thanks to my family for traveling with me on these weird and wonderful adventures, and for putting up with me as I insist we watch the *Planet Earth* snow leopard episode "just one more time."

I grew up on stories from my dad's days as a soldier in the Paras. In many ways my admiration for the Special Air Service stems back to him. There was never a war film that he didn't critique or a piece of military history that he didn't already know about. I just hope I didn't get any major military details wrong (crossing fingers). If I did—sorry, Dad!

I want to thank my brother and a childhood friend (KJ) who both work for the Ministry of Defence—not for the information they gave me, but for their tight-lipped refusal to say anything at all. It gives me hope for Britain's national security.

I want to thank my editor, Deb Nemeth, for doing such a wonderful job, and for knowing my voice well enough not to dilute, but rather to enhance the story.

Thanks for the encouragement and support of my beta readers, Maureen A. Miller, Laurie Wood, Marie Treanor, and Gary Anderson. Also, my long-suffering critique partner, Kathy Altman, who sees more rough drafts than any person should have to suffer. And thanks to Loreth Anne White for being my Skype buddy, and being there as we dip our toes into the self-publishing ocean. Let's hope we're not swallowed whole by great whites! Maureen A. Miller showed me some of the indie ropes and I thank her and love her to bits. And thanks to all the other indie authors who have been so supportive of fellow writers' publishing endeavors, especially Marie Force, Norah Wilson, and Dale Mayer.

ABOUT THE AUTHOR

Toni Anderson writes gritty, sexy, FBI Romantic Thrillers, and is a *New York Times* and a *USA Today* bestselling author. Her books have won the Daphne du Maurier Award for Excellence in Mystery and Suspense, Readers' Choice, Aspen Gold, Book Buyers' Best, Golden Quill, National Excellence in Story Telling Contest, and National Excellence in Romance Fiction awards. She's been a finalist in both the Vivian Contest and the RITA Award from the Romance Writers of America. Toni's books have been translated into five different languages and three million copies of her books have been downloaded.

Best known for her "COLD" books perhaps it's not surprising to discover Toni lives in one of the most extreme climates on earth —Manitoba, Canada. Formerly a Marine Biologist, Toni still misses the ocean, but is lucky enough to travel for research purposes. In January 2016, she visited FBI Headquarters in Washington DC, including a tour of the Strategic Information and Operations Center. She hopes not to get arrested for her Google searches.

Toni Anderson's website: www.toniandersonauthor.com

facebook.com/toniandersonauthor

twitter.com/toniannanderson

instagram.com/toni_anderson_author

tiktok.com/@toni_anderson_author

Made in United States
Orlando, FL
14 February 2023